INTO THE BLACK

Elise Noble

Published by Undercover Publishing Limited

Copyright © 2017 Elise Noble

C1

ISBN: 978-1-910954-65-2

Edited by Amanda Ann Larson

Cover art by Abigail Sins

www.undercover-publishing.com

www.elise-noble.com

Dedication. It's important to have this.

Dedication. It's important to have this.

CHAPTER 1

THE HORIZON GLOWED orange as dawn broke in Virginia. Or perhaps someone's house was on fire. Or I was hallucinating. Having been awake for the past day and a half, I was too tired to differentiate or even care.

Bradley, my assistant, nudged me. "The helipad's over there."

I glanced sideways, and a flash of colour caught my eye. "Pink? You painted my helipad pink?"

"It's fuchsia."

Oh, that made all the difference. "It's freaking pink."

He made that huffy little noise he always did when he thought I was being unreasonable, and right now, I was too exhausted to argue. I just wanted to go to bed, so I swung the helicopter towards the house, only for Bradley to shriek.

"Where are you going?"

"As near to the back door as possible."

The rotors were still turning as I stumbled out, leaving Bradley to deal with my luggage and the potted tree thing the downdraft had just blown over.

Home, sweet home.

I managed to keep my eyes open long enough to get past the retina scanner and fell inside. Was anybody else here? No, judging by the red light blinking at me from the camera beside the door.

"Zombie giraffes rule."

The biometric security system registered my voice print, and the light switch beside the door slid down the wall to reveal a touchscreen asking for my code. Six digits I'd never forget. The date I met my husband.

Bradley wandered in behind me, carrying my bag. "Do you want a drink? I've got bubble tea?"

I re-armed the system to monitor the perimeter only. "Nope. I'm going to bed."

"I bought you new pyjamas. Organic silk with matching cashmere-lined slippers."

Slippers? Who cared about slippers? I hauled my sorry self upstairs and collapsed on my bed fully clothed. Forget the sleepwear.

Fourteen hours.

Fourteen hours passed before I joined the land of the living. Darkness cloaked the room, broken only by the dim light of a crescent moon glittering on the rail of my balcony.

On the bright side, I'd woken in my own bed and my bad dreams had been blessedly mild. Too many times, I'd taken myself on sleepwalking adventures and ended up everywhere from the woods out back to the driver's seat of my Dodge Viper. Thank goodness I hadn't had the key.

As the fog in my head cleared, the events of the past week came back to me. The way I'd fled from England late last night, having spent the last five days hunting down a whack job who'd kidnapped my ex-boyfriend's sister and threatened to kill her. That freak's plan had involved Luke coughing up a chunk of change and some business secrets then conveniently dying, but I'd soon stopped that and managed to annoy Luke's mother while I was at it.

An achievement, huh?

Families. Having witnessed the chaos that could be unleashed by blood relatives, I was almost grateful I didn't have any.

No, my husband had been my only family, and after his murder, grief sent me running for England. I'd hoped time would help my soul to heal, but having spent a quarter of a year immersed in a new life, I found the grieving process had only been put on hold. The instant I'd stepped back across the threshold of the house we once shared, old wounds opened, raw and bloody.

I missed my husband more than I'd miss the sun if it stopped rising in the morning. Without him, my life was in perpetual darkness and that feeling hadn't abated in the three months, three weeks, one day, and ten hours since he'd been killed. And it never would, of that I was certain. All I could do was learn to tiptoe around the gaping hole his absence left in my heart.

And the life I'd left in England? Thinking of that hurt too.

Stifling a yawn, I rolled out of bed, desperate for a shower. Lank, greasy locks gave way to pimply skin, and my armpits smelled worse than a week-old corpse. Yuck. I cringed again as I caught sight of myself in the mirror on my way to the bathroom. Bradley had told me I looked terrible, and for once, he was right. Shh—don't tell him I said that.

It was eight p.m. according to the clock on my nightstand, which was kind of fuzzy seeing as I'd slept in the ugly brown contact lenses I'd hidden behind in

England. At least I could ditch the things now. I'd live with the dodgy tresses. A bad hair day hardly qualified as enough of an emergency to interrupt Bradley's evening, and I couldn't take any more of his optimism right now, anyway.

I blinked a few times, trying my best to get rid of the blurriness. What the...? When I'd left Virginia, my bedroom was done out tastefully in muted shades of blue and cream. Now it looked like the love child of a ripe plum and a pitcher of grape Kool-Aid had thrown up all over it. Good grief. How much time had Bradley spent decorating while I wasn't around to fasten him into a straitjacket? Did I dare venture into the rest of the house to find out?

Please, say he hadn't installed disco lights in the ballroom.

Procrastinating, I reached for the remote to catch up on the news headlines. Uh, where *was* the remote? Come to think of it, where was the TV? My forty-inch flat screen had been replaced with a print of an elephant painted by either a three-year-old or the elephant itself.

"Bradleeeeeey!" I screeched to empty air. "What have you done?"

To avoid murdering my assistant, I took a long hot shower then threw on a pair of jeans and an old T-shirt. No make-up, and I left my hair wet. Life was too short to waste on tarting myself up if I wasn't going out somewhere formal.

Hunger pangs hit me as I walked downstairs. I hadn't eaten since I picked at a salad on the trip back from England yesterday, and my stomach sounded like an angry bear.

What culinary delights awaited? On the plane, Bradley had mentioned that Toby, my nutritionist, had prepared a diet plan. On past form, a prisoner of war would eat better. Had Toby's instructions filtered down to Mrs. Fairfax, my housekeeper, or was there a possibility she'd left something edible in the fridge?

A steak. The makings of a cheeseburger. A lasagne. Something I could cook without burning the kitchen down or giving myself food poisoning. Knowing my luck, I'd find tofu and a crunchy salad.

But hold on, what was that? As I tiptoed through the silent house, the delicious aroma of frying meat drifted past. Who on earth was here? Few people knew I'd come back, and I certainly hadn't invited any of them over. Just the thought of being sociable filled me with a cold dread.

Perhaps I could turn around and go back to bed? Or better still, leave the country?

No, Emmy, you've got to deal with this.

Just in case, I popped open the hidden compartment in the oversized floral sculpture that dominated my atrium and grabbed a spare Walther P88, pausing to kiss the barrel. *Baby, I missed you.*

Probably a burglar wouldn't be cooking me dinner, but it always paid to be prepared. But why were my knuckles white as I squeezed the grip? I mean, the only way a burglar could get into my house without going through three layers of security was with a flipping rocket launcher.

I peered around the doorjamb.

"Carmen? What are you doing?"

She glanced at the pan in front of her and raised one eyebrow as if to say, "Seriously?"

"Okay, so you're cooking. But why?"

She didn't answer right away, just left the food and strode over to hug me.

"I missed you, *loca mocosa*."

Only Carmen could make calling me a mad brat sound like a term of endearment.

"Missed you too, hotshot."

Behind her at the kitchen table, Nate, her husband, sat tapping away on his iPad. He'd been my husband's best friend and one of his business partners. The other, Nick, had stayed behind in England to tie up loose ends in the kidnapping case.

"I thought you might be hungry, so I'm making fajitas. Although according to Toby's chart, today you're supposed to be having..." She turned to the fridge door and squinted at the list. "Grilled chicken breasts with steamed carrots and broccoli. But I won't tell if you don't."

"No chance of me spilling the beans." The organic haricot beans with no sauce and no seasoning. "What you're cooking smells great. Can I do anything to help?"

"We need plates."

Sure, if I could find them. Usually, they magically appeared on my counter complete with food. I wandered around, opening and closing cupboards.

"What's this?"

Carmen turned to take a look. "I think it's a panini grill."

"And this?"

"A waffle maker. Why? Does it matter?"

"Not really. Do I have a plate-warming drawer?"

"By the oven. Are you planning to take up cooking?"

Nate muttered something that sounded

suspiciously like, "Heaven help us all."

"Hey, I cooked in England."

"Did you hospitalise anyone?"

"No, I did not. Some of it was even edible."

Plates and placemats, cutlery and condiments. Water and glasses. A fancy candle. I set them all out on the table then escaped to the wine cellar to select a bottle of red. Hmm... French, Chilean, Australian... A nice vintage from a Californian vineyard I part-owned. Fifteen wasted minutes later, I sagged against a stack of crates. I couldn't put off speaking to Nate any longer.

Things had been strained between us since I came out of hiding, and his perpetually grumpy expression showed no hint of change as I slid into the seat opposite.

"Hey," I said, not quite sure how to start.

"Hey, yourself."

I rubbed a hand over my eyes. "I don't know what to say. Other than I'm so, so sorry for running off like that."

He reached over and took my hand. Strange. Nate never normally got touchy-feely. Touchy, yes, but not touchy-feely.

"You gave everyone a huge scare. I lost my best friend, and when you disappeared, it made things harder. None of us knew if you were safe or ever coming back."

I noticed wrinkles around his eyes that hadn't been there before, and his words made me even more disappointed in myself. How could I have been so selfish? For the past three months, I'd spent too much time worrying about me and not enough thinking of the people I'd left behind.

"I'll never do it again; I promise. I'll always let you know where I am from now on."

"Then we need to put this episode behind us."

I reached for the olive branch he'd extended and grabbed it with both hands.

"Okay."

"Just understand that if you disappear off the radar again, I'll hunt you to the ends of the earth, and when I catch you, you'll be getting one of those electronic tags like prisoners wear."

"Fair enough," I choked out a laugh then turned serious. "It's just Mack I need to win over now. She seemed off every time I spoke to her this week."

Along with Carmen and Daniela, who was still in England with Nick, Mack was one of my partners in crime. We worked together and we played together. Hard. I'd trust those girls with my life.

"Mack'll be fine," Nate said. "Yeah, she was annoyed about what you did, but she's mostly been upset this week because she split up with that guy she'd been seeing."

"Jerry?" She'd started dating that douche a month or so before I left. One of those pretentious idiots who charmed their way into a girl's knickers then acted like a spoiled toddler when things didn't go his way. "He was a grade A idiot."

"The one and only. And Mack realises he's an idiot now—he's been reminding her at every possible opportunity. Yesterday, he turned up at her apartment again, banging on the door until I sent someone over there to remove him."

"Great. I'd better talk to her."

Mack may have been a warrior behind a keyboard,

but she was also too sweet for her own good. I'd lost count of the number of undesirables she'd dated over the years. She had a habit of falling in insta-love, hard and fast, only for the objects of her affection to take advantage of her feelings.

Dan and I hated to upset her by questioning her judgement at the beginning of relationships when things were rosy, but we always ended up picking up the pieces several months later when life turned sour.

Even so, we never tried to discourage her. I hoped she'd find her Prince Charming one day. But Jerry wasn't him, and not-so-secretly, I was glad he'd left the scene.

"Dinner's ready," Carmen announced, interrupting my thoughts.

I savoured every mouthful, knowing that Toby's regime of twigs and berries would start in the morning. No doubt he'd padlock the wine cellar too, so I made my second glass of Burgundy last as Nate and Carmen caught me up on everything I'd missed.

"I'll get all the case details when I go to the office tomorrow," I said.

The pair of them looked at each other.

"Take a few days," Nate said. "You're not shooting anyone on your first day back."

"I'll try to last out the week," I joked, but even as the words left my mouth, apprehension built in the pit of my stomach.

Because my husband and I had worked as a team. He'd been my rock, the one who convinced me I could do the impossible. With him at my back, I'd felt a certain sense of invincibility as I put myself in one dangerous situation after another.

His death had rocked me to my foundations. I didn't fear death itself—that was inevitable. Rather, I was scared of letting people down if I was no longer good enough to do what I once did.

Was the old Emmy still lurking within me?

Or had she gone for good?

CHAPTER 2

OKAY, IT TURNED out the nightmares hadn't stayed behind in England. They'd hitched a ride across the Atlantic then rested up so they could kick the stuffing out of me properly. As darkness reigned, my husband's death played over and over again in my head, each time worse than the last.

With the amount of sleep I didn't get, Nate's idea of easing myself in gently seemed like a good one. As a newly initiated member of the walking dead, complete with jet lag and a leaky brain, I was in no shape to work. I'd never, ever felt so exhausted. At this rate, I'd be needing a zimmer frame soon.

Alone in the house, I made a half-hearted attempt to use the gym, but when Bradley bounded in midmorning, I took his arrival as a sign and staggered off the treadmill. What was wrong with me? The gym had always been my favourite room in the house, but today I couldn't wait to leave.

"Time to sort out your hair," Bradley said. "Blondes always have more fun."

The bag of cookies he handed me didn't hurt either. "Chocolate chip and raspberry? You really spoil me."

"I've seen Toby's menu, and I figured you'd need them."

"What would I do without you?"

"Starve, probably."

He knew me so well. Our closeness surprised people, but for the last decade, he'd been the sunshine to my Cimmerian shade. The glitter to my gloom.

Although our first meeting hadn't quite gone as planned, for either of us.

Deep in the throes of building my house, my husband and I had got sick of fielding endless queries from builders and carpenters and electricians and plumbers.

"If I get one more question about window frames, I'm gonna throw this phone off my half-built balcony. Why am I getting so many calls today?"

My husband looked across at me, and one corner of his lip twitched.

"You diverted your phone to me, didn't you?"

"I might have done that."

"You... You..."

"Yes?"

"You little git."

"Git, yes. Little, no. Look, just hire an assistant. Neither of us has time to deal with this right now."

Fine. I'd called an agency, and they assured me they'd have no problem finding a suitable candidate. "Our books are full of efficient and experienced personal assistants," I believe were their exact words.

I cleared half a day in my diary and rented an office suite for the interviews. Even back then, I'd hated bringing strangers home. My home was my sanctuary.

Three interviewees came and went, and as I spoke to the fourth applicant, I rolled up the sheaf of résumés I'd been given, ready to shove them up the recruiter's backside. The grumpy old battleaxe in front of me interpreted "efficient" as "I will arrange your life in the manner I see fit and woe betide if you don't agree with me." By the time the fifth prospect came in, a nervous girl for whom experience translated as having babysat for her cousin's children when she was sixteen, I'd resorted to plotting murder.

One person left to see, and I didn't have high hopes. Perhaps I could ask Nate to build me a robot?

I'd written half a snotty email to the agency when Bradley walked in, or should I say bounced? His pink T-shirt and artfully shredded jeans weren't typical interview attire, but after we'd chatted for twenty minutes about everything from the new model Corvette to the dire state of the Billboard 100, I figured I should ask some of the questions on my list.

At least, if I could get a word in edgeways.

"So what made you apply for the position?"

"Huh? What position?"

"The personal assistant position? The one this interview is for."

"Interview? I'm not here for an interview. I already have a job as a stylist." He indicated his own clothes as an example, and I had to admit the look worked for him. "I just want to rent an apartment. The receptionist said the realtor's temporary office was the third door on the right."

Well, at least Bradley could count. Shame the receptionist couldn't. This was what happened when staff got hired for the size of their chest rather than the size of their brain.

"Sorry, but I'm not the realtor."

"I wondered where the brochures were."

I may have lacked brochures, but I did have a few

empty apartments. By that point, my real estate portfolio was coming along nicely.

"What kind of place are you looking for?"

"Somewhere I can move into quickly."

"Hmm... I may be able to help."

As we walked around the corner to a property I owned, Bradley told me about his flooded home. "So, the guy upstairs left a tap running, the sink blocked, and the ceiling fell down. And the landlord's being soooo awkward. He thinks it's fine for the place to stay mushy and mouldy until he gets around to fixing it."

"Sounds like a real gem."

"That's only the half of it. The lady next door has a hearing problem and she plays her stereo loud enough to wake the dead." He shuddered. "And she only listens to Irish folk music."

Ouch.

I picked up the spare key from the concierge and showed Bradley around a nice place on the second floor. I'd bought the entire complex for a steal two years earlier from a guy with a gambling problem.

"What do you think?" I asked once he'd seen all the rooms.

Bradley looked out the window at the communal swimming pool. "I'm not sure it's in my budget."

"We can sort something out. Apart from that?"

"It's fabulous. So much nicer than my place."

"And mine."

"You have a nasty landlord too?"

"No, I have a building site. Right now, I've got no doors or windows, all the walls are bare plaster, and carpets are a distant dream. I don't know where to start."

So far, I'd only ordered the gym equipment.

"With decorating? Ooh, I love decorating! You need to get paint samples and decide on a colour theme for each room. Once you've done that, you can start with fabric swatches for the upholstery and then comes the fun part."

"Sleeping?"

He clapped his hands together in glee. "Buying furniture and accessories."

Wonderful. I genuinely hated shopping. "How busy are you with your stylist thing this month?"

"I'm between contracts at the moment. I'm sure I'll pick something up, though, and I always pay my rent on time."

"If you decorate my house, I'll pay you and throw in the apartment free for six months."

"Are you serious?"

"As a heart attack." Which was what I'd have if I tried to sort out the house myself.

Bradley leaned against the glass, tapping his fingernails on it as he thought. "I guess I could do that. Would it be a problem if my boyfriend lived here with me?"

"Is he an idiot?"

"No!"

"Then there's no problem."

Over the next hour, we hammered out the details, agreeing on a fair salary, a list of basic tasks that were needed, and rough working hours. That evening we sealed the deal with a handshake and margaritas.

Sometimes, the impulsive decisions you make in life turn out to be the best choices. Our original contract had lasted six months, but eight years later,

Bradley was still colour-coordinating my life. I'd be lost without him.

Bradley kept me company over lunch, although from the dirty looks he gave the salad, he regretted not stopping at the drive-thru on the way over.

"Thanks for staying, Bradley."

"That's why you pay me the big bucks, doll."

"I'll give you a raise if you can convince Toby to let me eat proper food again."

"No can do. I'll just have to stick with abusing your credit card instead."

I laughed, because I didn't care what he spent on my credit card and we both knew it.

I'd stopped caring about cash years ago. As long as I had enough to be comfortable, the extra zeroes on my bank balance didn't matter. Sure, I had toys, but most of them were there to save me time, like the helicopter and the plane. I never had enough time. Tick, tick, tick, tick... The seconds counted down, and then *poof*! You were gone. Material possessions? Well, I was just as happy wearing Walmart as Vera Wang.

And having money had proved a blight as well as a blessing. While I'd done good with it by starting a charitable foundation to help kids who'd been dealt a bad hand in life, it also meant I never quite knew who my friends were. Did new acquaintances see me as a person or a cash machine? The answer to that question meant I didn't trust many people, although I'd learned to spot money-grabbers a mile off.

Speaking of money-grabbers, I still had to deal with

my husband's Aunt Miriam. Ever the compassionate one, she was intent on suing me for his estate, convinced that as his only living blood relative, she was automatically entitled to everything. While I knew she wouldn't get a dime, the thought of a protracted battle weighed on my mind.

"Bradley, have you heard anything from Miriam?"

"She's been emailing you. Nate got your lawyer to write back, but that was only a couple of weeks ago, and I don't think she's replied yet."

Why didn't Bradley meet my eyes?

"And what else? Come on, I'm a big girl; I can take it."

"She turned up here one day."

"Here? Really?"

She'd spread her cheer at my husband's family home a few times, but never before darkened my doorway. Hardly surprising, since she hated me with a passion her husband could only dream of.

Fortunately, our paths hadn't crossed much over the years. I only saw her when we threw a party at the Riverley estate, which had belonged to her brother before it passed down to my husband. She'd turn up for the free booze, hoover up the canapés, complain a bit, then slither back under her rock until the next time.

"Yes, here. Mrs. Fairfax made the mistake of opening the door to her, and she started ranting as soon as she got inside. I asked her to leave, but she told me she wasn't listening to some fudge-packing little pixie and that this would soon be her house, anyway."

Bradley tried to smile, but his lip quivered. My mind flicked to the Walther I'd put back in its hiding place.

"Karma's gonna bite that woman in the butt one day, and when it does, the Kruger Clos d'Ambonnay is coming out of the wine cellar."

This time, he grinned properly.

"Karma can hardly miss, can it? Miriam's butt is the size of Texas. Dustin threatened to put a pitchfork up it if she didn't leave."

Dustin was the groom who looked after my horse, Stan, and he'd just earned himself a bonus. "Was that what got her to go?"

"No, her husband was with her."

Nine years had passed since Miriam got married, and the poor man deserved a medal for bravery. Or stupidity. "How did that help?"

"I told him I had a very special relationship with a member of the local press, who'd find her insults over my sexual preference about as funny as I did. Then I suggested he might want to get her out of here pronto if he didn't want her arrest for disorderly conduct to be splashed across the front page of the *Richmond Times*."

"Well done, Bradley, I've taught you well." I gave him a high-five, laughing.

"When I was trying to get rid of her, I just thought 'What would Emmy do?'"

"Yeah, I'd have totally done that. Except I'd have given her a couple of glasses of wine first so she made it into the drunk tank."

"She won't get this house, will she?"

"Not a chance, so you can stop worrying. This place is one hundred percent mine."

True, but what I didn't tell Bradley was that I fully expected her to stir up a real hornets' nest before she admitted defeat. Miriam was one stubborn woman.

But so was I.

The fifteen-thousand square feet of Little Riverley had always been in my name, although my husband had gifted me the land it was built on.

"Let's take a walk," he'd told me on the morning of my alleged twenty-fourth birthday.

"What kind of walk?"

Last time he'd suggested a pleasant amble in the countryside, I'd ended up in running gear, carrying a rifle for twenty miles while he jogged effortlessly beside me.

"You'll see."

"Do I need sweatbands and electrolytes?"

"Not today, Diamond."

We started from his house, Riverley Hall, and set off across the estate. I thought we'd stop when we got to the boundary, but he carried on, over the chain-link fence and through the forest belonging to the property next door. It was smaller than Riverley, but wildly overgrown, and an eerie stillness surrounded us as we crept through the tendrils of mist that lingered from a chilly night. The place had been empty the whole time I'd lived at Riverley Hall, although that hadn't stopped me from exploring. I knew we were heading towards the old house.

He pulled me to a stop in front of it, and I gazed up at the drooping facade. A fire had raged through the building many years ago, and between that and the storms that followed, the roof was left sagging at one end while charred timbers poked out of a hole at the other. Only two windows remained intact, the rest jagged shards of glass glinting in the morning sun. It was a sad shell of what had once been a majestic mansion. Like a wounded animal, it needed to be put out of its misery.

My husband put his arms around my shoulders and whispered in my ear, "Happy birthday, Diamond."

"Sorry, what?"

"I bought it. For you. I know Riverley's never been your dream home, so now you can design your own place."

"Oh."

Had he finally got sick of me living with him? Was this a really big hint that I should move out? Sure, our relationship had always been a little unusual, but I was happy sharing his house.

He took a step back. "Uh oh, don't give me that look. What have I done?"

"Giving me a whole estate is very generous, but do you not think there were easier ways you could have asked me to leave?"

"Leave? Why would I want you to leave? I was planning to live in the new place with you—we can share both houses." He sat on the edge of a broken fountain. "You always wanted a modern house, and when the old lady who owned this disaster died, the opportunity seemed too good to pass up. If you prefer, we can just take down the fence and use the extra land for riding."

You see why I loved him? He might have been cold, and he might have been slightly sadistic, but he knew me. And he wanted me to be happy.

"In that case, thank you!" I jumped up, wrapping my legs around his waist and my arms around his neck, clinging on like a demented monkey much to his amusement.

"That's more like it." He smiled, eyes twinkling, and hugged me back. "Let's go home and find an architect."

After Bradley and I finished lunch, I helped him to clear the plates into the dishwasher then he headed into town to run some errands. That left me at a loose end, which was why when Mrs. Fairfax returned with the groceries later in the afternoon, she found me cleaning my guns in an attempt to distract myself.

I wanted to do anything but think.

"What are you doing, child?" she scolded before giving me a welcoming hug. "You've got oil all over the table."

"I needed to do something mind-numbing."

"Things must be bad if you've resorted to polishing."

She was right. Of course she was right. But at least my Colt .45 was really, really shiny.

"I should get back to the office."

I couldn't put it off forever even though the prospect was daunting. Almost like the first day at a new school, and I'd had a few of those, what with having been expelled most years. Not only did I have to slot back into doing a difficult and dangerous job, I needed to do it without my number one partner in crime by my side.

My husband had always acted as my sounding board, and now the whole dynamic of how I did things, planned jobs, and thought them through would have to change. A rocky road lay ahead, one I wasn't sure I could navigate alone.

"No need to rush into work before you're ready," Mrs. Fairfax said. "How about I make you some supper?"

"Uh..."

Thankfully, Bradley arrived back and saved me from an evening of second-guessing myself.

"We're going out for dinner. I've made reservations at that Thai place you like," he told me.

I didn't relish the idea of dining out, but it was better than staying home alone. Home had too many ghosts and memories.

"I'm driving," I said.

"No, you're not. I've left my Valium at home."

"I'll drive slowly."

"Last time you said that, Mack had to hack into the police database and erase your speeding ticket."

"If you drive, we'll get there in time for breakfast."

We compromised and took a town car, which turned out to be a good move. Roadworks had left downtown in chaos. Rather than wait as our driver fought his way through road closures and detours, we decided to walk the last part. At least on foot, we could take a shortcut through the park. Fresh air and exercise were good for us, right? And I always carried a flashlight in my purse. Be prepared and all that.

Bradley and I were halfway to the restaurant, discussing the merits of green curry versus red curry, when I picked up on the soft pad of footsteps coming up behind.

I lapsed into silence while Bradley kept chattering enough for the both of us. The moon reflected off the metal bollards bordering the path, the only light at that time of night. I glanced around—the place was deserted. Only us and our new friend walked the narrow avenue between the overgrown trees and bushes, long past needing a trim. The tall evergreens and the damp air muffled any sounds. If anybody shouted for help, not a soul would hear.

Good. I never liked to have an audience.

I blocked out Bradley and concentrated on my surroundings. Our companion matched our pace twenty yards behind. I felt rather than heard him, and my sixth sense told me it wasn't simply someone out for an evening stroll.

Bradley realised I'd stopped speaking and turned to me. "What?"

I jerked my head back infinitesimally, indicating the trouble approaching. He knew me well enough that he understood.

"Here we go again," he muttered, rolling his eyes.

Chapter 3

I ITCHED TO reach for the pistol in my handbag, but I'd promised Nate I wouldn't shoot anyone today. Rats. I didn't fancy incurring his wrath quite so soon after arriving back, so I'd have to do this the hard way.

The footsteps grew louder as they left the grass and hit the concrete path. I spun around, shoving Bradley behind me as some little punk ran up. How old was he? Seventeen? Eighteen? He was taller than me, and heavier, but who cared? That only meant he'd fall harder.

Moonlight glinted off the blade in his right hand as he thrust it towards us. Good grief—his stance was all wrong.

"Gimme the bag and the watch," he demanded, then flicked his wrist towards Bradley. "Those earrings real?"

Bradley put his hands on his hips. "Of course they are. Do I look like the sort of man who'd wear cubic zirconia?"

Oh, Bradley. He'd rather be mugged than admit to wearing paste.

I went to hand my bag over, but before the kid could take it, I dropped it on the ground. Oops. As he bent to pick it up, I kneed him in the face, and there was a satisfying crunch as his nose broke.

Score one to me.

He let out a howl and straightened up, dripping blood down his shirt and all over the ground. Pain driving him, he ran at me with the knife held out in front. I sidestepped and twisted it out of his grasp. Amateur.

Bradley leapt back as I swept the guy's legs out from under him, and when he was flat out, face down, I pressed the tip of the blade into his neck.

"If I see you round here again, this knife'll be buried to the hilt. Got it?"

I lifted his mouth out of the dirt just enough for him to mumble, "Got it."

"Should I call the cops?" Bradley asked.

No way. "You should know better than to ask."

I'd been in the Richmond PD's bad books since I left for England, and if we got them involved, they'd bombard me with irrelevant questions for hours, just for the heck of it. Our dinner reservation wouldn't wait. Instead, I let the guy up, and in seconds he'd disappeared into the night.

"He won't be back here if he's got any brain cells left."

"I doubt he had any in the first place," Bradley pointed out.

"You're probably right. That went quite well though, don't you think?"

Despite being a little rusty, I'd controlled the situation with no problems and my worries about underperforming receded just a tiny bit. Not a bad evening so far, and I still had spring rolls and prawn fritters to look forward to.

Bradley squealed as he stepped forward and picked

up my handbag, holding it out in front of him as if it was poisonous. "No, I do not think it went well. He bled on your Louis Vuitton! And just look at the state of you."

Okay, so he had a point. My silk top, once a pristine cream, had taken on a tie-dyed appearance. Rats. I'd forgotten how much mess a broken nose made. The mouthwatering taste of crispy wontons receded into the gloom.

"Guess we're not going out for dinner anymore," I said. "We'll have to pick up pizza on the way home."

"I should have remembered how trouble follows you around." He rolled his eyes in the dim light and pulled out his phone. "Do you want jalapeños on yours?"

When we got home, Bradley and I curled up together on a sofa in my home cinema, wrapped up in a blanket, like we'd done many times over the years. He was one of the few people who ever glimpsed the soft side of me, the normal person hiding under the hard exterior. The outside world only saw serious Emmy, the hard-nosed woman totally focused on work. I kept the girl who chilled out with junk food and a soppy movie well hidden.

Only she'd been the Emmy who went to England. With Luke and his sister, Tia, I'd kept the darkness in me locked down, and for three months, I'd been free to act like a regular thirty-year-old woman. Just a couple of days had passed since I saw Luke and Tia, and I missed them already. Not the same way I missed my husband—think barbecue pit compared to the fires down below—but a certain sadness haunted me now I'd lost the only good things to come into my life in recent months.

Dan had messaged me last night to say Tia was holding up as well as could be expected under the circumstances, but that was little consolation.

Emmy: And how's Luke?

Dan: He blames himself.

Crazy, because only one man could have stopped what happened, and he was getting to know his new cellmate right now. For a second, the delusional part of me considered hopping on my plane and flying back to tell Luke not to be so hard on himself, but I soon put that idea out of my mind. I hadn't forgotten the look of disgust on his face when he found out I'd lied to him about my true identity. Hoping to slot back into the life I had with him was nothing more than a pipe dream.

Watching my husband die then seeing a bullet come within inches of Luke's head had brought home how short life could be. And now I had the choice of wasting mine or making the most of the remaining tatters. My crushed heart wanted to embrace the darkness but logic overruled, and I climbed out of bed as dawn broke the next morning to go for an early ride on Stan.

Being out on a horse at that time in the morning always felt magical. I changed into jeans and left the house, arming the security system before I took the short walk down to the stables where Stan lived with Dustin's old mare.

When I'd bought Stan as a half-starved mess in Spain, I could have kept him in the stable block next door, but instead I treated it as an excuse to have the old barn on my land renovated. I delegated that task to Bradley, and with his usual efficiency, he'd got the project finished by the time Stan was well enough to travel to his new home.

I should have known better.

As I'd been busy overseas, I'd given Bradley free rein to remodel in the way he thought best, and while he didn't know much about horses, he knew a whole lot about decorating and even more about shopping. The day I returned, he loaded me into a golf buggy before I had a chance to unpack and took me to see his masterpiece.

"What the...?"

My ramshackle barn had disappeared, replaced by a caricature of a Spanish villa.

Bradley stuck a sombrero on my head and tugged at my hand. "Come look inside."

It may have been six degrees Celsius out, but two steps over the threshold I stripped off my sweater.

"Why on earth is it so hot?"

He beamed at me. "Central heating. There's a solarium at the end as well so Stan gets a proper dose of rays all year round."

I did a three-sixty, taking in the eight-foot high mural of a clichéd Andalusian village and the artificial beach. Stan was happily ensconced in his new stable, munching hay and watching Spanish-language television.

"You realise he's a horse, right?"

"I wanted him to feel at home."

At least Stan wasn't French. Otherwise, I'd have returned to find a scale model of the Eiffel Tower planted in a vineyard.

The pseudo-villa had grown on me over the years, and Stan gave me a dirty look when I turned off the TV and led him outside into the cool Virginia winter. I gave him a quick brush before I went to fetch his tack. As I came back with the saddle and bridle, Dustin pulled up in his pickup truck and unfolded himself from behind the steering wheel, face impassive as always. My dog, Lucy, bounded out after him, hurtling over as fast as her legs could carry her when she realised I'd come home.

I braced for impact, but even then only narrowly avoided landing on my bottom. A fully grown Doberman weighs a lot. Lucy was supposed to be a guard dog, but at that moment she was bouncing around like a demented puppy.

"Look what the cat dragged in," Dustin drawled.

"Good to see you too. Have the animals been okay?"

"All fit and well. Lucy's been staying with me."

"I hoped she would be. Thanks for looking after them."

"Just doing my job, lady. Are you taking Lucy out with you this morning? She could do with a good run."

"Yes, she looks like she needs one."

Stan, Lucy, and I set off across the pasture, walking at first, but I urged Stan into a gallop once he'd stretched his legs. The wind tearing through my hair made me forget about the mountains of poop in my life, albeit briefly. Nothing mattered but the thud of Stan's hooves on the turf and Lucy panting as she raced along behind us, well, nothing apart from hanging on as Stan put in a couple of massive bucks out of sheer exuberance. At the far end of the grass, we waited for Lucy to catch up before taking a meander through the forest that reached all the way to the edge of my land.

Tendrils of mist lingered between the trees, and in the stillness, I could almost imagine we were the only three souls left on Earth. Sticky buds showed the trees would soon burst into leaf—new life and new hope in a world of gloom. Of course, Lucy shattered the illusion by shooting off after a rabbit, and Stan spooked as a deer jumped out of the bushes in front of us.

So much for a relaxing jaunt.

We made it back to the barn in one piece, just in time for Stan to watch his favourite Spanish chat show on EstrellaTV, and I decided to give him a good groom because it was calming for both of us. How lovely to be looking after my own horse after spending weeks working in a stable in England caring for other people's. I combed out his mane and tail then bent to brush his legs as he snuffled at my pockets for treats.

Then my phone fell out of my pocket and hit the deck.

Stan trod on it, no hesitation. He even turned his head to glare at me, annoyed at the crunching interruption to his program.

Normal service: resumed. I was back to destroying phones again. I managed it with astonishing regularity, and the guys in the office always had a pool running on how long they'd last. Except while I was in England, I'd managed to keep my cheap mobile working for the entire trip—almost three months. Maybe I should quit using my normal phones and just get three of whatever that one was. Or could it be an omen? While my phone was intact, my sanity wasn't, and vice versa? Perhaps breaking yet another fancy smartphone signified my life was getting back to normal. *Here's hoping, eh?*

After I'd salvaged my SIM card and dumped the broken remains in the bin, I led Stan out to his paddock and watched him have a good roll. Then I walked back up the path to the house with Lucy bounding around beside me. Didn't that dog ever run out of energy? The answer was no, but I preferred her like that than the half-dead puppy I'd brought home five years ago.

I'd been returning home late one night after visiting some acquaintances in a dodgy part of Richmond when I heard a small whimper as I walked past a dumpster. When I hopped up on an abandoned pallet and peered inside, Lucy's tiny head poked out of a plastic bag.

What kind of scum dumped a living creature like that?

I vaulted over the side, landing in something icky and ruining a pair of Jimmy Choo boots much to Bradley's despair. Out of five tiny puppies in the bag, only Lucy was still breathing. She couldn't have been more than a couple of weeks old. I sacrificed a Missoni scarf to make a makeshift bed for her in my handbag and rushed her to the veterinarian. It was touch and go for a few days, but a week later Lucy came home with me. I fed her around the clock until she was strong enough to eat by herself, and she grew into a beautiful dog, if not a little bigger than I expected. My reward? Her loyalty and companionship.

And also her drool and her muddy paws. She jogged into the house ahead of me, pausing to shake off the morning dew in the kitchen. Fantastic. Mrs. Fairfax wouldn't be very happy with us.

Lucy crunched her way through a bowl of doggy kibble while I started up the coffee machine. Caffeine was my drug of choice, and I needed a good hit first thing in the morning. While I waited for my drink to brew, I went to my phone cupboard and selected a shiny new model from the stack inside. Bulk discount, baby.

By the time I'd set my data to synchronise, the coffee was ready, and I poured myself a generous mug full of something dark, hot, and delicious. I'd just raised it to my lips, relishing the bitter taste, when it was removed from my hand and replaced by a cup of...

CHAPTER 4

"UGH, WHAT IS this?" I asked.

"Green tea with pomegranate," Toby replied, and I wasn't imagining the smirk on his face.

"Am I supposed to drink it? Or use it to ward off evil spirits?"

"Green tea's good for you. It's full of antioxidants."

"It's full of something. Can I have my coffee back?"

"No," he answered, pouring it down the sink. "You're on a detox this week."

Super. Rabbit food for every meal. The last time I'd been on one of Toby's detoxes, I'd been forced to sneak out in the middle of the night for a cheeseburger. Somehow he found out, even though I burned the wrapper and buried the ashy remains in a flower bed.

Toby went through my new diet plan with me. It could have been worse—at least I was allowed solids. Last time, everything had been pureed like baby food, which made me kind of queasy.

Grilled asparagus, steamed turkey, carrots with every meal. Mountains of protein. Not the tastiest in the world, but it saved me from having to think about what to eat. All I needed to do was look at the chart stuck to the fridge door, find the correct meal inside, and heat it up.

"See? I've labelled each box with the day," Toby

said.

Even with my brain's current underperformance, I could manage to decipher that.

I got out this morning's breakfast, a bowl of chopped fruit with yoghurt and nuts, and Toby took a seat opposite. I don't think he trusted me not to break out the waffles as soon as his back was turned.

And for good reason, I had to admit.

I'd just finished the last mouthful when Alex walked in. A curse hovered on the tip of my tongue, but I swallowed it down. Once, I'd have let it fly, but I'd made a bet with my late husband that I wouldn't swear for nine months, and I was determined to stick to it. Why? Firstly, because I liked to win, and secondly, because if I stuck with the wager, I could almost imagine he'd be coming back to pay up. And what was my prize? He'd promised to tap dance on stage. In Vegas. Topless. Yes, the logical part of me knew I'd never see it, but if I won, maybe I'd go to the city of sin myself. Take the girls. We sure could do with a break after this nightmare.

But I wouldn't get a break yet. Who told Alex I was back? He was my personal trainer, and he made it his mission in life to cripple me every day I saw him. When he walked into my kitchen that morning dressed in shorts and a vest, cracking his knuckles, I knew I was in trouble.

"You're not dressed."

I waved a hand at my jeans. "Uh…"

"Workout clothes. Now."

Stalin's modern incarnation made me run interval sprints for what seemed like an entire year. When my legs were so painful I could barely stand up, he moved onto my upper body, forcing me to do push-ups and pull-ups and dips until my arms gave way midway through a push-up and I collapsed into the mud.

Then he refused to give me a piggyback ride back to the house, although he did offer to drag me if I couldn't walk.

I staggered.

Alex let me have a brief respite over a lunch of quinoa salad with sliced turkey—thanks, Toby—then announced we'd be doing fight training in the afternoon.

"Who am I fighting?"

Please not him. I might as well lie on the driveway and get someone to drive a truck over me—back and forth, back and forth, back and forth—because it would have the same outcome but save an hour or so.

"Nick is here."

Oh, thank goodness. Seconds later, Nick pushed the door open and stepped inside. I flung my arms around him out of relief.

"Whoa! That's quite a welcome. You feeling all right?"

No, of course not. What was I even doing? I never showed emotion like that. Hurriedly, I dropped my arms and took a pace backwards. "How were things in England? Is Tia okay? And Luke?"

"Tia's got a therapist helping her, but she misses you. You should give her a call."

"I'm not sure Luke would like that. We didn't exactly part on good terms."

"He might have thawed a bit. I got the impression he'd been doing a lot of thinking."

"Is that a good thing or a bad thing? What if I make

things worse?"

"Promise me you'll consider it."

"I will."

I didn't promise I'd act, though. I'd already thought through the situation over and over as I lay awake at night, but I was no closer to working out what to do.

A shadow fell over us as Alex came over. "Are you ready?"

Nick seemed to shrink an inch or two under Alex's piercing gaze, and I couldn't blame him. Nick normally used his own trainer, but he'd heard my tales of Alex's particular brand of motivation. Or punishment, depending on how you looked at it.

"We will start off in the cage," Alex told us. "No gloves."

"At least you've already done your quota of nose breaking for this week," Nick said.

"Bradley's got a big mouth."

"He seemed quite annoyed. Apparently he got blood on his new Vans."

"That mugger was horribly inconsiderate. He made a massive mess."

"Stop talking and fight," Alex interrupted. "I am not waiting around all day."

For twenty minutes, fists flew. And feet, and overly polite non-curse words, from me at least. Nick thought my new un-potty mouth was funny, but he soon stopped laughing when I got in a good uppercut. Then he swore like the sailor he was.

"You're a sadist," he muttered during a brief water break. "And so is Alex. How do you put up with him?"

"Because he *is* so tough on me. The more I sweat in training, the less I'll bleed in a real fight."

"Or you'll just die in training instead."

"Well, that would mean I wasn't good enough, wouldn't it?"

And that was unacceptable.

Because I had to be perfect. Absolutely perfect. My husband had drilled that into me over the years. At first, I was convinced I wouldn't make it through the training tasks he and Alex set for me, but every time I cracked one of their evil games, I became a little bit stronger. Eventually, I'd believed I could do pretty much anything.

That confidence had taken a knock over the past few months, but every jab, cross, hook, and uppercut stirred my inner tiger. She was wide awake as I attacked the final sparring session of the afternoon. Alex made Nick come at me with a knife first, then a gun. It was my job to disarm him and take control of the situation.

"Nick, you're not giving it everything. You're holding back on me."

"I don't want to hurt you."

"You probably won't, and if you do, it just means I've got improvements to make. If I'm fighting with somebody who's trying to kill me, they're not going to back off because I'm a girl or because I've had a rough couple of months. Now just get on with it, will you?"

I'd always done that part of my training with my husband, and he'd never given it less than a hundred percent. I once had the broken arm to prove it. But I'd learned from that mistake, and he never came close to doing it again.

"Okay, okay. I'll push harder."

Nick flew at me, almost, but not quite, taking me by

surprise. I blocked him by the skin of my teeth, and for the next half hour, we must have looked to the outside world as if we were trying to kill each other.

"Enough!" Alex said, his Russian accent still thick despite having lived in the States for years.

I sank to my knees, sweat dripping onto the mat. A purple bruise already marred my pale thigh, skin that hadn't seen sunlight in too long.

Nick passed me a towel and laid an arm across my shoulders. "You okay?"

"Yeah. Sorry I grumbled at you earlier."

"Forget it. I knew you trained hard, but I never realised it was that bad." He jerked his head at Alex. "Is he always like that?"

"Sometimes worse."

Alex cleared his throat behind us. "I will be back in the morning."

"I can hardly contain my excitement."

Alex only laughed.

"I've got an early meeting tomorrow," Nick said as the door closed behind Alex.

"Lucky you. I don't get time off for good behaviour."

"Just tell him you need a break. You're paying him, after all."

I sat down on a weight bench and propped my elbows on my knees. "Tempting. But the training's good for me. My body's the best weapon I have. If I take care of it, it'll take care of me, and best of all, there are no problems getting it through security checks at the airport."

"I wouldn't want to come up against you in a dark alley," Nick said, chuckling.

Like a switch had been flicked, memories welled up

inside me. Despair overflowed as I dashed out of the gym, trying to outrun feelings I didn't know how to cope with. Without thinking, Nick had reminded me of how I'd met my husband. The official story was that we'd got chatting in a London wine bar, but in truth, our paths had crossed in a far less civilised manner, and yes, there had been a dark alley involved.

How could I stand my ground against a mugger but not face up to my own mind?

As I sped blindly through the house, the slap of rubber soles on the tile told me Nick was following. My head told me I should stop, but something deeper inside controlled my feet.

I ran faster.

Chapter 5

I'D REACHED THE music room by the time Nick caught up. I tried to pull the door closed, but he put his foot in the gap to stop me.

"Please, just leave me alone."

I didn't want him there. I didn't want anyone to see me in this state, let alone Nick, but I couldn't summon up the energy to push him away. The tears were coming, and I wasn't sure I could stop them.

"Sorry," he murmured, putting his arms around me and pulling me back into him. "I didn't think."

"It's okay. It's me. I'm overly sensitive at the moment. I need to give myself a good talking to."

I gulped in air, trying to swallow my sobs. Which didn't work, darn it. I'd already broken down on Nick once in England, and I hated the thought of embarrassing myself further by doing it again.

Nick spun me to face him, then gently lifted me onto the edge of the grand piano and caged me in with his arms. With anyone else, I'd have felt trapped and fought my way out, but this was Nick.

My makeshift perch put me at eye level with him, and I tried to look away. Staring into someone's eyes was like looking into their soul, and I didn't want Nick to see the pain and blackness tumbling through mine at this moment.

Except he wasn't about to let me off. He put a still-sweaty palm against my cheek and turned my head so I faced him again, leaning forward so his forehead rested against mine and I couldn't break his gaze.

"It will get better, I promise," he whispered.

"How can it?" Right now, Virginia felt bleaker than the Arctic. "Everything here reminds me of him. I'm sitting on a piano that only he ever played, in a room that was more his than mine, in a house he helped me to build. I could go into work, but if I did, I'd have to drive a car he bought for me to an office we shared at a company named after him."

Nick didn't answer, just softly stroked my hair.

And my words just kept tumbling out. "When I face people again, I know they'll offer sympathy, or pity, or avoid me altogether because they don't know what to say. Or they'll say something that reminds me of our life, like you did. Everything I see or hear or do or think brings back memories and makes me miss him more. And the nights are even worse."

"It'll get better because we'll make sure it does. All of us. You're not alone in this."

I sighed. "I appreciate you guys being here, really I do. It's just my head's a mess, and I can't fix it. I've never felt like this before."

"It's called grief, Emmy, and it's perfectly normal to feel this way. Your world got turned upside down. It's going to take time for the hurt to fade."

"I don't think it ever will. It hasn't so far. At least now I know I had a heart, despite what people said, because I can feel the massive black hole in my chest now it's been ripped out of me."

"It'll be like that for a while."

"How long did it take you? With Jana?" I whispered.

He stared at the wall beyond me, remembering too. "A couple of years before I could look at a picture of her. Double that to remember the good times rather than the end."

A tear ran down my cheek, the wet track cooling under Nick's breath. His eyes glistened as well.

"Forever isn't enough time," I said, my voice hoarse.

Nick pulled me forward into a hug. "I know, baby. I know. What can I do to help?"

"Nothing," I said weakly, my words muffled against his chest. "I thought about renting a place where I wouldn't be surrounded by reminders all the time, but I'll have to face up to things at some point. There's so much for me to sort out—his companies, his investments, the properties, the will. And Miriam's suing me on top of that."

"Miriam's suing you?"

"You didn't know?"

"No, nobody said."

"Yeah, well, she is. She wants his money. She won't get it, but it's just one more thing to deal with. I need a distraction. Somehow, when I was living in England all this didn't seem so real."

"How can I take your mind off things? Do you want to watch a movie? Have dinner? Go shopping? What about a holiday?"

"You're seriously offering to go shopping?"

If Nick would go that far, he must be really worried about me.

It was almost funny watching him squirm. "Uh,

Dan's coming back tomorrow. She'd love to go. Or Mack. I could cover for Mack at work while she takes you shopping."

"Thanks, but I'll pass. I always leave the shopping to Bradley, anyway. He knows what I want to wear far better than I do. No, I think what I need to do is get back to work. That's gonna be uncomfortable though— I'll be like an exhibit in a zoo."

"Do you want me to send a memo around telling everyone they should treat you as normal?"

"No! That would make me seem weak. Plus it's an open plan office. I can hardly avoid people."

"In that case, do you want to ride in with me in the morning? I could pick you up after my meeting?"

"Yeah, I'd like that. Assuming I'm still alive, that is."

After today's session with Alex, I had my doubts.

"I'll come over at ten and hang around till you're ready to go."

Nick lifted me off the piano and set my feet down on the floor. I nestled into him as he wrapped an arm around my waist, the way he always used to do when we were dating all those years ago.

"Come on, let's get a smoothie. We both need one after that workout."

He walked me through to the kitchen.

"I'll have strawberry and banana."

"Not the kale and wheatgrass Toby's lovingly prepared?"

"Don't. Just do— Oh, freaking fudge."

Miriam stared through the window, and her mouth curved into an evil grin when she saw Nick's hand resting on my hip.

Enough was enough, and I'd had it.

"Emmy, no," Nick said, but I ignored him and stormed out the back door towards Satan's pet manatee.

"Ahh," Miriam cackled. "Did I interrupt a session with your fancy man? Charles hasn't been dead for five minutes, and you've already taken up with someone else in your little love nest. I'll be adding adultery to your list of crimes."

It rarely happened, but I was literally speechless.

What did she know about my crimes?

Thankfully, Nick stepped in and answered for me. "Even if we were having a session, as you so charmingly put it, Emmy's husband would have to be alive for her to cheat on him."

Nick sounded calm, but I could feel from the way he gripped my hip bone that he was anything but. I moved a bit to release the pressure. Who wanted a hip replacement at thirty years of age?

"Well, you would defend her, wouldn't you?" Miriam said. "The pair of you were probably at it long before Charles died."

"Don't be ridiculous, Miriam," Nick snapped back at her.

"Not to mention the fact that everyone says she killed him. The Black Widow, that's what the papers are calling her."

I'd always prided myself on never losing my temper, but Miriam would try the patience of a saint. And I was certainly no saint.

"Miriam, I know why you're here. You want cash. I'm well aware of your financial situation and, unfortunately for you, I have the money and you don't. My husband didn't leave you anything. And if you think that walking into my house and accusing me first of adultery and then of murder is going to loosen my grip on the purse strings, I've got news for you; it won't."

"My lawyer says you manipulated Charles so he left me out of his will. He tells me I've got an excellent case. I am Charles's only living relative, after all."

Barely. If she kept that up, she'd be next in the ground. "Apart from me, you mean. I was married to him. For eleven years, Miriam. Eleven years, almost twelve, during which he probably spoke to you once every six months despite the fact that you only live fifteen miles away. And do you know why that was? Because he couldn't freaking stand you. Now get out of my face and get off my property before I have you physically removed. And best of luck to your lawyer; he's going to need it."

"Listen to you, Miss High and Mighty..."

"Enough! Now, I'm calling my security team. It'll be entertaining watching them cart you off. I'll remind them to bring the elephant gun, and then I'm gonna make popcorn."

I turned on my heel, stomped into the house with Nick, and slammed the door behind me so hard the glass rattled. Then I broke a nail hitting speed dial on my phone and absolutely didn't curse. Finally, I got through to the security guard on duty in the gatehouse.

"Get Miriam out of here. Right now. And while we're on the subject, why did you let her through the gates in the first place?"

The guard spluttered an apology. "I'm sorry. So sorry. She said she had an appointment. I did tell her she wasn't on the list, but she said it didn't matter because she was family."

"Just to make things crystal clear, I don't have any family. The only appointment I'll be keeping with Miriam is her funeral, and I'll only go to that so I can check that someone's put a stake through her heart. Now get rid of her."

I flung the phone down on the counter and a bit of plastic chipped off the edge.

"Flipping phone!"

"And breathe," Nick reminded me. "You're taking this not swearing thing really seriously, huh?"

"I am breathing. And yes, I've still got six months to go in my new non-sweary regime. But with Miriam around, you have no idea how hard it is."

"I can imagine."

"There just isn't room for that woman in my life."

I only had one go at it, and I didn't intend to waste either my time or anymore thoughts on her.

"There isn't room for Miriam in anyone's life," Nick said. "Literally. You can probably see her butt from space."

"If it got any larger, Earth would start orbiting it."

"And she'd block out the sun."

You know that old saying that you either have to laugh or cry? Well, today I laughed. Hysterically. Nick and I both did. I'm not sure whether it was about Miriam's butt being so big it had its own zip code, or at the sheer ridiculousness of the situation with her accusations and threats. At least I wasn't crying. That was a step in the right direction.

By the time security called back to say Miriam had left, we'd both collapsed on the sofa, spent.

"Are you staying for dinner this evening?"

"Uh, I actually have a date. But I can cancel it if you

want me here."

"Don't be silly. Go on your date. I'm perfectly capable of looking after myself for an evening, and Toby's already made me food."

Nick got to his feet. "If you're sure?"

"I am. I'll see you tomorrow."

"Just call if you need anything, and I'll come back. I don't mind. Honestly. I've been out with this girl twice already, and last time, she cooed over a baby at the next table which is always a bad sign."

Nick headed off to change before meeting the lucky lady. And she was lucky—women threw themselves at Nick with abandon, and wherever he went, he left a trail of disappointed females in his wake. Since Jana, none of his assignations had lasted longer than a few weeks, but I wasn't surprised—nobody wanted to risk that kind of devastation more than once in a lifetime.

Nick's departure left me at a loose end, so I made myself a coffee. Then I wrote a list of things to do at work tomorrow. Then I screwed that up and started again, scoring a bull's-eye as I threw the paper in the trash. After four attempts, I decided to bypass the writing stage and just lobbed the wadded-up pages at the bin instead.

After I'd wasted the entire pad of paper, I wandered out to the kitchen, made another cup of coffee, and ate a Snickers bar that Toby had somehow missed when he threw the edible food out of my cupboards. Then I felt guilty for ruining my diet. One Snickers wasn't so bad, right? After all, if a single bar weighed two ounces, I'd have to eat 965 of them to consume my own body weight. Plus they contained peanuts, and a girl needed her protein.

I made yet another mug of coffee and spent an hour watching YouTube. Perhaps I should get a kitten? They were so freaking cute.

Hold on. I hated wasting time on the internet. What was wrong with me?

Grief, Emmy. It's called grief.

I missed my husband, and I was doing anything to avoid thinking of him. But it hadn't worked, had it? Because there he was, front and centre of my mind again.

How about trying a different tactic? What had Nick suggested when we were back in England? Writing a letter to tell my husband how I felt. Letting all my pain out onto the paper and putting my agony into words.

Well, it was worth a try, because my current tactics sure weren't working. And if it didn't help, I could always stab myself in the eye with the fountain pen.

CHAPTER 6

I FOUND A fresh notepad and curled up on the sofa. Where should I start? The blank page and stationary pen taunted me, and I threw them down on the coffee table.

Why could I never think of the right words?

Eyes closed, I leaned back into the cushions. My mind was a blank canvas, and as images of my husband played across it, the words I wanted to say to him rushed into my head. Hundreds of them, pages of hurt and sorrow.

I picked up the pad and pen and began to write....

February 22nd

Of all the ways I'd considered letting you know how I felt about you, this one never came to mind. The trouble is that you're not here anymore, so I'm a bit limited on options. I suppose I could try a séance, but you're probably too busy flirting with the angels and playing poker with the saints to worry about pushing a glass around the alphabet. So it looks as if this is my only choice.

When we met, I felt many things towards you, but I can honestly say love wasn't one of them. In fact, I thought you were an arrogant git. I hardly kept this a secret—you'll recall I let you know at every possible opportunity.

Over the next few months and then years, though, my feelings went from fear, anger, frustration, and animosity to a grudging respect and finally to trust. I trusted you with my secrets, I trusted you to look after me, to make the best decisions for both of us, to keep us safe. I trusted you with my life, and you never abused that.

You forgave me a lot. One broken nose, a night-time knife attack, a crumpled Porsche, and a burned-out kitchen are just several of the incidents that spring to mind. Not to mention a few irritated clients before I learned not to blurt out everything in my head. But never once did you get angry with me. You had more patience than any saint, and heaven knows I tested it.

You were well aware of my disastrous forays into the dating world over the years. Indeed, what could have been more embarrassing than you having to drag me off Nick in the middle of the night when I tried to kill him in my sleep? But you never judged me for that, you just carried me back to bed and told me everything would be all right. And I knew it would be.

I knew, because you said it.

You.

It took me six years and one kiss to realise what was missing from all the men I'd ever tried on for size.

You.

None of them were you.

That night you kissed me, I was stupid, and I was a coward. Two things I'd always tried so hard not to be, but I failed miserably on both counts when it mattered most. You kissed me and I ran. I ran because

I was scared that if I spent the night with you, it would ruin everything else between us.

I didn't stop to think that it could actually make things better. That was the stupid part. I just didn't think. My brain eventually caught up with my emotions, and I spent the whole of the night working out what I needed to say to you. It was that night I realised I loved you with every atom in me.

The next morning you broke my heart for the first time when you told me that kissing me had been a mistake. But I smiled and agreed because I didn't want you to decide that the rest of your life with me was a mistake too. I don't think you ever knew how I felt inside. I was brilliant at pretending to be anything but myself by that point. Why? Because you'd made me that way.

Anyhow, I got through that. Because I still had you, in whatever way you were willing to give yourself to me, and I coped perfectly well until you went and died. That made all the other heartache fade into insignificance, a tiny ripple on a pond compared to the tsunami I felt when you left this earth.

I know I'll never be the same again. I'll exist, but I won't ever truly live. I love you with all my heart, and I always will.

You were it for me.

Your MB.

Well, there it was. I'd written the letter, and yes, in a strange way, I did find it cathartic. Nick had said I needed to leave it somewhere that I associated with my husband for the greatest effect, and I thought through the possibilities.

Not his grave. I hadn't been there since the funeral, and I struggled to match the charred remains in that hole in the ground with the person I'd known. His office desk was no good either, even if he had spent a lot of his time there—it was too impersonal. In the end, I decided to bite the bullet and go to his house. That was where the letter needed to be left—he'd lived at Riverley Hall his whole life.

"Lucy, do you want a walk?"

Of course she did, and I wanted her company. Not her protection, because I also took enough firepower to stop a small army. Old habits died hard, and it was almost midnight, after all.

On my way out, I stopped at the gatehouse to make sure the next guard shift had received the message about Miriam—affirmative—before continuing up the driveway. The night was cold and deathly quiet, a grim reminder of a soul departed. On the horizon, a yellowed full moon hung low in the sky, a constant in this world of uncertainty.

My husband's house was only a short walk away, and I arrived before I got the chance to chicken out of what I was doing. As I looked up at the imposing facade of Riverley Hall, the grotesque faces of the gargoyles along the roofline grinned down at me, their evil smiles mocking me for returning.

Could this place ever feel like home again?

I let myself in and flipped on a couple of lights. High above me, torches flickered to life in their iron sconces. As I walked across the overly grand entrance hall, my footsteps echoed off the stonework, carved by craftsmen so many decades ago.

The place was clean, just a little dusty, but the eerie

stillness said it was uninhabited and had been that way for a while. It reflected the man who'd once lived there, its spirit extinguished along with his.

I climbed the main staircase, which rose up both sides of the hall, and made my way through to the west wing where his bedroom was located.

The door creaked as I gingerly pushed it open. I'm not sure what I'd expected, but when I stepped into the room, the sheer emptiness of it hit me. The huge space was immaculate, not a thing out of place. Normally, there would have been signs of life despite Mrs. Fairfax's best efforts: a book open on the nightstand, a remote control tossed on the four-poster bed, discarded clothing draped over one of the leather armchairs.

But there was nothing.

The room was as lifeless as the man who'd once slept in it.

With a heavy heart and feet to match, I walked over to his nightstand and opened the drawer at the top. All of his stuff was still in there. A bottle of Tylenol, a box of tissues, a Beretta pistol. Loaded and ready, of course. And a Taser, just in case I had an episode.

I tucked the letter under the gun and quickly shut the drawer.

It was done.

Finished.

Over.

And just being in Riverley Hall had sapped all my energy. I debated staying for the night, but I decided I'd only feel miserable waking up there in the morning. Instead, I whistled for Lucy and went out the way I'd come, making sure the door was secured and the monitoring system set.

Lucy scampered around in the darkness as I trudged back to Little Riverley, and her exuberance only made me more exhausted. I glanced at my watch. Past two o'clock already, which only left me four and a half hours before Alex arrived for another fun-filled morning.

Please, let me get some sleep tonight.

Writing the letter must have helped, because for the first time in weeks, I slept through what was left of the night without nightmares.

I hoped it was a sign.

CHAPTER 7

DESPITE BEING RUDELY awakened by Alex at six thirty, I still felt more relaxed than I had in days by the time Nick showed up with breakfast at ten. My hero. A bacon and egg roll with ketchup and HP sauce, just the way I liked it, and a hundred times better than the sugar-free muesli allocated by Toby.

Once I'd hidden the evidence in the bin, I grabbed my handbag and hopped into the passenger side of Nick's shiny Dodge Ram.

"New truck?" He'd been driving a Chevrolet Silverado last time I was home. "You only bought the last one a month before I left."

"Yeah, I did, but it looked a little second-hand after Dan borrowed it to chase a pair of trigger-happy terrorists. The body shop said there were too many bullet holes to repair economically."

"Crikey. I take it Dan was okay?"

"Of course. She takes after you in that respect. When the cops dragged the terrorists out of the ravine they'd driven down to get away from her, they actually begged to be locked up rather than have to face her again."

Good old Dan. Guys tended to think that because she was small and cute, she couldn't pack a punch. Same with Mack and Carmen and me. We'd had a bunch of fun over the years showing them just how wrong they were.

Twenty minutes later, we arrived at the office. Rather than base our company in a high-rise building in town, we'd chosen a large estate in the country for our headquarters because that gave us the space to put our training facilities there as well. We also had a small office in Richmond for meeting clients, an hour away by car and a lot quicker by helicopter.

While we'd started off in Virginia, the company had expanded quickly, opening offices in New York and Washington, DC in our first year. Now we operated on six continents. If Nate ever made good on his promise to send me to Antarctica, we'd tick off the seventh. Forty-two countries and eighty-nine offices, not including the sixteen in the United States.

At last count, we had fourteen thousand permanent employees and probably the same again in regular contractors. From a humble start, with just my husband, Nate, and me working out of my husband's house with a secretary and a handful of part-timers, security had turned into big business for us.

"Look what the cat dragged in," Dan said as I walked into my office. She sat on my desk, swinging her legs. Abstract paintings and the occasional poem decorated the walls beside her, and, the bulletproof glass windows overlooked the outdoor shooting range beyond.

I stepped inside and closed the door before giving her a quick hug. I never showed my softer side to the rest of the employees. People needed to fear and respect me; they didn't have to like me.

"What fun awaits me this morning?" I asked.

She showed me jazz hands. "Management meeting."

"Oh, joy. I need coffee first."

"Overall, things are doing well," Nate said as I sucked down my third espresso. Of the eight people in the room, I was winning in terms of caffeine consumption. "Revenues are up, profits are up. Cash balances are good. The old mattress is overflowing."

"And operationally?" I asked.

"No serious problems since you left."

"Any minor ones?"

"Just the usual niggles." He looked down at the tablet in front of him. As head of the Technology Division, Nate would never resort to a pen and paper.

I, on the other hand, needed something to doodle with.

"There was a dispute with the local army in Pakistan," Nate continued. "They thought we were treading on their toes when we escorted a convoy of American businessmen through a conflict zone. We've smoothed that over now."

"And one of our celebrity clients in LA had a few hysterics," Nick chipped in. "The bodyguard we provided refused to let her fiancé backstage since he didn't have the correct pass."

I laughed. That kind of drama was why I happily left the Executive Protection Division to Nick. "Did the guard not recognise him?"

"He knew the woman was engaged to a rapper called T-Dog, but not what the dude looked like. When this kid wearing a pair of sweatpants with the crotch around his knees and enough gold necklaces to make a killing on eBay turned up, our guard didn't realise he was a musical prodigy."

"All that bling and no backstage pass? Our guy was just doing his job." We drilled our security staff time and time again: if people didn't have the right credentials, they didn't get past. Someone had obviously listened. "Send him a bonus. What's happening with Investigations?"

Dan shuffled papers on the desk in front of her. She'd headed up that division since my husband's death, a promotion by default. "Running smoothly." She gave us a brief rundown of the priority cases. "I've got a team flying to Puerto Rico tomorrow to try and find that missing kid and another heading for the Cayman Islands to hunt for the fraudster."

I poured another coffee from the carafe on the table, aware of fourteen eyes following my every move. Dagnabbit. I couldn't put it off any longer.

"So," I said. "Special Projects?"

That was my division. We took on the tasks others had decided were so difficult, so dangerous, so unusual, or so crazy that they were impossible. It was our job to make them possible. All the tasks nobody else wanted to touch flowed our way, and not just our company's problems. Governments, corporations, and oligarchs the world over flung theirs in our direction too. And they paid our outrageous prices.

What joyous tasks were on the list today?

"We've been telling your prospective clients you were working on a long-term project overseas," Nate said.

"That wasn't entirely untrue."

"If you count finding your sanity as a project, it's one you'll never finish."

Good to see he hadn't changed. As usual, I ignored him.

"Did they believe the story?"

"Some were suspicious, some were annoyed, but most just accepted it. The CIA was trying to track you down, from what I heard on the grapevine."

"Doesn't surprise me, but they didn't do a very good job." Lower Foxford, the English village where I'd been living with Luke, wasn't the type of place they cultivated assets. Lower Foxfordians got their intelligence from the local pub and the Women's Institute, and the CIA had yet to tap into those.

"Rumour has it they sent a team to Barbados."

"Wonder which genius got that signed off?" I took a cookie from the plate in the middle of the table. Sawdust and raisin—Toby had been around. "What's on my agenda?"

Nate stuck a bullet-pointed list up on the plasma screen. "Number one: A civilian contractor who's gone missing from his home in Afghanistan. The investigations team out there referred it up."

"Why can't the local office deal with it?"

"They've been looking into it," Dan said. "But he's been gone three days and the guy's employer, who's picking up our bill, is getting upset we haven't found him yet."

"The local team's more than competent, and they've probably got better contacts out there than I do. Three days is nothing for locating a hostage, if he even is a hostage. From this report, there's no evidence he's been kidnapped."

Dan nodded. "No signs of a struggle and no contact from any kidnappers."

"So get the local team to put a couple of extra people on it and tell the client we've brought in some experts to help. It's not like we're lying—they're all experts. If it turns into an actual rescue situation, kick it back to me. What's next?"

"Fancy a trip to Florida?" Dan asked.

"I could do with some sun. What for?"

"Eighteen-year-old girl found strangled in a hotel room. The police gave up and the parents hired us. We've traced the murder weapon to a local gang boss called Chainsaw."

"I bet his mother didn't name him that."

"No, she called him Cedric."

"Poor guy."

"Don't feel too sorry for him. When our agents stopped by for a visit, he threatened them with a shotgun then got a pair of Rottweilers to chase them off the property."

"I'll take that one. It's always interesting to chat with individuals from other sections of society."

Nate gave me a pointed look. "Emmy, it's your first day back. Is there any chance you could hold off on the jobs that might get you killed for just a week or two? You know, until you get back into the swing of things? And to give our nerves a chance to harden again."

His concern touched me, even if it was hidden behind a veil of sarcasm. "Relax, Nate, that job will be fine. It'll only take a few days. If it makes you feel better, old man, I promise not do anything really dangerous until you've had a chance to visit the doctor and pick up some Xanax."

Dan snorted and turned it into a cough. Nate glared at her.

Aw, he loved us really.

Out of deference to Nate's feelings, I turned down an undercover job with Interpol and an invitation from the CIA to hunt for chemical weapons in Syria. Even I could see that one was a suicide mission. That left one last item.

Evan Beck, our international coordinator, read out the details. "The UK police have requested assistance with a security training exercise in London. They want an independent team to act as the bad guys in a simulated terrorist attack."

"Haven't we done something similar before?"

"Last year." He smiled, no doubt recalling the chaos we'd caused. "They reckon they're better prepared this time."

"At least you won't come to much harm with all those cops around," Nick said. "You'd keep Nate happy."

Nate scowled at him.

I couldn't deny the last job had been entertaining, but one thing made me hold back. London was awfully close to Luke.

Part of me wanted to go there, to find him and speak to him and apologise for everything I'd done. To see if any part of our relationship was salvageable. But the coward in me told me I wasn't ready, that I was far better off on the American side of the Atlantic where he couldn't yell at me or tell me to get lost.

Beside me, Dan piped up. "It'll be men in uniform, Ems. I wouldn't say no."

"What's the timescale?"

"A little over two weeks," Evan said.

"That soon?"

"Apparently, they want to add an element of realism by giving those involved as little preparation time as possible."

"Including us." I took a deep breath and told myself I needed to be brave. "But I think we can do something reasonable in two weeks. Tell them it's a yes, if the money's decent."

"It's not great, but it's enough. A couple of hundred grand for us to send a full team."

"You're right, it isn't great. But I can borrow some bodies from the London office to save on travel costs. Dan, it looks like we've got planning to do."

CHAPTER 8

LUKE SAT AT his desk at work, looking at a tricky coding problem that had stumped his software developers. At least, that's what he was pretending to do. In reality, he'd doodled a row of circles and was busy colouring in every other one. First red, then green, then blue. Did he have a yellow pen anywhere?

He lifted his hands up to rub his eyes, fingers brushing against several days' worth of blond stubble. Shaving seemed like too much effort at the moment.

Nearly two weeks had passed since the life he'd enjoyed with Ash was thrown into chaos. First by his sister being kidnapped, then by the revelation that his girlfriend wasn't the sweet ex-housewife she'd pretended to be. It was five days since Ash rescued Tia then promptly disappeared, and the whole episode had left him shattered.

Tia's distress was all too obvious as well. "Please find her," she'd begged over breakfast that morning, stirring her Coco Pops into a soggy mess. "I've got to thank her. She saved me and changed my entire life over the last few months. I have to tell her that. I need her to know."

"I'll try; I promise."

Tia hadn't come out and said it, but Luke knew she blamed him for Ash's departure. He hadn't exactly been kind when she admitted her deception. Guilt over that gnawed away inside him, because despite everything, Ash had come through and got his sister back in one piece, even getting abducted at gunpoint herself in the process.

Then she left. He and Tia had been waiting for her back at their home, but she'd gone to the airport and got on a plane without so much as a goodbye. By the time he came to his senses and started looking for her, any connection had been severed. The friends she'd been working with didn't leave their contact details, and she'd taken her phone. The only evidence she'd ever existed was a handful of clothes at one end of his wardrobe and a couple of photos on his computer.

He racked his brain for anything useful. Was her name even Ash? He'd heard a few people call her Emmy, but when he'd brought it up, she'd brushed it off.

"Most people call me by a shortened version of my middle name," she'd said.

Ashlyn Emily Hale.

He repeated it over and over like a mantra.

Tia's wasn't the only life she'd saved. When Luke foolishly went to meet her kidnapper in the dead of night, Ash had followed him to an isolated forest and stopped the man from putting a bullet through Luke's brain. The concussion he'd received in the process made the wild ride back to civilisation hazy. She'd taken him to a huge house in London, but as they'd arrived and left in the dark, he didn't know whereabouts.

His vague recollection of what the street outside looked like hadn't been enough to narrow down the location. He thought maybe Chelsea or Kensington, Knightsbridge even, but he'd got his driver to take him around those areas and nothing had looked familiar. When he thought back to the events leading up to Tia's rescue, he realised he'd been kept carefully cocooned away from the action in the palatial abode while people worked around him.

Why hadn't he asked Ash's friends more questions? They worked at some sort of security company, but he'd never found out the name of it. When Dan visited for the final time, Luke had been dead to the world, the events of the last few awful days having caught up to him in the form of a dreamless sleep. She'd left a message with his housekeeper wishing him and Tia all the best for the future before she left as well.

The only other friend of Ash's he'd had contact with was a guy called Mack, who'd turned out to be a fellow hacker. Luke had sent him a message yesterday, but it bounced back, undeliverable.

He had nothing.

Nothing but an earful from his mother, anyway.

"That awful girlfriend of yours turned up at my house," she'd informed him when he admitted defeat and answered her eighth call.

"Which one?" Luke had several exes that fell into the "What was I thinking?" category.

"Ashley. She was incredibly rude. I've never seen Mrs. Squires so distressed."

Score one for Ash. Mrs. Squires made Hitler look benevolent. "When?"

"A few days ago. Right before my bridge supper with the Renwick-Smythes. She arrived in an Aston Martin, if you can believe it. Obviously stolen. Nobody refined enough to own such a quintessentially British vehicle would ever be so uncouth."

"What did she say?"

"She accused your father of having an affair. Where on earth did she get such a ridiculous idea?"

"I don't know, Mother."

Ash had been right on the money with her suspicions, but his mother lived in a world ruled by denial and social standing. He'd have more chance of crossing the Arctic in flip-flops than getting his mother to accept the truth.

"I suggest you find yourself a lady with some manners."

"Yes, Mother."

He sighed as he hung up. Never before had he let his guard down enough to actually start caring for a woman, but Ash had smashed through his defences and broken his heart.

When she'd ended up living in his house, nothing had felt so right. They'd spent every bit of his spare time together, and what's more, he'd enjoyed it. Not because of what they'd been doing—watching a movie or eating a takeaway were hardly the most exciting activities—but because she'd been by his side. Pre-Ash, the scariest word in the English language, the one guaranteed to send him sprinting in the opposite direction, had been *commitment*. Now the one that terrified him was love. What if he only had that one shot at it? And he'd missed.

Rubbing his eyes, Luke stared again at the code on the screen. He'd spent his whole life talking to computers, but in the last week, it seemed as if they'd suddenly started to speak a different language because the words in front of him meant nothing.

He carried on colouring his circles instead.

At four in the afternoon, a knock at the door made him jump. He peeled off a couple of paperclips that had stuck to his face when he'd fallen asleep on the desk and tried to look busy.

"Come in."

His secretary poked her head around the door. "Sorry to wake you, but Tia will be finishing school shortly. Do you want to pick her up or shall I arrange a driver?"

With Ash gone, he and Tia only had each other now. Nobody else understood what they'd gone through. After a heart-to-heart over pizza last night, they'd decided Tia would move in with him officially since she was seventeen and hated living with their mother. Luke quite understood why. He'd broken the news to her mother this morning, and her initial unhappiness at the idea had soon dissipated when she realised that not having to pretend to be a parent would give her more time to spend at the country club.

"No, I'll get Tia. Can you send her a text message to let her know I'm just leaving?" It wasn't as if he'd get anything done at work that afternoon, anyway.

"Of course, Luke."

He took the express lift down to the basement car park and bleeped open his silver Porsche 911. Normally, the roar of the engine gave him a buzz, but even the burst of acceleration as he pulled out onto the main road didn't make a dent in his misery.

Tia's school lay half an hour from the office, and thanks to his secretary's well-timed wake-up call, Luke pulled up outside just as Tia exited the building with

Arabella, her best friend for as long as Luke could remember. Secretly, he'd always found the girl a tad irritating.

"It's my turn in the front," Tia said as they neared the car.

"Well, make sure you pull the seat right forward," Arabella grumbled. "You know there's hardly any legroom in the back.

"Good day at school?" Luke asked.

Tia shrugged. "Okay. We've got a new project to do for art and a ton of chemistry homework."

"We've got a mock exam next week for chemistry," Arabella said.

"Better knuckle down then, girls."

The pair chattered away for the rest of the trip to Lower Foxford, discussing schoolwork, clothes, movies, and make-up the way teenage girls did. Not boys, though. Luke listened carefully for that, always in big brother mode.

At a red traffic light, Arabella told a joke and Luke glanced across at his sister, catching a half-smile, the first he'd seen since the kidnapping. That gave him hope. Perhaps with time, Ash's desertion would get easier for both of them.

Luke dropped Arabella home first, hardly a chore since she lived on the same street, then slotted the 911 neatly into his garage alongside his Porsche Cayenne. Yes, he had the mansion, the cars, and the money, and to anyone looking from the outside, his life was the picture of success. But on the inside? His heart ached with every beat.

Still, the world kept turning, right?

He hefted Tia's schoolbag over his shoulder and

pushed through the door to the house. In their new routine, he headed to the kitchen to grab a beer and Tia followed him.

"Have you heard from Ash?" she asked as she reached past him into the fridge and grabbed a can of diet cola.

"Nothing, Tia." He hated to dash her hopes, but he needed her to understand they'd probably *never* hear anything. "I'm not sure she'll get in touch, sis. She did leave the country, after all, and we don't know who she really was."

"But we were friends. I know we were. Even if she hates you, she still might call me."

Nice of his sister to be so tactful. "I suppose, but I wouldn't bet on it. Have you done your homework yet?"

"You sound just like Mother."

She grabbed a packet of crisps and stomped off to her room. The windows rattled as she slammed the door in the otherwise silent house.

Tia couldn't have meant that, surely? Luke had aspired to many things in his life, but being like his mother wasn't one of them. Should he lighten up on Tia a bit? He took a slug of beer and scraped a hand through too-long hair. Talk about being out of his depth. He only wanted the best for his sister, but being responsible for a teenager was *hard*. Ash had instinctively understood how to handle her, but he didn't share that magic touch.

A sigh escaped, so loud and heavy it filled the room. Food. Food would help. What had his housekeeper left in the fridge? A lasagne big enough to feed Luke, Tia, and half the village, it seemed. In true cooking-for-dummies style, the post-it note stuck to the top told him what temperature to set the oven at and how long to cook it for. Would Tia show her face to eat?

"Food's ready," he called once the timer dinged.

When he shouted for the third time, she slunk downstairs in her pyjamas, feet shoved into a pair of dinosaur slippers that Ash had bought for her. That was a good sign, right? That she'd reappeared? During dinner, he carefully avoided mentioning Ash, and they actually managed a pleasant conversation. Well, Tia talked about her horses and Luke listened. Three months ago, chatting like that would have been impossible. Tia had acted like a spoilt brat by default before Ash came on the scene.

He had so much to thank Ash for, but how?

A movie after dinner, alone, did little to occupy his mind, and he fell asleep dreaming of Ash's curves. Her smile. The way she'd curled against him in the evenings when they watched TV together.

Man, he missed her.

Please, let tomorrow hurt a little less.

Chapter 9

SINCE TODAY WOULD be my last day at Little Riverley for a week or two, I made the most of it with an early morning ride on Stan, who was his usual obliging self. First, he went backwards for about fifty yards before accepting the ride was going to happen whether he liked it or not.

"Get on with it, you little git."

When he hit the wall of the barn with his backside, he leapt forward, deciding he might as well get it over with so he could go back to his snacks. Eventually he settled, and we enjoyed a nice gallop across the pastures followed by a brisk trot through the wooded trails at the back of my property. Lucy bounded along behind us, occasionally disappearing out of sight as she caught the scent of a deer or rabbit.

When we got back, Stan's weekly fruit basket had just been delivered, courtesy of Bradley of course. I fed my beloved horse two apples and a banana, which he tried to stuff in his mouth at the same time. That earned me a dirty look when he couldn't chew properly. Honestly, I couldn't win.

Back at the house, I changed into running tights and a sports bra and headed straight out for a quick run. Quick because my flight for London left at six this evening and I had a ton of paperwork to catch up on beforehand—my least favourite thing in the world—but the report on yesterday's jaunt to Florida wouldn't write itself.

Lucy came too, lolloping along beside me with her tongue hanging out of her mouth. Where did she get her energy from? Because I desperately needed some of whatever she was taking. At least Alex had the day off, probably to weightlift with kryptonite or something, so there was a chance I'd still be able to walk this afternoon.

Although I couldn't complain too much about Alex —I'd only been home a fortnight, and I was already in far better shape than when I stepped off the plane thanks to his torture regime.

How much time did I have? Just enough to fit in a bit of shooting practice, and that *was* something I enjoyed. Thanks to the irritating British laws on gun ownership, I hadn't shot properly for months. The government in the UK had banned all the good stuff— only the criminals had access to that now.

I collected a nice selection of firearms from the weapons locker in my basement and headed out back. The grass airstrip behind my house doubled as a shooting range with targets from ten to a thousand yards set up along one side. To be honest, it was more of a shooting range that doubled as an airstrip, because it didn't get used for planes much. I had a Pitts Special in the hangar for fun and emergencies, but mostly I flew the helicopter or a jet if I needed to go long-distance.

Two hours, five guns, and a thousand rounds of ammunition.

I started with a Smith & Wesson Model 60 snub

revolver. It may have been tiny, but it was easy to conceal and handy for close range work. Next came the silenced Ruger Mark II .22—my favourite for jobs that didn't go through the books. If you weren't listening for it, the soft pffft as it fired could easily be missed.

Then came the ubiquitous AK-47. Given the choice of machine gun, I'd go for an M5 every time, but I didn't always have that luxury. If—when—I got stuck in a hostile country and needed something that went bang, chances were I'd be able to get hold of an AK-47 without too much trouble. Owning one was a rite of passage for any aspiring terrorist. I fired singles and three-round bursts out to a hundred and fifty yards until my bullets grouped nicely into the black.

Thankful it wasn't too chilly, I unfolded a mat and lay down with an Accuracy International sniper rifle, leaning into the bipod as I fired out to a thousand yards. I never used to be a fan of the long-range stuff, but as team sniper, Carmen had spent many hours teaching me the best techniques. I still had a way to go to beat her—she'd hit a dime at that distance every time while my skill level ran more to a watermelon—but you still wouldn't want to get on the wrong end of my scope.

Last came my favourite. I'd lavished my beloved Walther P88 with care and gun oil until it became an extension of my arm. Left handed, right handed, standing, lying, and sitting, I practised until I hit the centre of the target on instinct every time.

I could have happily stayed out there all day, but my computer was calling. Literally. I'd got fifty-seven emails in the last thirty minutes and Sloane, my office assistant, had taken the morning off to visit her grandma.

Back to the real world.

My black jeans looked fine for work, so I got the keys to my Dodge Viper out of the lock box on the garage wall, and half an hour later, I skidded into my parking spot outside the office. Why did the guard by the doors look so alarmed? I was great at the J-turn manoeuvre. He must have been new.

Upstairs, I couldn't bring myself to sit in my own office, not without my husband there to share it. Every time I looked at his empty desk, it made me breathless. Instead, I grabbed my laptop and camped out with Nick. He didn't mind as long as I kept his coffee topped up when I fetched my own.

"How was Florida?" he asked when I walked in and dropped my bag onto the round table he used for meetings.

I squinted at him as the sun burned through his window then walked over to close the blinds. "Fine, yeah, didn't take long."

"No?"

"A couple of hours poking around to see what was going on to start with. The guy might have been the leader of a gang, but he still lived with his mom. She went out to a viewing at a funeral home yesterday evening, so I figured it was a good time to talk to him."

"What happened with the Rottweilers?"

"I drugged them first and stacked them around the back. Chainsaw was so engrossed in pay-per-view porn he didn't notice they were missing."

"Often the way, isn't it?"

"Yep, stupidity always brings them down in the end. When I ambled into his living room, he pulled out the gun hidden under the sofa and took great delight in telling me everything he'd done to the poor girl he killed. Said he'd enjoy putting me out of my misery too, right before he did unmentionable things to my still-warm body."

"Was he serious?"

"Oh, he pulled the trigger. Trouble was, I'd taken the bullets out half an hour earlier when he visited the john. The look on his face was priceless."

"Wish I'd seen that."

"You can watch if you want—it's all on camera. Once I'd delivered him and his confession to the police station, I caught a late flight and got home by one. It should be an easy conviction. The idiot even told me where he hid the garrotte."

"Another job off the list, then."

"Easy money. Are you all set for this evening?"

Nick was flying to the UK with me as part of the police security exercise. Dan too, and I'd handpicked another eight guys from Richmond and New York plus ten from the London office. We had a briefing scheduled for nine the next morning.

"Sure am. I've just got a couple of calls to make and one meeting this afternoon. Speaking of which, I need a favour."

"What kind of favour?" I owed Nick one. He'd done enough for me over the past few weeks.

"The meeting's with Patrick Johnson at four. He wondered where you were for the last one, and you know how much he loves you to be there. Any chance you could come with me?"

Just what I needed—the delights of Mr. Johnson. We provided office security for his nationwide chain of insurance brokers, and he'd been a client almost since the beginning. Because of the amount of revenue he brought in, and that history, he always had his quarterly updates with one of the directors rather than a lowly account manager. As my husband initially landed the account, he'd usually taken the meetings, but now it seemed Nick had drawn the short straw.

And me. Not because I had particular expertise in the area of building security, or even because I knew anything about his account. No, Mr. Johnson liked me there because he was a pervert. In this age of laptops and light projectors, he still insisted on having a paper report. Then during the meeting, I'd have to sit next to him to turn the pages and point out the right figures.

Sounds straightforward? Not when the meeting overran because the old git kept getting distracted by looking down my top and "accidentally" brushing his hand against my leg. My husband had to repeat everything he said at least twice.

Far from being jealous, my darling husband thought it was hilarious, and we had a standing bet before each meeting over how many times I'd get groped. Each one scored a point. The person with the closest guess won, with the loser having to buy dinner that evening. I generally came out on top because by sitting next to Patrick, I had a bit of control over the situation. As a bonus, we'd charge Mr. Johnson an extra two hundred dollars for each point on his next quarterly bill, which more than paid for three courses. He'd never once questioned what these additional charges were, which was testament to how much attention he paid to figures of the numerical kind.

"Okay, Nicky," I half grumbled. "You know the drill, right?"

"Yes, your mercenary husband explained it to me over beers once."

"Good. My guess is thirty-seven points."

"Sheesh, that's high. Really? In a half-hour meeting? I'm gonna go with twenty-five. Surely he has to spend some time reading the report?"

I'd been playing this game a lot longer than Nick. "I want my steak rare and my wine expensive."

While Nick talked on the phone, I deleted half of my emails, forwarded one from Miriam's lawyer onto mine, and dealt with the rest. Sloane sashayed in with Mr. Johnson's printed and bound reports at three. And a plate of biscuits. Guess which one I preferred?

"Shh, don't tell Toby. You're going to the Johnson meeting, I take it?" she said.

"Wish me luck."

"You never need that. You'll knock him dead."

"I live in hope. He's on medication for a heart condition, so you never know." I made it my business to keep up to date on everything concerning my clients.

"Yeuuuch. You might have to give him mouth-to-mouth."

"Good point. I'd rather lose the account than do that."

"I'm finalising your schedule for the UK. I've tried to keep commitments to a minimum, but there's a fundraising dinner for your foundation on the evening after the security exercise. The organisers want to know if you'll be there?"

A fancy dinner? Showing my face in public was the last thing I felt like doing at the moment, but the charity was important to me and I'd spent years building it up. We always got more out of the donors if

I spent some time schmoozing with them at these events, so I figured I'd better put my own feelings aside and make an appearance.

"Nicky, will you be my date? Pretty please?" I wasn't going alone. Recently widowed or not, attending on my own would be an invitation for a whole host of insensitive idiots to hit on me.

"Sure, baby."

I nabbed a chocolate digestive and turned back to Sloane. "Put me down as a yes. Can you make sure we've got two tables? I'll take some of the other guys too."

"Sure thing. The committee members will be super pleased."

With those arrangements in hand, I changed for Mr. Johnson then met Nick in the lobby. A car was waiting outside to take us to the meeting.

He looked me up and down. "I hate you."

I smiled sweetly. Didn't he realise I always played to win? I'd dressed appropriately for the occasion in a push-up bra and left the top couple of buttons on my blouse undone. Yes, I'd worn a suit, but it was tailored to be tight, and the skirt was barely within shouting distance of my knees. A pair of four-inch spike heels completed the outfit. Perfect.

"I'm thinking somewhere with a couple of Michelin stars for dinner."

"That's the last bet I'm ever making with you. You'd think I'd have learned over the years."

"I'm surprised you didn't learn with the first one."

Ah, our first bet. We'd made it over a decade ago when I'd been learning to climb, and Nick had tagged along as my husband and I ventured out to Seneca

Rocks on a beautiful spring day. Only three months had passed since Nick left the Navy SEALs, he was twenty-four to my nineteen, and he considered himself to be an excellent climber. To be fair, he was pretty good.

As I fastened my safety harness, he'd laid down a challenge—a race up The Bell, one of the hardest climbs in the area. You have to consider we were both even crazier in our younger days, so we ended up making a silly bet. Last to the top had to get a piercing.

I won, of course. Mainly because Nick didn't know that my husband had been drilling me up and down that cliff every day for the past week. Even though the hole in Nick's ear had healed up now, the fact he'd had to get it in the first place was still a sore point for him, and he'd never let me forget it.

I straightened up, showing off my assets to their full effect. "You don't fancy wearing that nice diamond stud again?"

"Get lost."

The meeting went well. Forty-three points, my second highest score ever. Boom. Hey, I might as well use my genes to my advantage.

Once we got back in the car, I kicked off my heels, which I now knew were designed by a sadist, and stripped out of my suit. I'd stashed jeans, an old T-shirt, and a pair of Converse in the boot of the car to change into for the flight, so we drove straight to the airport. Neither of us needed luggage because we both kept everything we could possibly need in my London home, Albany House. After Virginia, it was where I spent the most time, and Bradley made sure my wardrobe stayed well stocked.

The rest of the team was already on the plane, our

Global 8000 this time, and from the smiles and laughter, they reckoned they were going on vacation. Probably not far wrong. We'd all be staying at Albany House—work together, play together was my ethos—and this job promised to be a fun one.

"Drink, boss?" one of the guys asked.

"Just coffee."

I took the pilot's seat with Nick beside me. I never slept on planes, anyway. In such a small space, I could do too much damage if I had an episode, so I might as well knock back the caffeine and drive.

Soon we were at forty-thousand feet over the Atlantic.

"Nice takeoff," Nick said.

"Thanks. Look out, London. Here we come."

CHAPTER 10

AFTER ALMOST THREE weeks, Luke came to the realisation that Ash, or Emmy, or whoever she was, had gone from his life. He hadn't heard a single word from her in all that time. Not even a whisper. But that didn't stop him from worrying about how she was coping.

Did she have enough money? He should have offered her some before she left, he realised now. After all, she'd only worked for a month while she was in England, and that job had paid minimum wage. And what about somewhere to live? Was she staying with Dan or perhaps that small, loud chap? What was his name? Bradley? He'd seemed friendly enough, albeit more concerned with what she was wearing than her welfare.

And that wasn't the worst of it. Ash's frame of mind worried Luke more than her physical well-being. The last few times he'd seen her, she'd had an aura of sadness, a pain lurking behind her soft brown eyes. What had happened in her past to make her that way? Why hadn't he spent more time talking and less time peeling her out of her clothes?

For the past fortnight, he'd done little more than sit around the house, trying to look after Tia and occasionally attempting to work, without much success on either count. At least Tia hadn't turned back into the devil-child she'd been three months ago. Hey, yesterday she'd offered to empty the dishwasher.

On Monday he'd ventured into the office, only to spend more time on Google than corporate affairs. Ashlyn Hale, Ash Hale, Emmy Hale, Emily Hale... He'd searched every possible permutation, but nothing relevant came up for any of them. After making a fool of himself in his first meeting because he couldn't remember key details of his own product, he'd dragged an intern to the next to take notes for him. Notes he still hadn't read. And worse, when he'd ventured to the break room to fetch a cup of tea, he'd interrupted a cluster of red-faced employees around the water cooler, whispering about his mental state.

"I'm going to work from home for the rest of the week," he told his secretary after that. "Call me if anything important comes up."

So, there he was, lying on the sofa at three in the afternoon, wearing the same pair of jeans and T-shirt he'd slept in for the past four nights. Evidence of the two king-sized Snickers bars and family-sized bag of crisps he'd eaten for lunch lay discarded on the floor beside him, and he'd absentmindedly watched four back-to-back episodes of *The Jeremy Kyle Show*.

Still, at least his beard was coming along nicely.

He picked up his can of beer and took a long gulp. Why stick to soft drinks when he planned to stay at home for the entire day? Arabella's mother was picking the girls up, which meant Luke didn't need to move until tomorrow morning.

Mental note: remind his housekeeper to buy another bottle of whisky.

Since the kidnapping, Luke had been holding onto a

thread of hope that Ash would get in touch, but now that was all but frayed through.

"Anything from Ash?" Tia still asked every day, but her voice was devoid of its initial optimism.

"No, nothing."

As the days wore on, Luke's hurt turned to confusion. Why had Ash left England so fast? Sure, he'd yelled at her, but he thought they'd got past that during their days in London. Yes, she'd been distant, but she hadn't blanked him like one ex did when he'd accidentally spelled her name wrong in her birthday card. Who spelled *Jessica* with a Y in it? No, Ash hadn't borne an obvious grudge. And didn't all couples have arguments? If they could only talk, he'd apologise for whatever he'd done, she could explain why she hadn't told the truth, and maybe they'd have a chance at a future together. All she needed to do was come back.

He shifted on the sofa because one butt cheek had gone to sleep. Perhaps he should invest in more comfortable furniture? One of those massage chairs or something, as long as he could order it off the internet.

Groaning, Luke blew out a long breath. Hadn't Ash felt the same way he did? In his head, he'd started planning a future with her by his side, one filled with love and laughter. Despite their different backgrounds, they'd clicked. But maybe they'd just been too different? Him, a millionaire with a crazy work ethic and a love of extreme sports, and her, the housewife turned stable girl who led a quiet life. Or so he'd thought.

What good was his money now? All those millions couldn't buy the normality he craved. Once, the status quo had meant flaunting a piece of arm candy that cost him plenty in clothes and jewellery but not much in terms of emotional involvement. Then Ash came along and he discovered the joy of companionship. Having someone to come home to each evening sure beat the parade of insipid socialites. But it had to be the right "someone."

Wow, this was all getting a bit too Sigmund Freud for a weekday.

The door slammed, breaking him out of his melancholy. Thirty seconds later, Tia arrived in front of him, hands on hips.

"Have you been lying there all day?"

"Pretty much, yeah."

"It's not even five o'clock, and you're already on your fourth can of beer. Do you really think that's a good idea?"

"No, you're right." He glanced at his watch for confirmation. "It's time I switched to wine. Can you bring me a bottle from the kitchen?"

"No, I can't! You need to get up and start acting normal again. You've been lying there for weeks eating rubbish and getting drunk. The gym's got cobwebs, and you stink."

Her mouth set in a hard line, and she glared at him.

"Okay, I'll get my own wine."

Tia whirled away and clomped up the stairs to her bedroom.

What was normal anymore?

The next afternoon, Luke rolled over on the sofa, accidentally squashing a packet of biscuits. Sheesh, they'd spilled out and melted onto the cushion. At least the dark chocolate matched the leather. He briefly considered clearing up, but soon forgot the mess as a particularly enthralling episode of *Bargain Hunt* distracted him. Who knew somebody would pay so much for an ugly porcelain cow?

Five o'clock, and the click of Tia's key in the front door made him glance over at the coffee table. He'd run out of beer again. Would she bring him a drink tonight, or was she determined to stick with the holier-than-thou attitude?

Footsteps sounded in the hallway, stopping outside the door.

"He's in there," Tia said.

A few seconds later, the door to the den was pushed open and a shadow fell over Luke. Uh oh. Tia had brought reinforcements in the form of Arabella's brother, Mark, and another friend of theirs, Rob.

"Good grief, mate," Mark said. "Tia warned you'd turned into a slob, but I didn't think it'd be this bad. Your jeans could stand up on their own. And what's with the beard?"

Luke struggled up into a sitting position. "I wanted a bit of 'me' time."

"What are you? A flipping woman?"

"I just felt like taking a day off. I do own the company. What are you doing here, anyway?"

"We're staging an intervention. You're not lying there watching..." Rob squinted at the TV screen. "Watching *Loose Women* any longer. Now, get off your pasty backside and take a shower. We'll wait."

"I'm not watching..."

Oh. Mark was right. *Bargain Hunt* must have

finished.

Luke toyed with the idea of telling the pair of them to get lost, but then he realised they were right—he couldn't spend the rest of his life slumped in front of the television, even if it was a fifty-inch flat screen with voice control and surround sound. And he didn't understand that program where a bunch of middle-aged women sat around chatting.

"Fine, I'll shower."

He dragged himself upstairs, reeling at the smell coming from his armpits. Nasty. Perhaps he should try bleach rather than a bottle of Lynx?

As Luke became reacquainted with his double-width shower stall, he couldn't help thinking of the times Ash had shared it with him. Would he ever get over her? He tried—and failed—to block her pretty face from his mind as he pulled on a clean shirt and jeans.

When he got back downstairs, Rob was bent over the pool table, and he potted a red as Luke walked into the den.

"Lucky shot," Mark said.

"That was pure skill, pal." He threw a glance at Luke. "Give me two minutes to finish thrashing Mark, then we're going to the pub."

"Whatever."

Anything to get out of this house and its constant reminders of Ash. One of her jumpers still lay draped over the back of the sofa, the faint scent of the Ralph Lauren perfume Luke had bought her still lingered in the air, and every time Luke moved something, he found another stray hair tie.

"Let's head into London," Mark suggested. "If we go to the pub in the village, everyone'll want to know why

Luke's channelling a hobo."

Not to mention asking where Ash was. No point in fuelling the local rumour mill—it did quite well enough without someone chucking a bucket of petrol over it.

"Fine."

"All those millions and you couldn't afford a razor? I'll donate one if you'll shave that scruff off your face."

"Pack it in, would you?"

Losing the beard wouldn't make much difference, anyway. Not when his eyes were bloodshot with dark circles underneath and his mouth had forgotten how to smile.

"This looks like a decent place," Mark said

Luke trailed behind him into the sports bar, grimacing slightly when his shoes stuck to the floor. Still, the prices were reasonable by London standards, and the barmaids worked fast enough to keep the queue short. Chelsea vs. Manchester United played on the big screen, and as Chelsea were two goals up, the atmosphere was positively jovial.

"Your round," Mark told Rob as they bagged a table with a good view of the screen. "Carlsberg for me."

Luke slumped into his seat, half drunk already. A few minutes later, Rob came back with pints for everyone.

"So," Mark started. "What happened with Ash, then?"

"I don't want to talk about it."

"Well, after venturing into your hovel, we deserve to know. So spill. We've heard about the kidnapping, if that's what's bothering you."

Mark and Rob were both in the Metropolitan police, and although they hadn't been present at the aftermath of Tia's abduction, clearly the force's grapevine rivalled that of the Lower Foxford Women's Institute.

"I'm not dissecting my love life over drinks." Despite Mark's earlier suggestion, he wasn't a flipping woman.

"You've got to give us something."

Luke sighed. "Tia's kidnapping put some pressure on my relationship with Ash, and after the situation with Tia got resolved, Ash didn't want to stick around to help pick up the pieces."

There, that sounded reasonable. Vague but plausible.

Mark leaned back in his seat, studying Luke through narrowed eyes. Now he knew how it felt to be interviewed under duress.

"See, that surprises me. I only met her a couple of times, but she seemed sweet. Thoughtful. The change she made in Tia was unreal, and it rubbed off on Arabella too. She's giving our parents far less grief now."

"Well, that's the way it happened. When you broke off your engagement with Carla, how did you get over it?"

If Mark was so keen on talking, he could dissect his own problems instead.

"Looking back, I had a lucky escape. But Carla cheated whereas Ash didn't." He paused. "Did she?"

Luke hastily shook his head. "Sorry, mate. I didn't realise Carla did that."

No wonder Mark hadn't wanted to speak about the split at the time.

"Don't worry. Like I said, it was better to find out she was a cheating cow before we got married rather than after. And as for the piece of slime she was banging, we clubbed together at work, and so far, we've given him thirty-seven parking tickets and nicked him for speeding twice."

"Good going. Ash wasn't involved with anyone else, though. She couldn't have been. She spent all her spare time with me and Tia."

"Revenge isn't everything. Yeah, it helps a bit, but I'd still rather Carla hadn't cheated in the first place." Mark paused to watch a goal replay as Chelsea scored again. "Why don't you try a different approach? I could set you up with one of Mandy's friends if you want."

Mandy was Mark's current girlfriend, sweet enough, but she never stopped talking about her job in PR—celebrity this, VIP that, freebies, freebies, freebies —and her habit of giggling after every sentence grated on Luke's last nerve.

"Don't think I'm ready for that."

Rob eyed up three women in short dresses teetering across the bar. "You want to find yourself a hot chick. Have some fun—just casual. Hit any club on a Saturday night and there's hundreds of girls, all gagging for it."

"I don't fancy incubating an STD."

"That'll only happen if you look in some dive. You should come out with me. I'll take you to places where the top totty hangs out."

"Thanks for the offer, but I'll pass."

Luke had never been one for a fleeting affair, although he had to admit, the idea of uncomplicated sex sounded more appealing after the burn Ash gave him.

Rob waggled his eyebrows. "Well, let me know if you change your mind."

"I will, but I'd rather enjoy the single life for a while. Do either of you guys fancy going skiing? I haven't been for ages, and I like the idea of some good snow."

Ironically, it was Ash who'd encouraged him to get back on a snowboard for the first time in years.

"I could do a long weekend, but not right away," Mark said. "We've got a big security exercise coming up at work in three days, and if it's anything like the last one, we'll all spend the next couple of weeks providing explanations to the brass for everything that went wrong. Then we'll have to implement a whole ream of new procedures so things don't get screwed up again. Rob? How about you?"

"Same. I'm in, but I can't go for a few weeks. Not just because of the security exercise—it's my sister's sixteenth, and Mother will go nuts if I miss the fancy dinner she's spent months organising." He turned to Mark. "But you're being too negative about this exercise. It'll go fine. We've spent the last fortnight planning for every eventuality."

Mark rolled his eyes. "You weren't here for the last one. We thought we'd do well on that, and it all went belly up."

"Yes, I know, but I've read the reports, and we've addressed the weaknesses they identified. Plus I heard Emerson Black has gone AWOL, so there's no way it can be as difficult as last time."

Excuses, excuses. Surely skiing was better than

work?

"What's this exercise about?" Luke asked. "And who's Emerson Black?"

CHAPTER 11

"WHO'S EMERSON BLACK?" Mark took another drink of his pint before answering Luke's question. "Sorry, mate. I keep forgetting you're not one of us. Basically, the exercise is a simulation of a terrorist attack for several police forces, working jointly. An outside company called Blackwood Security comes in to run it."

Rob jumped in to help. "Last time, it was a mocked up visit to a racecourse by a bunch of foreign dignitaries. Blackwood sent one team to play the terrorists and another to play the dignitaries, plus there were a few hundred extras pretending to be the general public."

"Sounds complicated," Luke said.

Mind you, his alcohol consumption made anything sound complicated right now.

"We were supposed to prevent a terrorist attack," Mark said. "But Blackwood killed off ninety percent of the dignitaries, eight police officers, and twenty-two of the public. The results got hushed up, so this doesn't go further than this table, but the upshot is that it was embarrassing. The chief constables are still giving us grief about it. This week's exercise is similar, except the venue's a conference centre rather than a racecourse."

"So, who's Emerson Black?" Luke asked again.

"Emerson Black's one of the owners of Blackwood

Security," Rob said.

"And he was tough to beat? Was he one of the terrorists?"

"She, actually. Yes, and yes. She's possibly the smartest, most devious woman ever to walk this planet. And some other planets too, seeing as the jury's out on whether she's even human. They never admitted it, but I'm sure she was the mastermind behind the racecourse debacle. She's one scary woman."

Mark shuddered. "Because of the finger thing?"

"That was just one incident. She's got balls, I'll give her that."

"What finger thing?" Luke asked.

Rob and Mark looked at each other.

"I'm not sure we can discuss it with a civilian," Rob said.

"Look, you just interrogated me over my relationship. The least you can do is give me something in return. And I won't tell anyone." Probably he wouldn't even remember tomorrow if the drinking went as he hoped.

"Okay, okay. So, Emerson Black heads up the Special Projects division at Blackwood, which essentially means she's psycho-nuts. A couple of years back, they consulted on a kidnapping case I was assigned to. The parents were loaded. The father was some hotshot in the telecoms industry."

Rob paused to take a swallow of his beer and glanced around. They were sitting in a quiet corner, the buzz around them loud enough that Luke couldn't pick out an individual conversation, but still, Rob lowered his voice before continuing.

"What I'm about to say goes no further than here,

got it?"

"Got it."

"The kidnapper told the parents not to call the police, so we had to keep our investigation under the radar. We'd got nowhere by the time the boy's finger arrived in the post."

Luke popped out in a cold sweat at the memory of Tia's fingernail turning up in a padded envelope. That poor family—at least Tia's nail would grow back.

"That's barbaric."

"You're telling me. The kid was five years old. Anyhow, by that point, the father wanted to do something—anything—that would help, and Sergeant Bridges suggested giving Blackwood a call. They charge big bucks, but like I said, the man had the cash, so he hired them."

"I heard Superintendent Flowers blew his top," Mark said.

"Yeah, big style. He didn't like having his toes trodden on. But he couldn't deny they got results because they found the boy in a day. The arrangement was that when they located him, they'd hand everything over to us."

"So that was good, right?" Luke asked.

"Yes and no. They called to say the kid was stashed in a townhouse on the outskirts of London, but the super's an idiot, so while he stood around in the street outside wasting time, it turned into a hostage situation." Mark put his head in his hands. "The twat actually started yelling at the kidnappers through a megaphone. Honestly, it made me embarrassed to be a copper."

"What happened after that?"

"Emerson took matters into her own hands."

"And?"

"From what I heard, she wandered around the back of the house and climbed up the outside of the freaking building. The cop watching her knew who she was and turned a blind eye because he thought the super was an idiot too. Apparently, she got a locked fourth-story balcony door open in five seconds flat. Might as well have had a key. It took another three minutes for her to get down to the ground floor, disarm and incapacitate both the kidnappers, and walk out the front door carrying the kid."

"Sounds like superwoman. Was she wearing a cape?" Luke asked.

"A pair of jeans. Looked as if they'd been spray-painted on. Anyway, it gets better. Before she left, she told the super exactly what she thought of him, mainly in four-letter words."

"Why does that make her scary? I'd have wanted to have a few choice words with the superintendent too, if I'd been in that situation."

"I haven't finished. When we went inside, one of the kidnappers was unconscious and the other was cowering in a corner, begging us to keep her away. When we cuffed him, we found he'd lost his little finger. And the doctors couldn't sew it back on because she'd stamped on it."

Luke let out a low whistle. "She cut it off?"

"She claimed his knife slipped in the struggle. Calm as you like. She wasn't even breathing hard when she came out of the house."

"Okay, I have to hand it to you. If that's true, she *is* crazy."

"It's true, all right. Every word. I swear."

"But she's not around anymore?" Luke asked. "Did she quit? What would someone like that move on to? It's not as if she'd take up a new career as a secretary is it?"

"My sources say she disappeared after her husband got murdered last year. The cops in Virginia tried to pin it on her, but they couldn't find any concrete evidence. Although if she did do it, there's no way she'd have left any evidence, so that's hardly surprising. But hey, disappearing doesn't look good in terms of guilt, does it? The press called her the 'Black Widow,' according to the internet. Get it? Emerson Black—Black Widow?"

Mark and Rob chuckled while Luke shuddered.

"She sounds like a real piece of work." What kind of man would marry a woman like that in the first place? "At least she won't be around for your exercise. You wouldn't want to end up missing body parts."

Mark turned deadly serious. "We don't know for sure that she's not around. Terry sat next to her at a conference a couple of years ago, and he didn't even realise. He was chatting to the guy next to him about how she was crazy but he'd do her anyway, then she got called up on stage to give a speech."

"Ouch," Rob said. "What happened? Did she hear him?"

"Oh, she heard him, all right. Came over after her speech, full of smiles, and said, 'If I'm half as crazy as you think I am, you'd better keep an eye on your crown jewels or you might wake up and find them missing.' Poor guy hardly slept for weeks."

"So he didn't know what she looked like, then?" Luke said. "Must have been a shock to find out."

Rob shook his head. "Nobody knows what she looks like. She's a chameleon. I've seen her three times now, and I still couldn't pick her out of a line-up." He looked around, eyes darting in all directions. "In fact, she could even be here now."

"The chances are pretty slim. And it's so noisy in here, we can barely hear you, let alone someone on the next table."

"He's right," Mark said. "Chill."

"Chill. Yeah." Rob picked up his glass, drained it, and pushed the empty towards Mark. "Your round. And speaking of Blackwood, are you still up for the Blackwood Foundation Ball on Saturday?"

"Open bar? Of course. But Geoff said to tell you he can't make it. His girlfriend's making him go to see *The Lion King* musical instead."

"Seriously?"

"That's what he said. I made him repeat it twice because I couldn't believe it either. That man is whipped."

"Okay, so we've got a spare ticket." Two sets of eyes swivelled towards to Luke.

"Luke, you'll come, right?" Rob said. "You need to get out of the house. No man should be sitting at home alone on a Saturday night."

If that house had beer and a computer, then being alone in it was perfectly acceptable in Luke's view. "I'd better not. Tia'll be on her own otherwise."

"Don't worry, Tia's going out with Arabella on Saturday night then staying at our place." Mark had temporarily moved back to his parents' home after a small incident involving a holiday and a moth infestation. "I heard them arranging it in the car on the way home today."

"You're out of excuses," Rob said.

"What's the dinner for? I'm not agreeing to anything without having all the information first."

"The Blackwood Foundation is a charity founded by the same people who own Blackwood Security. It works with young people in London by getting them off the streets and into work or education, and making sure they have somewhere safe to live."

Great. Another bunch of do-gooders wanting money.

Luke had been to those sorts of events a thousand times over, and quite frankly, his Xbox held more appeal.

How could he get out of this?

CHAPTER 12

"SO, IT'S A fundraiser?" Luke asked. "Can't I just send a cheque?"

Rob shrugged. "Yes and no. There's usually some sort of auction to raise money, but what they're really after is your time. Blackwood's always looking for mentors."

"Mentors? What do you mean?"

"They don't dish out free stuff to the kids. They teach them the skills they need to hold down a job and look after themselves. That's what they want people to help with."

Mark nodded his agreement. "You can say what you want about Emerson Black and her murderous tendencies, but she's put a lot of effort into the Blackwood Foundation. Their work's made a big difference to crime rates, especially in the East End. The number of rough sleepers is down too. I've heard Emerson even takes on some of the kids personally."

"I take it you two have got involved, then?"

"I'm working with a sixteen-year-old lad at the moment," Mark said. "We arrested him seven times last year for nicking cars, but now I've sat down and talked to him properly, I know he only did it because he needed the cash to survive."

"I can't believe there are kids living like that."

"Too many of them. Blackwood found this kid somewhere to stay, and now he's taking an automotive repair course at college. Getting good grades too."

"How about you?" Luke asked Rob. "What have you been doing?"

"My kid lives on one of the big council estates with his mum, but she's not all there. Dementia. Blackwood helped him to get the right care for her so he can go to college. When I caught up with him last week, he said the weight of the world's been lifted from his shoulders."

His kid? Rob had really been sucked in by this, hadn't he? "So you can see you're making a difference?"

"For sure, and that's only two kids. There are hundreds more who need help." The cheeky git caught the barmaid's eye and held up three fingers. Of course, she smiled and nodded. "You should try it. Blackwood provides every mentor with training and backup. You never know—it might take your mind off Ash."

Hmm, training? Perhaps that would give Luke some extra skills to handle Tia. He needed all the help he could get there. And although he hated to admit it, Rob and Mark were right. He did need something to occupy his newly created spare time now Ash wasn't there to share it with him.

"Fine, I'll come to the dinner thing, but I want to know more about this mentoring scheme before I commit to anything."

"I'll text you details of the place and time. It's black tie." Rob leaned over and poked Luke in the stomach. "If you can still fit into your tux after all the junk you've been eating, that is."

"Thanks for being so sensitive, mate."

Luke looked down then closed his eyes to block out the roll of fat hanging over his belt. Where had that come from?

A roar went up in the bar as Chelsea scored, and a group of blokes in blue team strips started doing a drunken dance in front of the bar. Luke surreptitiously switched to drinking water, suddenly concerned over whether he would in fact fit into his tux, or indeed any of his other suits. After all, the number of healthy meals he'd eaten over the past month was in single figures.

His diet started now.

With something to focus on, Luke found it easier to get out of bed in the mornings. He forced himself to use the gym before breakfast and ditched his beer and crisp habit in favour of protein shakes and salads. By the time Saturday came, he fitted into his tuxedo—just— and figured the trouser buttons would survive the evening as long as he didn't breathe too much.

Mark had insisted they start with a beer to line their stomachs before an evening of "poncey wine," and when Luke arrived at the pub across the road from the Black Diamond Hotel and Casino where the event was being held, Rob and Mark were already seated at a table. Chris, a doctor of something-or-other Luke had met a few times before, raised his hand in greeting.

"Got you a beer."

"Cheers." Luke took a sip to be polite, but he'd already promised himself he'd go easy on the alcohol tonight. He raised an eyebrow at Rob and Mark. "Why do you two look so glum?"

Chris grinned, while the perky pair glowered into their pints even more.

"They played some little security game yesterday, and it didn't go so well."

Mark dragged his gaze upwards. "Didn't go well is the understatement of the year."

"In what way?" Luke asked.

"At first, everything went to plan. We caught one terrorist at the entrance, and when he took a WPC hostage, we talked him down and arrested him. Except it turned out he was just a distraction for a bunch more bad guys to sneak in around the back."

Even to Luke's untrained ears, that sounded like a big problem. "What happened next?"

"Carnage. Pure carnage. Then it got worse. At the debrief in the conference hall, the dude playing the prime minister turned over the lectern he was speaking at and showed us the bomb built into the bottom of it." Mark leaned forward and smacked his head against the table. "We'd completely missed it."

"At least it didn't go off."

Rob half groaned, half snorted. "Our superiors didn't see it that way. And once the fake prime minister finished berating us for that error, someone shot him in the chest with a paintball. They had a sniper hidden inside the suspended ceiling at the back of the hall, and we hadn't checked it properly."

"And just to emphasise our utter incompetence, the gunman escaped before we could catch him," Mark finished up.

Luke couldn't help laughing, earning him dirty looks from his two friends. Before he got a thump in the arm, he checked his watch and pushed back his chair.

"Time to head over the road. We don't want to be late."

"I'm not sure I want to go anymore," Rob muttered. "I can't face anyone from Blackwood without wanting to sink into the floor."

Luke took hold of his arm and pulled him up. "You've dragged me away from a comfy sofa, and I've been living on rabbit food all week to fit into this penguin suit. We're darn well going."

Not to mention that when Luke checked the TV schedule earlier, there wasn't anything on worth watching. He didn't want to go home to sit through a reality show marathon again.

"And the tickets are like gold dust," Chris added.

"I'm only going for the alcohol," Rob said, sighing like a drama queen.

Right, time to get this over with. Mark finished his drink, and the four left the bar.

The drinks reception was in full swing when they reached the Black Diamond. The security staff on the door peered closely at their tickets and checked for ID. No doubt Blackwood had provided the four giants crammed into surprisingly well-fitted suits.

Inside the modern bar, gaggles of people stood around, cocktails in hand, chatting and laughing. An old pro at networking, Luke dove right in out of habit. He'd had to learn the art of meaningless small talk fast after his father died and he'd been forced to take over HC Systems. After half an hour, he'd spoken to fifteen people and had the pocketful of business cards to prove it.

The crowd proved to be a little different to the usual, though. Yes, Luke spoke to several captains of industry, a well-known football player, and an actress, but he also met a schoolteacher, two nurses, and a soldier. Every one of them brimmed with enthusiasm over the mentoring scheme, leaving Luke keen to hear more.

As a small woman with a big voice flitted from group to group, asking people to take their seats, Luke took a chance to admire his surroundings. The hotel was one of the nicer establishments he'd visited, the décor stark yet expensive. Abstract paintings added a splash of colour to the black and white theme in the bar.

The ballroom was done out just as tastefully. Purple orchids graced glass vases in the centre of each table, and the waitresses wore matching flowers in their hair. Luke slid into his seat next to Rob as the servers brought out warm bread rolls.

Perhaps this wasn't so bad, after all.

"I'm nipping out to the bar," Mark said. "I hardly got a wink of sleep after the disaster yesterday, and if I don't get a Red Bull, I'll be snoring in my soup."

Luke knew how he felt, except it had been thoughts of a certain brunette that kept him awake. "Make that two."

"Sure thing."

Ten minutes later, Mark returned with the drinks but without his colour. Luke had never seen anyone so white.

"What's up?" he asked. "You look as if you've seen

Hugh Hefner in a bikini."

"Emerson Black's here."

Rob's eyes widened. "Are you sure? I mean, we don't even know what she looks like."

"Well, she's standing with the bogus prime minister, and he just introduced her to the man next to him as Emerson Black. So I'd say there's a fair chance she is, in fact, Emerson Black," Mark screwed up his face the way he always did when he was pondering. "Plus she looks familiar. I'm sure I've seen her somewhere before."

"You'll be needing this." Rob pushed Mark's wine glass towards him. "So, she's finally reappeared. Maybe the rumours are true and she really is immortal. Say, I wonder if she was the shooter yesterday afternoon?"

"Is that all you can think about? Work? You never said how fit she is."

"Didn't I? Yeah, she's hot."

"Hot? She's smoking. No, hotter. Scorching. Does my hair look okay? Has anyone got breath mints?"

"Forget it. She's way out of your league."

"C'mon, let a guy dream. Anyway, it's not just me. I bet the gents' is full of guys jacking off over her. She's a walking wet dream."

"I'm glad there aren't any ladies at this table," Chris said. "One of them would have slapped you by now."

"Hey, I'm paying her a compliment."

"You reckon?"

Luke resisted the urge to roll his eyes. It didn't take much to get Mark's tongue hanging out, but Luke had to admit to being slightly intrigued by the mysterious Emerson Black.

Trying to be subtle, he angled his chair so it faced

the door. How long until she walked through it?

CHAPTER 13

AS NICK CHATTED away beside me, I questioned once again why I decided to come tonight. I'd already heard so many expressions of sympathy over my husband that if one more person said how sorry they were, I'd run screaming from the building.

Unfortunately, Nick read my thoughts and tightened his grip on my arm as he turned to introduce me to yet another benefactor.

"Emerson, this is Donald Watson. He runs a garden centre in West Sussex, and he's interested in joining our mentoring scheme. Donald, this is Emerson Black."

Donald stuck out a pudgy hand for me to shake. "It's a pleasure to meet you, Ms. Black." He addressed my chest, which was displayed a little too prominently in a red dress carefully selected by Bradley. "I'm sorry to hear about your husband."

Arrrgh. I gritted my teeth. "Thank you, but really, the pleasure's all mine. And I'm so happy you want to help with our work..."

After five minutes, I finally extricated myself from Mr. Watson's clutches. He'd seemed enthusiastic, but as he hadn't looked at my face during the entire conversation, I wasn't sure whether he was excited about the foundation's projects or my bra size.

Over at the bar, Ryan was drinking a pint of beer. A

quick glance around showed most people had already gone in for dinner, so I took the glass out of his hand and swallowed what was left.

"Bad day?" he asked.

"Nick keeps introducing me to morons. I think it's payback for the paintball incident yesterday."

"What do you expect? You shot him with pink. *Pink.* If you'd used blue or green, he probably wouldn't have been bothered."

"I don't think he was too thrilled with the bruise on his chest either, Ryan."

"Hey, that's part of the job."

"Is your speech ready?"

"As it'll ever be."

Ryan was one of the foundation's kids and a pet project of mine. We'd met five years ago on a dark and stormy night. Such a cliché, right? But it had been raining cats and dogs when I stopped to shelter under a railway arch until the downpour passed.

Turned out I wasn't alone. Some slimeball—a dealer by the looks of him—was shaking down a homeless kid for his last few quid.

"Leave him alone." My husband kept telling me to be more tactful, so I refrained from adding something impolite at the end of it. Are you proud?

As I'd hoped, the aforementioned slimeball turned his attention to me instead.

"How about you pay me what he owes instead?"

"What does he owe you for?"

"Rent. Everyone who sleeps on my patch 'as to pay their dues. And guess what? Now I'm charging interest."

"Really? In that case, hold on while I get my

chequebook out. Or do you take MasterCard?"

He paused, surprised, long enough for Ryan to come haring past and plant himself in front of me.

"Don't you touch her."

For goodness' sake... "Dude, I've got this."

"No way. You don't know what you're getting into."

"Oh, I think I do."

Ryan squared up to the slimeball. "You'll have to go through me to get to her."

Aw, that was actually kind of sweet. My husband never defended me that way. He just stood back and took notes so he could point out all my faults later.

But it was also stupid.

"Honestly, I'm good here."

"No, it's—"

The slimeball had enough of waiting and took a swing. Ryan ducked and sidestepped, and even managed a couple of good punches before the guy got him on the ground.

Then I knocked the slimeball's teeth out with one swift kick, and just like that, my night was complete. I got twitchy if I went too long without a good punch-up.

Anyhow, I'd liked Ryan's courage and his willingness to fight for what he believed in, so when the rain stopped, I took him out for dinner. And gave him a job.

Now twenty, he still worked in Blackwood's London office. Yesterday, he'd done a wonderful job of convincing the cops that he was a lone nut gunman while another eight guys climbed up the fire escape around the back of the conference centre and snuck in through a first-floor window.

My introduction and his speech were scheduled to

take place between the starter and main course. That would give the guests something to talk about over dinner, and it was easier than trying to get their attention at the end when everyone was drunk and half asleep. Far better to have the auction afterwards when the alcohol had loosened their purse strings. Bradley had managed to coax over thirty lots out of various acquaintances, everything from dinners to holidays to cases of wine. He'd perfected his tactics over the years —mostly he kept bugging people until they gave him stuff to go away.

Luckily, he had no shame.

Meanwhile, Nick came over and handed me a glass of white wine.

"Slightly more ladylike than the beer, my darling. Are we going in for dinner?"

"I thought I'd skip the starter." Carpaccio of beetroot with goat's cheese, apparently. Not my favourite, and I'd rather go hungry than be stared at like a zoo exhibit. "You go ahead if you want, though."

Nick stayed, and so did Ryan. We snagged a table in the corner and hid behind our glasses until a member of the organising committee came out to fetch us.

What was I doing here? I wasn't ready, not for this, but it was too late to escape. Nick took point, and I hung back as he picked up the microphone and got everyone to shut up. The room went silent as he introduced me.

"Now a few words from our founder, Emerson Black."

Everyone's eyes followed as I walked from the back of the ballroom to the stage. I hated being the centre of attention. The shadows were my home, and when I'd taken to the light in the past, I'd always had my husband's support. Without him, I felt naked. My nails dug into my palms as I clenched my fists, and I forced myself to relax. If I popped off an acrylic, I'd have to face Bradley's wrath.

But first, I had to face the audience. *Smile, Emmy.*

"When I started the Blackwood Foundation almost a decade ago with Nathaniel Wood and my late husband, little did I know how big it would grow. Nathaniel is unable to join us tonight, but like me, he wishes to extend his heartfelt thanks to each and every one of you for coming to lend your support. Thanks to your donations, we've been able to fund safe places for underprivileged teenagers to stay and counsellors to give them the support they need. Your expertise and time, so willingly given, teach these young adults what their parents have not."

I scanned the room as I spoke. Friends, colleagues, acquaintances, strangers. A not insignificant number of idiots I had to be nice to because they had fat bank accounts and useful connections. And then I saw him. Sitting at table number thirteen.

Guess it really was unlucky.

My eyes locked with Luke's and I tripped over my words. Even though I recovered quickly, Nick's head turned in the direction I'd been looking. Rats. My heart raced as I continued my speech on autopilot, the words sounding foreign to my own ears. Had anyone else noticed my slip-up?

"Tonight, you'll hear from two of our success stories. I first met Ryan when he was fifteen, and Michelle joined us at seventeen. Both of these individuals have shown extraordinary courage and tenacity in getting to where they are today, and they'll be giving you an insight into the foundation's work."

I spouted highlights from the past year and summarised new projects in the pipeline before I finished up.

"I'd like to remind all of you that we have an auction starting after dinner with some thrilling lots, including a two week holiday at the lovely Quinta Nova Vineyard in Portugal and a bespoke couture dress by up-and-coming designer, Ishmael. Finally, I'm going to add a pledge of my own. Whatever the amount raised tonight, I'll personally double it."

As I stepped down, murmurs of surprise travelled around the room. Good. Hopefully, that would encourage the wealthy to get their wallets out. A bit of competition could be a healthy thing.

"Good luck," I whispered to Ryan as he hopped up on stage to take my place.

One foot in front of the other, head up, back straight. Smile. As I sat down next to Nick, I tried to concentrate on Ryan's words rather than the fact that I'd just been outed to Luke.

Tried, and failed. Luke's wide-eyed shock played over and over in my mind like a bad horror movie.

I'd wanted to speak to him before I went back to the States, but not yet. It wasn't the right time. Not when my thoughts were still so jumbled, and I didn't know what I wanted to say to him or how to say it. Did I start by apologising? Or begging for forgiveness? Or should I just act normally and hope he did the same?

I snuck a glance in his direction, and of course, he was looking at me. Looking at me like I was a piece of doggy poop he'd just trodden in.

Great. I'd made things worse, hadn't I? Why hadn't I called him before this evening? Now he thought I was a rich kid with too much time and money on her hands.

"More wine, ma'am?" a waiter asked.

"Could you do me a favour and bring a gin and tonic?"

"Certainly. Hendricks, Bombay Sapphire, or Tanqueray?"

Did it really matter? "Hendricks. And make it a double, would you?"

I reached out for Nick's glass of red, but my hands shook so I stuffed them in my lap instead.

"You okay?" Nick asked.

"Never better."

Except I might have cracked a tooth from clenching my jaw so hard.

Thankfully, Ryan was oblivious to my drama and soon had the audience in stitches with his stories. My own laughter sounded mechanical. Or perhaps maniacal. After all, I'd lost my ever-loving mind. Half of the audience got to their feet and applauded as Ryan finished, and he high-fived me as he took the seat to my left.

Michelle started speaking, and I heard the nervousness in her voice. At least she'd made it to the stage—she'd been quaking more than San Francisco beforehand. My hug for her when she finished was genuine.

"You did me proud tonight," I told her.

"I thought I was gonna faint."

"Have faith, honey."

A waiter deposited a plate in front of me, but my appetite had deserted me. How bad would it look if I made a dash for it before dessert came out?

Nick reached under the tablecloth, grabbed my hand, and clamped it against his thigh, our fingers intertwined.

"I know exactly what you're thinking," he whispered.

"How delicious the food is?"

"You mean that food that you've barely taken two mouthfuls of?"

Guilty. "Okay, perhaps not."

"You're not running out on me."

Sometimes, I hated Nick and his psychic abilities. Besides my husband, he probably understood me better than anyone, and he was one of the few people able to read my moods. When we worked together, in situations where teamwork was crucial and the slightest miscalculation could result in *manger des pissenlits par la racine*, as the French would say, the whole mind-reading thing gave us a definite advantage. But right now, I wanted to shield my thoughts in lead and bury them in concrete.

"Me, run out? I'd never dream of it."

"This is your party. You're going to stay beside me until I say it's time to go, and you're going to enjoy yourself."

The git said that with a smile. Just another pleasant chat between Nick and Emmy.

"I'm not sure I can."

"Which one? Stay beside me or enjoy yourself? The second one's optional, but the first is mandatory."

Demanding much? It was almost like having my husband back beside me again. And that somehow made me want to stay.

"Fine. You win. But what about Luke? Seeing me here's got to be like rubbing salt into the wound for him."

"Well, there are three possibilities, aren't there? Either you go and speak to him, or he comes to speak to you, or you ignore each other. You're not going to pick option one, and option three won't cause you a problem. That leaves option two, and if he approaches you, then we'll face him together."

Nick made everything sound so straightforward. Three months ago, it would have been, but that was before my brain turned to mush. I carried on picking at my dinner, and what had been a beautifully presented salt-crusted sea bass with sautéed vegetable julienne soon became something even the most downmarket restaurant chain would turn its nose up at.

Even the Sachertorte that appeared for dessert made me feel sick, and I was the girl who'd once driven from Budapest to Vienna just to eat the original version. Eventually, Nick resorted to forking it into my mouth.

"Eat. I'm not carrying you when we hit the dance floor."

"You won't have to." Because I wasn't going anywhere near it.

After coffee, I got up on stage again to introduce the auction. Could anyone other than Nick tell I was falling apart inside? As the bids stacked up, my mood improved a little, enough for me to join the compère in a half-hearted foxtrot as he drummed up support for a course of ballroom dancing lessons.

Just don't look in Luke's direction, Emmy. You can do this.

Four grand for a crate of wine from Nate's California vineyard, sixteen thousand for Ishmael's wacky dress, and a round twenty for a week in the Florida beach house I rarely used. When the hammer came down on the final lot, the compère let out a whoop.

"Ladies and gentlemen, the total raised tonight comes to just under six hundred thousand pounds, meaning over a million will go to the Blackwood Foundation thanks to Emerson's generous donation."

Not bad for an evening's fundraising, but I had bigger things on my mind. Did I dare try talking to Luke?

As the applause died down, the band struck up. I'd left Bradley in charge of the music, and true to form, half an orchestra had arrived. He'd gone for classical with a rock edge—not what you'd normally hear at this type of function, but the guests seemed to like it.

"Come and dance." Nick held out a hand to me.

"I don't feel like it."

"Liar. You always want to dance."

"Not today."

"So you're going to abandon me to the cougars?"

Didn't he ever let up? "One song, that's it."

Only once I was on the dance floor, I couldn't get away. After a waltz, Nick pimped me out to the highest bidders from the auction, and I only escaped when a tipsy banker with a coordination problem crippled me. Would Alex still make me exercise with a broken toe? I grabbed a drink and settled back to watch Nick getting his backside groped by Ivy Kendrick-Holmes, a seventy-year-old in an electric blue cocktail dress. When I grew up, I wanted to be just like her.

Finally, as the opening bars of "Por Una Cabeza" played, Nick managed to extricate himself.

"Go on, I need one more dance with somebody who knows where to put her feet."

"I'm tired."

"Don't let Alex hear you say that."

"Good thing he's not here then, isn't it?"

Nick wrapped his arms around my waist. "Please, baby? You always make me look good."

That flipping smile. I'd never been able to resist it. Or the tango.

I'd shown Nick how to ballroom dance many years ago, after my husband taught me. My background was in a completely different kind of dancing, but it turned out to be a transferrable skill, and knowing a few steps came in useful at the tedious number of social functions we had to attend. My husband had learned his moves when he was young, at the insistence of a mother who'd decreed that all young men should know how to entertain a lady.

I was sure he had other, better ways of doing that, but I'd never got the chance to find out for myself. And now I never would.

The band seemed to up both the tempo and the volume as we got closer. Ryan stuck a fricking rose between my teeth, and for five blessed minutes, I got lost in the music. The click of my heels on the floor. Nick's heart beating against mine.

Then I opened my eyes and saw the man I'd considered spending the rest of my life with staring at us with barely disguised disgust.

Fantastic.

Well, at least that answered my earlier question: no,

I didn't dare to speak to Luke. A civil conversation would be out of the question, and I wasn't about to cause a scene at an event so many people had spent time organising. It would overshadow the whole evening.

No, now was the right time to leave. I could consider my next move from a safe distance.

I motioned to a waiter, and a minute later my coat appeared. Nick helped me into it. A couple of the Blackwood crew waved goodbye, but most simply groaned. That open bar had taken its toll.

A sleek black Mercedes waited at the kerb, engine running. Nick opened the door, and I lowered myself gracefully into the back. No tabloid moments for me. Nick climbed in too and the driver closed out the world, cocooning us in relative safety as he whisked us back to Albany House.

So, that went well.

CHAPTER 14

AS LUKE STOOD outside with Rob and Mark, he resisted the urge to kick something. Or better still, someone. He dug his fingernails into the palms of his tightly clenched fists while he waited for his chauffeur to show up, cursing under his breath.

So much for a nice night out to take his mind off Ash.

Not only had she magically reappeared with a new name and a new look, she appeared to have a new boyfriend too. She didn't hang around, did she?

Or worse, was he an *old* boyfriend? After all, Ash, or Emerson, it would now appear, had called Nick right after Tia got kidnapped. They obviously had a history.

What was she playing at? Had she been seeing Nick all along? If so, she must have been creative when she explained her time in England. What did Nick think she'd been doing while she shared Luke's bed? Working? Staying with friends? Maybe she'd lied to both of them, the cheating cow.

Whatever story she'd spun, Nick certainly hadn't seemed upset with her tonight, not with the way he'd gazed into her eyes. He'd fed her dessert, for crying out loud. And he certainly hadn't looked unhappy when they'd taken to the dance floor for a particularly grubby tango either. Most of the men watching had got hard-ons from her slinky moves, and the rest had probably forgotten their Viagra.

Well, apart from one. Luke was the exception, because watching that dirty little display on the dance floor had left him feeling nauseous. He'd wanted to storm out, but his feet had refused to move as he took in the delicate arch of her back... The way her hips swivelled in time to the music... The taut muscles in her calf as she wrapped it around Nick's thigh...

Enough!

He'd screwed his eyes shut, angry at his lack of self-control, and when he opened them again, it was just in time to see the scarlet swish of Emerson's dress as she left the ballroom on Nick's arm. No doubt they were en-route to some posh hotel to dance the tango horizontally instead. Or that enormous mansion in London where Luke had been sequestered while they searched for Tia. Who owned it? Did it belong to Nick? The man reeked of success in every way.

Looks.

Money.

The guy who always got the girl.

How many more lies had Emerson told? Luke thought back to the rumours flying around Lower Foxford when she first came to the village. Ash had been engaged, Carol from the Women's Institute told him in the bakery one day, but her fiancé cheated on her. Was Nick the guy who did the dirty? Had Ash forgiven his transgressions and taken him back?

If that was the case, the two were as bad as each other. Had Ash been blinded by Nick's money? Was she really a gold-digger out for what she could get?

Luke sidestepped out of the path of a drunk couple

as he considered Ash's motives. No, not the money. Luke wasn't short of a few bob himself, and she'd never been interested in his cash. So, what else? Did Nick give her a better time in bed?

"I'm sick of this," Luke muttered, kicking a discarded beer can into the gutter.

Was he a let-down between the sheets and none of his previous girlfriends had bothered to mention it? Or was it his personality? Had he not paid Ash enough attention? She'd never seemed particularly inclined to go out, but perhaps she'd been expecting Luke to take the lead in that?

Whatever the problem, Tia's kidnapping and Luke's botching of the initial ransom drop was the reason Nick had returned in the first place. Which meant Luke himself had been the unwitting catalyst that rekindled Nick and Ash's romance.

Marvellous. Just marvellous.

Luke booted the beer can further down the road, just missing a couple of girls staggering out of the pub he'd been in earlier. He didn't miss their disgusted looks.

"What's your problem?" one of them asked.

"Nothing." Everything.

"A woman. I bet it's a woman," the other said.

Luke's limo pulled up to the kerb and his driver leapt out to open the door.

"Evening, sir."

The first girl eyed up the car and her scowl morphed into a predatory smile. "How about we help take your mind off things?"

"Forget it."

Luke barely grunted at his chauffeur as he climbed

into the backseat and slumped back against the soft black leather. That type of girl was two a penny, sex a business transaction. Maybe he'd have been tempted once, but now he'd been touched by love and the sweet agony that came with it.

He wanted more.

Not since he got a D- in his GCSE geography mock had Luke felt like such a failure. And women confused him more as he got older. On the one hand, he hated Ash for her lies and cheating. But a part of him, the part that remembered what it was like to take a risk and win, still yearned for her. Or was it just a bad case of wanting what he couldn't have?

"You okay, mate?" Rob interrupted Luke's thoughts. "You've been distracted all evening."

"I'm fine. It's just been a long day." Luke spoke through gritted teeth, daring Rob to suggest otherwise.

But with a few drinks in him, Luke's lie skated right past. "Great night though, wasn't it? Plenty of food, and that music got the posh chicks up dancing. Did you see the sweet brunette in the green dress?"

"No."

"Oh. Well, anyway, I got her number."

"Congratulations."

Mark leaned forward, elbows on his knees. "Tell me you didn't miss Emerson Black dancing at the end? Talk about hot. What I wouldn't give to be Nicholas Goldman right now. I mean, the way she looked at him."

"I saw her." Luke gripped the door handle so hard it was a wonder it didn't snap.

"Way out of our league, though," Rob said. "Well, maybe not yours, Luke, what with you being loaded and all."

Mark nodded in agreement. "But I bet she's high maintenance."

Rob groaned. "Speaking of high maintenance, I got a quote to fix my car today. Two grand! Can you believe that?"

Luke sent Rob a silent thank you for changing the subject before he was forced to stick pins in his eyes. As the car purred along silent streets, Rob and Mark started an in-depth conversation about the benefits of LPG over diesel.

That left Luke to stew over his own thoughts the rest of the way home. Where was he? Oh, yes, Ash had got back together with her fiancé, and it was all Luke's fault. Worse, he obviously didn't have the moves to keep a decent girlfriend.

Apart from beer, life was terrible.

By the time Luke walked into his house, his bad mood had boiled over into full-on fury. He slammed the front door so hard a crack appeared in the plaster around the edge, then looked up to find Tia standing in front of him. The set of her mouth reminded him of their mother. She'd pursed her lips that way every time a teenage Luke had embarrassed her at the country club.

"Why aren't you in bed?"

"Good evening to you too, darling brother. What's got your goat?"

He threw his crumpled tuxedo jacket at a nearby chair. It caught on the arm and slid to the floor, not that he cared. "Well, I think it's safe to say I found Ash. And it's even safer to say she won't be coming back."

"What? You found her? Where? Did you speak to

her? Why isn't she coming back?" Tia spilled out questions Luke didn't want to hear.

"No, I didn't speak to her. She spent the whole evening cavorting with her boyfriend, and I didn't feel it would be appropriate to interrupt."

"Boyfriend? But *you're* her boyfriend?"

"Not anymore. Do you remember a guy called Nick from a couple of weeks ago?"

"About six foot two, dark hair, designer stubble, big muscles?" Tia tilted her head and smiled. "Kind of dreamy?"

"Yes. I mean, no. That's him, but not the dreamy part."

Did the man brainwash every woman who crossed his path?

"Nick was so kind to me. The day after I got rescued, he kept asking if I was okay, or whether there was anything he could do to help."

"Well, it seems he's Ash's fiancé. Except she's not called Ash. Her real name's Emerson Black."

"Are you sure?" Tia's eyes narrowed. "If you didn't even talk to her, how do you know that?"

"She was at the charity ball, which turned out to be for her flipping charity. She started it up a few years ago. Oh, and another gem—before she started shagging Nick, she was married to some other bloke. That woman she goes through men like most people go through toilet paper—just leaves all her mess on them and moves on." A hollow laugh escaped his throat. "On the bright side, at least she didn't get her claws any deeper into me."

"So what did she do, divorce her husband and take him to the cleaners?"

"No, she didn't divorce him. Apparently, she killed him instead. Her nickname is the Black Widow."

"That doesn't sound like the Ash I knew."

Luke heard the doubt in Tia's voice, and it only fuelled his anger.

"Then you didn't know her very well, did you? She's got a history of violence. Rob reckons she cut off some bloke's finger, and your kidnapper said she kicked him in the nuts."

Just thinking about those incidents sent Luke to the drinks cabinet in the lounge. Tia trailed behind as he slopped whisky into a glass and knocked it back.

Why was she looking at him like that? He wasn't the problem here, and neither was his drink.

Emerson Black was the problem.

Alcohol was merely the solution.

Chapter 15

TIA SQUARED UP to her brother. Honestly, for a grown man he could be exasperating.

"Good. The kidnapper deserved to be kicked where it hurts. And if Ash did chop off someone's finger, I'm sure there was a good reason for it."

Luke wiped his mouth with the back of his hand. "Stop defending her. What she did to me, and to others by the sound of it, was unforgivable."

"No, I won't stop defending her. Ash was my friend, and she saved my life. How do you know all that Black Widow stuff, anyway?"

Silence.

"Come on, tell me. What, did you watch a midafternoon documentary on some obscure satellite channel?"

Because Luke had turned into a world-class slob over the past few weeks. If he spent any longer on the sofa, he might as well upholster himself.

"No, Rob and Mark told me. They've come across her before, and apparently it's well known in police circles that she's one scary woman."

"Oh, so they discussed the details of a case with you? Isn't that illegal?"

Mark's sister, Arabella, had been Tia's best friend since they started secondary school. Tia spent a lot of

"You really are turning into Mother, you know."

Leaving Luke reaching for the whisky once more, Tia marched off upstairs. Why did her brother have to act like such a jerk? Yes, he'd split with Ash, but that was partly his fault, and drinking and sulking wouldn't fix a thing. She stormed into her bedroom, kicking the door closed behind her and cursing her stupid brother as she did so.

Men! She hated to lose the argument, but at least she'd stuck up for herself. Ash would have been proud.

Tia threw herself down on the bed, exasperated. Luke could be so closed-minded sometimes. Tia had already judged Ash too hastily once herself, back when she first met her last year. Guilty as charged. She'd assumed Ash was another gold-digger after her brother's money, same as the procession of shallow tarts who'd preceded her, but that turned out not to be the case.

No, Tia wouldn't make that mistake again.

She got her laptop out of its drawer and swept away the papers littering the surface of her desk to make room for it. Her gaze was drawn to the corkboard above, to the only photo she had of her and Ash. Just a simple selfie, with Ash smiling beside her into the camera, but as Tia looked at it now, she detected a hint of sadness in Ash's eyes. Why hadn't she asked Ash more questions back then? Maybe she could have found out more about her past.

But Ash had always hated talking about herself. Would she have answered if Tia asked? No, probably not. Ash had been a great listener, the best, and that was one of the things Tia had loved about her. Over the weeks, she'd opened up and told Ash her deepest secrets. Ash had never once reciprocated. When it came to Ash's feelings, Tia concluded that she'd never even scratched the surface, and she doubted Luke had got any deeper.

In front of her, the computer sparked to life. Tia opened up a search engine and typed "Emerson Black" into the box, tapping her fingers on the desk while the page loaded. Lower Foxford's internet connection came straight out of the dark ages, and even though Luke had installed some fancy satellite system for his work stuff, Tia was left with creaking broadband.

Finally, the page loaded, and she scanned down the results. A band called Emerson released their new album, *Black Moon*, last week. Emerson Knives Inc. had just brought out a new model of knife with a black finish. An author called Earl Emerson had written a book on a guy called Thomas Black. There were all sorts of permutations of "Emerson" and "Black," but nothing about a woman called Emerson Black.

Googling "The Black Widow" brought up a zillion references to spiders. Eeeuch, they were ugly little suckers. Tia shuddered at the more graphic photos. Luckily, they didn't live in the UK, although she did recall a creepy article on the news about one being found in a bunch of grapes at Asda in Watford. She hadn't eaten fruit for weeks afterwards.

Hundreds of results filled the screen, but still no Emerson Black. It was as if she didn't exist. Had Luke got things wrong earlier? He'd certainly reeked of whisky when he arrived home.

Tia made one last attempt by entering both search terms together, and was rewarded with a tiny paragraph in *The Richmond Times*, not a story but an apology for a previous article no longer available. The paper was profoundly sorry for any accusations made and accepted they had no basis in fact. What accusations? What were they talking about? Something to do with that murder nonsense her brother had been spouting?

Tia's sigh settled over the room. Somebody's lawyer had been working overtime, hadn't they?

Shoving her chair back so hard it fell over, she glared at the screen. The internet was a dead end. Whatever stories Rob and Mark looked at must have long since been removed like the article in *The Richmond Times*.

Why hadn't she paid more attention when Luke tried to teach her computer stuff? It would probably take him five minutes to write a program that searched dead web pages, but she didn't dare ask him for help. Even if she said she wanted to learn more about programming in general terms, he'd still be suspicious. She'd always glazed over at the first mention of his work in the past.

Arrrgh. This was so flipping frustrating!

Tia flopped back onto the bed, only to sit straight back up again as she recalled Luke's earlier words. Emerson had started the charity that ran the ball tonight, right? What was it called? She thought back to the conversation she'd had with her brother yesterday, the one where he'd been moaning that his tuxedo jacket was too tight. Blackstone? Blackrock? Blackwater? No, Blackwood. The Blackwood Foundation. That was it. She righted her chair, typed that into the search engine, and got a sleek-looking website. News of the ball took up most of the front page. *The Black and White Ball,* sponsored by Blackwood Security.

Tia tried searching for the name of the company instead. Surely they were connected? She clicked on the first website up, a global security conglomerate, and pored through the pages. Jeepers, Blackwood was big— the second largest security firm in the world if its advertising was to be believed.

Received death threats and need a bodyguard? No problem. Need a crime investigated? They had a team for that. Want assistance with training your own security team? Blackwood offered to travel anywhere in the world to do it. Got to have a state-of-the-art alarm system? They'd design something so secure even a mouse couldn't get in.

Eventually, on a page detailing the history of the group, Tia was rewarded with a small reference to the company's founders: C Black, N Wood, and E Black. Did the "E" stand for Emerson?

Tia trawled through the rest of the website, her heart rate increasing with every click, and found... Nothing. Not a single hint. With no other avenues to try, she returned to the "Contact us" page, selected her choice of country as the UK, and fired off a short message.

What was the worst that could happen? Only that someone would file it in the bin.

Covering a yawn, she changed into a pair of pyjamas, brushed her teeth, and climbed into bed. Sleep didn't come easily that night. Instead, Tia lay awake, watching the night sky out of the window. There wasn't a cloud up there, and the stars twinkled. She wished she knew the names of the different constellations. If Ash had been there, she'd have asked her. Ash knew things like that. Ash knew everything.

And somewhere under that same sky, Tia thought, Ash could be watching the stars as well. The question was where, and who with?

CHAPTER 16

"DID YOU SEE Luke's face?" I asked Nick as we rode back in the car. My fingers picked at the folds of my dress, and I couldn't stop them. A hole opened up near the seam. Oh, shiznits, Bradley was going to kill me.

"He looked slightly unhappy, I'll admit."

"Don't try to trivialise this. He gave me the look he normally reserves for something he's scraped off his shoe." I smacked the back of my head on the seat in frustration.

"Why didn't you try talking to him?"

"There was a rather large audience, in case you didn't notice."

"Fair enough, but you need to sort this out. Why don't you call him?"

"I'm not having that kind of discussion over the phone. I need to speak to him in person. But I'm not doing that until he's had a chance to calm down."

"So you'll go and see him tomorrow, then?"

Tomorrow? Tomorrow was less than an hour away. I broke out in a cold sweat at the thought of talking to Luke so soon.

"I think he needs a bit longer than that."

Like a few weeks, maybe. I didn't plan to be on the same continent as Luke tomorrow night.

"You're doing it again, aren't you?"

"Doing what?"

"Running away."

I let out a long breath. A thin stream of pain. "I can't help it. I hate confrontation."

"Liar. You thrive on confrontation. I remember last October when you stood up to that senator on the White House committee and told him just how wrong his assumptions on Iraq were. You didn't pull any punches."

"That was different."

"How was it different?"

"That senator was an idiot. I didn't give a toss if he ended up hating me. With Luke, I do care." I faced Nick head on, snapping because I couldn't help myself. "There, I said it. I care. Are you happy now?"

He chuckled as I crossed my arms and stared out the window.

"So she does have a heart, after all."

"Shut up."

Two hours later as I paced the lounge with a gin and tonic in hand, my mind was still racing. I felt like I was playing a game of chess, trying to second guess Luke as well as plan my own moves. But at the moment, I longed to flip the board over.

Because I'd screwed up yet again.

I hated being on bad terms with people I liked. Hated it. I mean, I was still friends with every single one of my other exes. Okay, so Alaric had been AWOL for a few years, but he still sent birthday cards.

How could I fix this?

"You're going to wear out the carpet," Nick said from his vantage point on the sofa.

"Then I'll buy a new one."

I took another drink, ignoring the line of fire that burned down the back of my throat. Perhaps I should have added more than a splash of tonic.

"Look, if you can't sleep, why don't you come out to a club with me? Take your mind off things?"

"Not in the mood, Nick." To my own ears I sounded petulant. None of this was his fault. I paused next to him and attempted a smile. "You go out if you want to. I'd only spoil your fun."

He reached up and took my hand. "I don't mind staying here with you."

"No, you go. Take the team."

"You sure?"

"Yeah, I'm sure."

Once they'd gone, I knew I wouldn't see any sign of them until tomorrow morning. That left me alone in the house. At least if I had a nightmare, which was happening with alarming regularity, nobody would hear me scream.

I switched to Scotch and swallowed a couple of fingers before heading to bed in the hope it would send me off. It didn't help. Instead, I lay there wide awake on my thousand thread count sheets, wondering how much worse things would get before they got better.

I'd had bad times before, and as I stared at the darkened ceiling, I thought back over what had happened in my life so far to land me in my present position.

Diamonds and darkness, blood and sweat, fear, friendship, and one fatal attraction.

I thought of how I met my husband...

CHAPTER 17

IT WAS A cold December night when I first saw him.

I glanced up at the sky as I hurried down the street, my footsteps soft in the darkness. The lack of clouds meant the temperature would drop a few degrees yet. The clock in the pawnbroker's window chimed the witching hour as I passed, muffled by thick glass and a security grille. My mouth opened in a yawn, and I didn't bother to cover it. Why fight the exhaustion? It festered inside me, the one constant in my life since childhood. A nemesis I'd never beat.

The eight to late shift was a killer, and in five hours I'd be up and working again, bleary eyed and faking a smile until I knocked off to study at one thirty. I'd have dearly loved to pack in my second job, the one in the evening, but it paid better than the first so I was stuck with it. Every day was the same. In order for me to get the recommended eight hours of rest, each day would need to have twenty-eight hours.

Still, I carried on. What other choice did I have? I was determined not to be stuck in dead-end jobs for the rest of my life, and my long-term plan involved sacrificing any kind of fun in my teenage years so I could enjoy my twenties and thirties.

I may have only been fifteen, but I had big ambitions.

Of course, nobody knew I was fifteen. If either of my employers found out I was two years and seven months younger than I claimed to be, they'd have kicked me right back out on the streets I'd fought so hard to escape. I got away with bending the truth because I looked older, and I looked older because fending for myself my entire life had matured me in a hurry.

On the bright side, appearing a little young for the eighteen years I claimed to be gave me a definite advantage in job number two. At Silk, the strip club—sorry, gentlemen's club—where I spent my evenings, acting like a horny schoolgirl paid decent money.

So decent that the other girls hated me, which was why, yet again, they'd hidden my clothes as I danced.

"Have you seen my jeans? And my jumper?" I'd asked Bambi, the self-proclaimed headline act.

"Are you sure you brought them? I wouldn't have thought you needed them on your street corner."

A crowd of her cronies stood behind her, sniggering. I'd balled my fists up, just seconds away from wiping the smirk off Bambi's make-up-caked face when I caught myself. I couldn't afford to lose that job.

Instead, I'd shoved my feet into the pair of trainers they'd thankfully missed, collected my coat from the cloakroom, and marched out into the night. Which was why I was currently walking home with a belted trench over my dancing outfit and my fishnet-clad legs stuck into a pair of genuine fake Nike's I'd bought at the street market for ten quid a week earlier.

Suck it up, kiddo.

Of course, it wasn't nice being so actively disliked, but I'd developed a thick skin, and the money I earned made the hassle worth it. I had this crazy dream, you see, to go to university and make something of myself.

Why crazy? Well, I'll give you three reasons.

First, I dropped out of school at twelve years old. That was what happened when you had no one apart from yourself to take care of you.

Second, the tuition fees and living expenses I'd rack up over a three-year course would add up to thousands. Rent, electricity, council tax, food, textbooks—they'd all need to be paid for, and I didn't have any family to help out.

Third, and perhaps the most difficult hurdle to overcome, was that people like me simply didn't go to university.

Right now, I was desperately trying to ignore point three while taking steps to address points one and two. Hence, the need for both jobs. In the mornings I worked at a gym, cleaning the cavernous room that housed the equipment then opening up, looking after the customers, and minding the front desk until the owner took over from me at lunchtime.

JJ's wasn't one of those posh gyms full of accountants and marketing executives jogging on treadmills while chatting on their mobile phones. The clientele didn't head off for a sauna and a smoothie so they could talk about share prices and which secretary they were shagging that week. There were no rows of perfectly made-up Lycra-clad women, all without a drop of sweat on them, cycling serenely on stationary bikes while counting down the minutes until their manicures.

No, JJ's had sweat, bruises, and occasionally blood. And muscles. Don't forget the muscles, including those of its owner, a gentle giant called Jimmy James. At least, he was gentle to me. At six foot five inches of solid bulk, you didn't want to get on his bad side.

After work, or sometimes during it if the place was quiet, I'd train for an hour or so to keep fit. Apart from Jimmy's wife, Jackie, I was the only girl who ever ventured into the place, so the guys had taken me on as their pet project. Not because they were weird perverts like the clientele at Silk. No, they'd decided changes needed to be made the day after I got mugged. I'd walked into the gym with a black eye that morning, a little embarrassed because I should have seen it coming and ducked out the way.

"What happened, Amanda?" one of the regulars asked.

"Just walked into someone's fist. That's all. It's nothing."

"It's not nothing. He take your money?"

I nodded.

"That's not gonna happen again, you hear? You're training with us now."

They'd even had a whip round and raised more than the amount stolen from me. When they handed the cash over, I got all sniffly and had to run off to the toilet to get my emotions under control.

I never cried, and certainly not in front of people.

Since that day, I'd done regular sessions of boxing, martial arts, circuits, or sometimes all three, depending on who was in the gym to help me. Nobody on the street touched me again, which was almost disappointing since I'd been itching to try out the new things I'd learned.

After training came studying. Maths was the bane

of my existence. I didn't care about Mary's inability to work out how much she could spend on tiles for her conservatory, and why on earth did Hannah want to buy 253 pineapples anyway? If I had cash, I ate. Simple as that.

And English? Whoever invented the language must have been smoking something. Why if the plural of mouse was mice did I have two houses and not two hice? As for pronunciation—broth and brother? Moth and mother? Give me strength. Karim from the mini-mart down the road had started teaching me Arabic, and although it looked a bit squiggly, spelling words like you said them seemed a far more sensible approach.

After I closed the books and grabbed a bite to eat, I'd get a couple of hours' sleep before I trekked to Silk again. Luckily, I didn't have far to go to bed, because I lived at the gym. The mattress in an old storage closet may have been basic, but it was mine, and it was safe.

Those two things alone made it better than anywhere I'd lived before. All in all, I'd stayed in some pretty horrible places, the worst of which was with my mother. Name something bad and she was addicted to it—drugs, alcohol, and men were her vices of choice.

I lived with her until the age of ten and hated every second of it. I spent most of my life outside the flat because it was easier to keep out of her way than bear the bruises. By the age of eight, I'd become an accomplished shoplifter, not for the thrill of it but out of necessity. Stealing food and clothes meant I only had to go home to shower and sleep. I'd finally left for good the night one of my mother's boyfriends paid me a visit in my bedroom. Over an hour, he was in there, but she'd passed out on the sofa, so hammered she didn't hear me scream. No child should have to go through that.

Even then, I'd kept going to school, but when my hygiene standards suffered, one of the teachers called social services. I'm sure there are some wonderful, caring foster parents out there, but I sure didn't meet any of them. So, I wreaked enough havoc to get kicked out of one home after another, each time hoping the next place would feel safe enough to stay.

But I never found my sanctuary. Every guardian was in the game either for money or because they had certain predilections frowned upon by society. Sometimes both, if I got particularly unlucky. Can you imagine a situation where a person had an unhealthy interest in young girls, and not only did the state deliver the object of their fantasies to their door, but paid the freak to "take care" of them?

No?

Think that never happened?

Well, let me tell you, it did.

By the time they ran out of foster parents for me, I'd been hit, burned, locked up, starved, and groped. The only way to escape from one particularly sadistic couple was by burning the house down. I'd only intended to damage my bedroom so I couldn't stay in it anymore, but who knew hairspray and perfume would go up with quite such a bang?

Next up was the children's home. When a so-called care-worker stole from me, for the second time, what wasn't his to take, I decided I'd had enough.

I quit.

I left the "care" system, and I stopped going to

school as well so they couldn't find me there and take me back.

After all, at twelve years old I was practically a grown-up, right?

Two years on the streets hardened me. The great outdoors may have been tough, but when I spotted the freaks, it was easy enough to avoid them. And over those months, I gained a whole new set of life skills, ones that didn't appear on the school curriculum.

I still remembered the thrill when I'd hot-wired my first car, my GTA mentor by my side.

"You got the lock barrel out?"

"Yep, I got it, Vinnie."

"Now, just twist the wires together."

The engine started with a roar, and a delicious shiver ran through me. I'd never driven a vintage Porsche before. I bet not many thirteen-year-olds had.

My shoplifting talents improved to the extent that I rarely had to do a runner from the security guards, and I perfected the art of the hustle. I'd act my little heart out for a cut of whatever the person running the scam managed to make. Accents, airs, graces, I could put on them all. In truth, I wasn't proud of the way I lived, but once I'd been turned down a one-way street, I had little choice but to keep walking.

I'd never been afraid to get physical, even before the mugging, but a lack of patience meant picking locks frustrated me. It took months to get the hang of it, but once learned, I never forgot. Even now, I still had the habit of carrying a couple of bobby pins for that very purpose.

So, what happened? What made me go straight at the grand old age of fourteen?

time at their house, but she'd never heard Mark mention any Black Widow. And Mark was always running his mouth off about police business, even though he wasn't supposed to. He had the discretion of a tabloid newspaper.

"No, Rob read about it on the internet."

"The internet?" Seriously? "So obviously it must be a hundred percent true then."

"Why are you taking her side? I'm your brother."

"And she was like my sister."

"She lied to you."

"Maybe so, but she also taught me not to be so quick to judge people. If I'm going to condemn her like you have, I want to hear what she has to say firsthand, not via Rob and Mark and the internet."

"You're not contacting her."

It wasn't the first time he'd used that firm tone with her, and on past form, he wouldn't budge. Hmm. More devious measures were called for.

She tried reasoning anyway, just in case. "Why not?"

"She's dangerous."

"Oh, don't be ridiculous. I spent as much time with her as you did, and she never showed the slightest inclination to harm me. Or you, for that matter. What she did do was stop other people from hurting both of us. You'll have to come up with a better argument than that."

"Okay, well how about because you're a minor living in my house and I say so," Luke said, hands on hips, just like their mother when she got cross. Genetics at work. Yes, Tia had listened in at least one of her biology lessons.

Well, my lifestyle came to a dead end one winter morning when I woke wrapped in a filthy blanket on the floor of an abandoned factory. My back ached as I rolled over and stretched, my fingertips touching the dude lying behind me.

"Sunny, you got any food?" I asked.

Sunny was six or seven years older than me, and his story mirrored mine, except he'd taken to self-medicating with whatever drugs he could beg, borrow, or steal so he wouldn't have to face his own mind anymore.

He didn't answer.

I scrambled to my knees, catching my palm on a nail sticking up from the floor. I still had that scar, barely noticeable, as a reminder of my previous life.

My breath puffed white in the chilly air as I wrapped a T-shirt around my hand to stop the bleeding, then I took a better look at Sunny.

"No," I whispered, unable to think of more words.

Milky white eyes stared back at me, unseeing, and I fell backwards, bumping my head on a pillar as I struggled to my feet. My wild run from the first of many dead bodies I'd encounter in my life ended outside JJ's, as I sucked in ragged breaths and tried to block Sunny's sagging jaw from my mind.

Cleaner wanted, the sign in the window read. *Hours by agreement, enquire within.*

My survival instinct kicked in, and after a quick trip to the nearest public toilet to make myself presentable, I went back, said I was sixteen, and landed the job. Jimmy didn't mind me coming in early to take a shower before my shift, but I started creeping in even earlier to sleep for the night.

Which I thought was a good plan until Jimmy came back unexpectedly one evening and found me sneaking into the storeroom.

"What on earth are you doing here?"

I froze, hand on the doorknob, unable to meet his eyes. "I'm sorry. Just give me two minutes, would you? I'll get my stuff and go."

Rather than getting angry, he'd laid a huge paw on my shoulder. "You should have told me, child. We knew things were bad for you, but not this bad."

I had a lump in my throat as I watched him clear out the room for me. When he told me I was expected for dinner each evening in the tiny one-bedroom flat he and Jackie shared above the gym, I could barely speak to say, "Thank you."

Jimmy and Jackie turned into the closest thing to parents I ever had, and their patrons became my family. It was one of them, Donnie, who gave me the job at Silk.

"I've seen you dancing around while you clean, love," he said to me. "If you're interested in making a few quid extra, reckon I'd have a job for you."

My first reaction had been, "No way," but how else could I get enough money for university? There weren't many jobs available to a person with no qualifications whatsoever, and even fewer that paid cash in hand, no questions asked.

Jimmy had been less than impressed when I told him my plan.

"You're too good for that place, Amanda."

"You gonna give me a pay rise?"

"Wish I could, but I can't. It's hard enough making ends meet in this place."

"Then I've got to dance. I know you hate it, and I don't like it either, but the money's too good to turn down."

"If anyone tries anything, they answer to me, you got that?"

"I got it. And Jimmy?" He looked down at me. "Thank you."

Hundreds of pairs of eyes roaming over my body made my flesh crawl, but I put it out of my mind as I counted my cash each night. Donnie looked after me and made sure the bouncers did too, partly because Jimmy threatened to put him in an early grave if he didn't but mostly because he was a decent guy who just happened to own a strip club.

I never did private dances or spent time alone with the customers. Any man who touched me got escorted from the premises in a headlock, usually after his instep had been introduced to my stiletto. I went to work, did my thing on stage, served a bunch of drinks, then got out of there as fast as humanly possible.

That fateful Friday night had been a quiet one at Silk. The local pubs were showing a big football match, and half of the regulars preferred to watch a bunch of overpaid boys running around a pitch rather than a bunch of underdressed girls dancing around a stage.

Tips were down, which meant I couldn't pass up the chance to make a bit of extra cash, legal or not. Living on the streets did that to you—the lines between wrong and right got blurred, and you learned to survive by whatever means necessary.

So, when I saw a tall, well-dressed man emerging from the steps of Aldgate tube station right ahead of me, tucking his tube ticket into his wallet and placing it into his right-hand jacket pocket, my synapses fired at a thousand miles an hour and came up with a plan.

The guy turned right and walked towards me, and I kept my head down, watching him out of my peripheral vision. As he passed, I tripped over the edge of a paving slab and stumbled into him, grabbing onto his jacket to keep from falling.

He caught me easily, one hand on either side of my waist.

"Are you all right?"

His accent was American. A tourist, most likely, or a visiting businessman.

"Fine, thanks, just tripped," I mumbled, acting embarrassed.

My smile was genuine—mission accomplished. He returned it, displaying a row of perfect white teeth as he set me back on my feet.

Just a simple mishap, right? I carried on my way, and he carried on his.

Except now I had his wallet.

CHAPTER 18

THE MAN'S FOOTSTEPS receded into the distance, and I resisted the urge to walk faster. Instead, I maintained the brisk-yet-casual pace expected of a woman out walking on her own at that late hour.

I must have been a couple of hundred yards down the road when a prickling of the hairs on the back of my neck told me something was wrong. The road curved to the right, and in the window of a clothes shop ahead of me, I saw the guy whose wallet I'd just liberated following me. Why had he turned around? He was close enough for me to see his eyes focused in my direction as his reflection floated eerily among the mannequins dressed up in evening wear.

My heart sped up as I considered my options.

Walking at my current pace, I could be mistaken for innocent. Maybe the guy changed direction because he was lost? If so, he'd have to find someone else to help with directions. Or perhaps he was an axe murderer? Oh, that was so much more comforting, but I could carry on walking and hope for the best.

Or I could run.

If he'd noticed the wallet was missing, running would make me look pretty guilty. If I ditched it, would he still come after me? Was he the forgiving type?

Another glimpse, this time in a car mirror. He'd

gained on me, still walking, but he looked to be about Jimmy's height and his legs were a lot longer than mine. Could I outrun him? I wouldn't win gold at the Olympics, but I'd had plenty of practice.

I risked a glance around.

You know that little sentence they print on wing mirrors? That objects in the reflection may be closer than they appear? Well, it was absolutely right. He was thirty yards behind me, and as I turned, his eyes locked on mine.

Oh, Jiminy Cricket. He knew.

I ran.

I hoped that as I was from the area and knew it well and he, being from the States hopefully didn't, I'd be able to give him the slip. The slap of his leather-soled shoes on the paving slabs told me he'd broken into a run, and that spurred me to sprint faster. What kind of shape was he in? Which of us would run out of steam first?

JJ's was a mile away, and I cursed myself for saving money by walking. Why hadn't I taken the Tube or a cab like a normal person? Oh, yeah, because it was harder to steal wallets while riding in a cab.

Silly me.

His footsteps got louder and I realised I had no chance of making it back to JJ's ahead of him, so I ducked left into a side street. The end was blocked, if I remembered rightly, by a fence with a small hole in it. A hole that should fit me but not him, and barbed wire topped the chain link, which was probably why some enterprising soul had cut the hole in the first place.

The road was narrow, little more than an alley, and with the high buildings either side, little moonlight got in. As I skidded to a halt at the end, a string of spluttered four-letter words spilled past my lips. The place had morphed into a building site. The fence I remembered had been replaced by a barrier of smooth wooden boards, at least eight feet high. Dim pictures pinned to it showed what the area would look like if the builders stopped drinking tea long enough to do any work.

I jumped at it and hooked my arms over the rough timber at the top. My ungainly scramble failed to get me over it, and I fell back to the ground, swearing again as I landed on one knee.

I glanced back.

The guy was almost on me, still moving fast. I didn't have time for another run-up.

Curses flew from my mouth. Why had I been so stupid as to get myself into this mess? I promised the big man upstairs that if I got out of this, I'd never steal a wallet again. Not unless the mark was clearly too unfit to run, anyway.

Despite the fact I'd never been to church in my life, I looked to the heavens, praying for divine intervention.

And got it.

Scaffolding stretched skywards, covering the façade of the building next to me. A yellow sign told me to *Keep off! Danger of death!*

Well, I'd never been one for authority, had I?

I went up.

Luckily, pole dancing had formed a big part of my repertoire at Silk, which meant I knew how to shin up one pretty quickly. I could spin around and hang upside down too, although I appreciated those skills weren't the most valuable in this particular situation. I shot up the scaffolding like I had a flamethrower behind me, hearing a muttered, "Are you insane?" from below as the man began climbing too.

And flipping heck, he was quick. He caught up with me by the sixth story, and as I heaved myself over the splintered edge onto the wooden platform, his hot breath washed across my neck. I rolled onto my back, feeling a fiery pain as something sharp ripped into my side. *Ouch!* As he crawled forwards over me, his dark eyes fixed on mine, and I did the only thing I could— swung at him with a vicious right hook while saying a silent "thank you" to JJ's and all who trained there.

There was a satisfying crunch as the cartilage in his nose gave way, and he reeled back, grabbing onto a protruding piece of scaffold as he narrowly saved himself from going over the edge. I sprang up and ran to the other end of the platform, cursing the dead end where it butted against a wall. Should I go up or down? Even running on adrenaline, I didn't have much strength left.

I hesitated too long.

He'd somehow recovered, and his arms snaked around me from behind and squeezed. Was the man part boa constrictor? I twisted in his grasp, bringing my right knee up, hard, and feeling it make a good, solid contact. The guy's eyes bulged slightly and even started to water a bit, but his grip got tighter and he backed me into the wall, blocking my legs with his so I couldn't try the same trick again.

What was wrong with him? Did he feel no pain? Was he even human?

He grinned, and without further warning, my legs were swept out from underneath me and I found myself lying on my back, my wrists pinned down either side of my head by his hands. He squashed my legs against the dirty boards as he sat on me, panting, blood dripping from his nose and landing on my face and chest.

What would it be this time? Murder or have him take what little innocence I had left? Having tried the latter twice, I'd almost have preferred to die. I had the idea that I should speak, start begging or something, but no words came out. Instead, I simply lay there, trying to burn through him with my glare.

He met my eyes. "So," he started, "you are one mad little brat."

"Are you going to kill me?" I couldn't keep my mouth shut any longer.

"Well, I wasn't, but I'm reconsidering now you've broken my nose."

"If I said I was sorry, would that make a difference?"

"Would you mean it?"

I tried to shrug, but I couldn't quite manage it. "Probably not."

"At least you're honest." He actually laughed. "What I really want is my wallet back. Where is it?"

"Left-hand pocket," I admitted.

He looked down, and I saw my coat had come open in the struggle. As well as the now-tattered fishnets, I was wearing a skirt so short Donnie called it a belt, a white shirt, also ripped undone, and a push-up bra. Thankfully, I'd taken off the tie and left it at the club, so at least the dude couldn't strangle me with that.

He stifled a laugh. "What on earth are you wearing?"

"Would you believe my school uniform?"

"Not a chance. You're a stripper?"

"Yeah, so? We can't all have city jobs, you know. And there's only a market for what I do because men like you want to get their rocks off."

Even though I didn't like my occupation, I still felt a bizarre need to defend it.

"You think I'm a city boy? Couldn't be further from the truth, sweetheart. And schoolgirls don't do it for me."

"You're not going to, well, you know, then?"

His eyes widened in genuine shock. "Of course not. I'm not a monster."

"You are lying on top of me."

"Only because you nearly shoved me off the sixth storey of a block of scaffolding. What's wrong with you, woman? Do you have no fear?"

"Hey, don't ask me what my problem is. Anyone would do the same if you started chasing them."

"I can honestly say this is the first time I've been in this position with a female. Usually, they're the ones chasing me."

"Ooh, arrogant much? And would you stop bleeding all over me? It's not pleasant."

"Demanding little thing, aren't you? If I move, are you going to try running off again?"

"Um..." I wasn't sure I wanted to commit to that.

"Because if you do, I'll come after you again, and I *will* catch you. And if that happens, our next stop will be the nearest police station."

My legs had been jelly before he sat on them, and now they'd gone numb as well. He was absolutely right —he *would* catch me.

"Okay, okay. Since you put it like that, I promise."

He let me up, and I clambered to my feet, trying not to show how much I was shaking. Standing close, the man was even bigger than I first thought. I didn't even reach his shoulder.

"Hey, you're bleeding too," he said, peering down at my side.

"I think I caught myself on a nail or something. I'll be fine."

"I'm taking you to get cleaned up."

I opened my mouth to protest, but he reminded me, "It's come with me or pay a visit to the cops."

"Fine."

I folded my arms and stared at him. If he planned to do something really nasty to me, surely he'd have done it by now? Or did he just want to get me somewhere it would be easier to hide my body?

Oh, heck. I didn't have much choice, did I? Maybe I could figure out a way to escape on the way to wherever he was taking me.

The builders had removed all the ladders away from the scaffolding, probably to stop people from climbing up it, so we had no choice but to climb down the outside again. I did my coat up and wiped my hands on it, trying to clean off the blood and sweat, then lowered myself over the edge. By the time I got to the bottom, the guy was already there, and as my feet touched the ground, he hung up his phone.

"There's a car coming for us. It's not a good idea to try taking a cab looking like this." He gestured at his nose and my side.

I looked down at myself and had to concede he'd made a good point—I did look as if I'd escaped from a slaughterhouse. But good point or not, I lagged behind as he took a few steps towards the end of the road because I really didn't want to go with him.

"Come on, Diamond," he said.

"Diamond?"

"You're pretty to look at and hard to scratch."

Diamond it was. I'd been called worse. I gave in and followed him, and two minutes later, a black limousine pulled up beside us. He opened the back door and ushered me inside, then with a click, the door closed, leaving my old world far behind.

CHAPTER 19

THE MAN BEHIND the wheel swivelled his head to look at us, his face a picture of astonishment under his peaked black cap.

"Not a word, Tony," my captor instructed.

The driver turned his eyes back to the road, and soon we were gliding smoothly through the streets of London.

"Er, I'd better give you your wallet back," I said, rummaging in my pocket and pulling it out.

"Give me the cards, but you can keep the cash. After the amount of effort you put in tonight, you've earned it."

Was he serious? I thumbed through it. There must have been a thousand pounds in there, all in crisp twenty-pound notes. I quickly flipped the wallet shut and handed it back.

"Nah, it wouldn't feel right. I'm sorry I took it." And surprisingly, I found I truly was.

"Sorry you took it, or sorry you got caught?"

"Well, both I guess. It's not every day I get chased up a building by a crazy stranger."

"You started it," he pointed out. "What's your name?"

"What's yours?"

"Black."

"Is that your first name or your surname?"

"Surname."

"Well, I guess that makes me Emerson."

My first name might have been Amanda, but I hated it. Mainly because my mother chose it for me. I suspected she gave it seconds of thought, sometime between deciding what to watch on TV and nipping to the shop for more cigarettes. Therefore, if I found an opportunity not to use it, I was going to take it. I figured if he was using his surname, then I could too.

"Now I'm not a stranger, Emerson."

"How about the crazy part?"

"You were probably right about that."

We lapsed into silence for the rest of the journey. My mind churned as I tried to think of a way to escape, and Black was no doubt working out how to stop me.

Unfortunately, I still hadn't managed to come up with a coherent plan when the car slowed. We turned into the driveway of a large, posh-looking building, and any hopes I might have had of doing a runner were scuppered when the driver pulled forward into an underground garage.

Six other cars were parked neatly in the bays, gleaming under overhead strip lights. I picked out an Aston Martin, a Porsche 911, and a BMW 5 Series, with two more sleek-looking vehicles hidden under fitted covers. A Land Rover Defender took the end space. Maybe one of the building's inhabitants had a pad in the country they retired to at weekends? There was obviously some serious money here.

Black must live in an apartment upstairs, I surmised. At least the abundance of cars meant his neighbours were home. If he did turn out to be a raving lunatic, there would be somebody to hear me scream.

Or so I thought.

He ushered me out of the car towards a lift in the corner and pressed the button for the ground floor. As the doors closed, I realised I didn't even know what part of London we were in. I'd rarely ventured out of the East End. That was my stomping ground and I knew it well, dead-end alleys aside.

This place might as well have been on Mars, for all the similarities it had with my home.

Actually, Uranus would have been more appropriate. Because at that particular point in time, I was convinced that was where Black hailed from.

The lift shot upwards, and seconds later, the doors opened. Instead of the hallway full of flat doors I'd been expecting, we emerged in a large room with staircases running up both sides. Tarpaulins covered a few pieces of furniture huddled in a corner, and a collection of paint pots and ladders stood off to the side. The place reeked of fresh gloss with an undertone of white spirit.

"Sorry about the smell," he said. "I've been having some renovations done."

I tried not to stare too much. "Is this whole building yours?"

"Yeah."

How could he act so casual about the fact he lived in a palace? I may have been hazy on the subject of property prices, but I bet this place cost more than the entire block JJ's was on. No wonder Black didn't care about the cash in his wallet.

I trailed behind as he walked to a vast kitchen and reached up into a cupboard for a first aid kit. I say kit, but from the size of the box, it was practically a hospital. He stuck it under one arm and took my hand to lead me up the stairs, and I was so busy staring at the chandeliers, I didn't think to snatch it away.

On the second floor, we went through what I assumed was his bedroom, a vast almost-empty space decorated in greys and blacks with the occasional deep-red accent. The blood seeping from the gash below my ribs coordinated perfectly with the curtain tie-backs. Just one room, for one man, and it was bigger than Jimmy and Jackie's whole flat. I paused to look but Black pulled me forwards again, into a luxurious en-suite bathroom on the far side.

While he peered into the mirror, I gaped at the marble shelves and taps that were probably made from platinum. Surprisingly, he didn't have a little woman stationed in the corner to wipe his backside.

He gingerly touched his nose. "You did a nice job on that, didn't you?"

Did he expect me to reply? I didn't think "Er, thanks" would be the right thing to say, so I kept my mouth shut.

"Hopefully it'll heal straight, but if it doesn't, it'll be a good reminder that I shouldn't underestimate people based on their appearance, won't it?" He grabbed a washcloth and wiped the worst of the dried blood off his face, then rinsed his hands. "Let's have a look at your side."

I hesitated, not sure I wanted to be half-naked in this bathroom with the soft-talking American. Even though I knew his name now, and he hadn't yet shown any indications of being a serial killer, the situation made me uncomfortable.

"Come on, I've already seen it all once," he coaxed.

"That wound needs to be cleaned up."

Oh, why not? I didn't fancy having to wake Jimmy up for the key to the medical cabinet when I got back.

If I got back.

I undid the belt on my coat and shrugged out of it, draping it over the side of the bath. The shirt was useless—it only had one button left and the bloodstains looked more gory than artistic, so I pulled that off and dumped it in the small bin next to the sink.

A quick glance in the mirror told me I looked like an extra in a horror movie. As well as the cut, I had bruises on my wrists and legs where he'd held me down and a nice purple mark coming up on the side of my face that I didn't even remember getting.

I sat down on the closed toilet while Black gently probed my side, cleaning off the blood then wiping it with antiseptic, which stung like a mother. I gritted my teeth so I didn't cry out. The last thing I wanted was to look weak, especially in front of him.

"This cut needs stitches."

"I'm not going to a hospital."

A doctor would ask awkward questions about my medical history, which would lead to an interrogation about my family, which would get me a one-way ticket back into care.

"I can do it. I've got sutures here."

"Really?" What would a toffee-nosed twat know about medicine?

"I've stitched people up before."

"Are you a doctor?"

That would go some way to explaining the amount of money he had, but for some reason, he found the question funny. His face softened when he smiled.

"What's so amusing?"

"The idea of me keeping people alive for a living."

I measured up the distance to the door.

His lips quirked up again. "You won't make it. Lean back. I promise I'll be as gentle as I can."

I didn't have much of a choice, did I?

He injected me with something that took the sting away then closed up the cut with six neat stitches. I admired his handiwork as he left me sitting there and disappeared into the bedroom. A few minutes later, he came back with a T-shirt and a pair of sweatpants, both huge and obviously his.

"Sorry I don't have something more suitable. I don't bring women here as a rule."

Really? What did he bring? Men? Four-legged friends? Blow-up dolls?

"Thanks."

After the way I'd behaved, he was kind to offer me anything, so I made do. I didn't relish the idea of walking back across London wearing a blood-stained coat and not much else. At least my trainers were still serviceable. I pulled on the shirt, which came to my knees, then put on the trousers. When I tugged the drawstring tight and turned the top over several times, they stayed put. I rolled the legs up as well. It wasn't the most stylish outfit, but at least it covered me.

He'd left me alone to change, and when I emerged into the bedroom, I found he'd done the same. Dressed casually, in a pair of jeans and a plain white T-shirt with his feet bare, he looked younger than I'd first thought. Mid-twenties at a guess. An air of danger oozed from him that his good looks and the dim lighting couldn't hide.

Black. The name suited him. His inky hair was spiked up on top, but just a little scruffy. All that money and he couldn't afford a haircut? Dark stubble a day or two past a five o'clock shadow speckled a strong jaw, and the bruise on his cheek was starting to turn a deep purple as well. Oops.

His T-shirt stretched across his chest, showing off his muscles, and from the way his jeans hung, he spent a lot of time working out. His light tan showed up more against the white shirt, suggesting he hadn't spent much time at the mercies of the British winter.

I rated him an eleven out of ten for looks. Manners, not so much.

His eyes were such a dark brown they were almost black too. They pierced me, like he had an uncanny ability to see right through to my soul. The way he stared, as if he was studying me, measuring me up, left me unnerved. An unwanted shiver ran through my torso.

"Are you hungry?" he asked.

"Yes, actually. I don't eat before I dance." I always made myself a sandwich before I left home and put it in the mini-fridge behind the reception desk, so I wouldn't wake Jimmy and Jackie by rummaging in the kitchen when I got back. "If you'll just show me where the door is, I can go home and get myself some food."

He ignored that. "I'll see what I've got."

Back in the kitchen, he opened a fridge the size of a small family car. The shelves held a variety of tubs and cling-film covered dishes, most of them with post-its stuck to the top.

"What's with all the notes?"

"My housekeeper," he said sheepishly. "She leaves

me instructions because she thinks I don't know how to cook."

"And do you?"

"No. Do you?"

"Not really. I can make a sandwich, but that's about my limit."

At home, I ate to live rather than the other way around. On special occasions, I'd help Jackie in the kitchen while she cooked up a Caribbean feast concocted from her childhood memories, but those times were few and far between. And mostly I got relegated to the washing up.

"Well, you can thank Ruth for her help in the morning then," he said.

He thought I'd still be around in the morning? "I won't be here. I could write her a message if you like."

"It's too late for you to go home tonight."

He waved at the clock above the sink, and I followed his gaze. Quarter past two.

"I don't have a choice. I start work at five."

"But you've just finished work. Surely there's not much call for strippers at five in the morning?"

"Of course not. But I have another job, and that starts at five."

"Can't you call in sick?"

"No, Mr. Moneybags, I can't call in sick. I've got to open up for customers at six, and I'll be the only one there. It'll be hard enough trying to explain the bruises, and I'm already gonna have to take time off from the club. I can hardly dance looking like I've been in a car crash, can I?"

"If you have to go back, I'll get Tony to drop you off for five. What time do you finish tomorrow?"

"One thirty. Why?"

"I'll pick you up at one thirty, then."

And take me where? "No, you won't. At one thirty I'm going to bed. I've already lost two hours sleep tonight, and I don't get enough as it is."

"Fine, get some sleep, and I'll pick you up later. If you can't work in the club, you'll be free in the evening."

"Nice try. I need to study when I'm not working. And what makes you think I want to see you again, anyway?"

"Money seems to talk with you, and I have a proposition. If it makes a difference, I'll pay you for your time this evening."

"I'm not a prostitute." I stared daggers at him. "I'll have you know I've never, ever slept with a man for money."

He chuckled. "If looks could kill..."

I put my hands on my hips and glared harder.

"Calm down, Diamond. It's not that kind of proposition. I'm talking about a business arrangement. I've already told you I don't go for the schoolgirl look."

"Well, now I know you're talking rubbish. I don't have any qualifications at all, and you've known me for less than a day. No way could you have a bona fide business opportunity to offer."

"Humour me. I'll pick you up at six. Does that give you enough time?"

"I guess." Anything to shut him up.

"Good. Now eat some food."

Part of me wanted to refuse on principle, but as my stomach grumbled, I gave in. The macaroni and cheese did look good. I added new potatoes and a bowl of vegetables and heated everything up in the microwave as per Ruth's step-by-step directions. If nothing else, at least I'd get a proper meal out of the visit.

And wow, Ruth could cook! The pasta had just the right amount of grease, and once I'd added a knob of butter, the vegetables weren't bad either. I felt an irrational jealousy at this man for having so much good food available. My shelf in the fridge was filled with whatever was on special offer or, if I timed it right, in the reduced section at the end of the day.

Black chose a healthier option, a salad with chicken breasts, and I made a show of chewing so I wouldn't have to talk to him. After we'd put our plates in the dishwasher, another luxury I didn't have, he showed me up to a spare bedroom.

"Get a couple of hours' sleep. I'll wake you up in time to get to work."

"Will you?"

He sighed. "You need to learn to trust me."

"Why?"

"I'll explain tomorrow."

What was he talking about? I had no idea, but my eyelids were drooping, so I decided I didn't care. A few hours, and he'd be out of my life.

True to his word, Black shook me awake at four thirty, at which point, if memory serves correctly, I told him to get lost, only not quite so politely, then burrowed back under the duvet. I was vaguely aware of being lifted up in his arms and bundled into the backseat of a car, at which point he nudged me awake again.

"You've got to help me out here—where are we going?"

I mumbled my address, which Black somehow translated for the driver, and before I knew it, I was being helped out of the car at JJ's.

"Sure you can't take the morning off?" Black asked again.

"No, I have to do this."

I turned my back on him as I punched in the combination to get into the building. The date Jimmy and Jackie got married, fourteen years ago now.

"Don't forget I'm picking you up at six."

"Whatever. Bye."

I stepped inside, gave him one last petulant glare, then slammed the door in his face.

Finally, the strangest night of my life was over.

CHAPTER 20

TO THIS DAY, I have no idea how I got through that morning. Not only was I knackered, I had to deal with Jimmy and Jackie's incessant questioning about the mess I was in as well as most of the regulars offering to go around and beat up whoever had caused it.

At twelve, Jimmy planted himself in front of me. "Go to bed, Amanda. I'm sick of you stumbling around reception like a zombie."

"I'm fine, honestly. I just didn't sleep so well last night."

"That's hardly surprising. If you tell me who did it, I'll sort it out."

"I'm grateful for the offer, but it's dealt with, Jimmy. This won't be happening again."

"It had better not. If it does, I'll hold you upside down myself and shake the truth loose. Now, get lost."

I half crawled, half stumbled back to my room, and despite the stiffness and aches plaguing me, I nodded off quickly. I wasn't quite dead, but I sure slept like it.

When six o'clock rolled around, I didn't notice because I was still fast asleep with the pillow over my head. I only woke up when the shouting started. Was that Jimmy yelling? He never yelled. He didn't need to —one sharp word from him and people generally cowered. I dragged myself out of bed and flattened my hair down with my fingers, grabbed a piece of chewing gum to cover up my disgusting breath, then walked out into the gym to see what all the fuss was about.

I found Black standing next to the boxing ring, facing off with a dozen scary-looking dudes led by my self-appointed guardian. Black's nose was swollen, and his face looked even worse than it did when he brought me back in the early hours.

Jimmy had his fists up as he raised his voice again. "You want to try fighting a man instead of my little girl?"

"I don't want to fight anyone." Black looked remarkably unruffled considering his opposition included a current heavyweight boxing champion and a dude who'd just been released from prison for grievous bodily harm.

"Well, you didn't seem to have a problem with it last night, did you, you monster? It *was* you, wasn't it? Have you seen the state you left her in?"

Oh, heck. I didn't want to be responsible for the inevitable beating that was going to happen if I didn't intervene. With little other choice, I rushed over and planted myself in front of Black.

"Jimmy, guys, back down. Please. It's not that I don't appreciate the sentiment, because I really do, but you've got the wrong man."

"Amanda, why are you defending him?"

"He didn't do this. It was some other guy. He jumped me, and I didn't see his face. Black pulled him off; that's how he got hurt." I pointed at his cheek, which glowed a tasteful shade of purplish-blue under the strip lights.

Okay, so that was a bit of a lie, but what was I

supposed to do? Tell the truth?

Like an outgoing tide, the tension ebbed from the room. Jimmy took a step back and stuck out his hand for Black to shake. "Why didn't you say so, son? Thanks for looking after her. Want a beer?"

The other guys clapped him on the back and wandered off to the weight pile.

Black reached out for his hand. "I'll pass, thanks. I'm just here to take *Amanda* out for dinner." He looked at me pointedly when he stressed my name.

Jimmy narrowed his eyes at him. "How old are you?"

"Twenty-five."

So my guess of mid-twenties had been bang on.

"You're too old for her. She's only eighteen," Jimmy informed him, turning to me. "He's too old for you," he repeated.

"It's not like that," Black said to Jimmy. "I only want to make sure she's all right after what happened last night. My conscience wouldn't let me drop her off and then wash my hands of her."

"Oh. In that case, Amanda, you'd better go and get ready. Sure you don't want that beer?"

Thanks, Jimmy. He may have looked like the Hulk, but he was a pushover.

Gah! I rolled my eyes, but it looked as if I was stuck going for dinner with Black, because I couldn't back out without Jimmy asking more questions. And I'll admit, I was a teensy bit curious over why Black wanted to talk to me.

I left him sitting on the sofa in reception and prayed Jimmy wouldn't blab too much about me to a man I barely knew. That thought made me hurry in the shower, and my jeans stuck to my still-damp skin as I pulled on the cleanest pair.

I didn't own much in the way of smart, and the closest I'd come to dinner with a man before was sharing the 2-for-1 deal at Chicken Cottage. But it wasn't like this was a date, so I figured the jeans and a plain black T-shirt would be fine with my dark purple jumper over the top. I didn't own a blow dryer and all my make-up was at Silk, so my face stayed bare and the soggy ends of my blonde hair brushed my shoulders.

Fifteen minutes later, I was back out the front with Jimmy and Black, who'd been joined by Jackie. The three of them were chatting away like long-lost friends. When Black saw me coming, he stood up and held out a hand to me.

Still playing the part for Jimmy, I linked my arm through Black's and smiled.

"The car awaits, my lady," Black said, charm personified.

Jackie grinned like she'd just won the lottery. "Oh, Amanda, he's such a gentleman. And don't you worry about working tomorrow morning, honey. I'll do your shift."

"You don't have to do that," I said through gritted teeth.

"Nonsense, you need to enjoy yourself sometimes." And that was her final word on it.

Black escorted me out of the door, and the second it closed behind us, I shoved his arm back at him. "I think we've safely established I'm not a lady, and I'm certainly not your lady, so you might as well cut the crapola."

Irritatingly, he just turned to me and raised an

eyebrow. "Amanda?"

"Look, have you ever had a name you really hated? I'm not going to use it if I don't have to."

"Sure I do. It's Charles. Why do you think my friends call me Black?"

"I'm not exactly a friend, am I?"

"Well, I'm working on that, okay? Good save in there, by the way. I especially liked the part where I beat up the mystery third assailant. That was a nice touch."

"I didn't do it for you. I just didn't want Nigel to get arrested again when the mob tried to kill you. He only got out of prison last week, and he'd be violating his parole."

"Oh. Well, thanks anyway." He stopped at a low-slung black sports car and opened the door for me to get in.

"No driver tonight?"

"It's his day off. Where do you want to eat?"

"How should I know? Do I look like the type of girl who dines in fancy restaurants? For me, eating out is a choice between McDonald's or Burger King, and you don't come across as a person who frequents either of those."

"I'm not, but if you want to go there...."

"Oh, for Pete's sake. If you insist we have to go out for dinner, just pick somewhere, will you?"

Black started the engine and put the car in gear then peeled out of the parking lot. He wasn't hanging around, and with a bit of speeding and some dubious calls at traffic lights, we soon pulled up outside a small Italian restaurant.

Once he'd abandoned the car at the kerb, he turned

and raised one of his dark eyebrows again. "I'm surprised. Most women would have told me to slow down at least half a dozen times during that trip."

"If you want to lose your licence, it's up to you. But it's nice that you're aware you drive like an idiot."

"I don't, normally. I was just trying to get a reaction out of you."

"Well, you'll be trying for a long time. I've been in cars with people who drive far worse than that."

"I'm not sure I want to know."

"Well, that suits me because I have no intention of telling you."

Some people who nicked cars drove them like idiots, not caring if they wrecked someone else's pride and joy. I hated being a passenger on those trips. When I stole a vehicle, it was either for the technical challenge or simply because I needed to get from A to B, and I drove mighty carefully. I didn't fancy explaining to the police why I was driving a borrowed car with no licence and no insurance, and I always left the car neatly parked once I'd finished with it.

Ever the considerate one, that was me.

Black walked around the car and swung my door wide open. I ignored his outstretched hand and levered myself out of the seat. He shrugged, a tiny movement, then guided me into the restaurant with a hand on the small of my back.

"I'm not going to get lost, you know. We're only twenty yards from the door."

He smiled faintly. "Politeness is wasted on you."

Well, I didn't want to be here, did I?

Inside, a tiny Italian man who introduced himself as Giovanni greeted Black warmly and showed us to what he professed to be the best table in the house, hidden in a quiet corner and softly lit by candles.

"You've got the wrong idea about this," I told the guy.

He ignored me and pulled a chair out.

"Sit," Black said.

"I'm not a freaking dog."

He sighed. "Sit, please."

I huffed and gave in. The sooner I sat, the sooner I could eat. And the sooner I ate, the sooner I could go home.

Black took over and ordered for both of us, asking for water and a decent bottle of wine, plus a plate of antipasti to start and a variety of pizza and pasta dishes to follow.

"I thought I'd order what I know is good, seeing as you apparently don't have a clue about restaurants, and the menu's in Italian," he said.

"Yeah, thanks. I'm sure someone as loaded as you seem to be wouldn't come somewhere the food's rubbish, though, so I don't suppose it would have mattered what I'd asked for."

"Are you going to be deliberately antagonistic all evening?"

"Probably. It's not like I asked to come, is it?"

Black inhaled deeply, the sign of someone hanging onto control by his fingertips. "I'm not accustomed to going out to dinner with a female who's so clearly unwilling to be here, so do you think you could try to be a tiny bit accommodating? To make the evening more pleasant for both of us?"

"Maybe. It would be even more pleasant if you'd take me home and pick up one of your oh-so-willing lady friends. Then I could go back to sleep."

I had another five o'clock start tomorrow, and I was still behind on shut-eye. Jackie might have offered to do my shift, but I had no intention of taking her up on it.

"That's not why I'm here tonight."

"Ah yes, your mysterious proposition. Well, what is it then? Spit it out."

"All in good time. We'll eat first."

How could he be so infuriatingly patient about the whole thing?

Giovanni brought the food, and it seemed as though Black had ordered the entire menu. Probably he did. I started eating, piling my plate high, and every dish tasted really, really good. So good, in fact, that I forgot to act annoyed and just savoured each delicious morsel. The wine slid down nicely, too, and I drank several glasses. Probably I should have mentioned that I was underage, but I didn't want to risk that little snippet of information getting back to Jimmy.

Besides, I'd been drinking since the age of twelve, albeit mostly beer and cheap cider rather than undoubtedly expensive grape products. This made a nice change.

The waistband of my trousers dug into my stomach as Giovanni returned to clear away the plates. Stuffed, I leaned back in my chair and tried to burp discreetly.

"Are you ready for dessert, or do you want to wait a few minutes?"

Dessert? There was more? If it was as good as the rest of the food then I wanted it, even if it meant staying in Black's company for a bit longer so I had enough room to eat it. In truth, he wasn't a bad dinner companion.

Conversation so far had stayed on safe topics—sports, London, Virginia where he was from, the weather, things like that. He seemed to know a lot about everything and conversing with him sure beat the monosyllabic grunts of half the guys I hung out with. It was a shock to realise I was enjoying dinner, despite my best efforts to the contrary.

Dessert arrived, or should I say desserts. Giovanni served up eight different ones, and Black and I both tried all of them, except I snarfed down four times more than he did.

Hey, I figured it might be years before I got food that posh again, so I wanted to make the most of it.

Black ordered another bottle of wine and poured me a glass. Then he topped up his own water. He was driving, so he'd only drunk one glass of red before he switched.

His face grew serious. This must be the important bit, I thought somewhat groggily, and through my alcohol-induced fuzz, I realised I had an issue.

Because although I didn't know what he was planning to ask me, I felt remarkably mellow. Far from my usual "uptight with a hint of crazy," probably due to all the wine combined with a total carb overload. At that moment in time, slumped back in my seat, watching his full pink lips move, I'd have agreed to anything.

Which presented me with a bit of a problem when I heard what he had to say.

CHAPTER 21

BLACK SAT BACK in his seat, watching me through soft eyes, relaxed but alert.

Mine kept trying to close.

"So," he started. "Last night was interesting, wasn't it?"

"I guess you could call it that."

"I think you have a rather unique skill set."

"And...?"

"Last year, I started up a company with a friend of mine, providing security and investigation services. We've encountered certain situations where having a female on the team would have been extremely useful, and we've spent months looking for the right woman without any success. But yesterday evening, I found her."

"Where?" Was I missing something?

"You, you idiot."

Oh, yes, the wine. I remembered now.

"Well, I think you've made a mistake. I don't know the first thing about investigating or securig... securitat...securitising."

"Or drinking more than one bottle of wine, it appears." He slid my glass away from me, laughing.

"Nope. Better than beer though," I giggled. What on earth...? Giggled?

He turned serious again. "I want you to come and work for me."

"I've already got a job. Two, in fact. And I even like one of them."

"I know. You'd need to leave them both, and it would be a big commitment. Jimmy told me you're saving up to go to university, and that's admirable. So, my offer is that if you work for me for six months and give it your all, I'll pay you two hundred thousand pounds at the end. After that, either one of us can terminate the contract. If you decide to come back here, you'll have enough money to study and put a down payment on a house as well."

"Seriously?"

He nodded.

"You're insane. You've only known me a day, and I'm not exactly a model citizen."

"I understand that. But I've also noticed your dubious talents." He started listing, ticking off the points on his fingers as he went. "You stole my wallet without me noticing."

I interrupted him, ignoring his dirty look. "You did notice."

"Only because I went to get some gum out of the same pocket. Pure coincidence, that's all. Then you knew I was following you without looking overtly behind and judged the right moment to start running. And when you took off, you were surprisingly fast. That climb up the scaffolding..." He shook his head and smiled. "That was impressive."

Okay, yeah, it was. I couldn't help grinning back.

He leaned forward, elbows on the table as he continued. "I spent several years in the Navy SEALs, and I barely kept up with you. Then you broke my nose and made me doubt for a few moments whether I'd ever father a child. I've been in fights with grown men who haven't come close to doing that. I seriously underestimated you. You look like an angel but you fight like the devil, and I want to harness those skills."

"And for six months you'd pay me two hundred grand? You've got more money than sense."

"Maybe, maybe not. If you're capable of what I think you are, it would be the best money I ever spent."

"So, just suppose I did agree. How do you see this crazy plan of yours working? Would I have to leave England?"

"Yes. You'd need to move to Virginia. But I come to London every couple of months, and you could tag along if you wanted to visit."

"I wouldn't know anyone. I'd be on my own."

And I'd never been completely alone before, not the way he was suggesting. In London, I'd spent years building up a network of acquaintances I could trade favours with, from the guys at the gym to the bouncers at Silk, local business owners, kids I'd been on the street with. Did I want to be by myself in a place I couldn't even find on a map?

"You'd know me, and I'd soon start introducing you to people. Despite your somewhat abrasive personality, people seem to like you, so I can't imagine you'd be lonely. And if you didn't want to live in your own place, I've got a spare room. Believe me, my house has got plenty of space for two."

"Is it as big as the one here?"

"Bigger. The pair of us could be there for weeks and never cross paths. Unless you wanted to, of course."

"What would I have to do?"

Had I gone quite mad? Why was I even considering his proper...propa...his offer? Was I that easily bought? I slumped in my chair, confused. The money sounded attractive; that I couldn't deny. And so did the posh house, especially if it came with a fully stocked fridge. And Black... He smiled, showing me his row of white, if slightly fuzzy, teeth. Boy, he was really pretty when he did that.

"Training. Physical fitness and fight skills. Shooting and knife work. Advanced driving, flying, scuba diving, parachuting, climbing, sailing a boat."

"Sounds like you want to turn me into Wonder Woman. Is there anything you've missed? Ice skating? Teleportation?" I nudged him with my foot. "Would I get to wear a cape?"

He scowled and ignored me. "Then there are the soft skills, like learning how to talk to people without swearing at them or getting them annoyed—that'll be the most difficult part for you. And you'd need to be able to do it in several languages. Towards the end, I might ask you to do a few simple jobs if I thought you were ready for them."

Joking aside, he was giving me the chance to do things I'd never even dared to dream about. Learning to fly cost a fortune, something that would be way out of my price range even if I did go to university and get a decent job. And the physical side of it appealed to me— the chance to take the training I'd done at the gym to another level.

Yes, I'd have to leave JJ's, but I'd never planned to stay there forever. Plus with two hundred thousand pounds, I'd be able to give Jimmy some cash as a thank you for everything he'd done for me. Maybe I could even hire him a new receptionist?

Then there was Black. He remained an enigma, but with all the stuff I'd dished out to him, he'd never once lost his temper or intentionally tried to hurt me. Quite the opposite, in fact. He'd treated me like an equal even if I didn't deserve it.

And in effect, he was offering me the world.

But I couldn't do it.

Not because I didn't want to. If he'd offered me the universe, my answer would still have been the same. Why? Because the little lie I'd told a couple of years ago came back to bite me.

I swallowed back a curse and stared at my hands, knuckles turning white as they gripped each other in my lap.

"I can't," I whispered.

"I know it would be a massive upheaval, but I'd do whatever it took to make it work. Is it the money? Do you want more money?"

"No, it's not that. I just can't."

"Tell me why. If you're at all interested, I'll find a way to fix whatever the problem is."

"I'm fifteen years old. Can you fix that?" Adding a couple of years to my age didn't matter in London. But if I needed to travel? My birth certificate, the one I'd liberated from my mother and kept folded up under my mattress, clearly stated my real birthday, and I'd need it to get a passport.

"Fifteen?"

He stared at me, eyes wide. I'd managed to shock him, and I couldn't imagine that happened often.

"You're kidding. Right?" he asked, a note of hope

creeping into his voice.

I shook my head and stared blankly at the table.

He swore under his breath. "And I've just given you a bottle of wine."

"Can you take me home now? And please, please don't tell Jimmy. He thinks my birthday's the fifteenth of May rather than December, and two years earlier than it is. I'd lose both my jobs for sure, and I really need them."

Black ran his hands through his hair, once, twice, three times, tugging so hard I thought he'd pull it out by the roots.

"So we're on the tenth of December now, which makes you nearly sixteen?"

I nodded.

"Do you have any family or friends, anyone who knows how old you really are?"

"No family, only Jimmy and Jackie. I haven't seen my mother since I was ten, and I don't ever want to. The foster care people don't know where I am either. I've been out of the system since I was twelve."

"I can't believe I'm even considering this, but doing what you did at fifteen... I can only imagine what you'd be capable of at eighteen. If it wasn't for the age thing, would you want to come with me?"

Would I? That was the question. If someone told me yesterday I'd be offered the chance to try things that I'd only ever seen on TV, and not just that, be paid six figures to do it, I'd only have asked one question: "How much crack have you been smoking?"

But here I was, and that possibility was sitting at the table in front of me.

"I'd have to sleep on it. I mean, all my plans, my

future—everything would change." The impact of the decision wasn't lost on me, drunk or not. One word, and life as I knew it would be over. "And I'd need to speak to Jimmy and Jackie. I can't leave them in the lurch, not when they've been so good to me."

"But you're not saying no?"

"I'm not saying no."

Black let out the breath he'd been holding and his smile flickered back, just for a second. "Thank goodness for that." His voice dropped, almost to a whisper. "I want you with me, perhaps more than I've ever wanted anything."

I realised at that moment, sitting in a little Italian restaurant in some back street in London, that I'd quite like to be with him too.

That evening, I went home with Black again. He offered to take me back to JJ's, but if I was going to end up living with him for six months, it seemed like a good idea to check I could still stand the sight of him after one night. Besides, he had better food.

Ruth turned out to be a plump, cheerful woman in her late forties, who was bustling around the kitchen when I went downstairs in the morning. Today, I was wearing a more appropriately sized tracksuit, which Black had handed me in a paper carrier bag last night.

"I bought you this."

A present? "More clothes?"

"I hoped you'd come back with me."

"Am I really that predictable?" I rummaged around in the bag and fished out something pink and lacy. "Knickers? Isn't that at bit...personal?"

He shrugged. "Not the first time I've bought underwear for a woman, Diamond. The sweats caused me the most trouble. I had to hunt for a sports shop."

I held the matching bra up by my fingertips. "But it's pink."

He sighed faintly and shook his head. "What colour do you normally wear?"

Uh oh. I shouldn't have started this conversation, and I felt my cheeks heat.

"Black," I whispered.

"What do you want for breakfast, dearie?" Ruth asked.

The only choice I'd had before was cornflakes with milk or cornflakes without milk.

"Whatever's easy; I don't mind."

When Black came downstairs, dressed in a suit undoubtedly made-to-measure on Saville Row, I was eating a plate of pancakes with maple syrup and bacon.

"I see you picked the healthy option," he said.

"I didn't pick anything, actually. Ruth did, and it's delicious. How are you not the size of a tank, having her here all the time?"

"You'll soon learn portion control." He reached over and snagged a piece of my bacon. "But this morning, I'll help you out."

I went to smack his hand away, but he was too quick. "Oi! That's mine."

Aaaannnnd...he'd eaten it. I really hated him at that moment.

"I have a meeting to get to, and after that, I'm going to see a man about our little problem."

The smug git actually patted me on the head, then leapt back as I tried to grab his hand. "Be good." His laughter followed him out the door.

Good grief. What had I done?

Ruth proved to be friendly but frustratingly unforthcoming with information about Black. From the snippets that slipped out, I gathered that he was an intensely private person, and she was a little surprised to see me there at all because he never brought women home with him. So there was no Mrs. Black, then.

While he was out, I took the opportunity to explore the house. With it being a Sunday, the builders weren't working, and Ruth looked busy in the kitchen with a huge array of baking products scattered on the counter. Keeping a careful ear out in case she came near, I went through room-by-room, starting at the top and working my way down. The place was surprisingly sterile, more of a show house than a home. And all the creeping around reminded me of my days as an amateur burglar.

On the whole, the place wasn't as interesting as I'd hoped. Half of the rooms were empty, and IKEA had more soul than the decorated parts. In Black's bedroom, I found one hefty safe behind a mirror and another set into the floor of his dressing room. That was next to a bag holding a set of handcuffs and a coil of rope. Was Mr. Black into a bit of kink, or did he have a fetish for kidnapping people? More to the point, did I really want to know the answer to that question?

By lunchtime, I'd been through all six floors apart from a locked room on the second. When I'd peered through the keyhole, it looked like an office, but I'd have needed tools to get inside and I'd left those hidden behind my makeshift wardrobe at JJ's.

The only other point of interest was the basement. Not because of the gym, the swimming pool, or the home cinema—those were quite normal, I imagined, if you were a millionaire. No, the strange thing was that the basement didn't fit with the floor plan of the house. My gut told me there should be more rooms, but I couldn't work out how to get into them.

I didn't get the chance to search any further because Black returned at lunchtime, looking cheerful. Or, at least, what passed for cheerful in his world.

"How did it go?" I asked.

"Not too bad. What do you want to do for the rest of the day?"

"That's all you're gonna give me?"

"Patience is something else you need to learn. Now, are you going to answer my question?"

"I don't know. I can't remember the last time I actually had a choice over how to spend an afternoon."

"Believe it or not, I don't often have free time either. We should get to know each other."

"Okay, so let's go out. What do you do for fun?"

He gave me a blank look.

"You know, fun?" I prompted. "Relaxing? Having a good time?"

"Fun isn't a big part of my life. What do you do?"

He had me there. "Uh, practice chemistry questions?"

We locked gazes for a second then burst out laughing. We were as bad as each other.

"Why don't we just go out and see where we end up?" I suggested.

"I don't normally do that either."

"You want me to change my life for you. I could do with a bit of give and take."

"Fair enough. Let's get our jackets."

We spent the afternoon doing stupid tourist stuff. I'd lived in London my whole life, but I'd never visited the Natural History Museum or been for a ride on a river boat. But then again, I'd never had anyone to do those things with.

And it was indeed fun.

Even sober, I found Black surprisingly easy to chat with. Although he clearly didn't like discussing his upbringing, as I didn't enjoy rehashing mine, we found enough to talk about that we barely shut up all afternoon.

As darkness fell, we ate dinner in a small Japanese restaurant in Belgravia, which turned out to be where his house was. I tried sushi for the first time, and strangely I liked it, despite the raw fish. Black taught me how to use chopsticks, although I nearly rammed one through his hand when he kept laughing at my initial efforts.

"Are you staying tonight?" he asked as we walked out into the freezing night. "I can drop you back early tomorrow."

"Why not?"

After all, I knew JJ's wouldn't be my home for much longer. I'd decided to go to America with Black. Crazy, maybe, seeing as I'd only known him for one weekend, but it felt like we'd been in each other's lives a lot longer. Despite coming from worlds that were as alike as a Lamborghini and a Lada, we clicked.

I didn't want to imagine the rest of my life without him in it.

Couldn't imagine it.

Which was why five days later on my genuine sixteenth birthday, I sat nervously clutching my new passport. The passport that proclaimed me to be Amanda Emerson, born on May fifteenth, two years and seven months earlier than I came into the world. It sure beat the dodgy driver's licence I'd bought in the pub around the corner from JJ's last year.

Beside me, Black thanked the flight attendant for the two glasses of bubbly she'd just handed him.

He passed one to me. "Happy eighteenth and a bit, Emmy."

I clinked my glass against his. "You should have bought the bottle."

"Don't push your luck."

I drained every drop then leaned back in my seat for the ride.

Dulles International, here we come.

CHAPTER 22

WHEN BLACK SAID the next six months would be hard, he hadn't been kidding. If it wasn't for the obscene amount of cash he'd promised to pay me at the end of it, I'd have jacked it all in during the first week.

Even then there were some days when Black nearly got his two hundred grand stuffed up his sanctimonious American backside while I caught the next flight home.

But I'll start at the beginning. Day one was all right. My first ride on a plane, in first class no less.

"I could get used to this," I said, settling into the plush leather seat.

"The novelty soon wears off." Black had his laptop open before the seatbelt light blinked out.

I hoped that was true, because after the initial thrill of take-off, I fell asleep, revelling in a bed far more comfortable than my mattress at JJ's. Black woke me when the food got dished out, and I forked down a tuna salad and a slice of chocolate cake, then I nodded off again. Perhaps my subconscious knew what was waiting for me.

After seven hours, we touched down on American soil just as the sun was rising. The fairy tale continued as Black ushered me into a chauffeur-driven car for the journey back to his house, Riverley Hall. If I'd known the nightmare that was to come, I'd never have left the airport.

But for now, I was blissfully ignorant, and when we turned through the enormous iron gates that guarded my new home, my jaw dropped.

"You weren't joking. It's huge!"

Riverley made the London place look like a council house.

"I never joke."

If the entire population of a small village, maybe even a town, ever found themselves evicted, the lot of them could have moved into Black's house with room to spare.

"It looks as if it came off a film set," I told him.

I'd only ever seen buildings like that in library books. Or films. Horror films. It had a gothic air about it, and hideous gargoyles stared down at me from the roofline. The huge stone columns flanking the front door dwarfed me, guarding walls with the same grey hue as a storm cloud.

"Are Morticia and Gomez home?"

"Sorry?"

"From the Addams family?"

He gave me a blank look.

"You know, on TV?"

"I don't watch TV."

Oh. "I just meant the house looks a bit creepy."

He shrugged. "I guess. I grew up here, so I'm used to it. A minor noble built it at the turn of the last century. He wanted something that reminded him of his mother country."

"Where was that? Transylvania?"

Black's lips formed a flat line. "England. He was

one of my ancestors."

"Freaking nobility. No wonder you've got a stick up your backside."

He followed me out of the car. "I do not."

"Do too."

He pushed open the front door and waved me through.

"What, no butler?"

"Good grief, why did I think this was a good idea?" he muttered, before taking a deep breath and turning to face me. "I'll give you a tour."

"Lovely. Will that include the crypt?"

No answer.

The mansion was a maze, the layout illogical and full of unexpected dead ends. And did I mention gloomy?

"Do you have a map?"

"You'll soon find your way around."

Really? Even at the end of six months, I could still see myself bumbling about like a blind hamster, desperately hunting for a way out.

Black led me upstairs, where he gave me the choice of sixteen bedrooms, each one expensively decorated and all but two with en-suite bathrooms. They may have been luxurious, but I didn't need a chandelier or seventeen throw pillows. I chose the plainest, a corner room on the second floor, third if we were speaking American, which looked out on a perfectly manicured kitchen garden and the lawns and woods beyond it. Little did I know I'd look out of that window every night for weeks dreaming of escape.

The bed was a king size, a far cry from my single at home, and I even had a small dressing room. While

Black went to make a phone call, I unpacked my suitcase then stood back.

"Isn't having an entire room for my clothes overkill?" I murmured to myself.

"Don't worry, you'll soon fill it." I turned to find Black had reappeared behind me.

"I don't like spending money just for the sake of it."

"You'll be spending my money, so don't worry about it. We'll go into town later. I'll show you around, and we can stock up on the things you'll need."

"Well, if you insist. I'm not going to turn down free stuff."

"Let's get brunch first."

Brunch? Another reminder the flight had landed on a different planet altogether.

As Black led me back through the labyrinth, I boiled it down to the basics. All I really needed to know was where my room was, where the kitchen was, and how to get in and out. Oh yeah, and how to find the gym, because according to Black, I'd be spending a lot of time in there.

When we got to the kitchen, I found Riverley Hall had its own version of Ruth too. She was equally plump and cheerful, but called Mrs. Fairfax.

"Omelette and salad?" she asked.

Black nodded while I grimaced.

"I stick to a healthy diet most of the time," he said.

"Is that why we have that?" I pointed at a bowl of fruit salad. "I was hoping for chocolate cake."

"Yes. You'll have to cut back on your junk food intake from now on."

That was my first indication of what was to come. It turned out a lack of cake was the least of my worries.

As promised, in the afternoon we headed into Richmond. I picked out some more workout clothes, a few pairs of jeans, and a jumper or two and tried not to feel guilty as Black footed the bill. Strange, because I'd rarely felt remorse when I purloined things back in London, but somehow it was easier to take stuff from strangers.

"You need a couple of nice dresses as well," Black said. "You may need to accompany me to dinner at some point."

"I'm not really into dresses."

He gave me a wry smile. "I'd noticed that, but you have to learn to pretend to be."

In the upmarket boutique he took me to, the sales girls swarmed around him like demented flies and looked down their snooty noses at me.

"Shop here often, do you? I didn't imagine you as a sequins-and-tiaras kind of guy."

"What man doesn't look good in a cocktail dress?" he answered, deadpan.

For a second, I wasn't sure whether he was serious. "I thought you said you didn't joke."

"It's a new thing for me."

He cracked a tiny smile. Progress?

Hmm. Where did I start in this fancy shop? The only time I'd bought dresses before, I was more concerned with the ease of getting out of them while cavorting around a pole than what they actually looked like. I shuffled through the rails, trying to look as though I knew what I was doing, but it was hopeless. I didn't understand the sizing, and I couldn't work out how to get into half of the outfits with all their hidden zips and twiddly buttons. I was drowning in a sea of silk and chiffon.

"How about this one?" Black asked, holding up a purple knee-length thing with sequins on the bodice. "It matches your eyes."

I snatched it off him. "Yeah, okay."

"Do you want some help?"

"No." I sighed. "Yes."

One snap of his fingers, and the nearest salesgirl started piling frocks into my arms. I caught sight of a price tag and dropped the lot.

"What's wrong?" Black hissed as I backed away.

"That dress costs three thousand dollars."

"And?"

"That's more than I earned last year."

The sales girl eavesdropped on our conversation, head going back and forth like she was at a tennis match. It took all my self-control not to slap her.

Black steered me back to the rail and bent to pick up the items I'd dropped. "My investments earned three thousand dollars while we were eating brunch. Just buy some dresses, would you?"

Trying to absorb that new piece of information, I plucked the top two dresses from him and hurried into the changing room. They fitted well enough, and I hauled my jeans back on.

"You want those ones?" he asked.

"Not really."

He turned to the cretinous woman still hovering at his elbow and handed her his credit card. "Could you wrap these up?"

She beamed up at him and scuttled off as I folded my arms and stared out the window.

"Now what?" he asked.

"I don't deserve those. I haven't even done any work yet."

He slung an arm around my shoulders and grasped my chin, forcing me to meet his gaze. "You will soon enough. I'll get my money's worth out of you, don't worry."

Why did my knees want to buckle when he said that?

"And we're having dinner with Nate later," he continued as the woman presented him with two bags.

"Who's Nate?"

He held the door open, allowing me to escape. "Nathaniel Wood. He's my business partner."

"Do I need to wear a dress?"

"Jeans will be fine. He's coming over to the house."

Super. Another person to be nice to.

We reached Black's Corvette, and I lowered myself into the passenger seat. That wasn't his only hot car—he'd shown me his garage earlier, full of automotive delights. I'd memorised the code number on the lockbox where he kept the keys, just in case an opportunity arose.

The engine growled into life, then we sped on to the next part of my adventure.

Nate arrived at Riverley not long after we did. He obviously had his own key because he came straight into the kitchen and helped himself to a beer. I felt like an amoeba under the microscope as he looked me up and down then turned to Black and raised an eyebrow as if to say, "Seriously?"

"Give her a chance."

"I thought we agreed to poach someone from the CIA? Or the FBI, even?"

"None of those candidates were right. I thought I'd try a different route."

Nate glowered at me. "What experience do you have in the security business?"

"Not a lot," I admitted. "And most of it's been from the other side."

He turned back to Black. "Have you lost your mind?"

"Quite possibly. But Emerson's staying."

The beef Wellington Mrs. Fairfax made was no doubt delicious, but I barely tasted it. Hostility rolled off Nate and filled the room, suppressing my appetite. I pushed dinner around my plate while Black and Nate talked business. The facts and figures mostly went right over my head, but Nate's suspicious glances in my direction every time Black mentioned anything about their current clients didn't. What, did Nate think I was some sort of spy for the competition?

Clearly, I had a lot to prove. Black had taken a huge gamble in bringing me here, even risking the wrath of his friend. Nobody but Jimmy and Jackie had ever shown that belief in me before. What if I let him down?

When Nate left an hour later, the temperature in the room rose again.

"Are you okay?" Black asked. "You were very polite. Not like you at all."

"He hates me." I sighed dramatically and collapsed over the table.

Black chuckled. "He's not your biggest fan at the moment, but he acts that way with everyone to start with. You have to earn Nate's trust. He doesn't give it out freely."

"An uphill battle, seems like."

"Yes, but you'll fight it, and you'll win."

Right now, I couldn't even fight my own body. By eight o'clock, I'd already yawned a dozen times as my brain got confused over time zones.

"You should get some sleep," Black said.

"I think you might be right." I couldn't resist adding, "For once."

"How has that mouth not got you into more trouble?"

"Must be my charming personality."

If Black rolled his eyes any harder, he'd have to go and retrieve them from his freaking tennis court.

"Charm or not, you'll have to keep getting up in the small hours. I train early."

Oh, joy. But at least I wouldn't have late shifts dancing sapping my energy at the other end of the day. The thought of eight hours of uninterrupted sleep made me smile as I journeyed to my bedroom. I only got lost twice. Not bad.

The next day, I reported for duty at the gym at five o'clock sharp, dressed for battle in running tights and a sports bra. How bad could it be? After all, I'd trained at least five times a week with Jimmy.

I soon got my answer. Every morning, a portal to Satan's dungeon opened up in the doorway of the gym, and I was contractually bound to step through it. More than once, I checked to see whether Black had grown horns and a tail. I wouldn't have been surprised if he'd started poking me with a trident every time I stumbled on the treadmill.

After four mornings in the gym with him, I struggled to walk. I had so many bruises in delightful shades of green and brown I didn't need to worry about wearing camouflage when he forced me to go running in the woods, and if I'd ventured out in public, I'd have needed to wear a burka to avoid getting dragged kicking and screaming to the nearest women's shelter. On the plus side, he might have got arrested, which would have given me a day off while his lawyer sorted out the mess. Black was the meanest fighter I'd ever come across, and at JJ's I'd met more than my fair share.

How I'd ever managed to break his nose, I had no idea. I couldn't even get him to break a sweat now. He'd start me off on cardio equipment, maybe eight miles on the treadmill or thirty on the stationary bike, before moving on to weights, then boxing or martial arts.

My muscles stiffened up overnight and by the next morning, I'd barely be able to move, but Black made me run, cycle, lift, and jump again anyway. On day five, he did at least bring in a physio to loosen my muscles before I seized up completely.

Fight training became my nemesis. I already knew how to box, but Black began drilling me with weapons too. He had a series of punchbags set up, all with layers of foam taped around the outside, and he taught me to attack them with knives first, because he expected me to carry one from now on. Once I'd mastered blades, he moved on to anything else that happened to be around —a golf club, a hammer, keys, a rolling pin, a flashlight, whatever we picked up on our way to the gym.

There were times—many times—I wanted to tell him what he was asking of me was impossible, but I swallowed down the words. Why? Because everything he made me do, he did it too, and I couldn't bring myself to admit defeat.

As I ate lunch after my third physio session, Black wandered in and sat opposite me. He'd already showered and moved with an ease I only dreamed of.

"I have to go away on business until the end of the week."

"Thank goodness." The words slipped out before I managed to stop them.

He looked at me sharply. "You still have to train, though. Gym at five, as usual."

I groaned, but I couldn't complain too much. After all, he was paying me a lot to be there. And without him watching over me, I'd just jog on the treadmill for half an hour then go back to bed.

Or so I thought.

When I got down to the gym on day six after a non-sanctioned lie in, I found Black had hired me a new trainer.

"You are late," he growled in a thick Russian accent, tapping his watch. "You will have to do extra."

Oh, great. Extra.

Alex, it turned out, used to be in the Russian army. I suspected they'd kicked him out for being too hard on the troops. Black was a pussycat in comparison, and I found myself counting down the seconds until his return. In my spare time, I plotted ways to murder Satan's older brother.

Shove him under a truck? Strangle him with barbed

wire? Simply shooting him as he slept seemed too kind.

On the plus side, when Black finally did get back, he'd procured me a UK driving licence to go with my passport, complete with international driving permit.

"After lunch, we'll start lessons," he said.

Thank goodness. If I was driving, Alex couldn't make me do push-ups.

Black sat me in the driver's seat of his Ford Mustang, apologising that it was the smallest car he owned, then proceeded to tell me what each pedal did, how to change gear, and what all the dials on the dashboard meant. He got halfway through his spiel before I got bored, started the engine, and drove off.

"Oh. Why didn't you say you could already drive?"

"You never asked. Once again, you made an assumption about me, and it was wrong."

"I'm going to have to stop doing that, aren't I? To save us wasting time down the line, do you have any other skills I should be aware of?"

"You already know about the pick-pocketing. Probably you could cut the lessons on shoplifting, lock-picking, and burglary short as well."

"Noted. Who taught you to drive?"

"Mostly a seventeen-year-old car thief named Vinnie, although some of it was trial and error when I started borrowing cars myself."

"Ah. So I needn't have bothered providing you with a key?"

"It wouldn't have been essential, no."

From that day on, I lost my afternoons to less physical tasks like offensive and defensive driving, shooting, and learning how to throw knives with deadly accuracy. It wasn't long before my evenings vanished too. Black started off by bringing in a French teacher, who spent three hours each day teaching me the language as well as French history and culture, which she claimed was as important as knowing the words themselves.

Sure, the lessons were hard, but learning how to converse abroad was far more useful than learning about the reproductive cycle of a dandelion. I enjoyed *L'ecole de Noir* far more than Forest Hill Comprehensive.

One of those co-opted into working with me was Nate, who turned out to be a whiz with electronics. He taught me a little about computers, as in how to hack them, search them, and take them apart. I also found out how to place bugs, disarm security systems, and monitor phone conversations.

I drank in everything he told me and developed a flair for blowing things up. It was possible to do an amazing amount of damage with things found in an ordinary household, and the day I created a spectacular ball of flame using a mobile phone battery and a few chemicals, I got a grudging smile and a "Nice job."

Hurrah! High praise indeed from Nate. That was the start of his thaw towards me, much to my relief. As he was Black's best friend, life would have been uncomfortable if the attitude he'd displayed at our first meeting pervaded for my entire stay.

After Nate came an old-timer named Herb, a botanist who talked to his greenery like it was human. Under his tutelage, I learned which plants were safe to eat, which had medicinal properties, and how the select few could be used to kill someone. With Herb's help and Black's permission, I started my own deadly garden out the back of Riverley Hall, fascinated as I watched my evil little fiends sprout and grow.

A mechanic of dubious origins improved my hot-wiring skills then taught me new ways to break into a car, the best methods to disable an engine, and how to sabotage parts of the vehicle to turn it into a death trap. I vowed to check my brake lines regularly from that point on because it was all too easy to damage them.

The high points in those first three months were few and far between. After physical training from five to twelve, I had half an hour to eat lunch then I'd carry on until nine with another thirty-minute break for dinner. My brain was worn out from all the studying, and at night I'd fall into bed wondering how I'd ever get through another day. Black had turned into the devil incarnate, and Riverley Hall became my living nightmare.

Think I'm kidding? I recall telling him that if he told me to "Just do it" one more time, I was going to just shoot him.

At that point in our lives, I didn't like him very much at all.

CHAPTER 23

AFTER THREE MONTHS with Black, I became aware of a gradual shift.

I'd stopped worrying whether I'd stick around until the half-year mark to collect my money and get out of there and instead started questioning if I was good enough. Would he want me to stay?

Rather than deliberately antagonising him, I found more and more that I was seeking his approval, although I still managed to irritate him effortlessly.

At the beginning of month four, he came down to breakfast smiling. I'd seen that look before. Usually, it meant I'd finish the day black and blue with my brain about to explode.

"What now?" Did he want me to learn Icelandic? Take on gang members armed with only a fork? Build a road bridge out of toothpicks? By that point, nothing would have surprised me. "Go on, give me the bad news."

He took his egg-white omelette from Mrs. Fairfax and added an avocado on the side. "I'm going to teach you to fly."

I put my slice of toast down. "What, like in a plane?"

"Unless you sprout wings between now and ten o'clock."

A plane it was, then. A T-34C Turbo-Mentor to be precise. The US Navy used them as training aircraft, but Black had scrounged one up from somewhere. He flew a few circuits of the airfield and explained the controls, then handed me a bunch of manuals.

"Some bedtime reading," he said.

I groaned. At least it was better than the book on rifle sights he'd made me read the week before. "When do I get to drive the plane?"

"When you're ready. And you're not to fly like you drive. I don't think my heart would take it."

"I've never crashed."

"Not for lack of trying."

Three more days passed before he let me get behind the controls. I was scheduled to fly for two hours a day, but I found myself extending that time because I enjoyed myself so much.

And once I'd mastered the plane, Black turned up on the back lawn in a helicopter.

"I thought you'd enjoy trying that too," he said.

My eyes lit up like a kid on E-numbers. "I think you might be right. Again."

Despite the time spent flying, Black didn't let up on the physical training. One weekend, he called in a favour from an old friend and took me along to the Naval Amphibious Base at Little Creek where he and Nate used to be stationed. They'd spent several years in the Navy SEALs before moving on to the CIA, in some special division they were both so cagey about that I didn't even know its name.

"I want to see you go around the assault course," Black said. "Find out what you're capable of."

"Is it difficult?"

"They call it the 'Dirty Name.'"

That didn't sound good.

Nate came with us, his usual happy self. People had obviously been informed of our arrival because a small crowd gathered to watch.

"Why is there an audience?" I asked.

"The last woman to attempt this got picked up by an ambulance before she got halfway around," Nate told me. "I guess they're looking for some entertainment."

As I stood around at the start, wearing a pair of woodland BDUs tailored to fit me, I heard people whispering. It made me nervous, something I was unaccustomed to.

"She's tiny—no way she's getting round," one guy said.

"What's this? Barbie does Navy?" another commented.

"She's with Black," a third put in. "Would he have brought her if she didn't stand a chance?"

And so it went on. "Are they running a pool on me?" I whispered to Black.

"I've just bet a hundred bucks that you'll get around in twelve minutes."

Great, no pressure or anything.

"Go," Black said.

First came the parallel bars. I had to shuffle along them, hop through a bunch of tyres, then vault over a wall higher than my head. And they called that the low wall? At least there was a rope to help me over the aptly named high wall that came next, but my arms burned by the time I reached the top. I got a mouthful of sand as I crawled under the barbed wire that came after it and headed for the cargo net.

"Two minutes," Black called from behind me. The git wasn't even puffing. The net stretched into the sky, almost as high as Riverley, it seemed like. Thankfully, I'd had some practice climbing up and down the balconies to avoid Alex and his boxing gloves.

The balance logs were easy, but the next obstacle not so much. That involved swinging from one rope to another via a hoop in the middle, but my arms weren't long enough. In the end, I leapt for it, grasping the ring by the tips of my fingers.

"Four minutes."

Next up came the beams that earned the course its moniker. I had to hop from one to the next, but if the gap was close enough to jump, the next log was too high. A series of wild leaps and a lot of luck got me over them. I glanced back in time to see Black and Nate springing between them gracefully, barely breaking a sweat.

The weaver was next, an arrangement of horizontal beams I had to wriggle under and over a few feet off the ground. I cracked my hip off one and didn't bother to muffle my curse.

Black laughed behind me. "Get on with it." What did he think I was doing? "Six minutes."

The rope bridge gave me a welcome break—I'd come across worse than that in the kiddie park in London—but the climb up a series of four platforms, each one six feet higher than the last, nearly killed me. Being shorter than the average SEAL left me at a definite disadvantage. To get down, I slithered along a zip line on my stomach. Navy men, it seemed, weren't allowed the "zip" part.

"Eight minutes."

The monkey bars came next, and I paused to wipe the blood off my hands. I'd cut my fingers on the rope, and if I wasn't careful, the wetness would cause me to slip.

The second lot of tyres and the wall I had to traverse sideways wouldn't have caused me a problem if I'd had to tackle them at the beginning, but looking up at the vertical surface after the horrors I'd already been through, I almost quit. I doubled over, hands on my knees, trying to catch my breath.

Black paused beside me while Nate carried on. "You can do it. You're not stopping now." He crouched beside me. "I'm not carrying you."

No way would I suffer that indignity. I straightened up and leapt across the wall before stumbling over the finish line in...

"Ten minutes." Black turned to the crowd. "Pay up, boys."

I leaned against a log, panting a sigh of relief that I hadn't needed medical intervention or let womankind in general down. I wanted to collapse, but that would have made me look weak.

One of the Navy instructors came over and clapped me on the back, nearly bringing me to my knees.

"I suppose you're planning to keep her?" he said to Black.

"Yes," he replied, the king of one-word answers.

"Shame. I'm sure the people at your old unit would be interested in offering her a job."

"She's not for sale."

"Hello? Living, breathing person here. Stop talking about me as if I'm an inanimate object."

Black smiled. "The people at my old unit would have a hard time dealing with her mouth. She never stops talking back."

I was nicely cross as he steered me back towards the helicopter we'd flown to the base in. "You might have effectively bought my life for six months, but I'm still human, even if you do expect me to act like a robot most of the time."

"Do I?"

"Yes. My life's an automated production line, one activity after another. No time to think. No time to relax."

He stopped mid-stride.

"Is that what it's like?"

"Surely you must have noticed?"

He pinched the bridge of his nose. "I only wanted to see what you could do. You've been so good at everything that I've just kept pushing you." He sighed. "I got carried away. I don't want you to feel like a robot."

Before we took another step, he got on the phone and cancelled my evening German lesson then found Nate and postponed my afternoon electronics session.

"When we get home, change your clothes and we'll go out. Anywhere you want."

"Really?"

"Sure. If you need a break, we'll take one. Now, you're flying back."

Once I'd parked the helicopter, I walked stiffly to the house. Despite my level of fitness, the Dirty Name had taken its toll on me.

"So, what do you want to do?" Black asked.

"Nothing. I want to do nothing."

"How about doing nothing in the Jacuzzi?"

"As long as you don't decide to see how long I can hold my breath underwater."

"Cross my heart."

After Black and I were both shrivelled, we went out for dinner.

"You pick the restaurant," I told him, since I still hadn't explored the local area. "As long as it's nothing too healthy."

I was sick to the back teeth of eating salad and grilled fish and chicken and steamed vegetables, which was what Toby, who Black had hired as my nutritionist the week before, fed me most of the time.

"Italian?" Black asked, looking hopeful.

I'd discovered that was his favourite. "Fine by me."

I ate until my jeans dug into my waist, and even Black, the epitome of self-control, leaned back in his seat and groaned. He was opening up to me more now, and I to him. We'd both been robbed of our childhoods, and I found it cathartic to talk. That evening, I told him things I'd never admitted to anyone, not even Jimmy. Black heard how my mother washed her hands of me as soon as I was old enough to crawl, and the moment I could walk, how I'd had to look after her rather than the other way around.

"Hey, you haven't lived until you've cleared up your mother's vomit after another heavy drinking session or thrown away her used needles."

I took another sip of wine. Black turned a blind eye to my age, and because he was with me, so did the restaurant owner.

"You should have been taken from her at birth. Couldn't anybody help you?"

"The care system was worse. At least with my mother, I had more freedom. In foster homes, there was always someone checking up on me. I hated it."

"Makes my life look idyllic, even if I didn't think so at the time."

Black came from old money, hence the massive houses and fancy toys. His ancestors had been big investors, first in gold, then property, and latterly oil. Although his early years had been pleasant, when his parents died in a car crash on the eve of his sixteenth birthday, he'd grown up fast.

"I was supposed to move in with my aunt, but Satan would have to live in an igloo before I'd set foot in her house. You'll meet her one day, and then you'll understand why."

"So what did you do?"

"A friend of my father's helped me out. He altered some records and got the court to appoint him as my guardian, then signed off so I could join the Navy at sixteen."

"When you say altered some records...?"

"When I said I was twenty-five, I meant twenty-four."

Suddenly, his willingness to help out with my age issue made more sense.

Black's father had split his job as a CIA agent with managing the family investment portfolio, and Black followed in his footsteps until he decided to quit the government agency and branch out with Nate instead.

"I was sick of the bureaucracy," he said. "Do you

have any idea how many forms you need to fill in when you shoot someone?"

"It's not a problem I've ever come across, no."

"And it's not only that. Some of the people who spouted enough half-truths to get elected had a habit of making messed up decisions, and I was stuck following their orders. If I'm going to die, I'd rather do it on my dollar."

"So you just quit?"

He laughed. "Not exactly. Now I'm a consultant. They don't have anyone else who can do what Nate and I do, so now we can charge what we like and kick the rubbish back to them."

"Is that where you go when you disappear?" He'd been gone a few times, ranging from a day to a week.

"Yes."

"What do you have to do?"

He stared at the wall over my shoulder as the mask he wore with everyone else slotted into place. Inside, I groaned. Just when I thought I was getting somewhere with him.

"Maybe one day I'll tell you. But not yet."

That hurt more than I cared to admit. I wanted him to trust me, but clearly we still had a way to go.

From that day onwards, Black made sure I got one afternoon off each week, and he nearly always joined me so we could do something together. Sometimes we'd go for a walk, or out in his plane, or even just sit in with a movie. We both liked action films, although neither of us could resist pointing out all the operational errors as we watched.

We spent a couple of days in England, with Black's house now blessedly free of decorators and paint smells. He still expected me to train, but I managed to find a morning to visit Jimmy.

He gave me a bone-crushing hug. "Amanda! We thought you'd forgotten us."

"I'd never do that."

"He treating you okay?"

"He's a tough guy to work for, but he's fair. I've learned a lot."

He looked briefly disappointed. "No chance of you coming back, then?"

Was there? I came to the realisation I didn't want to leave America. Riverley felt like home now. But what if Black didn't want to keep me when my time was up?

I pushed that thought out of my mind and shook my head. "Sorry, Jimmy."

He shrugged. "It was worth asking."

"What's up with the new girl?"

I'd said hello to her when I came in, and she seemed nice enough, but there was no way her chest wasn't surgically enhanced.

"Nothing. The men love her, and it was mighty kind of Black to provide her, as well as the cleaning crew. The only problem is she can be a little slow. It took her a week to learn how to swipe the membership cards, and she's still struggling with the computer."

"She'll learn. It just might take her a while."

Like a year or two.

The day we were due to fly back to the States, Black surprised me.

"I thought we'd go home via Paris. I have a meeting there, and it'd be good for you to practise your French."

Well, I wasn't going to say no to that.

While Black did his business stuff, I spent a pleasant morning climbing the Eiffel Tower, using the steps all the way. Not just because Black would have gone mental if he found I'd used the elevator, but rather my mindset had changed, and I'd have been disappointed in myself if I'd resorted to cheating.

At lunch, Black made me do all the ordering even though he was, of course, fluent in French, then we spent the afternoon exploring the Louvre. Black had several paintings on loan to the museum, so the director came out and gave us a personal tour.

The two-bedroom suite in the Ritz where we stayed for the night was easily the most beautiful place I'd ever been. Before dinner, we swam laps in the indoor pool then availed ourselves of the sauna.

"I should get one of these," Black said. "We could use it on our afternoons off."

"I'm surprised you don't already have one."

"I wouldn't have used it before. It's not just you who's changed in these last few months." He fell silent, thinking. I leaned back against the wall and nearly burned myself. Black laughed as I shot forwards, trying to look casual.

"We should go and get dinner," he said. "Before we cook all the way through."

"We're eating French tonight. Even you can't be so much of a heathen as to eat Italian in Paris."

The next morning we flew back to Virginia, and it was nose to the grindstone again. Or *rabotat' kak loshad'* as Alex, who was waiting for me when we arrived, would say. He insisted on teaching me Russian while I exercised—you know, kill two birds with one stone.

Or in his case, kill one bird with a set of dumbbells and a pair of running shoes.

While I was busy training, Black and Nate worked ever-longer hours as their company, Blackwood Security, Inc. got busier. In the last month, they'd rented an office in Richmond and hired a secretary to answer the phones and sort out their diaries. They'd also taken on a few permanent staff—a small team of bodyguards and a couple of investigators to start with, all carefully hand-picked and vetted—but they were still rushed off their feet.

A fortnight after we got back from Paris, Black arrived home late one evening, dark circles under his eyes showing how little sleep he'd got that week.

"Rough day?" I asked.

"Nothing unusual."

"Why do you do it?"

"What do you mean?"

"You don't need to work, do you? You could retire right now. Buy yourself a set of golf clubs and a tropical island."

He reached forward and tucked a lock of hair behind my ear. "It's the only thing that makes me feel alive."

I thought he was going to say something else, but

he took a step back.

"Even if it kills you?" I asked.

"I have to do it."

By then, I'd felt the rush that came with achieving the impossible. I understood what he was saying and gave him a small smile.

"Just be careful. Who else would I share the jacuzzi with?"

He laughed then turned serious again. "Diamond, I've got a job for you."

It was the first of many times over the years I'd hear him say that.

CHAPTER 24

MY FIRST JOB for Blackwood was a custody case, a young boy who'd been taken by his father while on visitation.

"The mother's distraught," Black told me. He leaned back against a bench press machine while I kept running on the treadmill. "The father called her to tell her she'd never see the kid again."

"How did we get involved?"

"An old comrade of ours from the teams. His wife's a friend of hers."

"Do you think we'll find him?"

He grinned at me. "Already did. The father's a convicted drug dealer, and he's surfaced in New Jersey. He just can't keep his nose clean. Quite literally, as he has a habit of sampling his products."

"So where do I come in?"

"I need a hand with retrieving the boy. When I snatch him back, I'll need to pick the right moment, and I can't spend too much time hanging around kids on my own without some over-zealous parent calling the cops."

I saw his point. Being arrested as a suspected paedophile wouldn't exactly help our case, and although I understood why parents got twitchy, I also knew firsthand that the most dangerous child molesters selected their victims in more devious ways.

But thankfully, nobody in New Jersey batted an eyelid at Black and me strolling hand in hand along the street, or out shopping, or in the park, gazing adoringly past each other to our target as he played on the swings.

I snapped a few photos of Black and got a good one of the child as well. His mother confirmed almost instantly by return email that we had the right boy.

Now all we needed to do was get him back.

Our chance came two days later. The father catered to the upmarket set, those whizz kids who couldn't get through a Friday night without snorting their bonuses. At nine, he swaggered out the door in a cheap-looking suit and drove his Mercedes to a party ten miles away.

"It's a work night for him. He'll be there for hours," Black said. "If we move fast, we can clear the state line before he realises what's happened."

Under cover of darkness, I broke in through a back window. Black skulked in the shadows outside, ready to alert me if any unexpected visitors stopped by.

Just to demonstrate how right the judge had been to grant the mother custody, the child was home alone, huddled on a threadbare sofa under a blanket that was too thin. He looked at me with wide eyes.

"I'm here to take you home," I whispered. "To your mom."

He stayed silent, with not a murmur of protest as I picked him up and carried him out of the back door. The first time he spoke was when he saw his mother, six hours later, and the huge smile that erupted as he ran into her arms was enough to make the last five months worth it. When I looked at Black, the king of the blank mask, just for a second, I saw the same joy I felt on his face.

Black gave me more work from that day on. A surveillance shift here, a touch of breaking and entering there, maybe a bit of search work on the computer. He also let me loose with clients, even if it was only to give them updates and act as liaison for the others. I slowly began to master the art of being polite and making inconsequential small talk, much to his relief.

"I don't worry about you putting your foot in it when I take you out in public any more," he told me one evening as we were getting ready for a black-tie affair.

When he bought me another dress for the occasion, I'd even managed to stare down the snobby shop girl.

Each time a new person started at the company, I gained another friend. My colleagues became the family I'd never had, and work wasn't some nine-to-five chore. Blackwood was where I belonged.

Despite feeling like I'd found my calling, I struggled to settle. Black stayed worryingly quiet about my future, and if he told me to leave when my six months was up, devastation wouldn't have begun to cover it. Just thinking of that possibility made my chest go tight.

Then one week before my deadline was up, Black asked me to do another job with him and Nate.

"We're after a grade-A freak who's jumped bail. A cool million. We get ten percent if we bring him back."

"What did he do?"

"Double murder. His wife and her lover. Hammered a stake up the guy's rectum, by all accounts, and made the wife watch."

The logistics of that made my stomach turn. "How on earth did he get bail?"

Black shook his head. "The stupidity rife in our legal system never ceases to amaze me."

I sat on the edge of Black's desk and swung my legs. "So, when are we off?"

"As soon as you can get your bag."

For the last couple of months, Black had made me keep a "go-bag" packed with essentials ready and waiting in case I needed to take off at a moment's notice. "It's in the trunk of my car."

Crunch, the freak in question, hung with the Hell's Angels in Randomville, North Carolina, a town famous for its annual hot dog festival and a serious drugs problem. Black wanted me to travel with them to this delightful place to take Crunch into custody. Problem was, he spent all his time with his biker brothers, who carried enough firepower to give a small army cause for concern.

"Why do you need me?" I asked. "Can't you catch him on your own?"

I'd worked with Black a few times now, and his ability to reduce grown men to shadows of their former selves within two minutes of meeting them was almost disturbing. I thanked my lucky stars I was on the same side as him, and from what I'd seen of Nate, he was just as tough.

"Dealing with the bikers isn't a problem," Black explained. "But we'd prefer to avoid bloodshed if possible. The paperwork's a nightmare."

"That's where I come in, isn't it? You need a distraction?"

He gave me a cunning grin. "You're good at driving

grown men crazy, Diamond."

With hindsight, I'd rather have filled out the forms.

Crunch spent his evenings in a biker bar, and the only thing he'd leave his pack for was a woman. Lucky for us, he seemed fond of jailbait, and that was why on a muggy June night, I popped open another button on my checked shirt and bent over the pool table in Lou's Hog Shack. I had a nicely placed red in front of me and a dozen of the ugliest, meanest men I'd ever had the misfortune to meet staring at my sweet patootie.

Black had helped with my outfit, which meant the shirt was two sizes too small, my D-cups stuck out the top, and when I leaned forward to pot the ball, the whistles from behind told me my knickers were clearly visible.

Fifteen minutes later, I'd successfully manoeuvred my bottom into Crunch's fetid crotch, and between fetching him drinks and waving my girls in his face, I hinted I wouldn't be averse to a trip out to the parking lot.

Where Black and Nate were waiting.

After I'd sunk my last shot, Crunch snatched my pool cue and threw it down on the table. My stomach clenched as he grabbed me with his clammy paw and shoved me roughly towards the door. So far, so good.

Well, not good, exactly, but you know what I mean.

Thanks to Nate, Crunch's Harley had developed an engine problem, so the ugly freak had driven to the bar in an ancient Ford pickup. Apparently, he didn't understand the concept of DUI. The truck was parked in the shadows created by a spreading maple tree, and as we got closer, I expected Black and Nate to step from the darkness and relieve me of my pervert.

But they didn't.

We reached the truck, and without further ceremony, Crunch yanked the door open and threw me backwards onto the bench seat. He followed me in, landing on top of me and forcing his tongue into my mouth. As the taste of beer and stale cigarettes invaded my mouth, I struggled to keep from gagging.

"Fancy another game of pool instead?" I mumbled as he rasped a breath.

His only response was a grunt, which might have been appreciation since he'd paused to squeeze my girls. It would seem he didn't know the meaning of taking it slow, because his hands soon wormed their way downwards.

Black and Nate obviously didn't know the meaning of taking it fast because WHERE WERE THEY?

Suddenly, my mind filled with an image of mother's disgusting boyfriend crawling over me when I was ten, and my heart stuttered as panic welled up inside me. I wanted to tell Crunch to stop, but with his mouth on mine, I couldn't form words. Then, before I was able to process things, he was touching me down there.

"Get off!"

I tried to push him away, but he weighed three hundred pounds to my one twenty, and I couldn't get the leverage. *What to do? What to do? What to do?* Finding my senses, I bit his tongue hard, and he reared up. The back of his hand crashed across my face with enough force to make me see stars.

"I like a girl with some fight in her," he said, moonlight glinting off his grimy teeth.

He forced me down again, and his sweat mixed with mine, a juxtaposition of excitement and fear. Even today, the stench made me gag whenever I thought about the incident. I squirmed, sliding on the cracked leather seat, and finally got a hand free. My fingers raked over his cheek, gouging, and he roared like a demented gorilla as an acrylic nail snapped off and embedded itself in his pudgy face. I was trying to get at his eyes when Black and Nate hauled him off me.

In my peripheral vision, Nate stun-gunned the freak then hog-tied him like the pig he was while I crawled out of the truck and puked in the bushes at the edge of the parking lot. The low rumble of our SUV drowned out my retching as Black manoeuvred it to block Crunch's twitching body.

"You okay?" Black asked.

What a stupid question. Possibly the stupidest question in the whole of history.

I tugged my torn shirt around me, not trusting myself to speak as Black hauled me to my feet and brushed gravel off my knees.

"Emmy?"

I shook my head, and he scooped me up in his arms. Crunch had wet himself and the delightful aroma of urine drifted over from the boot of the car. Black climbed into the backseat with me clinging to his neck.

"Is he going to wake up?" I croaked.

"Not with the amount of ketamine I gave him," Nate said. "He'll be out the whole trip."

Black held me on his lap all the way back to Virginia. I made a half-hearted attempt to move to my own seat, but he wouldn't let me go, so after a couple of tries, I gave up and dropped my head against his chest. The sound of his heartbeat soothed me, so steady in comparison to mine.

At the precinct in Richmond, we offloaded our package. Crunch had snored so loudly on the trip that Nate had suggested strapping him to the roof—the only lighthearted moment in a dark day—although I think he might actually have been serious. Black stayed with me while Nate got the body receipt, then we went back to Riverley. Home, sweet home. But for how long?

Nate drew up outside the house, and Black carried me inside. It seemed as if he, like me, knew my legs weren't to be trusted tonight.

"Drink?" he asked after he'd set me on the sofa.

He didn't bother to wait for an answer before he poured two glasses of Scotch. His preference, not mine.

"Are you going to speak? What happened back there?"

He moved me back onto his lap, but I couldn't look him in the eye. My gaze fell to the far wall where the second hand of the grandfather clock ticked its way through the numerals.

"I panicked. I thought you weren't going to come." A little hiccup escaped. "I'm sorry."

"We had to wait a minute because half a dozen of Crunch's buddies walked out front for a smoke. We'd never have abandoned you. You have to know that."

"Logically, I do. But I just couldn't think. It brought back memories, and I freaked out. I'm so, so sorry."

"What do you mean, brought back memories?" Black's voice turned low and dangerous.

Oops. I'd never intended to pop the top on that can of worms.

"It doesn't matter."

"Yes, it does."

I'd kept my secrets for years, but now I owed Black

the truth. After all, he'd given me a chance and I'd screwed up.

"It's not the first time I've been in that position," I said quietly. "It's happened twice before. When I was a little girl."

"How far did it go?"

He turned colder than liquid nitrogen, and I stayed frozen in his arms.

"All the way," I whispered.

His glass flew across the room, smashing in the fireplace on the far side. I'd never seen him lose his cool like that, not once, even when I was deliberately winding him up. "You never said anything."

"What was I supposed to say? It's not exactly something you drop into casual conversation."

"I'd never have asked you to do that tonight if I'd known."

"Which is partly why I didn't tell you. Bad enough that it happened, without it affecting the rest of my life. I promise I won't react like that again. Crunch just surprised me, that's all."

Black turned me on his lap and cupped my cheeks in his hands. "Emmy, you need to talk in future. Seeing you practically catatonic on the ride back scared me half to death."

"I didn't mean for you to worry." My fingers twisted in the remains of my shirt. Dare I ask? I didn't want to, but I had to know. "Is there a future, then?"

"What are you talking about?"

"It's nearly been six months. I'm not sure if you want me to stay."

"Of course I want you to stay, you mad little brat. Never doubt that for a moment. You'll be a big part of the business going forward. I've spoken to Nate, and we want to offer you shares in the company if you'll join us permanently."

"Even after my performance tonight?"

"Especially after your performance tonight. You were battling demons no one else knew about, but you still got the job done. Will you stay?"

"Yes, I'll stay."

"Thank goodness for that." He pulled me tighter against him and held me until the chiming of the hour broke the spell. Then he pulled back and looked me in the eye. "What happened to the man who attacked you?"

"Men." The muscles in his jaw clenched, and I hurried to continue before he cracked a tooth. "Two different ones, two years apart. I don't know what happened. I never saw either of them again."

Black fetched another glass and filled it almost to the brim. No ice, just fifty quid's worth of Jura. Then he made me tell him everything I could remember about my mother's boyfriend and the care worker who'd attacked me. I'd never had much faith in the old adage of "a problem shared is a problem halved," but as I spoke, a little of the tension that wound around my guts loosened. Perhaps there was some truth in it after all?

"Do you believe in karma?" Black asked once I'd finished spilling my soul.

"Do you?"

"I believe in justice."

Exhausted as I was, his words barely sank in. And the next morning, he was gone.

At seven a.m., Alex walked into the gym, drinking a

smoothie rather than his usual protein shake.

"Today we do running. And maybe some weights. Just the light ones."

"What's wrong with you? Why are you being so nice?"

He shrugged. "Boss told me to take it easy."

Oh he did, did he? Because of last night? Because he thought I couldn't handle the load? Well, screw him. I didn't want special treatment over something that happened four long years ago. That made no sense.

"Forget Black and his 'take it easy.' Train me how you normally would. No slacking."

Alex picked up the pace, although I knew he was still holding back. Nobody crossed Black, even a brutal ex-commando.

And speaking of my darling mentor, where was he? I asked Nate when he stopped by after breakfast to pick up some files.

"Have you seen Black?"

"Something urgent came up overseas. He said it wouldn't take long."

I didn't bother asking for details because I knew I wouldn't get any.

The next day, a courier arrived with an envelope. Apart from a Christmas card from Jimmy and Jackie, that was the first piece of mail I'd received. Ever. Inside, I found a statement for my new bank account, balance two hundred thousand pounds, as well as a charge card for Black's account and a note from him saying to spend whatever I wanted. After the initial temptation to buy myself a shiny new sports car wore off, I vowed not to use any of his money. I decided I'd rather make my own.

After all, I'd done it, hadn't I? Somehow, against the odds, this little girl from the rough end of London had crossed the Atlantic and survived.

That sense of achievement beat any buzz I'd get from buying a Ferrari.

A week later, I came down to breakfast and found Black sipping an Americano as he read the paper. No cuts, no bruises, and for Black, he looked remarkably relaxed.

"How did it go?" I asked. "You know, whatever it was?"

"Problem's dealt with." He smiled and poured me a glass of juice. "It's about time I bought a new car. Want to take a trip to the Porsche dealership?"

"Why not?"

That evening while Black used the gym, I ran a couple of computer searches, curiosity driving me now the past had been dredged up. My mother's disgusting ex-boyfriend, the one who attacked me, had died of a drug overdose three years ago—there was an appeal for relatives in the local paper. Neighbours took five days to find the body, and in August that couldn't have been pretty.

And the care worker who'd forced himself on me in the back of his ancient hatchback had, by some freakish coincidence, come to a nasty end just two days ago. His car had left the road and crashed into a ravine, and the police were searching for witnesses.

I knew they wouldn't find any.

Black was too careful for that.

CHAPTER 25

NOW I OFFICIALLY worked at Blackwood, I spent less time learning new skills and more time consolidating existing ones. Yes, I still had to keep ridiculously fit, but it was no longer a chore. Thanks to Black and Alex, I now tackled tasks that had seemed impossible just a few short months ago with ease.

And I was onto my fourth language—Spanish—when Black asked me if I fancied spending a month in Mexico. Tanning and tequila? Too right I did.

"Sure, I'd love to. I can inflict my terrible linguistic skills on the locals. Uh, what do you need me to do? Break into somewhere? Follow someone?"

"Not exactly. It's more of an undercover job." When he said that, I didn't realise he meant it literally. "We're lending you to the CIA, and they owe a favour to the DEA, who heard about you on the grapevine and requested your assistance with a little problem. They don't have anyone else with the right, er, attributes."

"The DEA? What kind of problem?"

"There's been a flood of drugs into Southern California recently. Intelligence suggests it's coming from one particular resort on the Mexican coast, but nobody's been able to work out how it's getting from A to B."

"So why send me? The closest I've come to the

drugs trade is the odd bit of recreational use at parties."

Black rolled his eyes at me. "Yeah. Don't mention that. And they want you to go because none of the men working for them looks good in a bikini. They might create a distraction but not in the right way, especially as it's a couples' resort."

"So basically, you've spent the best part of a year playing slave driver at me so I can parade around on a beach, half-naked."

He shrugged. "Think of it as a holiday. Now, do me a favour and go pack."

"When do we leave?"

"*We* don't. I've got things to do here."

"But you said—"

"I know."

"Then who are you sending me with?"

I could deal with pretending to be Black's girlfriend. But no way did I want to be pimped out to some government pervert with wandering hands.

"Nick Goldman. He's an old friend, a good guy. Nate and I used to work with him when we were with the agency, and he came up through the SEALs too. We've been trying to convince him to join us at Blackwood, so if there's anything you can do in that respect, I'd be grateful."

Right. So all I had to do was pretend to be in love with a guy I'd never met, work out how illegal cargo was getting shipped into the United States, and do it well enough to convince said guy he wanted to quit his secure job with the infinite resources of the US government behind him and come to work with us.

"You don't ask for much, do you?"

Black gave me a smile, the sly one he wore when he

was cooking up a scheme. "Just remember, you don't have to be good, but you do have to be perfect."

When I opened the door of the government car sent to take me to the airport, Nick was already inside, phone clamped to his ear. Wow. I'd expected a middle-aged dude in an ill-fitting suit, not a young James Bond. With extra muscles. And dimples.

Oh my.

He hung up as I slipped into the seat beside him, and I willed myself not to blush. Recalling Black's training in social graces, I figured I'd better introduce myself. Should I shake hands, kiss him European-style, or simply throw myself at his feet?

After a few seconds of awkward silence, I gave him a little wave and said, "Hi."

He grinned wider. "Hi. Emmy, right?"

"Uh, yeah." I fumbled with my seatbelt and finally got the flipping thing done up. "So, we have a month in Mexico..."

"We do. And four weeks in the sun can't be as bad as the three weeks I just spent in Moscow. Snow everywhere, and it was colder than a penguin's foot." He looked me up and down. "Company's better too."

And just like that, the ice was broken.

After a slightly evasive game of twenty questions, I found out Nick had joined the Navy six years ago at the age of seventeen.

"As a way of giving my old man the finger, I suppose," he said. "We never saw eye to eye. He wanted me to work in the city."

"Moscow's a city."

"Good point."

He gave me *that* smile again, eyes crinkling, and I knew right then the trip wouldn't be as bad as I'd feared. He talked, I talked, and we were almost at the airport when I remembered this was supposed to be work.

"What's the plan, boss?"

"We're newlyweds on our honeymoon. Vegas wedding, baby."

He passed over the picture the CIA had thoughtfully provided as a memento of our joyous occasion. Our heads had been artfully photoshopped onto a couple standing under bawdy neon lights shaped like wedding bells.

"Ugh. That dress is hideous," I said. "The woman's practically falling out of the top, and it does nothing for her waist."

"The guy's not much better. Someone should have fixed his tie." Nick looked at his reflection in the window glass. "And my skin's three shades darker in that photo. I need some sun."

I nodded my agreement as he took an envelope from his pocket and tipped out a pair of trashy-looking gold rings. Eighteen years old, and the closest I'd got to the beach was the Dirty Name at Little Creek.

"Nice," I said as Nick slipped a ring onto my finger.

"I should have gone out and bought these myself. Everyone's gonna think I'm cheap."

I batted my eyelashes at him. "You, cheap? But honey, you've shelled out for the honeymoon suite."

"At least the expense account's generous."

The plane ride passed quickly as I flipped through

the file of suspects, memorising names and faces. Once I was happy I'd recognise them, I switched my attention to a map of the area so I'd be familiar with the terrain when we arrived. I wanted to ace this job for Black.

And, I realised, for Nick.

The honeymoon suite turned out to be a secluded villa that fronted onto the hotel's private beach. Nice. Perhaps I should become a smuggler? They sure had chosen somewhere idyllic to do business.

"Not bad, is it?" Nick said as we walked inside.

"It isn't quite the Ritz, but it'll do."

"The Ritz?" He raised an eyebrow. "Black, I take it?"

"Yeah."

"Well, Black probably has more money than the CIA, so I'm afraid we're slumming it."

Nick ordered us a late lunch of grilled fish and pineapple, and we sat under a shady palm on our terrace to formulate a plan. My plan would have been to lie out on a sun lounger all week, but it was the CIA's dollar, so unfortunately we had to do some work.

"I thought we'd go for a walk this evening to see the lay of the land, then we should get an early night," Nick said.

"Sure. Do you have plans for tomorrow?"

He nodded, and my stomach dropped as I recognised the same look Black gave me on many occasions. Right before he made my life a misery.

"Tomorrow, I'm giving you a scuba diving lesson. Black said he hadn't gotten around to it yet."

Wonderful. My week on the beach had just disappeared underwater. "What about equipment?"

"I brought it all with me."

"I wondered why you had two suitcases."

"The second one's full of sunglasses and hair products." Nick's hair, the colour of freshly ground coffee, was half an inch long.

"Tart."

He grinned back at me and pretended to fluff his hair. Did I mention he'd taken his shirt off? Well, he had, and those tight pecs and perfect six-pack were incredibly distracting.

As my heart flipped, I blew out a long breath, forced myself to focus, and wondered how far he planned to go with this marriage charade.

The main hotel building turned into the Mary Celeste in the evening. We had the restaurant to ourselves for dessert, a bored waiter and a by-the-numbers pianist our only company. What with it being a couples' resort, I could well imagine why. I ordered an extra slice of chocolate cake to-go. And an individual cheesecake. And a small portion of churros. What? Without Toby's beady eyes on me, I could eat what I liked and I was determined to take advantage of it, especially with the CIA paying. The chef packaged it up for me in a cardboard box covered in multi-coloured hearts and gift ribbon.

"Carry this for me?" I asked Nick.

"Not on your life."

The soft chirp of crickets sounded from the bushes

at the side of the path as we ambled back towards the villa just after eight, hand in hand. After a short walk up the beach to get an idea of the locale, we decided to call it a night.

"What are we doing about sleeping arrangements?" I asked, seeing there was only one bed. An enormous bed with enough cushions for an entire sorority to have a pillow fight, but still only one nonetheless.

Nick made a face. "Black told me before we left I'd be sleeping on the floor. I brought a camping mattress. Don't worry, I wouldn't want to tread on his toes."

"What do you mean?"

"Well, spending the night in bed with his girlfriend would hardly help our future working relationship, would it?"

"I'm not Black's girlfriend."

Nick turned and stared at me. "You're not? I just assumed you and he were...well...you know..."

"We're not."

"But I thought you lived together?" Nick raised an eyebrow.

"I have a bedroom in his house. I didn't know how long I'd be staying in Virginia initially, and he had sixteen to spare, so he let me use one. And sometimes at parties, we pretend we're a couple so neither of us gets bothered by unwanted attention."

"Oh. Right. Why's he so protective of you then?"

I shrugged. "I've had some experiences with men in the past that have been less than ideal. I think he's just looking out for me."

Nick flipped back the lid of his suitcase and pulled out the mattress. Before unrolling it, he paused in front of me and put a gentle hand on my shoulder.

"I promise I'll be the perfect gentleman."

"Thanks. I appreciate that."

But the question was, did I want him to be?

Scuba diving soon became my second favourite activity, not quite as fun as flying but close. A magical world existed under the surface of the water, full of colour and beauty, and I found a peace down there that escaped me on land. Nick warned me it wasn't always like that, and that diving in the balmy waters off the Mexican coast was a far cry from being tossed overboard in the North Atlantic and being expected to swim in near-freezing conditions to a landing point two miles away. But for now, I revelled in the power of the ocean, bewitched by its charms.

As a former SEAL, Nick made an excellent teacher. He lacked Black's pushiness and Alex's impatience, and I looked forward to each lesson. Even the horrid parts, like the mask-off drills and having to remove all my diving gear underwater then put it back on again, didn't seem so bad under his tutelage.

Sunbathing on the beach wasn't exactly a hardship either, and by watching the comings and goings at the nearby marina, we soon noted patterns of unusual activity. People would get on yachts at dawn and never disembark, and a couple of boats had endless boxes of cargo loaded without ever leaving to deliver it. Occasionally, we'd spot another ship on the horizon, and Nick took photos with a long lens while I cavorted in a bikini in the foreground.

"Left a bit. Now smile."

Who did he think he was, David Bailey? I glanced over my shoulder just in time to see the ship disappear over the horizon. Even with a telephoto lens, there was no way those pictures contained anything useful.

"You git."

He gave me a heart-stopping grin, and two women to the right of me sighed.

"I'm having fun. Aren't you having fun?"

I marched up to him. "What are you planning to do with those?" I pointed at the camera. "Keep them as souvenirs?"

"What if I said yes?"

"I thought you were a gentleman?"

He pinched my bum then grabbed my hand as I went to slap him. "I lied."

Nick's colleagues confirmed several of the suspect boats had been seen in the Gulf of Mexico just off Texas, but they'd never docked in the United States. Despite careful surveillance by the coastguard, nobody saw their crews throw anything overboard, either.

We'd have to keep digging.

There was only so much time I could spend on a sun lounger without turning into a lobster, and we couldn't skulk in the shade without looking suspicious. So, with the CIA's funds at our disposal, we solved that problem by signing up for all sorts of water-based activities.

"How on earth do you stand up?" I asked, after my attempts at wakeboarding resulted in a near-drowning. Nick, of course, had probably surfed out of the womb.

"Try pointing your toes," he called from his position in the back of the boat.

What do you know? It worked. Before long, I was

zipping from side to side waving one arm in the air. At least, until I tried to copy one of Nick's jumps and gave myself whiplash.

"Don't worry, baby. I'll massage it better later," he said, purely for the benefit of the boat captain of course.

At least, I'd assumed it was for the benefit of the captain. Turned out it wasn't.

After flying and diving, Nick's fingers became my new favourite thing. Actually, maybe they even topped that list. Our married couple act became natural, and I held his hand through instinct rather than obligation. Kissing him was hardly a chore. When his lips touched mine, the golden sands outside our veranda weren't the only thing feeling the heat.

"You might as well share the bed with me," I told him at the end of the first week. Hearing his spine crack every morning as he rose from the tiled floor was giving me a backache.

"Are you sure Black won't mind?"

"Even if he did, it's my decision, not his."

Despite starting off on separate sides of the mattress, my subconscious had other ideas, and I woke up in Nick's arms. In that floating, dream-like moment between sleep and wakefulness, I nuzzled into his neck, relishing the warmth of his body in the chill of the air conditioning.

"Uh, Emmy?" he whispered.

Oops. "I'm sorry!" I rolled away, putting some space between us as I re-joined the land of the living.

"I'm not." He stretched out his arm, inviting me back in.

I gladly went.

The more time I spent with Nick, the more I liked him. After the challenge of Black and his complexities, Nick's easygoing charm was exactly what I needed. With Black, I constantly had to listen for what he wasn't saying. Read between the lines. Nick was straight-up, and did I mention hot? Yesterday alone, three women had walked into solid objects after being distracted by him, and we had a side bet as to what the total would be by the time we left.

Double figures, for sure.

At the beginning of the third week, a hotel security guard caught us sneaking around the boathouse on the edge of the marina. His face clouded as he reached for his radio.

"What are you doing?"

I thought back to the glimpse of Nick I'd caught in the shower last night, which made my cheeks redden rather nicely.

Nick's lips curved up in a cheeky smile as he pulled me tight against him. "What do you think?" he asked the guard.

"You shouldn't be here."

"Don't worry, we're leaving."

Nick swept me up in his arms, and I gave a convincing shriek. The guard followed at a distance, still suspicious as Nick carried me back to our room. On the doorstep, Nick paused, checked discreetly behind us, then attempted to find my tonsils with his tongue while he fumbled with the lock.

At times like that, I couldn't believe I got paid to do

this job.

We stumbled into the villa, landing on the bed as the door bounced off the wall and slammed behind us. Nick kept up his search, and I was only too eager to assist. His hardness pressed into my thigh and I ground against it, my body taking over as my mind went blank. As I wrapped my legs around him, he levered himself up and we paused, nose-to-nose.

"Nobody's watching anymore, baby," he whispered.

"Good."

"Do you want me to stop?"

Time slowed as I thought of my past. Of the other times I'd been in that position and how it made me feel. Used. Dirty. But Black had laid those demons to rest. Quite literally, in the case of one of them.

I bit my lip. Nick was offering me a way out. But the very fact he'd offered meant I didn't want to take it.

I shook my head.

"No, I don't want you to stop."

Nick continued my education for the rest of our time in Mexico, when we weren't busy working, of course.

"I don't know what the future holds, baby, but I know I want to hold you until we go home," he said.

"Black's probably planning my life as we speak, but you're right—we should make the most of this."

After all, Black had told me I didn't need to be good.

The job still took priority, though, and having ruled out other avenues, Nick began to suspect the use of submersibles in the smuggling operation. As the sun rose one ordinary Wednesday morning, we made a dive into the marina and found cleverly concealed doors in the hulls of two of our suspect boats. The crew had covered the cracks with fake barnacles, and unless you were inches away, the openings were impossible to spot.

Three days later, Nick visited the harbourmaster to enquire about the possibility of berthing his imaginary yacht there in the marina for a couple of weeks. Alas, the cost proved prohibitive, but as he dropped his cigarette into the wastebasket of the operations office, he still managed a smile. The paper smouldered for a while before the flames took hold then chaos broke out. Smoke poured from the windows, blurring the view as I snuck onto our target boat with Nick's camera.

"And?" he asked half an hour later as I slipped back into the villa.

"A mini-sub. I need your laptop to upload the pictures."

There was clearly big money in drugs. As well as the mini-sub, I'd seen stacks of cash, gold coins, and even a photo of the yacht's owner with his pet tiger.

"Here, I'll help."

As the encrypted email flew through cyberspace to Nick's bosses, sadness swept over me. I almost wished we hadn't found the submarine, because now Riverley beckoned. My last night in the honeymoon suite wasn't something I'd forget in a hurry, though. Even now, I still flush thinking of the things Nick did to me.

"Could you put your seat belts on, please?" the flight

attendant asked as the plane descended towards Dulles.

I buckled up and turned to Nick, resting my hand on his thigh. "Thanks. For everything. I'll never forget this."

"You'd better not. I'm hoping for a repeat performance one day." He leaned over and nibbled my earlobe. "Maybe in Virginia."

"Does that mean you'll give some thought to working at Blackwood?"

"Yeah. I'll call Black and have a talk about it."

I couldn't hold in my smile—mission accomplished, even if I'd used slightly unorthodox methods. One last kiss before the plane landed, and I was soon on my way back to my mentor.

"Job well done, Diamond," Black said. "My contact at the DEA's a card-carrying member of your fan club now."

A week later, Black beckoned me into the conference room for a call with the DEA. One of our boats had been raided by the DEA and the coastguard as it crossed from international waters off the coast of California.

The haul? Six million dollars' worth of heroin, plus four illegal immigrants.

Not bad.

"Makes the two hundred grand they paid for my holiday look like a bargain, doesn't it?" I said to Black.

"I'll charge them double next time."

Next time? I kept my fingers crossed.

CHAPTER 26

NOT ALL JOBS were as pleasant as my Mexico jaunt, as I found out a couple of weeks later. Black lent me to the NSA, and a day spent undercover on a college campus took a turn for the worse when a young religious extremist decided to take an inexperienced agent hostage rather than be arrested. I stared through a rifle sight for three hours while the lunatic fiddled with his suicide vest, trying to convince us to come around to his way of thinking.

Black's voice played over in my head. "Keep breathing, Emmy, until you see your shot. Steady. In and out. Then stop while you pull the trigger."

My bullet punched through the guy's left eye as I dispatched him to discuss his views with Allah in person.

I thought I was okay with it. It was an outright kill, a single shot, and there wasn't even that much mess. I mean, I'd even got a round of applause from the agents on site.

I went home, wrote up my report, then had a pleasant supper of roast chicken and assorted vegetables with Black before I snuck up to my room to eat the Reese's peanut butter cups I'd cadged off a local cop. Half an hour in the newly installed sauna, and I was relaxed and ready for bed. Sure, I'd had to shoot someone, but in my new line of work, that wasn't entirely unexpected, and it was either him or that poor schmuck from the NSA. In a way, it was a relief to get my first kill over with.

I fell asleep.

But not for long.

That fateful Wednesday, the devil in my head paid his first nocturnal visit. I saw the terrorist's eyeball disintegrate, the splash of blood on the wall behind him so vivid I could smell the metallic tang. In life, he'd crumpled, but in my dreams, he stayed standing, staring at me with his good eye as he reached for his vest.

Over and over and over and over again.

"What's going on? Emmy?"

Black's shouting woke me, and I came to with a jolt. Why was he in my bedroom? And more importantly, why did he have a gun in his hand?

"Is there an intruder?" I grabbed my own gun from under my pillow and thumbed the safety.

He stared at me.

"What?" I asked.

"You were screaming."

"No, I wasn't." Surely I'd have heard myself?

"Yes, you were. And you've gone white."

"You must have been dreaming."

He sat down on the bed and squeezed my hand. "Diamond, I think *you* were the one dreaming."

I shook my head, as if by denying his words, they wouldn't be true. How could I have made enough noise to wake Black without even noticing? His gaze flicked downwards, and I realised my Walther was still in my hands. I dropped the gun as if it had burned me and struggled to sit up.

"I wasn't... I couldn't..."

The reality wasn't something I wanted to consider.

But I had no choice.

Nightmares plagued me, ever more frequent as I added to my back catalogue of triggers. Talking things through with Black helped some, but they kept coming, relentless.

Something inside me broke that day, and nothing could ever fix it.

Over the next year, the jobs Black gave me got tougher, as did the ongoing battle with my demons. Black was always by my side, though, and Blackwood grew like it was on steroids. The profits made the decision to expand overseas an easy one, starting with an office in London.

While Black and I scoured the UK property listings and hunted an art thief in LA, Nate surprised us by getting married. He took a trip to Mexico to deliver a hostage negotiation training program in partnership with the Mexican authorities and came back with their best sniper in tow. The High Command GAFE had been less than happy to lose Carmen, and Black spent two weeks placating them while Nate and his new bride took off for a honeymoon in Australia. To this day, we still gave the Mexican Special Forces a discount on our services.

Nick finally agreed to join us, and Black and Nate each signed over five percent of their shares in Blackwood to him as an incentive. I'd kept in touch with him over the months, our meetings mainly dinners of the room service variety. Our discreet liaisons suited us both, as did our string of dirty text messages.

After the ninth or tenth such occasion, Black found out. Nick dropped me back at Riverley one evening and kissed me goodbye with a little too much tongue. When I turned towards the house, I saw Black step back from the window. Our secret wasn't a secret anymore. Would Black say anything?

I half expected him to, but when I said goodnight, all I got in return was a grunt as he poured himself a glass of Scotch.

"That's a good thing," I muttered to myself as I climbed the stairs.

Like I'd said to Nick, what I did in my own time was my business, but I still didn't want to talk to Black about the sordid details. He may have controlled my working hours, but he couldn't take over my entire life.

Oh, who was I kidding?

Two days later, Black beckoned me into his study after my morning workout.

"I've got a project for you. A new challenge."

"What kind of challenge?"

"We've just signed the contract to buy an office building in King's Cross, and I need you to fly to London and oversee the setup."

"How long for?"

"At least a month. Maybe two."

"That long?"

"The contractor's behind, and they've already installed the wrong type of partitioning on the top floor."

"Seriously? You want me to monitor builders?"

"I thought you might like to catch up with your old friends as well. Jimmy... Jackie... That kid who taught you how to boost cars."

I might have grumbled, but Black was right. Yes, I missed Nick, but I had a ball catching up with the guys at the gym. Jimmy helped me to keep up my training while I learned the ins and outs of business and investments. Profit and loss, balance sheets, government regulations, marketing. Boring, but it sure came in handy later when I needed to look after my own money.

Unfortunately, with my frequent flights between the UK and the US, I also learned about jet lag and the joys of airport immigration queues when you don't have a US passport. I had a citizenship application in progress, but the constant barrage of questions on every aspect of my life and job from US Customs and Border Protection officers drove me nuts. Interviews, forms, visa renewals. Hours of my life wasted. Not only that, my hazy status caused difficulties getting security clearance for some jobs, and while I could obtain the information in more creative ways, it wasted valuable time and energy.

After one such painful trip through McCarran International, I sat in a Vegas hotel bar with Black and Nate, ready to plan a security test we were due to undertake for one of the big casinos out there. I'd arrived late, annoyed, and tired, and I quickly swallowed the glass of white Black pushed in front of me.

"Problems again, Diamond?"

"What's new? I can't even be sarcastic because then

they insist on a cavity search. Which you gentlemen may get excited about, but let me assure you, it's something I could live without."

"I'll order another bottle of wine."

"Can't you just get me a fake US passport? You got me a UK one."

"Under a different name, yes, but we need to keep Blackwood above board, at least on the surface. If you leave under one name and come back under a different one, suspicions will be raised. How about I buy a jet instead?"

"That wouldn't help. I'd still have to go through the same channel at immigration and the jobsworths keep asking questions about my employment. They struggle to believe a twenty-year-old is a partner in a security company, and it's not as if I can go into lots of detail. Half the stuff I do is classified."

"Maybe if you told them you were a secretary instead?" Nate suggested.

"I don't think having an admin job and nothing else to tie me to the States would be conducive to my application for citizenship, which will take years, by the way, since I've got no family here. I need more wine."

Black signalled to the bartender, but I couldn't wait. I grabbed his glass of red instead.

Nate drummed his fingers on the table then snapped them in front of my face. "I've got an idea."

"Please, I'm dying to hear it."

"Why don't you two get married?"

Black choked on an olive, and I spat out the mouthful of Merlot I'd just taken.

"Exactly how much have you had to drink, buddy?" Black asked.

"Only a couple of beers. And a whisky or two."

I started laughing, ignoring Nate's indignant look. Black waved at the waiter again and asked for a jug of water.

But Nate wasn't finished. "Just think about it. Emmy, you'd get your green card faster and save time at the airport. And if Black had a ring on his finger, he wouldn't keep getting chased by horny women with dollar signs in their eyes."

"Nate, I know you've had some crazy ideas in the past, but that one's special," I said, patting his hand.

Even so, part of me felt oddly pleased. Nate had hated me when we first met, and now he was trying to marry me off to his best friend? This was progress.

"Ems, it's not that crazy. How long does it take to get permanent residence after marriage? Three years?"

"Something like that," Black said.

"And you could get divorced afterwards. If you keep your fingers crossed, marrying Emmy might even give your Aunt Miriam a heart attack."

Should I be pleased or insulted by that?

Black took a sip of his fresh glass of wine. "Perhaps the idea does have some merit."

"I can't believe you're even considering it," I said.

"Diamond, you were the one complaining about immigration. And neither of us likes Miriam."

Nate nudged me. "A heart attack, get it? Marriage... Valentines... Hearts... Never mind."

I'd only met the irritating cow once, and I'd been forced to have a chat with the punchbag in the gym afterwards. When Black and Nate put it that way, the pros did seem to outweigh the cons.

"Fine. Let's get married then." I slammed my glass

down. My third glass. My third, large glass. That was the wine talking. "How do we even do that?"

Black turned to Nate. "This was your suggestion."

"Okay, okay. I'll ask the concierge."

Three hours later, I stood in front of a fat bloke dressed as Elvis with Black beside me. Thanks to the concierge, we had the licence thingy and a bouquet of flowers, and Nate had bought us rings.

Black squinted at one of the cheap gold bands. "They're engraved?"

I leaned forward to see for myself. CB & MB 4EVA?

"What's with the text speak?" Black asked.

"Chief Petty Officer Black and the Mad Brat Forever. Appropriate, huh? And it's your initials as well, sort of. Get it?" He poked me in the arm. "Get it?" he asked again before noticing our exasperated looks. "What? The engraving was free. We might as well take advantage of it."

"Thanks, buddy," Black said dryly.

A lady with bouffant hair and a clipboard marched up, her face arranged in a fake smile.

"Ma'am? You'll need to put the wine bottle down before the ceremony starts."

"What?" I glanced at my hand and realised I was carrying a bottle of rosé. "Oops. Here, take it."

"Have you written your own vows, or would you like to use the standard ones?"

Vows? I could barely even speak without slurring. "Uh..."

"The standard ones," Black said.

He looked remarkably calm for a man about to sign his life away. My bottle disappeared, replaced with red roses, and Elvis coughed in front of us. Boy, his collar was really shiny.

"Dearly beloved, we are gathered together here in the sight of God to join Charles Edward Black and Amanda Emerson in Holy Matrimony..."

After one small hiccup where I told Black I took him to be my wedded wife, we got through the ceremony and mugged for the camera while Elvis snapped a picture. Bouffant lady handed it to us minutes later in a cheap cardboard frame, our only reminder of this oh-so-momentous event in our lives.

"I'll always be by your side, Diamond," Black mumbled. "In spirit if not in body."

Where had he got that whisky from? I wanted some, but Nate confiscated the bottle.

"Time to go, buddy."

The wedding package included a limo, one of those tacky stretch ones with fancy lights and vaguely sticky seats, and we returned to our hotel as Mr. And Mrs. Black.

At that point, I was just trying not to puke.

"Now what, Mr. Black?" I asked as we staggered into the Bellagio.

"Bar, Mrs. Black?"

"A marvellous idea, Mr. Black."

We could barely walk at all, let alone straight, and instead of ending up in one of the many lounges, we found ourselves at a poker table in Club Privé. Black shoved a pile of cash at a croupier as my buy-in.

"Happy wedding, Mrs. Black."

He pressed his lips to my forehead then stumbled

off to the speakeasy-style bar. He didn't come back. Through drooping eyelids, I saw a slender blonde dressed in stilettos and feathers leading him by the hand as they headed towards the bedrooms, and although an irrational spike of jealousy flared in my chest, I quickly extinguished it with a gin and tonic. Black was my husband in name only. At least one of us would be getting some on our wedding night.

I didn't even make it to bed, let alone with a man. When I woke in the bathtub the next morning, blotchy circles covered my skin, imprints from the pile of poker chips I'd fallen asleep on. Half a million dollars, I found when I counted them up. That was a lot of splodges. Really, I should play poker drunk more often.

Back home in Virginia, we had a late wedding reception for appearances' sake. Neither of us could be bothered with the details, but the party planner went all out. Black knew loads of people and a few hundred turned up to offer congratulations, toasters, cutlery, and bed linen. Miriam arrived with a set of polyester napkins. Unfortunately, she didn't keel over and die, but her face did go disturbingly purple as she berated him for his lack of prenup.

"Did you leave your brain at home when you went on your gambling spree?" she hissed. "Because I can't see any other explanation. Where did you find her, anyway? On a street corner?"

"We met in a wine bar in London," Black said, sticking to the cover story we'd concocted for the occasion. He gazed down at me adoringly. "And

Emmy's my soul mate. We'll be together until the day I die."

At the time, I didn't realise how prescient those words would be.

"Well, I hope you've got a good lawyer." Miriam spun around, caught herself from overbalancing with an inelegant lurch, and stormed off.

I could quite understand why Black's opinion of her was so low he needed a backhoe to find it.

Eventually, we both got bored with mingling and small talk and settled into the library with Nate, Carmen, Nick and a good bottle of Scotch.

"How long do you reckon before they all go home?" I asked nobody in particular.

"Ages, I expect," Black answered. "They'll probably hang around as long as there's food and drink left."

"Oh, good grief. For a pretend wedding, this sure is turning into a hassle."

"Pretend wedding?" Nick asked.

I realised neither of us had filled him in yet. I thought he'd been a bit quiet.

"Kind of. We got married for real, but mainly to help out with my citizenship application."

"You're all invited to the divorce party in a couple of years," Black added.

"So you're not really together, together?"

I shook my head. "No, nothing's changed except we get to wear these classy rings Nate picked out, which probably cost twenty cents each."

"Yours cost forty-nine dollars, you ungrateful wench," Nate said.

"Such generosity."

The grandfather clock near the window had chimed

two by the time the last of the guests trickled out. One of the party organisers stuck her head around the door. "That went amazingly fantastically!"

Her perkiness was unnatural at that time in the morning. I managed a grunt in return.

"Well, we'll be back tomorrow—oops, later today—to clear up. Y'all have a fabulous night!"

Black finished his drink and got to his feet. "I'm going to bed."

"Same." I paused then leaned into Nick. Sitting beside him all evening had left me with a wanton ache between my thighs. "Want to join me?"

"Black won't mind?"

"No. You heard him." Besides, he'd spent our wedding night with a showgirl.

Nick followed me to the door, but Black changed his mind and poured himself another whisky. Well, at least if he was hungover, he wouldn't notice if I had a lie-in.

Upstairs, Nick gave me a reminder of our Mexican jaunt, and I was grateful that in the days when Riverley was constructed, they built proper, solid walls with plenty of soundproofing.

Otherwise, that night could have got a little embarrassing.

Life continued as normal. What passed as normal for Black and me, anyway. The only noticeable differences were that I lived it with a ring on my finger, albeit a nicer one than Nate bought, and I changed my name.

"Pretend or not, no wife of mine is wearing a forty-nine dollar ring," Black told me.

I bought a second ring for him in return, but we kept the original engraving. Tacky, but it seemed fitting. Amanda died a death, appearing only on official paperwork, and with my new surname, Emerson became my semi-official first name.

As I filled out one form after another, I asked, "Do you want me to sign a proper prenup?" We'd scribbled out something on the back of a cocktail napkin, but it probably wouldn't stand up in court. Black was loaded, and I didn't ever want money to come between us. "Well, I guess it would be more of a postnup now?"

"Don't be so stupid."

"But what if I decided to go out and buy a house with your charge card?"

He took me by the shoulders. "Diamond, when my parents died, their estate was worth just over nine billion dollars, and it all came to me. I've probably doubled it since then. So you'd have to buy a really big house for me to notice, and even if I did notice, I wouldn't care. Spend what you want."

Wow. I knew he had a lot of money, but I didn't realise it was *that* much.

CHAPTER 27

I MET DAN six months after I got married. I'd started making decent money by that point, and I wanted to donate some of it to people who hadn't been given the chances Black offered me. One dreary Saturday, I took a trip into Richmond to visit a homeless shelter. I'd met with the people who ran it the previous month, and their ability to do so much with so little funding impressed me. What could they do with a bit more cash?

Two cheques crinkled in my pocket. I'd written the first, and back then, those ten thousand dollars were a lot to me. Although we charged a bomb for my work, my income was sporadic as we ploughed all our profits back into Blackwood's expansion rather than paying ourselves inflated salaries.

The second cheque came from Black. When he heard my plans, he'd offered to help.

"It's a good cause, Diamond," he said, as he ripped it out of his chequebook. "I'll always match whatever you want to give."

The staff had been wiping their eyes when I left the shelter. That was the first time I'd ever made someone cry in a good way, and it gave me a warm glow inside. Rainbows and sunshine, but sadly the weather outside didn't agree. I paused in the foyer and groaned at the sheets of rain. Did I bring an umbrella? I rummaged through my bag, but all I found was an extra knife and two kinds of pepper spray.

"*Oof*. What the—"

I stumbled backwards as someone ran into me, then remembered Black's training. *Manners, Emmy*.

"I'm sorry..." I started, looking up to find a dark-haired girl in front of me. Tears soaked her cheeks as she held her hands up to ward me off. Her swollen belly protruded from a coat too thin for the time of year and blood trickled from her nose.

"Hey, what happened?"

She shook her head then doubled up in pain, clutching her stomach.

"You need to get to a hospital."

"I can't." She shook her head again. "I don't have any insurance."

"It's an emergency. They have to treat you."

"He'll find me there."

"I'll sort it out. Just get in the car." Whoever "he" was, I hoped he did turn up because I wanted a word with him for leaving her in that state. The girl doubled over in pain again, but she let me guide her into the passenger seat of the Ford pickup I drove back then, and I put my foot down as soon as I leapt behind the wheel. Her pale face scared me, and she gripped the seatbelt as her breath came in short pants. Was she about to have a baby? Even the cop who pulled me over for speeding took one look at her and waved us on our way. If only it were that easy every time I got stopped.

In the ER, I paced up and down as the doctors worked. I didn't even know the girl's name, and nobody would tell me anything because I wasn't a relative. But

I couldn't leave her there on her own. Finally, I overheard one nurse whispering to another that Daniela di Grassi's son had been stillborn, and my heart sank. That had to be her, right? And she'd lost the baby?

I paced the waiting room until shift change then told the new receptionist I was Daniela's sister. I'd got my American accent down to a tee by then, and even though the woman gave me a dubious look because I was blonde and Dan had dark hair, dark eyes, and olive skin, they still let me through to see her.

"Hey."

She dragged her gaze in my direction, blinking tears away. Now what? I didn't deal well with emotions.

"He's gone," she whispered. "I named him Caleb after my grandfather, and he's gone."

Turned out I did know what to do. I gripped Dan's hand as she wept into her pillow and stayed by her side until the doctors kicked me out.

But I came back the next day, when the doctor told Dan she'd never have children, and the next, and the next. Even though Dan barely spoke, just stared at the wall, I wanted to be there for her. Black didn't protest, even when I skipped workouts and meetings. He may have been cold on the outside, but he had a vein of compassion lurking deep under the surface that others rarely saw.

Finally, the doctor said Dan could leave, and she slid off the bed with the reluctant demeanour of a condemned woman.

"I can drive you wherever you want," I told her. "Do you have family nearby?" She'd refused to talk about it so far.

"The shelter. I don't have anywhere else to go."

"But you need to rest, for six weeks at least." I'd been listening to the doctors, even if she hadn't.

She shrugged, then winced as something inside her tore. "I don't have any choice."

"Okay, okay. I'll take you there."

But I didn't. I took her to Riverley instead. Not just because she'd had major surgery but because she'd been reduced to a shell of a person, and she wasn't going to heal sitting by herself in a ten-by-eight box. She needed to talk. Black still had fifteen spare bedrooms—he'd barely even notice her.

Over the next few days, Dan alternately cried, sat and rocked, and stared into space. A week passed before she began to speak.

"Who did this to you?" I asked as soon as I thought she was strong enough to answer.

"My ex. He said no way was he going to spend the rest of his life paying for an accident." More tears fell, and I passed another tissue. "But I didn't even ask for money from him. I just hoped he'd get to know his child, but he didn't want to be a father."

Well, not to worry. Once I'd paid a visit to that sorry waste of space, fatherhood wasn't ever going to be an issue for him. I'd learned from the master, you see.

As Dan recovered and found herself at a loose end, she started joining me as I trained in the mornings. Black got a gleam in his eye when we discovered she could run, jump, and shoot better than half of the men we knew, but that wasn't where her true talents lay. In the afternoons she took to sitting in the library surrounded by Blackwood's cold case files, and after she'd cracked four of them, it became inevitable we'd offer her a job. Seven months after I met her, she became a permanent member of the team as well as my partner in crime, sometimes quite literally.

I'd never had a proper girlfriend before, and Dan had never had any money, so for three wild months we drove Black nuts with our antics. Dan was eighteen, a year younger than my real age, but I'd made the contacts to get us fake driving licences by then so bar hopping became our new favourite thing. A little shorter in height than me and a lot shorter in her choice of hemlines, Dan brought life to any party. Looking back, I don't know how Black put up with us.

Like the night we arrived home in the early hours and accidentally set off the alarm system. I'd lost my shoes, and Dan was still clutching a half-empty bottle of champagne. We collapsed in the hallway in a fit of giggles as Black shut off the noise and stood over us, one dark eyebrow raised.

"What's so funny?" he asked.

"I can't quite remember." I looked at Dan, which brought on another fit of laughter.

"Me either," she said. "There were cocktails?"

Rather than being mad, Black carried us up to bed, Dan first, then me.

"I'm sorry," I said as he deposited me under my quilt. "I think I may have been a bit bad."

He bent and kissed me on the forehead. "I'm glad to see you both happy. But you're still in the gym with Alex at five thirty."

Dan was still staying at Black's a few months later when

I did something not just bad but utterly terrible.

I'd been on one of my now-frequent excursions overseas, this time at the behest of the CIA. Those trips were seldom pleasurable—the break in Mexico with Nick had been the exception rather than the rule—but rarely did they make me sick to my stomach like this week's did. In the course of stopping a people-trafficking operation, our joint task force had uncovered a boat hold full of rotting bodies—those poor souls promised a better life overseas who hadn't made it.

The stench of the corpses sent me running to the side of the ship to throw up, clutching the rail as I hung my head over the ocean. The smell lined my throat and crept into every pore. Even after I'd scrubbed myself three times in the shower, I couldn't get rid of it. Worse, we stayed on board for three awful days while we sailed out to sea to lose the rusty cargo vessel in the deepest part of the ocean so nobody found the six dead snakeheads stashed in what had been the captain's quarters. As for the captain, we'd found the poor man stuffed in his wardrobe, a single bullet hole between his eyes. It was only after the evidence had sunk to the bottom of the ocean that a Navy vessel plucked us from our life raft and returned us stateside.

Riverley stood silent as I arrived home. I left my car in the garage with the windows open to get rid of the smell, which had ingrained itself everywhere not least in my mind. Inside, a mess of pizza boxes covered the coffee table in the lounge, and I knew who'd left them there. Nick. Because Nick was a slob and no amount of nagging got him to change. Black would at least have carried them through to the kitchen and piled them up ready to go out in the trash the next morning.

I crept upstairs, avoiding the squeaky thirteenth step that might announce my presence. Nick lay in my bed, his steady breathing telling me he was fast asleep. He barely stirred as I crawled in beside him. Home, sweet home. Exhausted from the past week, I nodded off quickly.

And found myself back on the boat again.

Four of the snakeheads came at me, three with guns and one with a wicked-looking machete. I shouted for my team and shot two of the targets. They dropped to the deck, but when I turned after knocking a third out, they were getting up again. Why wouldn't they die? I killed them again, with the same result. Again, again, again. I was stuck in my own personal horror film. Sweat dripped down my forehead as the traffickers kept coming. My team—where were they?

Panic kicked in as another man grabbed me from behind. I lashed out, feeling his nose give way before he pulled me backwards, kicking and screaming in a bear hug. Black's words played on repeat in my head: *Get them before they get you.* I twisted, going first for the solar plexus then for the xiphoid process—that fragile piece of bone which, if you get the right angle, can be driven through a person's liver.

Thank goodness I didn't get the right angle. Because the next thing I knew, I was being pulled off Nick, who curled up on the floor groaning as blood poured from his face.

Tears streaked Dan's cheeks as she rushed over to help him, while Black threw me on the floor and held me down.

"What are you doing, Emmy?" he yelled.

I couldn't speak, firstly because my face was smushed into the carpet, and secondly because I didn't know what to say. I had no clue what I was doing.

Nick spluttered behind me, wheezing as he struggled to speak.

"She was asleep. She was asleep!"

The pressure on my back eased slightly as Black took some of his weight off me.

"Are you awake now?" he asked me.

"Yes!" I gasped.

He dragged me over to the wall and propped me against it. "Stay there. I need to deal with Nick."

I watched from the corner, arms wrapped around my knees, as Dan and Black stemmed the bleeding from Nick's nose then helped him onto the bed. Except it wasn't me watching. No, I was a stranger. Because this couldn't be happening, not to Nick, not in my bedroom. *What had I done?*

"One broken nose, gouges from her nails, a couple of cracked ribs, a bunch of bruises on your calves, and a black eye," Black assessed. "And you need to get that cheekbone X-rayed."

"That it?" Nick asked, still sarcastic even though he must have been in agony.

"Count yourself lucky, buddy. When she broke my nose, she got me in the balls too, and I couldn't walk properly for a week."

Dan helped Nick to get dressed then fetched a car to take him to the hospital. As he shuffled out of the bedroom, I struggled to my feet and stumbled towards him.

"I'm sorry. I'm so sorry, Nick."

He paused and squeezed my hand. "It's okay, baby.

I know you didn't mean it."

Black wrapped a blanket around me, and I realised I was still naked. Just great. Nick bent to kiss my cheek before trailing Dan out into the hallway. At least he didn't seem to hate me, although how, I wasn't sure.

I certainly hated myself.

Their footsteps receded, leaving me alone, and I slid down the wall with my head in my hands. I'd sleepwalked in the past, but this... This was a whole other category of messed up. Usually, I just woke up somewhere else in the house and went back to bed with bruised shins from walking into things. My eyes prickled as I thought of Nick's mangled face, and I cursed my training. Over the past couple of years, I'd become a machine, taught to react automatically to any sort of threat, and my subconscious had done exactly that.

Black came back and lifted me up, his face impassive as he carried me through to his bathroom and lowered me into his swimming-pool-sized tub. The heat of the water stung, but I didn't care. I deserved the pain. It was nothing compared to what I'd inflicted on Nick.

"You okay?" he asked.

"No."

"Physically?"

"I'm fine."

He washed Nick's blood off me, the water turning pale pink with the evidence of my crime. Despite my claim to be okay, he checked me over, and when he didn't find any damage, he bundled me into a robe. I expected him to lead me back to my room, but he picked me up again and tucked me into his bed.

"Sleep, Diamond." He leaned over and touched his lips to my forehead. "I'm going to check on Nick then I'll come back and take the couch."

"You shouldn't be in a room with me. What if I hurt you too?"

"Don't worry. I'll bring a Taser." My darling husband, ever the practical one. "I want to keep an eye on you tonight."

It was all very well him telling me to sleep. As I lay still, watching the full moon hanging in the sky over Black's balcony, I wasn't sure I'd ever sleep again.

Soft footsteps and the squeak of a spring signalled Black's return. On any normal day, he'd have told me to suck it up and get on with things, but tonight he somehow knew I needed sweet, and he gave it to me.

See? He wasn't always a monster.

That was me.

CHAPTER 28

THE NEXT MORNING, Black helped me to switch bedrooms. I'd never lie in my old bed again without feeling the crunch of Nick's nose under my elbow or look at the wall by the door without seeing his bloodied body slumped against it.

My new room was beside Black's. Nate installed a motion sensor on the door, and once set, if I tried to open it without punching in a six-digit code first, an alarm would sound. Surely even I couldn't enter six numbers in my sleep?

And having Black next door meant he could deal with me if the worst happened. An interconnecting door, bolted from his side, would let him in to shoot me with a tranquilizer dart, Taser me, something. Anything. Anything to stop a repeat of last night.

He carried in a pile of towels and stowed them in my new bathroom, bigger than my old one but I didn't deserve the extra space.

"That's the last of it."

"How do you cope?" I asked. "You must have seen things every bit as horrible as I have."

"I block it out," he answered softly. "If I didn't I'd never sleep."

"I wish I could. I try. While I'm awake it's okay, mind over matter and all that, but the moment I close my eyes, the devil comes out to play."

"Want me to see if I can find someone to help?"

"What, like a psychiatrist? How do you see that going? 'So, Emerson, tell me about your day.' 'Well, I shot three people and that was fine, just an interesting technical challenge. But I could have done without getting lowered on a rope into a dark hole full of rotting corpses to check for survivors. That made me feel a bit queasy.' They'd have me committed."

"Point taken. Is that really what happened?"

"Yes. I was the smallest and lightest, so I got the pleasure of going down there, and no, there weren't any survivors. Then I threw up over the side of the boat until there wasn't anything left inside me. I was in good company though—everyone else on the team lost their lunch as well."

"Well, if you need to talk things through, talk to me. I'll always be here."

"Thank you," I whispered.

My life might have been messed up in ways most people couldn't even imagine, but at least I wasn't alone in it.

I'd hoped I wouldn't have to take Black up on his offer, that the awful night with Nick was a one-off, but little did I know. My sleep would remain on FUBAR status for years to come. Black was to become my sounding board, my confidante, my outlet for the horrors that threatened to consume me.

But back then, I was still blissfully ignorant, and I mustered up a smile when Nick came home later in the day, clutching X-rays that showed two cracked ribs and a broken nose but thankfully no cheek fracture.

"The hospital staff believed my story about getting

into a bar fight."

"Thanks for telling them that."

He slung an arm around my shoulders and gave me a squeeze. "It was less embarrassing than admitting a one-hundred-and-twenty-five-pound girl did it in her sleep. They probably wouldn't have believed me if I'd told them that, anyway."

"I'm so sorry, Nicky. I don't know what came over me."

He turned me to face him and put a hand on each of my shoulders. "It wasn't your fault, baby. I heard you cry out, and when I tried to cuddle you, it triggered, well, something. You weren't even there. I mean, your eyes were open but they were vacant. You almost gave me a heart attack."

Nick may have forgiven my actions, but I struggled to cope with them myself. Space. I needed space. Some time away to process things in my own head. So I ran. I flew to London under the pretence of building up business at the new office and spent a month speaking to clients and helping with paperwork.

At night, I stayed in Albany House, but I trained each morning with Jimmy. Whenever a job came up, I foisted it onto someone else. Although I had Ruth on hand to cook for me, I joined Jimmy and Jackie for dinner whenever I had a free evening, mucking in with the washing up and getting in the way. Like in the old days, JJ's became my sanctuary, except without the cleaning or the stripping parts.

Even though I'd been away from the East End for a while, Jimmy acted as if I'd only been gone overnight. I was beyond lucky to have him in my life. And I wanted to repay the kindness he'd shown me over the years, so one day, I borrowed the folder where he kept his important documents, visited his bank manager, and paid off the mortgage on the gym.

I felt quite pleased with myself until he found out.

"Amanda, you can't just give us your money. You worked hard for that."

"Yes, I can. I can do whatever I want with it."

"Then I'll repay it. I don't like being in debt."

"I'll tear up the cheque."

"I'll write it anyway."

"He's a proud man," Jackie said after Jimmy left the room. "He doesn't want to take charity."

"But it's not charity. You guys did so much for me and you didn't have to. You could call that charity too. I just see this as returning the favour."

Jackie settled herself onto the sofa and patted it for me to sit beside her. "Can you afford it? Be honest."

"Yes, I can. It was sixty thousand pounds. I made that in the last month."

Jackie's jaw dropped. "I had no idea you earned so much."

"Well, I do. And I'm so busy working I barely have time to spend a penny."

"You need to take a break, darling girl. You'll burn out."

"I like work." A month ago, I'd have said those words with more conviction. I did enjoy work *most* of the time—it was just the odd nightmare-inducing jobs I could do without.

Jackie squeezed both of my hands. "Then thank you. I'll speak to Jimmy, see if I can get him to accept it."

I gave her a hug. "It would mean a lot to me."

In England, I slept alone, the house silent apart from the creaks and groans as it settled. I spoke to Black most days, and although I was getting kind of lonely, I kept thinking of new reasons not to go home. Eventually, having grown tired of hearing my ever more ridiculous excuses, Black sent Nick over. Ostensibly for a meeting, but the real reason was to drag me back to Virginia.

"I'm not sure I'm ready to leave," I grumbled to Black.

"You've got to face up to things, Diamond. You can't keep running away from reality. Now, get yourself back over here. I've got things for you to do."

He was right, of course. Nick acted like his normal self, and any tension between us was all in my head. We soon fell back into our old friendship, the only difference being that I never attempted to spend the night with him again.

Weirdly, I discovered that when I went on a job, the nightmares stayed away. A kill switch, if you like. For one crazy moment, I considered moving to a war zone to escape from my own subconscious, but Black quickly vetoed that idea.

"Are you out of your mind?"

"Not on the frontline, no. That's the whole point."

"Forget it, Diamond."

Over the next couple of years, I learned to live better with myself, and Black kept his promise; he was always by my side. Despite our initial plans to divorce, we stayed married. Our relationship remained platonic, but neither of us met anybody we liked enough to warrant filling out the paperwork. I stayed at Riverley Hall, gradually influencing the decor until it was a little less stuffy and formal, while Dan moved into an apartment in Richmond.

I couldn't entertain the thought of a serious relationship, not after what had happened with Nick. Nor could I bring myself to have the one-night stands that Dan seemed to favour. Instead, I preferred discreet liaisons with a few men I knew well enough to trust with the true reason why I got dressed and left before midnight.

After Nick came Xavier. Edgy in the bedroom, brutal out of it. At that point in our lives, neither of us liked ourselves much, and our time together reflected that darkness. Then there was James, who showed me sweet and kind but only behind closed doors. Those days were...difficult. He wanted more, but I couldn't give it to him, not when his career aspirations were so incompatible with mine. Our relationship was always doomed to fail.

I went through Gideon and Alaric, neither of whom could be termed easy, before I found Jed. Jed made no secret of liking the ladies, but his easygoing nature made a refreshing change. Not to mention he sure knew how to make me smile.

Black got his kicks too, although I never saw his women. He took them to an apartment in Richmond, and Bradley told me the place was devoid of any personality. No colour, no personal items, no soul.

I asked Nate about it once, why Black didn't just bring a girlfriend back to Riverley, but he said Black didn't want the emotional entanglement. That if a woman saw the size of the estate, they'd also know the size of his wallet, and he'd never get rid of her.

Suited me.

Although I didn't care so much at first, I grew to hate the nights Black spent in Richmond. Those were the nights I lost myself in Jed.

The business went from strength to strength, mainly because Black, Nate, Nick, Dan, and I spent most of our waking hours working. Carmen took a step back after she and Nate had their first child, a boy they named Joshua. The rest of us regularly worked through several time zones each day, and I collected so many airline toiletries I could have stocked my own pharmacy.

In the end, Black did buy a jet, which allowed us to avoid baggage restrictions and meant I could stick my knife in my pocket rather than having to find a creative hiding place every time I went through airline security.

I had ever-growing demands on my time, especially when I followed Black's lead and diversified my investments. I bought into other businesses, watching them grow alongside Blackwood. And as a person, I grew too.

Despite our hectic lives, Black and I were always there for each other. Even on opposite sides of the world, I knew he was only a phone call away. He was my rock, the one thing that kept me grounded and enabled me to deal with my demons and keep doing the job I did.

Until all that changed one fateful day when a stranger with an itchy trigger finger stole him from me.

My sanity, balanced on a knife-edge for so long, was in serious danger of falling into the abyss below.

CHAPTER 29

AFTER A NIGHT of reflection and regret, I stumbled into the bathroom at Albany House early the following morning. I might as well not have bothered going to bed, for all the good it did me.

Yesterday evening at the Blackwood Foundation Ball had been a monumental screw-up. Why had Luke been there? I'd checked the guest list in the afternoon as I always did, and his name wasn't on it, which meant he must have taken someone else's seat.

I leaned forward, hands on the mirror above the basin, and stared at my puffy eyes. *Good going, Emmy.* Although in the cold light of day, the situation wasn't the end of the world. No, the apocalypse had already happened, last year in the parking lot of the Green Mountain Hotel.

Yes, Luke knew who I was now, and yes, his dislike for me had been confirmed, but what impact would that truly have on my life?

Probably not much of one.

So his presence had made me uncomfortable? Compared to some of the situations I'd been in, on a scale of unpleasantness from zero to ten, being in a room with Luke came so low I'd have to limbo. If Black were alive, he'd have told me to man up, and I intended to do exactly that.

Things became easier when I left the country at noon. I had a jungle survival exercise scheduled in the Belize rainforest, and it only took a phone call to fly out there a few days early.

Just imagine, seven days of peace and quiet—me, a bunch of special forces guys, and nature. Okay, so there was a bit of crawling around in the undergrowth required, I got bitten all over, and I had to survive on things that certainly wouldn't feature on your average menu. Chilli fried grub anyone? But there were no meetings, no paperwork, no awkward people to deal with, and no technology demanding my attention every five minutes.

Of course, Nate had given me a satellite version of my red phone, together with instructions to keep it with me and turned on at all times, but it fell out of my pocket and smashed on a rock when I was climbing a tree on day two. I heard the despair in his voice when I borrowed a phone to inform him he'd have to communicate with me via base camp from now on, but secretly I found it liberating.

A week later, I returned to the UK relaxed and rested. Sure, I had some bites and scratches, but my tan looked good and Bradley could fix my hair. I sauntered into the office, getting several odd looks when I smiled. Nobody had seen that from me in a long time. I'd even stopped off at Krispy Kreme and bought donuts. I hid them in the break room where hopefully Toby wouldn't notice, then continued to my desk.

My mood soon dropped when I saw my email inbox and the pile of papers waiting for me.

Welcome back to reality.

It took me the rest of the morning to get through it

all, and there were some real nasties in there. First up, a message from the Metropolitan Police asking if I'd testify as a witness in Tia's kidnapping trial. My answer? Not voluntarily.

I hated court and never went unless I was subpoenaed. Even then, I'd do anything I could to get out of it. Two years ago, I'd even gone so far as to get one of the Joint Chiefs of Staff to write me a note.

Dear Judge,

Emmy is away on very important and very classified government business so she won't be able to attend the hearing today.

Sorry.

Of course, the language was more officious, but you get the gist of it. It cost me a super-expensive box of cigars, and I had to fly to Cuba to pick the stupid things up then smuggle them back into the country.

I sat back in my chair and folded my hands behind my head. How could I get out of court this time? A light bulb pinged, and I made a quick phone call.

Black's Aunt Miriam was on the warpath too, demanding a copy of his will and a bunch of money. Well, she could get lost. I told my lawyer to tell her so, in those exact words if necessary. I knew—because Black had told me—that she had financial problems, so we could play a game of legal tennis all year. She'd run out of cash long before I did.

I'd built up a nice nest egg over the years, and I was still making money faster than I could spend it. I hadn't done anything about the will yet because I didn't need Black's assets as well. There was no hurry.

When I got to the bottom of the pile, I found a message that had been forwarded around to several people before landing on my desk with a coffee stain and a post-it note saying *Yours?* stuck to it. I took a mouthful of my own Americano and started to read.

Subject: For the attention of E Black
   Hi Emerson (I think),
   Luke came home tonight and told me your name, but I'm not sure this is the right person? If it is, I want to say thank you for saving my life (again!)
   I wish you'd stayed because I miss having you around, but Luke really hates your guts now so I guess I can't blame you for leaving. If ever you are in Lower Foxford, and you feel like going out for lunch or something, it would be nice to see you. Luke told me not to contact you, but I could sneak out and he wouldn't even know.
   If not, then I understand, and I hope you are happy and that life goes OK for you.
   Love from Tia xxx

Looked as if I'd never escape from the past, didn't it? Although Tia was one part of my past I didn't mind coming back. Hanging out with her was like having a little sister, and while I'd never admit it to her brother, I admired the rebel in her. Luke may have behaved like an idiot, but I didn't see why I should cut Tia out of my life because of it.

   So I fired off an email.

From: EmmyBlack@blackwood-security.com
   Subject: Emerson
   Hey Tia,
   Hope you're doing OK after your tangle with

Simon. Try not to get into any more trouble while I'm not around, eh?

Lunch would be good. If you tell me when you're free, I'll clear some time in my diary. I can pick you up, but best not from Lower Foxford, or it would get back to Luke before we even left the village. If you need any hints on sneaking out, let me know. I've had plenty of practice at that, lol.

I've put my number at the bottom—text/call me whenever you want to chat.

Ash / Emmy x

That was my last bit of paperwork. I decided to celebrate with a donut, only to find the vultures had eaten them all, and when I went to the mini fridge in my office, starving, it was filled with carrot sticks and celery. For crying out loud, I'd eaten better in the rainforest.

"What on earth is this lot?" I asked Tina, my London assistant.

"Er, Toby gave me a shopping list."

"If I give you a new shopping list, would you be a darling and pop out to get me something I can actually eat?"

She shuffled awkwardly from foot to foot and refused to meet my eyes. "Toby told me I couldn't. He said you'd ask, but you're on a strict diet."

"Fine."

I walked out to the break room and found one of the junior analysts eating a sandwich.

"Hi. Gareth, isn't it?"

"Uh, yes?"

"Gareth, I'll give you fifty quid if you'll nip out and

get me a Subway."

"I-I-I can't," he stammered. "Toby said you're only supposed to eat the food he prescribed."

"Did he tell everyone in the whole office this?"

"Uh, yeah, he sent a memo around."

Toby was officially in my bad books now. "A strict diet" meant the fridge at Albany House would be filled with chicken, fish, lean cuts of beef, vegetables, fruit, and cottage cheese. Protein shakes. Eggs. Not a chocolate bar in sight. I'd starve.

I looked at my watch. Half an hour until my next meeting—just enough time to find some proper lunch without being late. I jogged down to Subway and ordered a turkey foot long and a bag of cookies to go with it, turning down the cashier's offer to add a soft drink for only fifty pence. I never touched that fizzy stuff. Artificial sweeteners, colour, preservatives—those things could kill you.

The cookies made me happy, but silly things still made me miserable, like Black's toothbrush sitting beside mine in the bathroom off our shared office. The alternative was to throw it out, though, and I couldn't bring myself to do that. Not yet. While it was still there, if I didn't think about it, I could almost believe he was coming home.

My last meeting of the day was at New Scotland Yard, a one hour debrief that turned into three as we rehashed the mess they'd made of the security exercise at the conference centre. In a typical display of public bureaucracy, they'd sent sixteen people to the meeting when four would have been perfectly adequate, and they all wanted to have their say.

After I escaped, I headed back to my old haunts.

You could take the girl out of East London, but you couldn't take East London out of the girl, and over the years I'd kept in touch with some of the people I grew up with. After a quick visit to JJ's and a drink at the pub opposite, I stopped for a catch up with Vinnie, the guy who'd been generous enough to share his knowledge of car theft when we were younger. He tended to work late, as that was when most of his cars were nicked, so I knew I'd find him awake.

He was underneath what had once been a Mercedes S Class when I arrived. I poked him with my foot, and he shot out on a wheeled plank, banging his head and cursing.

"Don't you ever knock?"

I shrugged. "Nope."

"Why are you here? Anything important?"

"Nah, just thought I'd stop in to say hello."

"In that case, put the kettle on, would ya?"

We caught up over a cuppa, reminiscing about the old days and the people we knew back then. When Vinnie got called away to deal with a wiring problem on a Porsche, I went to check on one of the kids I mentored through the Blackwood Foundation, leaving the BMW X5 I was driving in Vinnie's care. It wasn't a good idea to park it on the street around there, although I suppose there was a certain irony in leaving it at a chop shop for safekeeping.

The lad's new job at Harry's Fish Bar meant he had a steady income and as much free food as he could eat, and he served me up a portion of chips with plenty of vinegar, just the way I liked it. Better than Toby's baked sweet potatoes, that was for sure. I ate them out of the paper on my way back to Vinnie's.

"Don't be a stranger," Vinnie said as I picked up my car.

"I won't."

"Come over for dinner next time. You can meet my daughter. She's a real daddy's girl."

"What, she dismantles the Lego cars instead of playing with Barbie?"

"Something like that."

This evening had been my kind of night out on the town, and I was smiling as I started the BMW. Vinnie had even topped up the oil.

Thank goodness for old friends.

CHAPTER 30

I WAS TWO miles from home when my phone rang. Okay, which git had set my ringtone to the "Macarena"? I stopped caring as Tia's name flashed up on the car's display screen right next to the time. One o'clock in the morning? What was so important it couldn't wait until tomorrow?

I hit the button on the steering wheel to answer, and the car filled with the sound of sobbing.

"Tia?" I clenched my fingers around the hard leather.

"Ash? Is that you?"

"Yes, what's wrong?"

"I'm lost." Seconds passed as she gulped in air. "I'm in some woods, and I don't know where I am."

"Why are you crying? And what are you doing in the woods at one a.m.?"

"I was with this guy, and he wouldn't get off me, so I pushed him and he hit me. Then I jumped out of his car and ran."

Looked like I wasn't going home after all. "How's your phone battery?"

"Uh, eighty percent."

"That's good. Leave your phone on, and I'll track you."

Thank goodness for technology. Tia was in no state

to work out her location.

I hung up and made a quick call. If anyone could help with the problem, it was Mack—her first language was techno-speak. Nate had tempted Mackenzie Fox away from the CIA not long after I split from Nick, and as well as speaking fluent computer, she had a handy sideline in wreaking havoc and mayhem. When we first met, she'd lived a little further east in Colonial Beach, but she'd recently bought an apartment in Richmond to cut down on commuting time. Despite that, she spent most evenings hanging out at Riverley with Dan, Carmen, and me. Our new best friend, not least because she could hack into the police database and erase our speeding tickets.

That night, she put me on hold for five minutes as she worked her magic. "Tia's by the side of the road about a half hour from Lower Foxford. Forty-five minutes from you."

"Forty-five minutes of my driving or yours?"

"Your driving. An hour for any sane person."

"Thanks, honey."

I called Tia straight back. "Right, I'm on my way. I'll be about three-quarters of an hour. Are you hurt? Cold?"

"A bit cold. I'm only wearing a party dress but I'm not hurt apart from my face and that aches where Theo hit me." That rush of words was followed by more sniffles.

"Sit tight, sweetie. I'm on my way."

Worried for Tia and furious on her behalf, I drove far too fast and made it to the area in thirty-five minutes. As I got nearby, Mack guided me to Tia's precise location. I took a few deep breaths before I got out of the car because being cross wouldn't help matters. Anger wasn't an emotion I often felt. Although I saw a lot of nasty things, that was normally in the line of duty and the people involved were strangers. I found it easier to stay detached that way.

Now that I was in a situation involving someone I cared about, my emotions threatened to make an appearance. The strange thing was, I hadn't yet felt anger over Black's death when by rights I should have been furious. Every day, grief overrode my sanity, coupled with enough numbness to give me an out-of-body experience. I needed the rage to come—it would be easier to deal with.

Ten feet into the forest, I found Tia sitting on a log, arms wrapped around herself and mascara running down her face. The bottom of her dress hung in tatters, and her eye already looked nasty and purple. Lovely. I squinted in the gloom, taking in the cut on her cheek and her busted lip as I helped her up.

"Where does Luke think you are?"

There was no way he'd have let her stay out at a party this late.

"At Arabella's. I told him I was staying the night."

I got a blanket out of the boot and wrapped it around Tia's shoulders before helping her into the front seat. Once I clipped her seatbelt on, she started shaking, and even when I leaned in and gave her a hug the tremors didn't stop.

"Don't worry, we'll sort this," I whispered.

"How?"

I knew what Luke's reaction would be if I took Tia home, and sympathy wasn't it. I figured I should do my civic duty and save him from an aneurysm.

"If Luke's not expecting you back, I'll take you home with me, and we can get your face looked at. What happened?"

"There was this boy I liked. Arabella said he wasn't a nice person, but I went out with him half a dozen times, and he took me to fun places and bought me things. I thought he cared."

She gave a sniffle, and I passed her a packet of tissues from the door pocket. Thanks, Bradley.

Tia paused to blow her nose before continuing. "We went to a party tonight, and after a couple of beers, he acted just like all the other guys. He only wanted one thing."

She squirmed in her seat as she talked, and she wouldn't meet my eyes.

"You didn't..." I began.

"NO! I refused. That's when he started to get rough with me."

"So the guy drove while he was drunk then tried to force himself on you? Nice."

"I feel so stupid for trusting him. I honestly didn't think he'd be like that. Maybe it was because he'd been drinking? Or I did something to encourage him?"

"Don't you dare blame yourself. Alcohol only exacerbates tendencies you already have. It doesn't change your personality completely. A few drinks wouldn't have made this guy into a monster if he didn't already think that way. If you told him to stop, he should have stopped, no questions, no hesitation."

She fell silent for the rest of the journey. I had no doubt she was playing the evening's events over in her head, especially when she started to sob quietly. As I reached over and squeezed her hand, I vowed I'd do my best to fix this.

Back at Albany house, I parked in the underground garage and led Tia into the lift. Once the doors opened on the ground floor, I guided her through to the kitchen and helped her onto a stool at the breakfast bar. The lighting was best in there, and I took a better look at her eye.

"Is it bad?" she asked.

Nothing seemed broken, but she'd have one nasty bruise in the morning.

"No lasting damage."

I fetched an ice pack and got her to hold it on. After a minute or two, her breathing evened out and she looked around the room with her good eye.

"Is this your house?"

"Yeah."

"It's really nice. Why on earth were you living in a caravan at Hazelwood Farm if you had this?"

"I needed to get away for a while. Hazelwood Farm made a convenient place to lie low."

"What, because of your cheating fiancé? He must have really hurt you if you chose to stay in that awful caravan instead of here."

"The whole fiancé thing wasn't exactly true, I'm afraid."

"Then why?"

"It was still man trouble. I used to be married and someone murdered my husband."

She went quiet for a second. "Luke said that, but he's been drinking so much lately, I thought he'd made the story up. He thinks you did it."

"Do you?"

She shook her head, then clambered off her stool

and hugged me. I froze for a second before hugging her back, careful not to squeeze too hard.

"It's not been a great few months," I said.

"I'm so sorry," she mumbled in my ear. "I must have made things even worse for you. I was so nasty when we first met. If I'd known what had happened, I'd never have been mean like that."

"It's over and done with now. No matter how much we'd like to, we can't change what happened in the past." And I didn't particularly want to discuss it either. "How about we both go to bed? I don't know about you, but I'm knackered."

"I'm super tired too. Do you think I could borrow some pyjamas and maybe a toothbrush? I literally have nothing but my phone. Not even my handbag. I managed to leave it in Theo's car when I jumped out."

In this place, we had spare everything. Most of my friends treated it like a hotel. "Sure, I'll show you where my wardrobe is—borrow whatever you want. There are spare toothbrushes in every bathroom. Did you have anything important in your bag?"

"My wallet and some antibiotics I've been taking. I had a bad chest last week." She groaned. "And my house keys. I guess I'll have to ask Luke to change the locks. He's gonna be really mad at me, especially when he sees my eye."

"We'll worry about that in the morning."

"Perhaps I could just keep out of his way and not tell him? At least he's gone back to work now, so he's less likely to notice if I'm not there. He moped around the house for ages after you left."

"Did he? He looked as though he wanted to poke my eyes out when I saw him the other day."

"Oh, that was only after he found out you were still engaged. He said he felt used."

I didn't know whether to choke or laugh. "Engaged? Who am I engaged to?"

"Nick, he said. The guy who helped rescue me?"

"Where on earth did he hear that? I'm not and never have been engaged to Nick."

"I don't know. I think maybe one of his friends told him? Luke came home that night and said you and Nick were dancing together."

"Dancing, yes. But that doesn't automatically mean I'm going to marry the guy."

"So you've never been involved with Nick?"

"We had a thing once, but that was almost a decade ago." I thought I might as well put that on the table. "We've only been friends for years."

"Oh. Luke got completely the wrong end of the stick, then."

"Looks that way, doesn't it? What's Theo's surname?" I changed the subject in an effort to avoid getting into a deep analysis of my failed relationships with my ex-boyfriend's sister.

"Baldwin. Theo Baldwin. Why?"

"And do you know his address?"

I put the kettle on to make coffee. At this time of night, instant would have to do. I'd changed my mind about going to bed.

Tia reeled off an address near where I'd picked her up. "Why do you want to know?" she asked again.

"So I can get your bag back." And give Theo a piece of my mind, although I wasn't about to tell Tia that.

"You can't! He's almost six feet tall!"

"Trust me, it won't be a problem. Does he live

alone?"

"Yes, his parents bought him the flat. But please don't go. My bag doesn't matter, and I don't want you to get hurt."

"I promise I won't get hurt. One thing: if he calls you, pick up."

I led Tia upstairs, still fretting, and found her a pair of pyjamas and a spare bedroom. I always slept in an old T-shirt and a pair of boxers, usually stolen from Black or Nick, and Mack favoured the kind of frilly stuff people wore in movies, so the pyjamas were Dan's.

Then I went out in search of Theo. It was just before sunrise when I drew up outside a tidy Victorian converted into two apartments. One up, one down. Theo lived in the bottom one. The lock was so basic a child could have picked it, and it only took me a few seconds to get inside. A pair of muddy boots lay abandoned by the mat in the small, unkempt hallway, and a couple of coats hung on a doorknob. I spotted Tia's Michael Kors bag dumped on a side table next to a set of car keys and a dying spider plant.

I peered in the top. Her wallet was in there, plus a small bottle containing her pills. Good. I'd pick it up on my way out.

Theo lay snoring on the bed, half covered by the duvet in a room that reeked of stale sweat. The moonlight shining through the gap in the curtains showed Tia was spot on about his height, but he wasn't in great shape. He'd gone pudgy around the middle.

As I stood there, I felt the way I had many times before. No joy, but a touch of anticipation and the satisfaction that I was about to fix one more problem with this messed up world.

I flipped the light on. "Rise and shine, sweetheart."

Theo woke, groggily at first, then he suddenly came alive when he realised somebody was standing in his room.

"Who are you? What are you doing in my house?"

I ignored the first question but answered the second. "I'm here to give you a little lesson on how to treat women."

I picked his phone up off the desk and thumbed through it, but he didn't like that much.

"Hey! Put that down!" He sprang out of bed and charged at me, arms outstretched. Smooth, Theo, real smooth. I stepped to my left and used my leg to sweep his feet out from underneath him. He landed with a resounding thump, and I grabbed the chair next to me. Before he could get up, I positioned it so the strut between the back legs was over his neck then sat down.

He flailed around, but he was trapped. I waited patiently until he went still then put the phone next to his hand. "You're going to call Tia and apologise."

"Get lost," he spat.

"Not gonna happen. I don't go for the forceful type. Now, make the call."

"In your dreams."

"We've been over that. And take as much time as you like. I can guarantee I'm more comfortable than you."

After fifteen minutes, Theo got a cramp in his leg and finally decided to dial Tia. But his apology was somewhat half-hearted.

Not good enough.

I used my foot to press down a bit harder on his windpipe.

"Once more, with feeling."

He did better that time, and once he'd dropped the phone, I let him up and took a few steps back, waiting.

As soon as he scrambled to his feet, he came at me again, winding his arm back to get a good punch in. I ducked to the side and, no kidding, he actually ran into the wall.

Did you ever watch those cartoons where Sylvester runs at Tweety, Tweety neatly sidesteps, and Sylvester knocks himself out? Well, there you go. There was a sickening crunch when Theo hit the bricks, then he slowly crumpled to the floor. I waited for the little stars to start twinkling around his head, but nothing. Zilch. Real life was nothing like the movies.

I prodded him with my foot, but he was out cold. His pulse beat steadily, and I only hoped his stupidity had knocked some sense into him. Ten minutes passed, twenty, and I answered a handful of emails and took a phone call from Tokyo while I waited for Theo to rejoin the land of the living. I'd just started playing solitaire when he started to blink.

Once he'd mumbled a few choice phrases and rolled onto his stomach to puke, I made my exit, remembering to grab Tia's bag on my way out the door. An early morning dog walker gave me a strange look and a wide berth as I hurried along the pavement, probably because I was laughing like a drunk.

But honestly, I needed that.

Laughing was better than crying.

CHAPTER 31

WHEN I GOT back to Albany House, I grabbed a couple of hours sleep then checked on Tia. Her bedroom was on the floor above mine, and I knocked softly on the door to see if she was awake.

"Come in," came her groggy reply.

I stepped inside, dropping her bag on the dresser as I went.

The curtains were open, and in daylight, her face looked even worse. Despite the ice we'd put on her eye last night, it had swollen into a puffy mess and she couldn't open it properly. I felt a small pang of regret that I hadn't knocked out at least one of Theo's teeth.

"How are you feeling?"

Tia struggled to sit up, blinking her good eye in the midmorning sun. "Like I just did ten rounds with a cage fighter."

"Can you move over by the window? I want to take a closer look."

She climbed out of bed and shuffled over. Outside, there was barely a puff of cloud in the sky. Would it be one of those glorious crisp, clear winter days? Oh, who was I kidding? This was Britain—we'd have rain by lunchtime.

I turned Tia to the right angle and peered at her damaged eye. The bruising had blossomed overnight and turned a lovely shade of plum, which by freakish coincidence matched the ridiculously ostentatious curtains chosen by Bradley. The cuts on her cheek and lip had both scabbed over into ugly crusts, and while the lip looked worst, I knew from experience it would heal the fastest.

"I'll give you some anti-inflammatories to help with the swelling. And I'll bring up a hydro-colloidal dressing for your cheek. It may look hideous, but it'll help the cut heal faster."

"Thank you," she said.

My bigger concern in all this was her mental state, and perhaps more important, how to deal with Luke's reaction.

"How are you feeling up here?" I asked, tapping my head.

"Pretty stupid."

"It's not you who caused the problem. Always remember that."

"I guess. I just can't believe I didn't realise what he was like before I said yes to going out with him."

"It happens more often than you'd think. If you tell me the name of the next guy who reckons he's good enough for you, I'll run a background check. Deal?"

She spluttered on the water she was sipping, then her lips quirked up in a smile. "You'd really do that?"

"Of course. I don't want you to go through a night like that again." I paused. "Or what happened when you got kidnapped. How are you holding up?"

She shrugged. "Okay, I think. I was drugged for most of it, so really it's more like a bad dream. Luke sent me to some therapist, but she was a patronising old biddy. Kept asking, 'Soooo, how did that make you feel?' I managed two sessions then for the third, I went to the cinema with Arabella. Channing Tatum made me feel better than the counsellor ever could."

I cracked a smile. Tia seemed to be coping with things better than I was. "I'm glad you're doing okay."

"I'm a bit worried about the trial though," she confessed.

"Don't fret over that. You won't have to testify."

"But I'm a witness."

"Trust me. The trial isn't an issue. I promise."

I pulled her into a hug, and we sat there for a few moments until she mumbled into my hair.

"What happened when you went to get my bag?"

"Theo didn't appreciate the interruption. He does have a violent streak, and not just with you."

She pulled back and stared at me, wide-eyed, checking me up and down for damage.

"Did he hurt you?"

"He tried, but he was never going to succeed. He's probably feeling slightly uncomfortable this morning."

"Oh my gosh! Do you think he'll call the police?"

I laughed. "Not a chance. First, he'd have to tell them what he did to you. Second, most of the damage happened when he managed to run into a wall all by himself. Third, he'd have to admit he got bested by a girl. Trust me, it's not going to happen."

When I recounted the story of how Theo knocked himself out, Tia was soon laughing almost as much as I had last night.

"I don't know what I'd have done if you hadn't been there," she said.

"Well, I was, so don't start dwelling on 'what ifs.' Now, we need to work out what to do next. I'm assuming Luke doesn't have a clue about the party last night?"

"He doesn't know anything about Theo. I told him Arabella and I were working on an art project."

Tears gathered in the corners of Tia's eyes, and I knew what she was thinking. Telling her brother what happened wouldn't be easy.

But did we have to?

I'd be in Europe for a week, and the bruising would fade in that time. The cuts should also be well on their way to healing, and any remaining lumps and bumps could be hidden with make-up by that point. Trust me, I'd had plenty of practice with that.

"How do you feel about staying here? Would Luke believe you were at Arabella's for a whole week?"

Yes, I know, I shouldn't have encouraged Tia to lie. But with all the other bad things I'd done in my life, that little fib paled into insignificance.

"With you?" she asked.

"I have to work, but I'll be around a bit."

"That's okay. I'd love to!" She perked up. "He'd totally believe I was at Arabella's. I used to stay there loads before...you know. I've got spare clothes there and everything. She'd absolutely cover for me, and her parents have gone to their villa in Marbella this week. Mark won't notice whether I'm there or not. He spends most of his time at his girlfriend's."

"Okay, that sounds like a plan. Even if I'm not around, someone else should be here most of the time. Does the school know Luke and I split?"

"Probably not. Luke hasn't exactly been broadcasting it."

"That helps. I'll be able to call in and tell them

you're sick without having to imitate your mother."

"Thank you, thank you, thank you!" I got another hug, which was followed by an "ouch" as Tia smushed her face against me then remembered she was hurt.

I showed her how to get to the kitchen, where I introduced her to Bradley and Mack, who'd arrived at some point in the morning.

"Just rummage through the closets and help yourself to clothes. We all share stuff and nobody'll get precious about you borrowing things. If you need anything else, Bradley will sort it out," I told her.

"Sure thing, sweet pea," Bradley confirmed, speaking around a mouthful of Lucky Charms.

"Bradley, how come you get those while I have a wheatgrass smoothie?"

"I guess Toby's too busy looking at my pretty face to notice what I'm eating."

I took the Aston Martin to the office, where I had a meeting with a new client followed by a day of operational planning. I'd barely driven the car since I bought it, and I'd almost forgotten where all the buttons were. At one point, I turned on the wipers when I tried to flash a moron who jumped a red light. Kind of embarrassing, but at least the sweet burble of the V12 engine under the bonnet was music to my ears.

Thoughts of Tia at home made me scoot out of the office at six. When I got home, the others were clustered in the lounge, tucking into a half-empty Chinese takeaway. I grabbed a container of Kung Po chicken and a pair of chopsticks and joined them. I'd deal with Toby and his apoplexy in the morning.

"Are you out all day again tomorrow?" Tia asked.

"I'm going to hit the gym first thing, then I've got a video call for most of the afternoon and a business meeting in the evening. What are you supposed to be doing at school? Anything important? Didn't you mention art?"

"Yes, I have art coursework to do. And it's science week. I'm supposed to be doing experiments for physics and chemistry."

"Fine. Tonight, you make a list of the equipment you need and the books you're studying. We'll get all the stuff, and you can do the projects here or at Blackwood. Mack can help you. She likes that kind of thing. Right, Mack?"

"Science is my life."

"Do I have to?" Tia asked.

"Just because you're having a week off school doesn't mean you're getting a holiday."

"At least I won't get behind." She nibbled on a prawn cracker, looking thoughtful. "Do you think I could come to the gym with you? One day, even if it's not tomorrow?"

"Sure, but why? You don't need to lose weight."

"I know... It's just... I thought that if I ever came across someone like Theo again, if I was fitter I might be able to defend myself. Luke's got a gym, but I don't know where to start."

"Have you ever been to a self-defence class?"

"No, never. Nothing like that."

I looked at Mack, and she looked at me. "JJ's?" I asked.

"JJ's," she agreed.

"Okay, but it'll be a six a.m. start. Just make sure you find some leggings or tracksuit bottoms and a pair of trainers that fit before you go to bed. We're not looking for those at five thirty in the morning."

Tia was ready right on time the next day, much to my surprise. She'd never been much of a morning person. We piled into a shiny new crew cab pickup I found in the garage, and off we went with me driving. I always liked to drive. Mainly because of Dan. If you'd ever been in a vehicle with her behind the wheel, you'd never want to be a passenger again either, trust me.

"Nice truck. Whose is it?" I asked Mack.

"Yours, I think."

Oh. I guess Bradley had decided it was time for a new car. I parked it behind JJ's and punched in the security code that let us in through the employee entrance, past the staff room and my old storage closet. When we emerged onto the main floor of the gym, two guys were already sparring in a boxing ring ahead of us. A handful of regulars trained on the heavy and speed bags, and a few others pumped iron over at the weight stack in the corner.

"What is this place?" Tia whispered.

"It's a boxing gym."

She crinkled her nose. "Smells sweaty."

"The sweet aroma of muscles and men."

I looked to the side in time to see Jimmy walking through the door marked *Private* that led from his apartment upstairs. Usually, he didn't come down this early, but I'd messaged him last night to let him know we'd be visiting.

He strode over and enveloped me in a tight hug.

"Good to see you, Amanda," he whispered in my ear.

Mack got the same treatment, then he turned to Tia with open arms. She looked a bit dubious but stepped forward and gingerly embraced him as he engulfed her.

Stepping back, he held her at arm's length and surveyed the mess of her face. "Girl, what happened to you?"

I answered for her. "She had a coming together with a guy who wanted more than she was willing to give."

Jimmy's eyes and voice went hard. "Did you fix it?"

"Of course."

"Proud of you, sweetheart."

I did an introduction. "Tia, this is Jimmy. I lived with him when I was a teenager."

"Pleased to meet you, Tia."

"And you, Jimmy."

"Are you ready to start? Emerson here said you wanted to learn the basics of self-defence."

"I'm ready."

Jimmy and Tia headed for the mats, where Jimmy started by teaching her about the easiest parts of the body to inflict pain—something I firmly believed every girl should know. Mack and I went over to the bags to train. We'd spent an hour on punches and kicks when Jimmy ambled across.

"You gonna spar before you go?" he asked me.

"Sure, if there's someone for me to go up against." It had been a while since I'd fought in the gym, although I'd had the odd bit of practice on the street.

"Darnell could do with a bout," he said, pointing at a black kid who looked to be around twenty, pounding away on a heavy bag.

I skipped over to my old room, which was where I still kept my boxing headgear, shoes, and the gloves I liked to fight in. Time to play.

Darnell made a reasonable opponent. He had a couple of amateur bouts under his belt, of which he'd won one and lost one. He was strong, but he needed to be faster. We went a few rounds, with Jimmy and I both giving him pointers. After me, Mack hopped up into the ring and did some pad work with Darnell while I headed off in search of Tia.

"How's it going?" I asked.

"Jimmy's taught me how to do an uppercut. Look!" She walloped the bag in front of her, grinning. "I just imagine it's Theo's head and I can hit really hard."

"That's great. Now try leading with your shoulder to get more power behind your punches."

"Like this?" She had another go.

"Yeah. You want to come back later in the week?"

"Can I? I'd love to. I'm going to see if Luke'll let me do more classes when I get home. I won't tell him I came here, of course," she added hastily.

Jimmy winked at me as Tia went back to swinging at the bag. She had a long way to go, but she was enjoying herself, that was the main thing. All in all, it was a good session for the four of us.

CHAPTER 32

I DROPPED MACK and Tia back at Albany House to set up Tia's school projects. In his typical efficient manner, Bradley had organised the necessary equipment while we were at the gym. Then I carried on to the office, where my diary was full with meetings until late afternoon. The cloudy sky matched my mood as I headed in for a fun-filled day of paperwork.

When Black was alive, he'd taken on his share of the admin, but at the moment, I had to carry part of the extra load until we trained someone to help. Probably several people, as no one person would be able to do everything he had. More than anything, I wished I could avoid meetings altogether because they bored the stuffing out of me. At least I had "proper" work to do this evening.

But before I headed out again, I stopped off at home to find Tia had been busy.

"How's the project going?"

"Really well. I've done most of the experiments; I just need to write it up. Mack's awesome."

"She's pretty good at all that stuff, huh?"

"Yep, and she makes it fun. We're going to JJ's again tomorrow morning. Can you come with us?"

"I have to start work early, I'm afraid."

"Oh." Tia's face fell, but only for a moment. Then

she smiled again. "I found the pool. And the cinema in the basement. We're gonna watch a film."

"Have some popcorn for me."

Tonight's job was simple. All I had to do was break into a house belonging to a trio of suspected terrorists and see if there was any evidence that might confirm my client's suspicions. I did a quick recce of the three-bed detached and studied the photos and movement logs while I waited for the surveillance team on duty to confirm the suspects had gone out.

Once satisfied the property was empty, I slipped inside and spent an hour or so going through the contents, coming to the conclusion that there was nothing to worry about. The suspects just had really bad taste in YouTube videos. At least the organisation that contracted us to do the job could now concentrate their efforts in other areas.

The next morning, Mack and Tia arrived back from the gym before I got up. When I shuffled downstairs with every atom in me crying out for caffeine, I found the kitchen island resembled a chemistry lab and the place stank. The pair of them stood there in goggles, watching something bubble away in a conical flask.

I wrinkled my nose at the acrid smell. "Dare I ask?"

"We're finding out the concentration of ethanoic acid in white wine vinegar," Tia explained.

"Is it supposed to stink like that?"

"I think so."

"In that case, I'll leave you to it and get breakfast at the office."

On my return, the dining room resembled an art shop. The table was stacked high with pads of paper, canvases, pens, pencils, paints, and brushes. As I wondered whether Tia planned to do her own coursework or perhaps the entire country's, Bradley bustled in with yet more bags.

"Got enough stuff?"

"Perhaps I did get a bit carried away," he admitted.

Tia came in behind him and stared at the mountain of supplies. "I only asked for some acrylics and a couple of canvases. Plus a box of pastels and a pad. I don't need all that." She waved her arm at the stacks on the table.

"Don't worry about it. I asked Bradley to buy me a dress once, and he came back with nine different ones and the designer herself in tow."

"Hey, she offered!"

"I know. I'm just trying to demonstrate your lack of restraint to Tia."

"Oh." He turned to Tia. "Restraint. She's right. I have none."

"I take it you're going to be painting something next, then?" I asked.

Tia pointed at what looked like half a greengrocer's, stacked in boxes on the sideboard.

"The teacher wants us to do a twist on the traditional still life bowl of fruit. We have to copy a modern artist's style."

"Sounds fun. Which artist have you picked?"

"I haven't decided yet."

"How about Damien Hirst?" Mack asked, wandering in. She picked up an apple and started munching. "If you pickled the fruit, we could spend the rest of the time shopping."

Tia looked at me, questioning. I glared at Mack.

"No pickling. You have to do it properly. I'm sure your art teacher doesn't want you lugging a tankful of formaldehyde into the classroom."

"I need inspiration. Can I use the internet? And a printer?"

"Sure."

"Or do you think I could go to a gallery? If I arranged my hair over my face, it would cover most of the bruising."

"I'm sure we can sort something out. Or there's a few modern paintings upstairs if that's any use?"

"What paintings? I need somebody well-known."

Good question. What did we have here? Black had looked after the art, and most of our collection was either loaned out to museums or back in the States. The gallery on the ground floor at Riverley Hall housed the modern pieces, and the expensive stuff lived in a smaller room on the second floor. His father and grandfather, who needed something to spend their wads of spare cash on, had both been keen art collectors. Black not so much. He bought the occasional painting, but only because he liked them, not because he had any particular aspirations of them skyrocketing in value.

"There's a Picasso, something by Dali, and a couple of David Hockneys. Oh, and one by MC Escher we bought years ago, but that would be difficult to copy." The Escher lithograph was one of my favourites. "The rest of the stuff is by lesser-known artists."

"Cool, can I have a look? It sounds odd hearing you say 'we.'"

"It makes me feel odd that there isn't a 'we' any longer."

She stepped over and gave me a hug. "I'm really sorry he's not here."

"Not half as much as I am."

I led her up to the study I'd shared with Black. The security for that room had been upgraded to accommodate the expensive paintings, and I flipped back the light switch next to the door to stare into the retina scanner. While Bradley bought entire shopping malls, Mack installed electronic gadgetry.

"That's wicked! I've never seen one of those in real life," Tia squealed.

How lucky for her that she'd never needed to.

I'd barely ventured into the study since Black's death. Of all the rooms in the house, it was the one that reminded me of him most. I picked up his Montblanc pen from his desk and twirled it around my fingers before carefully putting it back, a wave of sadness rippling through me. It was also the only room that held any photos of us. Neither of us had been big on personal mementos, but we'd made an exception in there.

Tia stood in front of the wall behind my desk, leaning forward to look at the largest picture of Black and me. We'd been about to go climbing, at Red Rock Canyon in Nevada if I remembered correctly. My grin stretched from ear to ear, and while Black had his customary mask on, he'd taken off his shirt and looked particularly hot. Just seeing us made my breath hitch.

"Was that him?" Tia asked.

"Yes."

She gazed over the other photos—some of us alone,

some with our little gang. There were pictures of us on his yacht, at home, all of us together skiing, and a few of a memorable holiday at his villa in the Caribbean.

"He was really handsome," she said.

I didn't answer. I couldn't.

Tia must have sensed I didn't want to talk about Black, because she moved over to the wall of paintings, arranged so we both got a good view from our desks.

She peered at one portrait. "Who did this? It's really good. I know Picasso did the original, but this is a copy, right?"

"No, that's the original."

Black's father had bought it from Christie's a couple of decades ago, apparently blaming the purchase on one too many glasses of sherry at lunch when his wife got upset. I could understand her reservations. Black always said I was a heathen, but I did prefer a face with a nose in the right place.

Tia was gaping open-mouthed at the gaudy painting. "Seriously? This is a genuine Picasso? And are those actual David Hockneys?"

"Yes, and yes."

"Oh my gosh! They must be worth millions!"

"So the insurance company tells me." By making a conscious effort, I managed to use "me" instead of "us" this time.

It didn't take long for Tia to decide. "I love the Picasso, but I'm not sure how I could translate that to fruit."

"A pineapple with the green bit sticking out from the side?"

She shook her head. "Nah, I'll go with Hockney. I can do blue apples and pink bananas."

She stepped closer to the paintings again, enthralled. Happy that she was happy, I got Mack to update the security system so Tia could get into the study and left her to get on with it.

Chapter 33

BY THE END of the week, the bruising around Tia's eye had faded enough to be hidden with make-up. Bradley had done exactly that for her yesterday and taken her out shopping. When I got home, there were bags everywhere, and Bradley was Tia's new best friend.

Then on Friday afternoon, Dan rocked up and announced that as nobody had plans this evening, we were all going out.

"I think I have something on," I told her.

"No, you don't. I already checked your schedule."

Super. Why did Sloane have to be so efficient? "Dare I ask where?"

For Dan, going out could mean anything from a belly dancing class to hopping on a plane to Rio for the carnival. Although to give her credit, that was one awesome trip.

"I haven't quite worked that out yet, but it'll be fantastic, I promise."

Just what I was afraid of.

"Can I come?" Tia asked.

Dan looked at me and raised an eyebrow. Tia had only turned seventeen a couple of weeks ago, and Dan didn't understand the concept of a tame night out. Last year, she'd promised a quiet dinner, which turned out to be served on the smooth, tanned body of a naked cowboy. Well, almost naked. He left his boots on. No, I could hardly inflict Dan's perversions on Tia. But then again, I'd be a hypocrite if I criticised doing stupid things at a young age, wouldn't I?

"Sure. Just promise you'll stay sensible."

"Woohoo! Bradley, will you help me pick out something to wear?"

"We'll make you look fabulous, darling." He gave her a high-five, and she grinned at him. Women loved Bradley.

When had I last been out for fun? Not for months. Since Black died, fun had been the last thing on my mind. Guilt needled at me—guilt for not being a better friend, guilt that I might have a good time, guilt that I was alive and Black wasn't.

How could I get out of tonight's activities?

I sat quietly, staring out of my "thinking window," a glass oval above the window seat at the end of the second-floor hallway that overlooked the garden. Bulletproof glass, of course. Black had insisted. Soft footsteps announced Nick's approach, and he dropped down beside me.

"When did you arrive?" I asked.

"Just got in. And apparently, now I'm just going out."

"Dan can be quite convincing, can't she?"

"You don't want to go?"

"Not really. It doesn't feel right."

"Because Black's not with you?"

"Yeah. He's in a hole in the ground and I'm still

here. It doesn't seem fair that I enjoy myself."

"I don't know whether there's anything after death, but if there isn't, Black won't care what you do. And if there is, he's up there watching over you, desperately wanting you to be happy. No way would he want you to mope around for the rest of your life."

"I guess."

"I don't have to guess; I know. Come on, join us for a little while. I'll come back early with you if you're not having a good time."

Nick's sweetness convinced me. Since I'd got back, he'd taken it upon himself to act as my protector in Black's absence, at least after he'd got over his hurt from me disappearing. I'd never needed someone to shield me before, but something inside me changed when Black died, and I constantly doubted myself. Right now, I wasn't confident I'd ever get back to being the old me completely.

New me was alien, a stranger who'd taken over my body. She felt things. Emotions. Anger, hurt, love, frustration. I'd always managed to lock those away before. Somehow, Nick knew this and sheltered me from the outside world as best he could while at the same time pushing me to repair myself. I was beyond lucky to have him around, and I owed it to him to try.

"Okay, I'll go. I can't stay out too late anyway because Tia's coming with us."

"Whenever you want to leave, just say the word."

I reported for duty at the appointed time, and from the outfit Bradley had laid out on my bed, I guessed we were going to a nightclub. Where else would I wear a pair of tight black jeans and a top made entirely from zips?

Zips? Seriously?

Did Bradley think I needed ventilation? Because I had no desire to show any flesh otherwise. At least he'd picked out my favourite boots, black leather with studded snakes slithering up the front. I'd had them for years, and Bradley was under threat of losing a limb if he ever threw them out.

Still not feeling the vibe, I climbed into the limo parked outside with Tia following. Dan already had a glass of champagne in her hand, but I shook my head when she offered me one.

"Where are we going?" I asked her.

"Just Black's. Things got busy at work this afternoon, and I ran out of time to organise anything else."

"Black's is fine."

At least we'd get good service there. As you can probably guess from the name, the club was another of my investments.

I enjoyed a night out dancing, or at least I used to, but I hated clubs filled with stinky sweat and watered-down drinks and too much noise to have a decent conversation. To solve the problem, I'd opened a small chain of exclusive clubs so I could have a good night out, drunk or sober, all over the world. Thanks to my marketing team, they were always packed.

"Are you talking about *the* Black's?" Tia asked. "As in the best club in London? The one it's almost impossible to get into?"

"That's the one," Dan said. Turning to me, she

added, "At least somebody's excited."

"Will I even get in there? I'm only seventeen. I have a fake ID, but Arabella got it for me, and it's not very good."

"Yeah, you'll get in. We're all on the guest list. I know the owner," Dan said.

"Awesome."

Thankfully, Tia's experience last weekend didn't seem to have affected her too much. What with that and the kidnapping, she'd proven to be remarkably resilient. Although she was the youngest in the car, she'd grown up a lot since I first met her, and I felt proud of the woman she was turning into.

The journey didn't take long at that time in the evening, and we soon pulled up outside the club. The line stretched halfway along the block, as usual. My bank manager would be thrilled. Oh, oops, that was me. Following Black's death, I owned his Swiss bank as well.

We walked straight to the velvet rope, and the bouncer let us in without bothering to glance at his clipboard. We got a few jeers from those waiting at the front of the line, but such is life.

"Thanks, Tyrone."

He gave me a gold-plated grin and a salute. He'd worked at the club for three years now, another graduate from the Blackwood Foundation.

Black's had two floors—the lower level housed the main dance floor, DJ, and bar, and the upper, quieter level had a dining area, another bar, and the VIP rooms. The floor was cut away in the centre so partygoers could look onto the dance floor below, and a staircase led down from each side of the balcony.

The club manager met us as we checked our coats then ushered us into a VIP room. Squashy sofas sat either side of long, low tables, already set out with a selection of snacks. This one also had a private bathroom and its own waitress.

"Things going okay tonight, Ricky?" I asked him.

"One minor disagreement between a group of punters earlier, but we clamped down on it sharpish. Apart from that, everything's peachy."

"Good." I settled back into the grey leather. "Could you send in enough beer to keep this lot happy?" I motioned to the other guys. "And some water and a couple of bottles of wine?"

"Sure thing, boss."

When the drinks arrived, I checked out the menu and ordered dinner. There was none of the usual fried rubbish. Brown food, Toby called it. He'd assisted with the recipes, which consisted of semi-healthy tapas-style dishes that wouldn't have been out of place in a restaurant, and because it tasted great, we could charge a packet for it.

The alcohol flowed and more people turned up from Blackwood. Dan must have spread the word when she visited the office this afternoon. The room filled to overflowing, and she rose a little wonkily from the sofa, tugging down her tight skirt.

"It's getting claustrophobic in here. Who wants to hit the dance floor?"

She looked at me, and I declined with a shake of my head, but two-thirds of the people in the room followed her downstairs. Phew. The rest of us had space to breathe again.

Tia was one of those left behind, along with Ryan. It

wasn't lost on me, the glances they kept giving each other—Ryan when he thought I wasn't looking and Tia shyly from under her eyelashes. Which of them would make the first move? I didn't think it would be Tia, not after the events of last weekend. And Ryan was watching me out of the corner of his eye, wary of upsetting momma bear.

I contemplated giving them a bit of space, but my red phone buzzing on the table in front of me interrupted my thoughts. Normally a message on that phone would concern me, but when I looked, it was only a text from Nick.

Nick: Help!

I doubted he could have got into an emergency situation in the club. Or at least, not what I classed as an emergency.

Emmy: What??

His reply came a few seconds later.

Nick: Being mauled. By the bar.

Even though he couldn't see me, I rolled my eyes.

"What?" Tia asked.

"Nick has a small problem. He's got separated from the herd, and now he's being hunted by a pack of women who are out for blood. He wants me to rescue him."

"This I have to see."

Tia scrambled off the couch, and I noticed Ryan got up as well and trailed behind, his eyes dropping a little too low for my liking. We left the relative peace of the VIP area and descended into the main room of the club, the beat of the music getting louder with every step.

By the time we reached the bottom, the volume made talking a waste of breath. I grabbed Tia's hand to keep her close and used the locator app on my phone to find Nick amid the writhing mass of bodies.

He was pinned down by the bar, a trio of silicone-enhanced women pressed up against him. One of them had her hand inside his shirt. He removed it, only for it to be swiftly replaced by the lime-green talons of one of her friends. It was like watching *Dawn of the Dead* with Barbie doll wannabes rather than zombies.

With Tia in tow, I fought my way over. This was one of those rare moments when I regretted the club being quite so popular. Nick saw me coming, and I caught the glimmer of desperation in his eyes. The irony wasn't lost on me. Here stood a man who'd managed to survive some of the most difficult combat situations I'd ever known only to be brought down by a swarm of spray-tanned stick insects.

I parked Tia six feet out, and mouthed, "Stay here."

She confirmed with a nod, and I saw Ryan take her back.

I pushed through the crowd to Nick, elbowing girls out of the way as I got close. He relaxed as I plastered myself to his side and wrapped my arms around his waist.

"Oi!" Barbie number one said, or rather, shouted.

Nick gripped me tighter, and I stood on tiptoes to lick a trail up the side of his neck, stopping at his ear to inform him, just loudly enough to be heard over the music, that he was a massive idiot.

He only grinned.

Hands tugged at my top, and I turned to face the gaggle of irritated girls. It was too loud to make out most of what they were saying, but I think my interpretations of "we saw him first" and "find your own" probably weren't too far off the mark.

Tempting though it was, I refused to get into a catfight in my own club, so I executed plan B instead. Sadly, it wasn't the first time I'd had to help Nick out in a situation like this, so he knew the drill. I lived in the hope that one day he'd learn to avoid these problems, but for a smart man, he could be annoyingly oblivious when it came to his effect on women.

Nick cupped the back of my head with a hand and brought his mouth down on mine. Which should have been hot, but it felt like I was making out with my brother.

Had the women left yet? If not, I'd need to switch to plan C, which meant hauling them out of the club by their hair extensions and dumping them in the river. Although judging by their overly inflated chests, there was a good chance they'd float.

"Gone?" I asked.

Nick nibbled my earlobe. "They disappeared a while back, but I was enjoying myself."

I smacked him on the backside. "Idiot."

Nick only grinned, and I dragged him back over to Tia. She hadn't moved an inch, but her mouth had dropped open.

"Just giving an old friend a hand. No need to look so surprised," I said.

"Uh, okay. It's just odd seeing you with anybody but my brother."

"I get where you're coming from, honey, but I'm sorry to say that's over. Your brother's a great guy, but I'm not the one for him. Our relationship was all kinds of screwed up. I hope one day he'll meet a sweet girl who'll give him what he needs, which is someone with considerably less baggage than I've got."

She pursed her lips for a second or two, thinking. "I'd like it if you guys got back together, but I understand if you don't want to."

That was what she said, but the wistfulness in her voice made my breath hitch. She still dreamed of happily ever afters. I knew they didn't exist.

"I'll always be there for you, though. You know that, right?"

She brightened a little. "Really?"

"Call me any time, day or night. There may be moments I can't answer because I'm in the middle of something, but if that's the case, I'll always phone you back. You can talk to me about anything."

"Uh, there is one thing..."

"Yeah?"

"Do you think if I asked him, Ryan would dance with me?"

"Way he's looking at you, honey, I think Ryan would do anything if you snapped your fingers. The only reason he hasn't is because I'm here, ready to chop off parts of him he'd quite like to keep if he does anything inappropriate."

"You wouldn't do that, would you?"

Bless her, she looked so worried.

"Maybe not to Ryan, but any man who hurts you, I'd make their life pretty miserable."

"Thank you. I think."

"Now, go dance."

Tia smiled and walked over to Ryan. I saw her talking and gesturing, and then they both headed for the dance floor.

I pulled out my phone and fired off a quick

message.

Emmy: Keep your hands above her waist or you're on surveillance duty for the next six months.

Ryan checked his mobile, then our eyes locked and his chin tipped up as he acknowledged my words. I knew he'd look after her. Ryan was a good kid, and Tia needed that.

"Come and dance!" Dan grabbed my hand and dragged me into the heaving sea of bodies.

Nick repaid my earlier favour by keeping eager men at bay, but my heart wasn't in it, and after a few songs I escaped back to the VIP room, now empty, thank goodness. Boy, I really was the life and soul of the party tonight. I knew I should have stayed at home. Even the tapas tasted like cardboard as I waited for the rest of the gang to come back.

"You okay?" Tia asked, red-faced and obviously buzzed.

"Fine. Just not really feeling it tonight."

But she was. I knew this because when she sat down, she did so on Ryan's lap. His arm stayed loose around her waist, and I noticed he was careful not to drop it any further downwards.

Good man. See? I trained them well.

"What's that?" Tia poked the top of my arm. One of Nick's girls had tugged a zip open, leaving my skin exposed. A multi-coloured skull glowed through the gap, and my lips curved into an involuntary smile.

"It's a tattoo. A special one that only shows up in black light."

"Why a skull?"

"It's a sugar skull. I thought it was cute."

Not only that, sugar skulls were a part of the Day of

the Dead, which was what I created when I was on form. My skull showed up under black light because it was under Black that my skills to create my own *Dia de Los Muertos* first emerged. The design was symbolic, but I couldn't tell Tia that.

And now, as the skull shimmered under the ultraviolet spotlight above me, I thought of my husband and knew where I'd be going the next day.

Luckily, Tia's attention was taken by her phone ringing. I glanced at the screen. What did Arabella want at this time of night?

Tia picked up and answered, "Hey, what's up?"

Then her face went ashen.

"L-L-Luke," she stammered. "I can explain."

CHAPTER 34

TIA LOOKED AT me, wide-eyed in panic.

Luke must have gone over to Arabella's and found Tia missing. Rats. My streak of bad luck was holding, and the cat was out of the bag. Our cover was blown. The beans were well and truly spilled.

"I'm just with some friends," Tia told her brother. "Yes, I do have friends apart from Arabella. No, not the same ones I used to hang out with." Tia screwed up her face. "No, I'm not taking drugs."

Tia held the phone away from her ear as Luke lost it and started yelling. I didn't catch most of it over the music.

"No, I'm not with a guy," she said.

Except Tia, what with being sat on Ryan's lap and all, sounded well and truly deceitful.

"It's just friends, honestly. No, I'm at one of their houses. The stereo's on really loud." More yelling. "I can't turn it down. Er, the remote's gone missing."

Ouch. Tia was such a bad liar it was almost painful. We'd have to work on that.

But not tonight. I reached over and took the phone out of her hand.

"It's Ash." Now it was my turn to hold the phone away. "For goodness' sake, stop shouting. It achieves nothing. Look, this is my fault. I called Tia earlier and asked if she fancied a night out with me and a few friends. She was planning a quiet evening with Arabella, but I encouraged her. I'm sorry."

"She's my little sister! What have you done, dragged her out clubbing?"

Luke didn't lower the volume, but our waitress held out a pair of earplugs on a silver tray.

"We are in a club, yes, but it's perfectly safe, and Tia's had one of us with her at all times."

"Clubs aren't safe. All sorts of bad stuff happens. There's sex, drugs, alcohol. Someone could have spiked her drink."

"Not in this club. The door policy's strict. Anyone even thinking of trying that would be out on their backside." With my boot up it.

"You don't know that."

"Yes, Luke, I do. You want to know why? Because it's my club, and I set the door policy. And as I hardly ever come here, but I'm in here now, the staff are all on their best behaviour. If someone so much as took a cough sweet this evening, they'd get questioned. Tia's had one glass of wine, which, I'll point out, is far less than I've seen her drink when you've taken responsibility for her."

That took the wind out of Luke's sails a bit. "Whatever. I want her home, right now."

"Fine. But just remember, this was on me. Don't punish Tia for something that wasn't her fault." I hung up and turned to Tia. "Gonna have to go now, honey."

"I know." She hung her head. "I'm sorry."

"I've called for a car," Bradley informed me, ever efficient.

"Thanks, Bradley."

"You want me to ride with you?" Ryan offered.

"Can he?" Tia asked me.

"Sure."

The journey back was quiet. Tia sat in the middle of the backseat, curled into Ryan, who had his arm wrapped around her shoulders. I stared out of the window, contemplating how I'd managed to mess things up yet further with Luke. In the game of Bad Girl Bingo, I'd managed to check off covering up a crime, lying to a teacher, and corruption of a minor all in one week. Go me.

All too soon, we drew up at Luke's home in Lower Foxford. I hadn't been there since the night of the kidnapping, and it was back to how I first remembered it—a peaceful mock Tudor mansion rather than a hive of crime scene activity.

Tia turned and gave me a long hug. "Thanks for sticking up for me tonight."

"That's what friends are for. Just pile everything on me. I'm already in Luke's bad books; a bit more manure slung at me won't make any difference. I'll get Bradley to send your artwork over to Arabella. At least you can pretend you did the project at her place."

"Love you, Emmy." Tia hugged me tighter, tears glistening in her eyes.

Apart from Dan when she was drunk, people didn't often tell me they loved me. In fact, the last person to do so had been Tia's brother, and I never did say it back. Emotion was something I didn't do well and now was no different. Words stuck in my throat.

I squeezed her back, breathing deep. "Take care of yourself, yeah? Call me when you can."

Tia gave Ryan a quick hug as well then walked to

the house, dragging her feet. Luke's silhouette appeared in the open doorway, hands on hips. Still angry. Great.

He moved aside to let Tia past, and I felt his glare, even though I couldn't see it. When the front door slammed behind them, Ryan tapped on the privacy screen and our car slowly pulled away. Another perfect end to an evening involving Luke.

Would the storm clouds hanging over us ever clear?

Chapter 35

I DIDN'T HEAR from Tia the following day. Or the next one. The day after that, a Monday, I got a text message from Arabella.

Arabella: Tia says thanks for her schoolwork. Luke's confiscated her phone and her laptop and she's not allowed to use the house phone. She's waiting for him to calm down and then she'll call you as soon as she can.

I fired off a quick reply.

Emmy: I understand—tell Tia to keep her chin up.

On Tuesday, I returned to the States. I had things to do there—some good, some not so good—and with no further news from Tia, there was nothing to keep me in England.

I couldn't wait to see Stan and Lucy, and Carmen called to say she'd organised a teppanyaki night. One of my regular clients also sent through a couple of interesting projects, and they'd keep me and my team occupied for a week or two. Not so enjoyable were the meetings with my accountants and investment managers—yawn—talking to my lawyer about Miriam, and dealing with paperwork.

Oh, and Alex was waiting for me to land, with bated breath and cracking knuckles.

The icing on the cake was my new tattoo, the one

I'd got on Saturday, which itched like poison oak as it healed.

I'd thought I couldn't sink much lower after the run-in with Luke last week, but Wednesday proved me wrong. Most mornings, the senior team met to discuss upcoming jobs, and today was no different. One look at Nate's face when I walked into the conference room and I knew there was something on the agenda he wished he could erase.

Still, he kept me guessing while he dealt with the mundane stuff.

"Come on, spit it out," I said when he umm-ed and aah-ed then launched into a detailed account of an elderly widow's missing cat. A cloned cat worth $25,000, and the old lady was a wealthy heiress, but a cat nonetheless.

Nate sighed and fiddled with his tablet. "Okay, so we've had a request in from the CIA. They want a team, meaning Emmy, to go into Syria and look for evidence the Syrians are building chemical weapons they claim not to have."

"Isn't that the same brief they gave us a few weeks back?" I asked, recalling the request I'd knocked back just after I returned to Blackwood. "The one that was more of a suicide mission than a spying job?"

"Exactly the one. Except now there's a new twist. After you blew them off, the CIA sent their own team, which has now disappeared. So the job's gone from looking for weapons to looking for weapons plus hostages if they're lucky, bodies if they're not."

"From the way the Syrians treat their hostages, I'd say being dead was the better option. Why can't the CIA send their own people, being as they seem to think this mission actually has a chance of being less than a total disaster? A sentiment I have to say I don't share."

"The CIA already sent their best team."

"So their best team couldn't do the job, and now they want us to sort out their mess?"

"Emmy, they already sent their *best* team."

Oh. My blood drained to my feet as I realised what Nate meant.

"Jed?"

"Jed," he confirmed. "Plus one other, a guy called Phillip Farrow."

Now I didn't know Phillip Farrow. But I knew Jed. And Jed's bosses at the CIA knew I knew Jed. And as they knew a lot, even if it wasn't quite as much as they liked to think they did, they likely knew how well I knew Jed.

So now they were asking me to go into Syria to find him and complete their job while I was at it. Manipulative little... I had to hand it to them. It was something I'd have done myself.

"So..." I started.

"You're not doing it, Emmy," Nate jumped in.

"That's got to be a decision *I* make, Nate."

"You've already made it. I saw it on your face the second I mentioned Jed."

"So you understand there's not much you can do or say to change my mind."

"Unfortunately, yes. But it doesn't mean I won't try. You've only been back a few months, and without Black here your head's not in the right place."

"I know as well as you do I'm not playing with a full deck at the moment. But I'm still going."

"I'll come with you," Nick said.

Nick's proposition meant he was literally putting his life on the line for me. But I had to turn him down.

"No, Nick. Not that I don't appreciate your offer, because I do, but that's not a part of the world you're used to operating in."

"Who do you want, then?"

"Logan Barnes, if he agrees to it. Plus the support of everyone around this table because I'm going to need it."

"Goes without saying that you've got our support, Emmy," Nate said. "That doesn't stop us all wishing you wouldn't go."

"I have to."

And not only because of Jed. When I started working with Black, he showed me I could make a difference. Some of the things I did, although unpalatable, would ultimately lead to a greater good. If I gathered information on weapons the Syrian regime didn't want people to know about, the world could act. Would I trade my life for the potential to save many? In a heartbeat. It was why I existed—I'd just got lucky so far.

Nate knew that, and he sighed as he hit a button on the intercom.

"Someone find Logan, please."

And that was why, a little over a week later, I sat in premium economy eating shrivelled peanuts as the plane descended into Damascus.

"Want one?" I offered the packet to Logan.

He mock-shuddered. "I can only stomach those

with beer."

What I wouldn't do for a pint. We were off alcohol until we got back, not that it was easy to come across in the Middle East, anyway.

The first miracle befell us as the ageing plane landed in one piece, and the second happened when the rickety luggage carousel cranked into life and all our bags appeared on it. Logan picked up the hefty case holding his cameras. We'd travelled under the guise of freelance reporters, both on French passports. Logan had his French accent tuned to perfection, and it did squishy things to my insides just listening to him. I'd already made him read the weather report twice.

Of course, flying commercial limited us somewhat in the weapons we could bring. The knives hidden in our suitcase frames would have to serve us until we sourced something better. The CIA had promised their support—I'd have settled for nothing less seeing as it was them who'd messed up in the first place—but I never completely trusted them. On past experience, I'd found the CIA looked out for the CIA and screwed everyone else. I'd sent them a shopping list two days ago, but whether they delivered any of it remained to be seen. I certainly wasn't holding my breath.

The hotel we spent the night in claimed to be five-star, but turned out to be five-cockroach. Logan and I took it in turns to keep watch, and as the call to prayer echoed off the battle-scarred buildings the next morning, we packed up for the next stage of our journey. At least our CIA contact had turned up with just over half of my requests. I felt happier with a gun under my baggy shirt.

The driver of the decrepit taxi hunched over the

wheel, listening to crackly pop songs the whole way to Homs. Occasionally he sang too. I should have brought those earplugs from Black's along.

"Home, sweet home," Logan muttered as the car pulled up outside the dilapidated apartment sourced by the local CIA station chief.

I wafted exhaust smoke away as I pulled my kit out of the trunk. "This is luxury. It's got a roof and everything."

Plus two lumpy mattresses, a hotplate I wouldn't have dared to turn on even if the electricity worked, and a whole variety of insects. If it flew, climbed, crawled, or scuttled, there was a specimen. An entomologist's dream.

"Look on the bright side," Logan said. "If we get hungry, we can fry them on the windowsill."

No, there was no air conditioning either.

We dumped the bags inside, careful to keep anything valuable with us. The rusty padlock on the door wouldn't keep anyone out. The sun beat down on us as we stepped into a war zone just feet from the front door. No matter how many denials the government issued, there was no mistaking the reality.

A tiny child ran up to me, hand out. I placed a few of the *livres syrienne* I'd brought for the purpose in his palm, which only attracted more kids. I hated places like this. The West could donate pound after pound, dollar after dollar, but aid seldom got to where it was needed most. Handing out notes on a street corner made me feel better for an all-too-brief moment, but it was like trying to stop a leaking reservoir with my thumb. Pockets empty, I backed away with the mission on my mind. Helping to cut the legs off the so-called-leaders who'd brought this country to its knees was the biggest way I could make a difference.

Those youngsters might have tugged at my heartstrings, but the older ones got to me more. A twelve-year-old boy walked past with an AK-47 slung over his chest, pausing to look at me with dead eyes. Just one of thousands who'd lost their humanity.

Time to go to work, Emmy.

The base we were investigating lay four kilometres outside town. When we set out at dusk a couple of days after we arrived, I'd changed into a loose-fitting abaya, complete with veil and gloves. Logan walked alongside me, acting as my *mahram*, the male guardian who accompanied many ladies in the area. Our first two trips out there had been uneventful, preliminary excursions to see the lie of the land.

Tonight, we hunkered down at the boundary as we prepared to test their security. We'd seen roving patrols walking the fence line, but what else did they have?

As midnight passed, I threw a handful of stones at the chain-link fence then stuck my fingers in my ears as a siren wailed. A jeep pulled up and five guards leapt out, guns drawn. They spent several frantic minutes running up and down the fence line before their movements slowed.

"*Lashai*," the leader muttered. Nothing.

The group piled back into the vehicle again and took off back to the cluster of buildings in the distance. Reality TV and coffee beckoned, no doubt. Lucky people. My mouth watered at the thought of the latter.

The second time the alarm sounded, they rushed out again, still alert, but they didn't look around quite so hard. The third and fourth times, they left their weapons in the jeep, and I heard their muttered curses from my hiding place behind an abandoned car. That was the last we saw of them, and the eighth time I threw the stones, the alarm remained silent. Obviously, they'd come to the conclusion the system had malfunctioned and shut it off.

Perfect.

I beckoned Logan forward from the derelict building thirty feet behind me, and together we hopped over the fence. Sticking close, we crept towards the main part of the base. Only my eyes showed from under my niqab, my freshly dyed black hair hidden away. Dressed as I was, I blended into the background, almost invisible. I could have been the cook, the cleaner, the shadow you weren't quite sure existed.

As well as being deadly in all the right ways, Logan easily passed for native. A few days in the sun gave him a tan to make an Essex girl jealous, and he'd spent enough time in Syria to adopt the colloquial Arabic spoken by the locals. We'd liberated his Syrian military uniform from an unlocked car two days ago, and I'd traded food in return for his machine gun with a little girl who couldn't have been more than ten. The AK-47 wasn't in the best nick, but it still worked—we'd taken it for a quick test run in the desert. Nobody around here batted an eyelid at the noise anymore. Gunfire was engrained in daily life.

Keeping alert for signs of the enemy, we combed through the base, slowly and carefully, a section each night. When we got back to the apartment, we'd use our satellite phone to send the photos we took back home, hundreds of them. That base housed a lot of interesting stuff.

The fence alarm was still down on the fifth night. Clearly, maintenance crews had been on the list of government cuts. We snuck past the buildings we'd already checked, along a dusty track, and stumbled across the underground weapons facility. Quite literally. I almost tripped over the emergency exit, a trap door set in concrete alongside a ramshackle warehouse.

"Good going," Logan whispered once we'd shimmed the padlock and opened the hatch. "Do you want to go first, or shall I?"

"I'll go."

Lead from the front, that's what Black taught me.

The extra guards didn't present us with too much of a problem, but the sprawling maze of tunnels meant we didn't find Jed and Phillip until our seventh night of trying. I'd nearly given up by then, convinced they must be dead, their bodies either buried or left in the desert for the birds to pick at.

Which might have been the better option. When we found them, I almost wished we hadn't.

The two dingy cells, each no more than ten feet square, festered at the end of a darkened passage far away from the main storage area. Probably so the soldiers wouldn't be disturbed by the prisoners' screams.

I opened one door, and Logan took the other.

I got Phillip. And the only reason I knew I got Phillip was because when Jed limped into the room, his arm over Logan's shoulder, he slumped forward and choked out a string of profanities.

Words weren't enough. Words would never be enough.

Phillip had been crucified. Rusty nails pierced his palms and ankles, thin rivulets of congealed blood seeping from the holes and taking their natural course towards the floor. His head slumped towards his stomach, where his intestines spilled out through a ten-inch gash. Some monster had caught them in a bucket, and they lay swollen in a pool of blood and faecal matter. The stench choked me. Putrid fumes coated the back of my throat like a thin layer of fur, and I gagged as my stomach tried to evacuate. Flies rose around my head as I stepped forward with my camera, ready to take an identification photo. I hated to do it, but I'd been trained to complete a job no matter what. Work came first.

Work always came first.

Then Phillip coughed.

If I'd felt ill before, that quiet splutter multiplied my urge to throw up by a factor of ten. I hated this part of my work. The part that fuelled my nightmares. The part I needed to talk out with Black afterwards to keep my sanity.

"Leave," I told the other two.

"We have to do something..." Logan began.

"Leave."

Jed caught my eye and understood what I was about to do. He backed out of the room with Logan following.

I walked over to Phillip and caressed what was left of his cheek. If nothing else, he'd know at the end someone cared. "I'm so sorry," I whispered.

Then where the back of his neck was exposed, I drove my trusty Emerson CQC-7 through his brain stem. One twist of the knife, and the light in his remaining eye blinked out.

He wasn't suffering anymore, but that didn't make it any easier. *Turn off the emotions, Emmy.* I grabbed my tiny camera and snapped a burst of photos: face, torso, mangled extremities. *Don't think; don't think; don't think.* For a brief second, I'd been glad it was Phillip hanging there. Why? Because it wasn't Jed.

And I hated myself for that.

As I stepped into the corridor, a commotion sounded from around the corner, followed almost immediately by the *pew pew pew* of a rifle on full-auto. The horrors of the night were far from over.

Instinct took over, and I jumped over the body of a guard, lying on the floor as he breathed his last. Footsteps echoing off the concrete walls told me reinforcements were on their way. I stripped off the abaya so I could move properly and grabbed the dead guy's still-warm rifle from the stained concrete.

"Move," I barked at the other two. We didn't have time to waste.

Jed tried to hide his injuries, but every time he landed on his left leg, his face twisted up in pain. Logan half carried him as they ran, which left me to cover the back and sides. I sensed movement to my right and took out two soldiers before they raised their guns. One round each. I needed to conserve ammo. Up ahead, Jed shot another, using the hand not hanging on to Logan.

Things only got worse outside. Soldiers appeared from every direction, forcing us backwards. We ended up hunkered down between an old tank and a raised bank as the moon lit up the grim scene before us. I glanced back at the carnage we'd left in our wake. The nearest body was still twitching.

Fascinating though that was, I blocked out the sight and willed my brain to think.

"How much ammo have you got left?" I asked the others.

Jed dropped his magazine out. "Nineteen rounds."

"Seventeen," Logan said.

"Same."

I slammed my gun back together and flattened myself to the gritty earth as another barrage of bullets flew at us. A car was on fire, and in front of the wild flames, shadows danced as the guards milled around, plotting how to get us out of our hole or, better still, kill us in it.

We had something in common. I was plotting how to get us out of there too.

"You remember you once complained I never took you anywhere exciting?" Jed asked.

"I never said that."

"One night on the sofa when I was feeding you chocolate ice cream. You said, 'movie and junk food, what could be better?'"

"Huh? I enjoyed that."

"Oh. I thought you were being sarcastic."

"Guys," Logan interrupted, waving his arm at the trained killers in front of us. "Hello? Gunfight? Would you mind rehashing your failed love life later?"

"Sorry."

I got back to thinking about the situation we were stuck in. There had to be at least two hundred soldiers out there by that point, so unless they helped us out by lining up four deep, we didn't have enough bullets to go around.

Jed was injured, and despite his sense of humour

being intact, his body wasn't. The sharp angles of his jaw hadn't escaped me, nor had his hipbone digging into my side. He'd been starved. How much use would he be when the Syrians started shooting? He'd fight all right, to the death, but death might come sooner rather than later if I didn't come up with a decent plan.

Our only advantage was that they didn't know who they were up against. The troops were currently being cautious, waiting for us to make the first move. Their patience wouldn't last, though. We didn't have long.

I looked to the heavens for inspiration, and amazingly, it came. In the bank above my head, a black opening yawned from the gloom. Some sort of pipe? I plastered myself against the dirt and stood on tiptoe. The mouth gaped at me. Maybe it was part of an old drainage system? I hadn't seen it on any of the maps I'd studied, and where it went, I had no idea. But I was about to find out. I whispered my plan to Jed and Logan.

"You're crazy, but what's new?" Jed said.

Logan just rolled his eyes, the whites glinting in the moonlight, but they both knew we didn't have any other options. Either I could try to find a miracle, or we'd die together.

"Help me up?"

Jed leaned over and kissed me roughly, desperation in his lips. Was that a final goodbye? Please say it wasn't. I could still taste him as Logan squeezed my hand in a silent show of support then gave me a boost into the pipe.

Welcome to a new nightmare...

CHAPTER 36

A FEW FEET in, the pipe curved to the right and my world turned pitch black. Something skittered over my leg, and I resisted the urge to swipe at it, not that I had the room to sit up even if I wanted to. As I got deeper, the muffled gunfire outside faded. Would this be my tomb? I carried on crawling through pools of fetid water, pulling myself forward on my elbows, deeper into the unknown. How far did this duct go, and more to the point, what would I find at the other end? Was it leading me away from the nightmare or closer to the inferno?

While I inched along, I had plenty of time to contemplate what on earth I was doing there. Why, when my bank accounts ended in more zeros than those of some countries, was I slithering through rat pee when I could be having a pool party or shopping in Harrods? Why was I dodging bullets when I could be eating lunch at a country club or trying to stay awake at the opera?

Then it hit me. Because it made me feel alive. I may have been in some dismal sandpit with half an army trying to kill me, but adrenaline ran through me in a way it hadn't since Black died. Danger called to me like a siren, and I couldn't resist her lure.

A dim glow broke the gloom ahead as I reached the

end of the pipe. So much for this being the easy option. A metal grille blocked the exit, and moonlight taunted me from the other side. Once upon a time, I might have felt claustrophobic, but Black had foreseen that and wedged me in enough small spaces over the years to tamp down the sense of panic that threatened to take hold.

I took a closer look at my nemesis. The thing went from one side of the pipe to the other with barely an inch around the edge. I grabbed it and gave it a shake. It rattled, and the coating of rust scraped at my fingers. The grille had been there for a while.

I wriggled around so I was pointing feet first and slammed both boots into it once, twice, three times. The sound of Syrian guns covered up the noise I made, but I feared for Jed and Logan. Then the grille started to give. I kicked it again and again, the impact jarring up my spine, and finally—finally—it plopped onto the ground. I breathed a sigh of relief and clambered out, dropping down ten feet or so onto sand.

I'd emerged into a deserted compound. Three hundred yards away, fires still burned where the hostiles focused on the excitement I'd left behind. A jeep sped past on a rutted road just ahead of me, and I ducked back into the shadows. Judging by the soldiers' excited shouts, Jed and Logan didn't have long left. I needed to cause a distraction.

Something big.

Weapons became a priority. I couldn't do much with the handful of rounds and the single knife I had on me. A row of abandoned trucks rusted into the sand on my left, and twenty feet to my right sat a low building, beige paint peeling from its walls. I jogged over to it.

The padlocked door and lack of windows indicated some sort of storage unit. More interesting was the plastic lawn chair abandoned outside the door, fresh cigarette butts scattered around its legs. I'd bet my Aston Martin there would usually be a guard sitting in it. He'd gone to watch the Jed and Logan show, no doubt.

Good news for me. If the building contained something worth guarding, it was something worth having. I just hoped that whatever it was would prove useful in my current situation.

I made short work of the padlock with the set of picks I kept on my belt, silently thanking the locksmith Black had hired to refine my skills as a teenager. The building was as dark as the pipe, and I risked flicking on a flashlight once the door closed behind me.

Well, hello Christmas.

My grin grew so wide my jaw cracked. Guns lay everywhere. Big guns, little guns, fat guns, thin guns. It would have given any good redneck a hard-on. I pried open some of the crates stacked at the side then hit the jackpot. A Stinger. A freaking Stinger missile. I was pretty sure they weren't supposed to have that, but it didn't matter. They wouldn't have it for much longer.

I picked a couple of guns from the selection—a Heckler and Koch assault rifle and a Glock Model 17— plus the ammo to go with them, and put them quietly by the front door. Then I went back for the Stinger, snapping a quick picture of the serial number before I picked it up.

Now, I'd never fired one of these before, but I knew the theory, thanks to Carmen, who was somewhat of an expert on anything that went bang. Time to test it out.

I hauled the Stinger to the exit and inserted the coolant unit into the handguard, praying the batteries still worked. They were notorious for failing. The display lit up, indicating it was good to go. So far, my luck had held. I peeked around the door, noting the guard was still AWOL, then hefted the missile onto my shoulder. A once in a lifetime opportunity. If I did the Facebook thing, that would have made a great profile picture.

Hmmm, where to aim? Decisions, decisions. I picked a building behind the circling guards, to the far side of the spot where Jed and Logan were hunkered down. If I hit that, I'd have a clear run to get back for them.

I took out my phone, still miraculously intact at that point, and dialled Logan. On this operation, we didn't bring proper comms gear because if we'd been caught with it, it would have been a little hard to explain. We'd decided the cons of having it outweighed the pros, although now, as I juggled the handset and the missile, I was beginning to rethink that.

Logan picked up immediately. "Tell me you have a plan."

"Sure do. Keep your heads down."

I held my breath and fired.

Then watched in fascination as the heat-seeking missile decided that it didn't like the building I'd aimed at and swerved off to the right. It flew on its own path towards a squat warehouse right behind the guards, closer to me than I'd planned.

I dove for cover.

An ear-splitting blast shook the earth, followed by a fireworks display, Syrian style. Holy shiitake mushrooms. The Stinger had hit an explosives store, judging by the mess, and screams mingled with the whiz and pop of various armaments going off as flames leapt high into the night sky.

Well, the good news was the Syrian soldiers no longer seemed to be too concerned with Jed and Logan, from what I could see. They were occupied with trying to put themselves out because quite a lot of them were on fire.

The bad news was the wall of flame blocked my route back to Jed and Logan.

The unmistakable smell of burning flesh filled the air, mixed with the fumes of melting plastic. It got into my throat and made me gag as I dialled Logan again.

"Uh, that went a little more boom than I expected."

"No kidding. Glad you told us to keep our heads down. A fair few of the Syrians have lost theirs."

"Are you both okay? Can you escape?"

"Yes, and I think so."

"Good, just get out. I'll meet you back at the apartment. Uh, I'm gonna have to go. I think they've realised where the explosion came from."

"I'll help you."

"You will not. You're taking Jed and leaving."

"But—"

"Or I'll come back and murder you myself."

I dove sideways as someone shot at me, and the phone went crunch as I landed on it.

Oh, sugar honey iced tea.

I ran, shooting at the two men chasing me as I went. Thankfully my aim proved more accurate than theirs because I made it into an aircraft hangar and they didn't.

A pilot in full flight gear stood on the wing of a plane, watching the carnage outside through a grimy window. I took him out with one to the head before he could form a thought. He tumbled from his vantage point and landed in a heap on the concrete.

My priorities had changed. If Logan did as instructed, and he'd freaking well better have, he and Jed would be almost back at the fence by now. Without having to worry about saving them, I needed to switch my attention to staying alive myself. That meant getting off the base.

And it just so happened the quickest way out of there was sitting right next to me.

Judging by the suited-up pilot, I'd come across the Syrian equivalent of a "Ready-Five" aircraft. It would be flight-checked, fuelled, armed, and ready to go. All the Ready-Five needed was for someone to hop into the driver's seat.

My new best friend was a MiG-21, the most common supersonic jet in the world, flown by air forces on four continents for over half a century. An old design but still a good one. And thanks to Black's money and his indulgence of my love of flying, one I'd had the pleasure of piloting on the odd occasion.

My brain went into overdrive as I formed a plan on the fly, no pun intended. By my reckoning, I only had a minute or so. With so many people around, it wouldn't be long before someone noticed me skulking around in here, and then I'd be back at a disadvantage.

In the harsh glare of the strip lights mounted on the ceiling, I took a rapid inventory of the hangar, my eyes sweeping from one side of the grease-marked floor to the other. Two planes in the middle, tool chests on the left-hand side, a battered desk on the right. What was that on the desk? It looked like the pilot's dinner. And a crate of bottled water sat underneath it. I grabbed the food and as many of the bottles as I could carry and threw them into the nearest cockpit.

On my way to the hangar door, I shot out the tyres on the other plane. I didn't want anyone following me. Then I hauled on the dirty chain that would open up my escape route, and it slid slowly upwards, inch by creaking inch. They may have maintained the planes, but the buildings not so much. Once I had a path out into the night, I took a running jump and scrambled into the cockpit of my new best buddy. No ticket, no money, no passport. Just a wing and a silent prayer to Loki.

Please let this work, you devious git.

Then I fired up the engines.

As the plane's nose poked out of the hangar, another huge detonation rocked the base. I think even the CIA had underestimated what the Syrians stored there. In all the chaos, nobody noticed as the plane taxied over to the runway. They sure noticed as I took off, though. I mean, it's hard to miss it when a fighter jet whistles over your head. But since I'd stolen their Ready-Five aircraft, shot the pilot, and taken out the only other plane that looked good to go, I'd bought myself a few minutes. All they could do was shout at me and fire their baby guns pointlessly into the air.

Okay, time for the next phase of my plan, which wasn't so much a plan as desperation. The full fuel tank gave me a range of just over a thousand miles. I only needed to fly four hundred, according to my impromptu calculations.

The plane cruised at five hundred miles an hour, with a top speed of thirteen hundred. Flying that fast would kill the fuel consumption, though, so I settled in at six hundred. It took me twenty minutes to reach the Syrian border, and as I crossed it, the radio traffic started up between Syria, Israel, and Jordan. The words themselves were a bit crackly, but the gist of the message was "Land, now."

When I didn't land, they added "Or else" onto the end of it.

I carried on, of course, and sped up instead. One hundred and fifty miles to go. Seven minutes at top speed. I no doubt scared a few camels with the sonic boom, but I was long gone before I could apologise.

A ping from the radar alerted me to another plane behind, and I could see it gaining. I ran through a mental list of possibilities. The Israelis had F-15s and F-16s, both of which were faster than my MiG-21. The Jordanian air force had the F-16 too. Worse, the Syrians favoured MiG-25 interceptors, which flew at over two thousand miles an hour and scared the stuffing out of me. Whatever was following, I didn't want to be there when it caught up.

I kept a careful watch on my GPS coordinates, thankful I had a crazy good memory for stuff like that. I'd only ever travelled to my destination on the ground before, and I remembered watching the SatNav from the passenger seat of a battle-scarred jeep as Black drove.

The numbers cycled around, almost faster than I could follow. As I approached my target, I slowed hard, snatched up the food and water and clutched it to my chest, then pulled the ejection handle.

Kapow.

I shot up a hundred feet before floating back down again, and the MiG carried on over the horizon without me. I'd never had cause to use an ejection seat before—another first for me today—and I wished with all my heart I could tell Black about it. As far as I knew, he'd never ejected either, so I was one up.

As I neared the ground, the shadow of the chasing jet swooped over me, but it was too dark for me to identify it. When I saw the flame of a missile being released, I was pretty freaking glad I hadn't hung around to find out.

I hit the desert floor with a gentle bump. What a ride! I know I really shouldn't have enjoyed it, but that was the most fun I'd had in ages. Adrenaline pumped through my veins as my fingers fumbled to release the seat harness, and I stumbled into the sand with a loud whoop. Despite the horrors I'd left behind, I felt freaking elated.

I dragged the seat under an overhanging rock and waited for my heart to stop racing. While I might have felt ready to take on the world at that moment, I knew that was just hormones talking.

When my breathing had steadied, I took stock of the situation. Vast and inhospitable, the Jordanian desert was a rocky wilderness covering eighty-five percent of the country. The Bedouin who called it home eked out a living by herding goats, sheep, and camels, although many of the tribes had turned their backs on their traditional way of life, preferring the sprawl of urbanisation to the rigours of the vast, scrubby plains. At least I'd picked a good time of year to visit. The temperature swings weren't so great at the end of April.

I'd enjoy mid-twenties Celsius in the daytime with a drop to high single figures at night.

My biggest problem would be running out of water before I got to my final destination. You're probably thinking hey, you're an expert in survival, surely you can find water in the desert? Well, forget what you've read in those pocket guides about peeing into a hole or eating a cactus. It doesn't work. You'll use up more water digging the darn hole, and if cacti even grew in the Jordanian desert, which they didn't, I wouldn't fancy eating one because most of them were poisonous.

On the plus side, I wasn't worried about being found by whoever had been chasing me. The Syrians and Israelis couldn't simply waltz into Jordan to look, and if my pursuers were Jordanian, they either thought they'd shot me down or I'd crashed, and my plane was miles away from me now, anyway.

I leaned back in the seat and ran through the next stage of the plan. I knew where I wanted to be, and thanks to the GPS, I had a rough idea of my present location. The problem lay in the "rough" part. It was hard to be precise flying at several hundred miles an hour while trying to keep an eye on the enemy aircraft on your tail.

The night sky twinkled, and I stepped forward to get a better look. I was fairly sure I'd undershot, which meant I needed to head south. By following the first rule of desert survival, I'd move at night, which meant not only would I keep warm and conserve water, I'd be able to navigate by the stars.

The parachute flapped in the gentle breeze that swept over the dunes, and I used my knife to cut it free. I'd need it to give me shade in the daytime while I slept.

Sunburn may not kill me, but it could make life flipping uncomfortable.

Right now, I needed to get moving. All being well, I'd be able to cover a few miles before the sun came up. The aircraft seat came with a handy survival kit stowed in the base, although the contents depended on the locality, so it was potluck as to what I'd get. I rummaged through it and found a tiny torch as well as a compass that would keep me on track and glucose tablets to give me energy. But what on earth was I supposed to do with a pair of rubber gloves and a pencil?

I bundled the contents up in the parachute, together with the food and water. I wouldn't drink for the next twenty-four hours to kick my body into survival mode. Who knew how long I'd be out here? Eager to get on my way, I trudged off into the darkness, hoping Lady Luck had hitched along for the ride.

CHAPTER 37

LUKE SWORE UNDER his breath as he dodged around the portly grey-haired man ambling along the corridor. What was it about this place? Everything seemed to run at half-speed.

The meeting he'd just been in had lasted four hours when it should have been over in one, and when they'd served coffee halfway through, it had been both instant and cold. Public sector bureaucracy at its finest. He rubbed his temple with his free hand, and it throbbed. At least the paracetamol he'd taken half an hour ago was starting to kick in. Why did government procurement processes have to be so tedious? He'd been chasing this job for over two years, and nobody had made a decision yet.

Still, if they could clinch the contract to provide a new data protection system to whatever branch of the security service this was—they wouldn't even admit that much—all the sucking up, security clearances, and endless pitch documents would be worth it. It wasn't that Luke found the project boring—the firewall architecture fascinated him—it was the hoops that he and his staff had to jump through to secure the work that frustrated him.

The beady red eye of a CCTV camera watched him as he stepped into the lift, and he jabbed at the button for the ground floor three times before the doors finally closed. Did they program them like that? To waste a little bit more of everybody's lives each day?

"Can I take your visitor's pass, Mr. Halston-Cain?" the receptionist called as he emerged in the atrium. He never normally used his full double-barrelled surname, but every other person in this place seemed to, and he didn't want to be left out.

He handed the badge over to the overly efficient brunette and pushed through the turnstile. The lobby was packed, and when he looked through the glass doors to the street outside, he saw fat raindrops splashing against them. He'd have to wait in here for his car to arrive.

Luke fished his phone out of his jacket pocket and turned it on, but before he could call his driver, the screen lit up with a slew of incoming messages. He closed his eyes and groaned. Two days and—he quickly counted—thirty-six texts. If this kept up, he'd have to change his number.

He dialled his chauffeur. "Where are you?"

"Five minutes out, sir. Traffic's worse than I've ever seen it."

"I'll be waiting by the door."

The night before last, Luke had given in to Mark's insistence that he needed to get over Ash and gone out on his first date since she left. The girl, a colleague of Mark's girlfriend, had clearly looked him up on Wikipedia because she claimed to be an expert in every single one of his hobbies. Even bird watching, which he'd only put on there as a joke. He'd had a modicum of fun convincing her to perform the mating call of the Lesser Spotted Woodpecker in front of the restaurant's patrons, but then she'd started talking again.

And her squeaky voice hurt. It actually hurt, and that was when his headache had started.

At half past eight, he'd got out his phone, feigned a server-related emergency out of desperation, and made a run for it.

Then the messages started. He politely declined her offers to meet him at home later, cook him breakfast, or meet up for lunch, then simply stopped replying. She hadn't got the hint.

He sighed, feeling his stomach strain over his belt. He'd lost a few pounds before that horrendous charity thing, but he'd piled it all back on since. And last week, well, that had just sent him straight to the biscuit tin.

He'd stopped off at Mark's place, hoping for a beer and a game of pool while planning to check on his little sister at the same time. She'd called on Monday to say she'd be staying with Mark's sister to work on some school project, and he hadn't seen her all week. She used to drive him nuts, but he'd found himself missing her. Go figure.

But Tia wasn't there, and not only had she lied to him about that, she'd driven the knife in by going clubbing with Ash. Ash, his ex-girlfriend who'd turned lying into an art form then left him for a fiancé who cheated on her. She'd even had the gall to introduce the man to Luke before she hopped back into bed with him. Just the memory of it made him feel sick.

Ten days later, Luke was still fuming about Ash corrupting his sister. How dare she encourage Tia to go out drinking and who knew what else with her and a bunch of her cronies?

And when he called her on it, she'd accused him of

being the irresponsible one!

Luke had grounded Tia, of course, and taken away her phone and laptop. He'd even unplugged the house phones and hidden them in his sock drawer. She needed to understand she couldn't get away with lying to him. After all, she was only seventeen and even after being kidnapped, she was still hopelessly naïve. Luke worried that she'd get taken advantage of, especially by teenage boys. He'd certainly been no saint at that age.

He thought he'd done the right thing trying to protect her until he got home and found the note saying she'd gone back to live with the mother they both hated. That hurt more than he wanted to admit.

Luke's phone chirped, and the sight of another message from Charmaine almost made him throw the stupid thing against the marble-tiled wall. What did she want now?

Charmaine: I have a surprise for you! It'll be waiting for you when you get home!

In case he was left under any illusion as to what she might mean, she'd helpfully included a photo of herself dressed in a PVC nurse's outfit with a lacy red bra peeking out the top.

That did it. His thumbs flew over the screen.

Luke: I'm not interested. Stop—

He got no further as he hit a warm body and his phone went flying. A flurry of red hair blocked his vision, and the woman he'd knocked into tumbled to the floor. Luke barely kept his own footing as he tripped over a pair of long, pale legs, which ended in a pair of black patent stilettos that made his trousers tighten. In the other direction, the legs led to a pair of slim hips and a slender waist, and Luke's gaze lingered a little too long on a chest hidden by a demure neckline. Forcing his eyes upwards, he found a face that made Charmaine look like a Picasso painting.

"I'm so sorry. I wasn't looking…" He trailed off as he came to his senses and reached down to help her up. As she put her hand into his, he was already changing his plans for the evening. A takeaway and a DVD no longer held the slightest attraction. Thank goodness he'd brushed his teeth after lunch.

He pulled the woman to her feet, surprised when she stood eye-to-eye with him. Sure, she had *those* shoes on, but even so, she was tall. Their gazes connected for a split second before she looked down and gasped. The contents of her handbag lay strewn across the polished tiles, and she crouched to pick the mess up.

Luke bent to help her, and their foreheads met with a bump.

"Ow!" Her hand flew to her brow.

Once again, Luke tried to apologise. "I really am sorry. For knocking you down and for walking into you in the first place. I wasn't looking where I was going."

"It's all right, these things happen. Karma's out to get me today."

Her American accent caressed his ears. And those lips! Luke was already imagining them wrapped around things he shouldn't.

"I'm sorry," he said again, lost for words.

"D'ya know what this chaos is?" she asked, looking around.

"Tube strike. It was all over the news earlier."

She swore under her breath, the words sounding foreign coming from such a beautiful creature.

"Nothing's running at all?"

Luke shook his head as a cacophony of horns sounded from outside. Gridlock didn't bring out the best in people.

The woman fumbled in her bag. "Where's my phone?" she muttered.

Luke spotted it under a chair and picked it up. "It's cracked. I'll buy you a new one."

"Don't worry about it. As long as it works—I need to call for a car."

Luke was desperate to make amends. "My driver will be here in a couple of minutes. Can I give you a lift somewhere?" Anywhere. Her place. A restaurant. A hotel. His house, if he managed to hit the jackpot. Could he convince her to shed that dress?

"I don't want to put you out."

"It's no trouble."

Luke had always prided himself on looking after the women in his life. He'd treated them well, been interested in their feelings, and got to know them before taking them to bed. And look how that had worked out.

He'd never tried the "wham, bam, thank you ma'am" approach before, but Rob assured him it worked. What better way to get over Ash than to replace her with an upgraded model?

And there was something about the redhead in front of him that made his head go funny.

She took another look outside. Two men squared up to each other, ready to come to blows over the only black cab in sight.

"Really, it's okay," she said. "It was just a little spill, and I can call for a car myself. I should have done that in the first place, but the Tube's usually quicker."

Luke saw his chance slipping away. "I insist. I promise I'm not a serial killer or anything."

He tried to lighten the mood because, for a beautiful woman, she looked incredibly sad.

"I'm not worried about that," she replied, lips flickering into what Luke hoped was a smile. "If you're able to give me a lift, it sure would save me a lot of time."

"No problem. Follow me."

Luke's car drew up seconds after they reached the front of the lobby. He wished he had an umbrella to hold over the redhead as they dashed through the rain to his black limousine, but he'd forgotten to bring one. He wrenched the door open as they reached the vehicle and helped her into the back. Her skirt rose as she slid into the leather seat, and Luke could barely drag his gaze away from her legs as he climbed in beside her. She gave the driver her address, then Luke wound up the privacy screen.

"So," he said, trying to break the ice. "Why are you having such a bad day?"

Men were supposed to ask things like that, right? It made them seem caring. He'd lost his touch lately, and he needed to get it back.

Her forehead crinkled with worry lines, and she bit her plump bottom lip. *Adorable*. Luke felt a movement in the trouser department as other parts of his anatomy agreed with him.

"A friend of mine's gone missing, and I'm helping with the search. I'm worried in case we don't find her."

"Have you tried all the usual places? Friends, relatives?"

"It's not that straightforward. She was on, uh, vacation when she disappeared."

"Have you got the local police involved?"

"Unfortunately, the police in that locale aren't all that helpful."

"She'll probably turn up. Most people do. Maybe she just had one drink too many and wandered off?"

Mark had gone missing in France three or four years back, and they found him in the next village, clutching a bottle of Calvados with no recollection as to how he got there.

"We know she didn't do that. It's been days now." The redhead gave a sniffle.

Luke's chest tightened. Crying women scared him, and he was never quite sure how to handle them. The situation got worse when she turned to the window and swiped at her eyes, then her shoulders shook as the tears came.

Oh dear. Now what? Luke pulled a handkerchief out of his pocket and offered it to her. He carried one out of habit, drilled into him long ago by his mother.

"Th-th-thanks."

He gathered her into his arms and hugged her. All thoughts of a good time floated away on her river of tears, but he didn't know what else to do. She tensed at first, but after a few seconds, she relaxed and dropped her head against his shoulder. Like she was made for him, she fitted perfectly into his arms, and one arm wrapped around his chest and clutched at his shirt. She quivered against him as she choked back fresh sobs.

"I'm s-s-sorry," she wept. "I don't even know you, and I'm breaking down on you."

"It's okay," Luke reassured her, keeping his fingers

crossed the tears didn't get worse. "I'll take care of you."

He was surprised to find he meant it. Unable to resist, he dipped his head and kissed her hair. What was it about the sweet scent of vanilla that made him lose his senses?

She gripped him more tightly, and Luke felt her heart beating against his chest like the fluttering of a butterfly's wings. He had an urge to kiss her properly, but he held off. That wasn't what she needed right now.

The snarled-up traffic cleared as they got further from the river, and soon they were moving faster. It wasn't long until the driver interrupted through the intercom.

"We're here, love. Albany House."

Luke peered out onto the dimly lit street. They were on millionaire's row. Maybe even billionaire's row. These homes made his look like a Lego house. Who was this lady?

She extricated herself from his arms, biting her lip again. "I'm so sorry. I don't know what came over me. I've never broken down on a complete stranger before."

"Luke," he said.

"What?"

"Luke. That's my name. I'm not a complete stranger now."

"Oh. I'm Mackenzie."

An awkward silence ensued as they waited in the car outside Mackenzie's house, Luke's arms still around her. Much to his embarrassment, he couldn't help stifling a yawn, which seemed to spur her into action.

"I guess I should go inside," she said, reaching for the door handle.

"If you need someone to talk to, I can lend an ear."

"You're tired. I'm sorry for keeping you up."

"It's been a long week. I'll get some coffee on the way home, no problem."

She stilled a moment, as if turning over her thoughts before coming to a decision. "Uh, do you want to come in? I have coffee here. I could make you a cup as thanks for the lift?"

Something about the woman piqued his interest, and it was more than just her figure. A collision certainly wasn't how he'd usually meet a girl, and on any other day he'd have run a mile at the sight of tears, but he was drawn to her.

"I'd like that."

Mackenzie gathered her belongings and Luke picked up his briefcase, letting her climb out of the car first. It wasn't entirely altruistic—he enjoyed the view as she stooped to get through the door. After seeing her upset, he knew he shouldn't be thinking the thoughts he was, but something more primal had taken over his mind. Mackenzie's hips swayed in front of him as he followed her past the colourful winter pansies that edged the path, and he wished the lighting was a little better.

She unlocked the huge wooden door using a numbered keypad, a fingerprint scanner, and finally a key. A pang of jealousy hit him. He'd been toying with the idea of installing a similar system at his own house, but the forms were still sitting on his desk, shoved aside in favour of cat doodles as he'd wallowed in self-pity.

Why did she need such a complicated set of locks? Seriously, who was she? He'd barely had time to contemplate the question when she swung the door open and sashayed into the stark white entrance hall.

The first thing Luke saw was an ornate chandelier made from multi-coloured sculpted glass. By Chihuly, if he remembered correctly.

There weren't enough four letter words in the dictionary to convey how Luke felt.

Because he recognised this house.

Chapter 38

A CURSE SLIPPED out of Luke's mouth, and Mackenzie turned to stare at him.

"What?" she asked.

"I've been here before. This is Nick's house, right?"

She raised a perfectly plucked eyebrow. "Nick's house? Do you mean Nick Goldman?"

"I guess so."

"No, it's not his house. He just stays here sometimes. You know him?"

"Not exactly. I met him a month and a half ago. With Ash. I mean Emerson. She brought me here when my sister was kidnapped."

Mackenzie went whiter than the sofa in the hallway as she sank onto the soft leather.

"Oh my gosh. You're that Luke? Emmy's Luke?" Mackenzie stared at him, her green eyes wide. "I didn't ever see a picture of you. I never knew what you looked like. Nate dealt with most of the kidnapping thing while I was in California. Then when I got back, everyone was walking on eggshells around Emmy, avoiding the subject."

He crouched in front of Mackenzie. "Yes, I'm that Luke. But I'm not Emmy's Luke. We broke up."

"I'm not sure you should be here," she said, but she made no move to show him to the door.

He had to admit it was a little awkward, being in Emmy's territory, but at the same time, he wanted to give her a piece of his mind about what happened with Tia. She'd sped off the other night without so much as a word, and she needed to understand it wasn't acceptable to take Tia out to nightclubs.

"Where is Emmy? Did you know she tried to corrupt my little sister? She called her up and encouraged to go out clubbing of all things. Tia's only seventeen, for crying out loud."

"Emmy hardly called her up. It was the other way around."

"She told me she called Tia." Luke may have been hopping mad that evening, but he certainly remembered the conversation.

"That's not how it happened at all. Tia called her. In the middle of the night. Tia had a problem, and she rang Emmy for help. Ems got me up at three in the morning to track Tia's cell phone so she could find her."

"Tia did that?"

"You have any other sisters?" Mackenzie's voice held a hint of sarcasm, but that was better than tears.

"Well, no."

"And neither of them told you?"

"No. Emmy told me she phoned Tia on the Friday and asked her to go to a club with her. Why would she say that if it wasn't true?"

"I imagine she knew you'd be angry, and she was protecting Tia. She's like that. She looks out for people she cares about, which includes your sister."

"Are you sure?"

"Positive. Tia was here since the previous Sunday."

"What?"

Did nobody tell Luke anything?

"Tia was in a fight, I think. She had bruises on her face and a split lip. Emmy arranged for her to go to self-defence classes. I even took her to a couple myself. Tia's a sweet girl." Mack smiled, and Luke's breath hitched. "You must be proud to have her as a sister."

Luke pushed aside the feelings he didn't understand. "You met Tia?" He thought back to the note she'd left. "She won't even speak to me now."

"Sure did. I helped her with her science homework. Physics and chemistry. She had an art assignment as well, but Bradley worked with her on that. Did you meet Bradley? Anyhow, Emmy only let her go out that Friday once she'd finished all of her projects. For a treat."

Luke felt like his brain was working at half-speed. Perhaps he'd be at home on that government project after all. "Can we back up a bit? Bruises? Who gave Tia bruises?"

"Could you forget I mentioned that?" Mackenzie took half a step back. "You'll have to ask Tia if you want to know anything else."

"Look, if someone hurt my little sister, I want to know who. As her brother, I should do something about it."

"If something needed doing, then Emmy did it. Trust me on that. And if Emmy took care of it, she'd have made sure the person who hurt Tia got the message loud and clear."

Luke heard the pride in Mackenzie's voice when she talked about her friend, although he wasn't sure he shared her opinion.

"Then maybe I should ask Emmy exactly what she

did. Is she here?"

Luke watched in horror as Mackenzie's face crumpled, then she turned her back on him and began sobbing again.

"What did I say? Whatever it was, I'm sorry." Luke sat on the couch beside her and pulled Mackenzie into his arms, trying to work out what he'd done to upset her. Why did he keep messing things up with women lately? He never used to have this problem.

Then it came to him. "It's Emmy who's missing, isn't it?"

"Y-y-yes," Mackenzie choked out between sniffles.

"Well, hey, she'll probably come back. Last time she left, she was with me, wasn't she? And nothing really bad happened to her that time."

Except for when his sister got Emmy fired from her job. But Emmy had seen the good in Tia and got past that. Then Tia got kidnapped and Emmy brought in a team to hunt down the kidnapper, then she personally rescued his sister from wherever she was being held before single-handedly capturing her abductor.

Okay, so there was some good in Emmy, but she'd still cheated on him with Nick. The knife twisted in Luke's chest every time he thought about it.

"You don't understand," Mackenzie said. "It was different that time. This time she disappeared during a job. Right in the middle."

"What do you mean 'a job?'"

"I can't tell you. You probably know more about Emmy than most people, especially now, but I can't discuss work." Mackenzie looked at her watch. "I'd better make you that coffee then I can get back to the search."

"It's ten at night. What are you going to find at this time?"

She shrugged. "The internet never sleeps."

"You're going to look online?"

"It's what I do."

The woman was gorgeous *and* she loved computers? Luke was intrigued. "That's what I do for a living too."

"I know. We had an exchange about it back when we were looking for Tia."

"We did?"

"Yeah, you found out I'd been in your company system and thought I had something to do with Tia's kidnapping."

"Wait a minute, you're Diablo? The hacker? Of course, Emmy said your name was Mack. I just assumed I was talking to a guy." Worse than that, Luke had pictured Mack as a two-hundred-pound dude with too much body hair who hung out in a basement and lived on pizza and energy drinks.

"People do tend to make that mistake."

"So not only are you beautiful, you're also ridiculously smart."

"I don't really know how to answer that." Mack blushed and looked at her feet.

"You don't have to. I was just stating a fact." The number of women he'd met who claimed to be techno-whizzes but didn't have a clue what to do with a command prompt was into double figures, yet here was Diablo, who he suspected knew even more about the inner workings of the world's networks than he did. He wanted to find out what went on in her mind. Perhaps he could learn something? "Why don't I stay and help you? Two heads are better than one, and all that."

"It's not so straightforward. The work Blackwood does is confidential. I can't give a stranger access to that information."

"I'm not a total stranger—I know Emmy."

"But you've never worked with her."

"Couldn't you deputise me or something? Or make me sign a non-disclosure agreement? I'm not about to start blabbing your secrets."

"We don't deputise people. Blackwood's a private company." Mack leaned back on the sofa and closed her eyes. "But truthfully, I could do with some intelligent help. There's so much I need to look through, and I've already spent three hours today trying to break through a single firewall."

"Which one?"

She paused for a few seconds before whispering, "The Jordanian defence department."

"I did that one last year. They might have changed it since then, but I doubt it. Too expensive."

She stared at the wall beyond him as she came to a decision. "I'd have to ask Nate and Nick. They're in charge in Emmy's absence."

Nick? Fantastic, just who he wanted to see. He was tempted to make an excuse and leave, but his intrigue over Mack won out. Luke rarely worked with a partner, but a collaboration with Diablo promised to be a fascinating experience. "Well, call them up, and we can get started."

Mack led the way into a ground-floor control room that was part-NASA, part-Fortune 500. One entire wall was covered in video screens.

"This is a mini replica of our operations centre at

Blackwood House. If there's an issue there, we can switch everything over here and carry on functioning without missing a beat."

It made Luke's home setup look like a teenager's bedroom. "Very impressive."

"Wake up," she commanded. Monitors and consoles whirred into life as she turned to Luke. "Many of the systems are voice controlled, and we also use biometric security to prevent unauthorised access." She took a seat at the centre desk. "Call Nate."

Seconds later, a tanned face popped up on the screen, its features arranged in a scowl. The caption at the bottom of the picture told Luke it was 5:00 p.m. in Richmond. This had to be Nate.

"Anything?" he asked.

Mack's shoulders dropped. "No, you?"

"Nothing. She's gone without a trace. What did the French say?"

"They're looking, but none of their people on the ground have heard anything about a woman being killed or held hostage. Just a lot of rumours about the explosion."

"Who's that behind you?" Nate caught sight of Luke lurking on the edge of the picture.

"Uh, it's Luke. You know, Luke Halston-Cain? I ran into him at Sector 8. Public transport was in chaos, and he gave me a lift back here. I, uh, mentioned Emmy's missing, and he's offered to help with the search. I could really do with an extra pair of hands."

"He's a civilian."

"I know, but..."

"But what?"

"We've got no time, Nate."

"He the genius hacker Emmy seems to think he is?"

"From what I know, yes."

On the monitor, Nate rubbed his temples. "I can't believe I'm even considering this."

"We need all the help we can get, and he says he'll sign a non-disclosure agreement."

"That's just paper. Luke, do you give me your word you'll keep your mouth shut if we let you in?"

"Absolutely."

"And you understand that if you don't, I'll hunt you down myself and the outcome of that wouldn't be something you'd enjoy?"

"Yes, sir."

"Then welcome to the team. Mack'll fill you in. She's right—we need whatever assistance you can offer."

Nate signed off, and Luke took a seat next to Mack. "Go on then, what happened?"

"Okay, so Emmy took a job in Syria for the CIA. A dangerous job, too dangerous, and she shouldn't have done it. She knew she shouldn't, even admitted it, but she went anyway."

"Why would she do that?"

"Because part of the task involved searching for two men who'd disappeared attempting the same mission, and one of them was an old friend of hers. She said she couldn't just leave them there."

"And what happened?"

"She took one other person with her, a former special forces guy called Logan. They were looking for evidence of chemical weapons on a military base, and they found it. Then they found the hostages. They couldn't save one of them, but the other made it back with Logan. Emmy didn't."

"Why not?"

"They got spotted as they left, and a whole company of Syrian army troops pinned them down. Jed had a broken leg, so Logan stayed with him while Emmy crawled through a pipe to escape. She called Logan to say she had a plan to distract the soldiers, and then somehow she blew up the whole place."

Mack couldn't be serious? Luke looked for a sign she was joking, but her expression didn't change. One person couldn't blow up a whole military base, surely? And not Ash. She'd struggled to bake a cake without it collapsing in the middle.

Mack saw his disbelief and answered his unspoken question. "No kidding, she levelled it. They saw the explosion from space. She spoke to Logan one more time and told him to get Jed out of there, but the line went dead in the middle of the conversation. According to Logan, the troops took off towards the other end of the base, and there was a whole lot of shooting. Nobody's seen or heard a thing from Emmy since."

"So you think she's been captured?"

"Either that or killed. And after what they did to Jed and the other guy who didn't make it, being held prisoner by the Syrians is not something that bears thinking about."

"Could she have escaped?"

"Anything's possible with Emmy, but this all happened six days ago and there's been radio silence. We reckon she broke her phone, which isn't a surprise because she destroys every phone she gets her hands on, but if she was free and able to, she'd have begged, borrowed, or stolen another to let us know she was safe."

"What's our plan? Look for anything in Syrian internet traffic that refers to a prisoner or a woman being killed?"

"Exactly. So far, we've found nothing, but that doesn't necessarily mean much because they kept quiet about Jed and Phil too. From what we've heard, they're writing the explosion off as an accident with a munitions store."

"And if we don't find anything?"

"Nate and Nick are organising a team to go back to Syria, but if they do have Emmy, they'll be expecting us, and it's got the potential to turn into a bigger bloodbath than it already has."

With that hanging over their heads, Luke pulled his laptop out of his briefcase and Mack flipped open the lid on hers. Side by side, they hacked, hunted, and translated until the early hours of the morning.

All to no avail.

Eventually, Mack slumped forward onto the desk and Luke yawned until his jaw ached.

"We need sleep," he said.

"I know. But I feel awful going to my bed when some psycho could be torturing Emmy on the other side of the world."

"You can't help her if you're snoring on your keyboard."

"I know." She gave a resigned sigh. "MI6 has agreed to help search, and I've got a meeting with them in the morning. I need to stay awake in that. And I don't snore."

Luke pushed his chair back and got up, stretching his arms out above his head. Mack looked as if she hardly had the strength to move. Unable to resist, he scooped her up and carried her over to the lift. She let out a little squeal then relaxed in his arms.

"Which floor?" he asked.

Mack reached out and pushed the button for the second.

Following her directions, Luke found himself in a room decorated in eggshell blue with a large, comfortable-looking bed against one wall. He walked over to it and lowered her gently onto an intricate quilt decorated with birds.

"Do you stay here a lot?" he asked.

The room looked lived-in, not something reserved for guests. The furniture matched perfectly, artfully made in distressed wood that didn't go with the rest of the house. Tubes of make-up littered the dressing table and clothes were folded over the back of a chair. Luke took a closer look at the pile of magazines on a low table by the window—*Wired, Cosmopolitan, The Linux Journal*, and something on arts and crafts.

"I spend most of my time in the States, but I come to Europe once a month or so. Emmy and Black always wanted us to feel at home here, so I decorated my room how I like it. My grandmother made the quilt." She smiled as she looked down at it. "It reminds me of my real home."

"Where's that? And who's Black?"

"I'm Texan, born and bred. Black was Emmy's husband."

Ah yes, the dead one. Another reminder of Emmy's darker side.

"I heard a rumour that Emmy did him in."

Mack rounded on Luke, hands on hips. "Even the

idea of that's ridiculous," she snapped.

He held his hands up in a gesture of conciliation. "That's just what someone said."

"Who?"

"A mate in the police."

"Well, it's not true." Fire flashed in her eyes.

Great. So far in his company, Mack had gone from crying to cross, and Luke wasn't sure which one scared him most. Time to go to bed before he put his foot in it again.

"Where should I sleep?" he asked, taking a step backwards.

She simmered down a little. "The room to the right of this one's empty. Use anything you want from the wardrobe or bathroom."

Luke found enough energy to clean his teeth with a spare toothbrush from the drawer under the sink, then he stripped off his clothes and climbed into bed. It was a king size, and the expanse of cool sheets stretched out on either side of him. He had to admit, he missed spending the night with a woman. In all his time with Ash, she'd insisted on sleeping in the spare room.

As he drifted off, he couldn't help thinking of a very different woman sleeping alone. He imagined her red hair spread over that pale blue pillow, those long limbs splayed on the sheets. *Cain, don't think about Mack that way.*

He'd never dated a redhead before, and with Ash in the picture, he didn't dare consider it.

CHAPTER 39

I STUMBLED OVER a rocky outcrop, losing my footing as part of the surface gave way beneath me. A bolt of pain shot through my ankle as I reached out, barely hanging onto a jagged ledge as I stopped myself from falling. Six days in the desert had slowed my reactions.

The agony in my ankle faded as a new throb started up in my hand. I looked down in fascination as blood oozed from my palm. On a normal day, it would have gushed, but dehydration left my blood thick and sticky. My heart struggled to push it around my veins, or at least that's what it felt like. Every beat vibrated through me, reminding me I was still alive, but not for long.

The sun blinded me as I stepped around a boulder, burning into my retinas as I tried to blink. Even my eyes were dry. Up ahead, a cliff promised shade from the heat to come, and I forced myself to keep going. Just a few more yards, then I could rest. Or die.

I'd had the same thought yesterday, but my body hadn't given up. Would today be my lucky day? I began to think that death was the better option. Anything would be better than...this.

I looked around at my prison—mile upon mile of emptiness. The only sign of human existence had been a discarded flip-flop a mile or two back. Why did someone leave a single shoe behind? A couple of times

I thought I saw people on the horizon, but nature liked playing tricks. The first time a rock formation confused me, the second it was a dead tree. At least I wasn't hallucinating completely. Right?

Black whispered in my ear, his breath making my skin tingle. "Don't give up, Diamond."

All very well for him to say. I spun around but he'd gone, floating away on the warm breeze that tormented me in my waking hours. It gave the illusion of coolness, but in reality, it robbed me of moisture and liquid was the only thing separating me from the Underworld.

I stared at the bottle containing the last of my urine. On day two, it had been pale yellow, the colour of a summer cornfield back home. Now it took on the hue of the setting sun, and it tasted disgusting. I allowed myself another sip, resisting the urge to spit it out, then fished the last glucose tablet out of my pocket. It'd take the foul taste away, but once I'd eaten it... Apart from a lizard I'd caught on day three, the packet of sweets was all I'd eaten since the crash. The waistband of my trousers gaped as it clung to my hipbones. At this rate, I'd be heading down the catwalk when I got back. No, not when. If. If I got back. Black always told me I'd find a way out of anything, but this problem left me stumped.

The cliff grew bigger until it filled my vision, and I looked for somewhere to hunker down for the day. Or maybe eternity, who knew? A soft patch of sand would be good, or a smooth rock. Anywhere out of the fast-rising sun.

What was that shadow? I stepped closer. A cave? I dropped to my knees and crawled inside, my eyes slow to adjust to the darkness as the hollow widened beyond the entrance. My hand hit something. What was it? I felt around the object, smooth, leathery, and covered in tattered cloth.

A body. A freaking body. Well, wasn't that motivational? The poor guy had lain here for years judging by the state of him. What was his story? Intrepid backpacker? Elderly Bedouin? Or, like me, just in the wrong place at the wrong time? Whatever, I'd be sharing his resting place for the next twelve hours. Perhaps his tomb too.

A thought struck me, and I crawled back to the entrance where I could see a little. If I died here, I should leave a message. Finally, I had a use for that pencil. On a pale rock face, I scrawled my initials just in case anyone found me. MB. As an afterthought, I added + CB 4EVA, choking both on my fat tongue and the memory of Black on our wedding day. Well, I'd be seeing him again soon at this rate.

I took one more sip of liquid, wrapped the remains of the parachute around me, and sank onto the floor of the cave. Whether I'd see another dusk was out of my hands now.

I blinked, trying to adjust my eyes to the gloom. Was I alive or dead? My back still hurt from my adventure with the ejector seat, and I reached out until my fingers touched my new friend. Yup. Alive. I wasn't sure whether to be pleased or disappointed.

I rolled onto my side until I saw the entrance to the cave. Orange light seeped in as the sun left for another day. Time for me to walk. Then again, could I be bothered? Soon, I'd have been searching the desert for a week with nothing to show for it but a handful of scrapes and a twisted ankle. Why not stay here? Sure, it may not have been five-star, but the company was good. Quiet, no endless chatter, just the way I liked it.

Except now he was screeching. For Pete's sake, shut up! I turned to give him a few choice words, but he reached out and caressed my face.

"Oi, get off me!"

He touched me again, and I flipped my knife out, ready to introduce the pair of them. Only his hand had gone again. I took a step forward. What was he doing?

Then it hit me. Literally. A bat! There were bats everywhere. Somewhere deep, I found a reserve of energy and leapt at the roof of the cave, plucking my prize down by its wings.

Saved. By freaking Batman. Who says comic books aren't real?

Within seconds, I'd drained the bat's blood into my throat. Then another, and another. In the last of the light, I took my booty outside and skinned it, swallowing down the good bits like a glutton at a Michelin-starred restaurant.

With food came strength, and with strength came sanity. For the next few hours, I killed and ate what I could grab, and drained the spare blood into my empty water bottles. The pile of bodies made me feel guilty, but I had no choice. It was them or me. And with Black's spirit coursing through my veins, I understood it wasn't my time yet. As the stars twinkled overhead, I set my compass south and started walking. I didn't want to die in this desolate patch of sand. After what I'd survived in my life, that would be insulting.

Black's voice rang in my ears with every step.
Never give up.
Never ever give up.

CHAPTER 40

THE TINNY SOUND of "I'm a Barbie Girl" blasted through the wall behind Luke's head, and he woke with a start. Was that Mack? If so, she had terrible taste in music.

The din stopped, and he leaned back on the pillow, but it started up again seconds later.

When Barbie wailed about being wrapped up in plastic for the third time, he gave up and swung his legs out of bed. The clock on the wall told him he'd had five hours sleep—that would have to do.

When he found Mack in the kitchen, her hair was wet, and she'd twisted it up into a knot on top of her head. Even without a scrap of make-up on, she put most other women to shame.

"Coffee?" she asked, and without waiting for an answer, she poured him a cup.

"Cheers. I'm already awake, though, thanks to Barbie."

"It's awful, isn't it?" Mack admitted sheepishly. "But I'm so bad at getting up in the mornings, I set my ringtone to a song I really hate so I'll answer it to make it stop."

"I suppose that makes sense."

"I sleep through almost anything. That's why I have the control room call me until I get out of bed, or I'd stay there all day."

Hang on—Blackwood ran a state-of-the-art, multi-million-pound control room, staffed with highly trained operatives, and Mack was using it as an alarm clock? Cute.

Then again, Mack really didn't look like a morning person, judging by the way she was stumbling around the kitchen. Luke figured he'd better lend a hand.

"Do you want me to make you some breakfast?" He wasn't an expert in the kitchen, but he could butter toast and scramble an egg.

She looked at her watch, a Tag Heuer on a slim, gold band. It complemented her eyes. "I've only got time for a bowl of cereal. The car will be here in five minutes to take me to my meeting." She rummaged around in a cupboard and pulled out four different kinds of muesli. "Ugh, it's all horrible."

Luke picked up one of the boxes and turned it over. "Toasted quinoa, chia seeds, and dried goji berries?"

"It's Emmy's nutritionist. He throws the good stuff out. I'll stick with the coffee."

"Maybe I'll have toast."

Luke opened the fridge, but when he picked up the seventeen-grain wholemeal brick inside, he changed his mind. Mack was right; coffee was definitely the way to go. It might help him to lose a few pounds, anyway.

Mack poured a gallon of milk into her own coffee then gulped it back and shoved the cup in the dishwasher. "Gotta dash." She gave him a little wave before disappearing out the door.

Left in the house by himself, Luke took the opportunity to have a quick look around. When he'd been here before, exploring had been the last thing on his mind, and he'd only seen a small fraction of the rooms. As he wandered the corridors, he soon found Albany House was even bigger than he first thought.

He saw few personal touches outside the bedrooms. No notes stuck on the fridge. No shoes lined up in the hallway. No books on the coffee table in the lounge. His thoughts turned to the house's owner. Emmy had proved to be an enigma. Who was she, really?

He'd only find out one way, and that was by finding her. After one more cup of coffee, he returned to the control room, ready to work. Mack had set him up as a user the previous day, albeit not with full access rights, so when he commanded the systems to turn on, they did.

The monitors spanning the wall showed live feeds of similar rooms the world over. He read the captions at the bottom. Paris. London. Los Angeles. Berlin. And Richmond. Luke groaned as he spotted Nick seated at a desk, head down as he stared at a sheaf of papers.

Should Luke just ignore him? Tempting, but sooner or later they'd have to speak. Might as well get it over with.

"Good morning," he said. Could Nick hear?

Nothing. He clicked on a speaker icon and tried again. This time Nick looked up.

"Morning, Luke. Nate mentioned you'd come in. It's been a few weeks, hasn't it? How are you doing? And Tia?"

How indeed? The truth was, Luke had avoided the subject. He didn't want to think about the kidnapper or the shadow that man had cast over his life and Tia's. The police liaison officer had called the other day to say they'd transferred the man to Broadmoor, which was probably the best place for him.

"I'm just trying to get back to normal."

Or as normal as things could be with Emmy involved. And now Mack. Her luscious face filled his mind again, and it took a second for him to realise Nick was speaking to him.

"Sorry, what was that?"

"I asked if Mack gave you a briefing?"

"Yes, she explained the situation. She wanted a hand getting into the Syrian military networks."

"We all appreciate any help you can give. Emmy seemed to think you were good at looking into places you shouldn't be."

"That's one way to put it, I suppose. I'm planning to carry on where Mack and I left off last night, unless there's anything else you'd rather I do?" Luke erred on the side of politeness. After all, who knew what Emmy had told Nick about him? Maybe she'd played them both.

"No, you get on with that. We've found no sign of Emmy after her phone cut out. Nate's been analysing satellite feeds while Mack's team's been searching through internet traffic. Dan's acting as liaison with various intelligence agencies, and I'm planning a possible rescue mission with Logan and Jed. Plus we've got another seventy or so staff supporting us."

"That's a lot of people."

"Yeah, well, it's Emmy, isn't it? Just give one of us a shout if you find anything, no matter how insignificant it might seem. We've got the manpower to run down every lead."

"Will do."

Luke worked steadily, but the translation took too

long. After persevering for a couple of hours, he stopped and re-jigged some of the language algorithms in his search program. It may have taken him ninety minutes, but when he settled back into the hunt, he found it worked much faster.

He left the chatter from the Richmond control room on in the background. Staff bustled back and forth, a hive of quiet efficiency. Despite the obvious tension, there were no raised voices, no tempers flaring. He couldn't help being impressed by the organisation.

At one point, he heard some of the men discussing Emmy's mental state. Nate and Nick were involved, as well as Logan and a guy with shoulder-length dirty blond hair and a large, greenish bruise spreading across his cheek. From his leg, encased in plaster and propped up on the desk, Luke assumed that was Jed.

"So, how was she doing?" Nate asked. "She admitted before she left that she still wasn't herself but insisted she'd be fine."

Luke felt a little guilty for eavesdropping, but curiosity got the better of him, so he turned the volume up.

"That was the strange thing," Logan said. "When we got to Syria, the old Emmy came back. There was none of that hesitancy or lack of confidence she'd been showing since Black died. She knew exactly what she was doing."

Jed confirmed that. "She took charge, got on with things. Even when she saw Phil, she did what she had to, no hesitation. It was vintage Emmy. I saw no issues with her performance at all."

"How do you think she'd hold up if she got

captured?" Nate asked him.

"Not sure. Nick?"

"She definitely wasn't right a few weeks back. Whether she sorted her head out enough between then and now to withstand the nightmare they put Phil through, I don't know."

"When did she last do a hostage drill?" Jed asked.

"With Black and Alex about three months before Black died," Nick said. "A full drill—four days. Sleep deprivation, starvation, stress positions, messing with her senses, torture, the lot. Alex was waterboarding her when I saw them. And Black put her in a picquet before that. She was doing fine, but she'd never have broken with Black there anyway."

"The question is, how would she do with him out of the picture?" Nate asked.

"Not sure. I'll have a chat with Alex and get his take on things."

When the men stopped talking, Luke ran an internet search to find out what a picquet was. He'd seen waterboarding on the news, and he thought that was horrific until the results for picquet popped up.

It had taken him several goes to get the right spelling, but when he did, he wished he hadn't. The gruesome mediaeval device involved tying one hand high above the victim's head, either by the wrist or by the thumb. They balanced on their opposite foot atop a rounded spike, not sharp enough to draw blood but definitely pointy enough to hurt. When the pain in the victim's hand got too much to bear, they'd transfer their weight to the foot until that too became unbearable. This shifting of weight continued until the victim confessed or died from the pain.

And Black had put his wife in one? Luke had no words. Only a monster could contemplate that. A sadist.

Until that point, Luke had felt many things for Emmy, but pity wasn't one of them. Now he felt a twinge of sadness as he thought of how she'd been treated, and guilt that he'd added to her problems.

This latest news spurred him on, leaving him more determined than ever to get to the bottom of what happened to her.

Chapter 41

LUKE DECIDED NOT to mention the torture parts to Mack. If she didn't know, he'd rather avoid upsetting her further. It might not be true, anyway. All he had was second-hand information, and Nick could have misunderstood the situation.

Mack came back a couple of hours later, carrying a bag from Starbucks.

"You're a genius," Luke said as she unloaded pastries onto a plate.

"I don't know about that." Her cheeks went adorably pink. "I just wanted some food that didn't taste of cardboard."

Luke cast his eyes over the selection of cakes and danishes. "You made a good choice."

"I only eat sugary food when I'm stressed. Normally, I'm quite good."

"You and me both. I need to diet, but I keep telling myself 'tomorrow.' How did the meeting go?"

"Dead end, for the moment." She stuffed half a maple-pecan twist into her mouth and chewed mechanically. "They've said they'll keep looking, but Syria's difficult right now."

Luke reached over and squeezed her hand, trying to show support. She stared at his fingers on hers, but didn't pull away.

"We'll keep looking too," he said.

They carried on through the day, but it was hopeless. Luke found nothing, and each time Mack sighed, he knew her luck wasn't any better. When his eyes started to ache, he pulled Mack back from her screen.

"What are you doing?" she asked.

"You'll end up with eye strain if you don't take a break. Sometimes a bit of time away from the computer shakes something loose. That's what I've always found."

"I want to look for Emmy."

"We'll just stop long enough for dinner. How about that? We could go out—"

"No time. Ruth will cook us something."

"Ruth's the housekeeper?" Luke had heard her vacuuming earlier. Not close. On one of the other floors.

"Yes, the housekeeper."

Apart from her sugar hit in the morning, Mack had barely eaten all day. Dinner was no different. She picked at the lasagne Ruth cooked for them, shoving it around her plate until it turned into an unrecognisable mush. Even the chocolate cake left out to tempt her had no effect.

Luke tried to keep her mind off things, sticking to safe topics of conversation like movies and computer programming, but it didn't work, and the subject kept coming back to Emmy. Luke decided he might as well try to find out more about her.

"I got a shock when I found out Emmy was...well... Emmy."

"I'll bet. She lived with you for what, two months?"

"About that. But I feel like I barely knew her at all."

"If it's any consolation, I've known her for nine years, and I haven't totally figured her out," Mack said. "I don't think anyone ever has. Except for Black, of course."

"Her husband."

"Husband, soul mate, best friend. I'm not sure she'll be the same now he's gone, even if she does come back."

"I suppose if he was here now, he'd be having an awful time worrying about her."

"That's the irony. He'd be the calmest out of all of us. I can picture him now, sitting in the control room, cool as ice, saying 'trust her, the brat is indestructible.'"

"He'd call his own wife a brat?"

"And a lot worse besides. But she gave as good as she got. It wasn't exactly a conventional marriage, but then again, nothing about Emmy or Black could ever be described as conventional. I mean, within a week of their first meeting, Emmy quit London and moved to the other side of the world to live with him."

Gazing at Mack, the idea of moving to the other side of the world to be with someone didn't seem that strange to Luke. Because he wanted to get to know her, and as she lived in America, he foresaw a considerable amount of travelling in his future.

Was that crazy? Probably, but the more time he spent with her, the more time he wanted to spend with her. Mack was sweet like candy. Nothing like the new Emmy, a little like the old Emmy, but mostly just Mack. He wanted to unwrap her, layer by layer, and find out what was hidden within.

"Isn't that romantic rather than unconventional

though?" he asked, getting back to the subject of Emmy's life. "It wouldn't be the first time a couple fell in love at first sight."

"I don't think there was a whole lot of romance involved. The first thing they did when they met was have a fight, then Black insisted she went home with him so he could patch her up."

"Patch her up?"

"She needed stitches. Black didn't come off any better, and Nate said that was the reason Black hired her. Not many people could have taken him on and not ended up unconscious."

"Hired her? So she moved to America to work for him? Not because she was in love?"

"I don't think she even liked him at first."

"But that must have changed, right? I mean, they got married."

"A couple of years later. But that wasn't out of love. Emmy wanted US citizenship and Black and Nate wanted her to commit to staying at Blackwood. So one night when they were drunk in Vegas, Nate suggested Black and Emmy get married, and they thought they might as well."

Luke choked out a laugh. "No big white wedding, then?"

"Not a chance. Emmy hates being the centre of attention."

"What's she really like? She was quiet when she lived with me, but I'm not sure how much of it was just an act."

"She's got so many different faces. You never know what she's thinking, and she can change her whole demeanour as if someone flicked a switch. One second she's devastatingly upset, the next absolutely furious, then she turns around and her face is completely blank, no hint of emotion there at all. It's freaky to watch. If she were in Hollywood, she'd win an Oscar. Black was very similar." Mack's expression turned wistful. "They understood each other."

"That must have been difficult to deal with."

"Not really. She's always ranged from quiet and a little detached to snarky as anything. But you couldn't ask for a more loyal friend. If anyone she cares for gets into trouble, she'll go above and beyond to get them out of it. Why do you think she went on this job in the first place? I'd never ever want to get on her bad side, though. Life can get very uncomfortable, or just plain short, if you annoy Emmy."

"That's just great." Luke closed his eyes and rubbed his temples. "I think I've annoyed her quite a bit lately. The last time I spoke to her, well, shouted at her, it was over the phone to chew her out for taking Tia on the lash."

"Don't worry about that. She got where you were coming from, and she said as much. She'd never fly off the handle over something so trivial. Besides, since she got back, she's been different. Less like a robot and more human."

"Is that a good thing?"

"I'm not sure. The old Emmy was cold as a Siberian winter, but I kinda preferred that to miserable Emmy. Who knows what we'll get if she comes back from Syria?"

Mack's face crumpled, and Luke took her hand as she struggled to hold herself together.

"If she's out there, we'll find her." He hoped he

could keep that promise.

A tear leaked down Mack's cheek, and he reached out and wiped it away with his thumb.

"It's us against a whole country. Sometimes, it seems like an impossible task," she said.

He pulled her into a hug, liking the feel of her slender arms around him far more than he should.

"We can still win."

In bed that night, Luke tossed and turned. Visions of Emmy lying beside him swam through his mind. He'd push her away, but then her face would morph into Mack's, and as he tried to pull her back again, she kept slipping away, just out of his grasp.

He got up and stared out the window. The view of the private park across the road looked almost the same as it did all those weeks ago when they were looking for Tia, but now he had a different kind of problem eating away at him.

Mack. He liked Mack. His head and his heart both knew it. Not only was she beautiful, but he could talk to her about his passion for computers, something he'd never been able to do with another woman.

The question was, did she feel the same? And if she did then what, if anything, was he going to do about it?

CHAPTER 42

SEVEN DAYS. SEVEN days and seven nights I'd been stuck in this sorry piece of desert. I know I always said I liked hot places, but now I was rethinking that. At that moment, I'd have sold my soul for a bat blood slushee.

I was annoyed because I was baking in my own skin. Annoyed because my boots were filled with sand and I had blisters. But mostly annoyed because if I didn't get to where I needed to be quickly, I'd die in this horrid bit of wasteland. My luck in the cave may have brought me a brief reprieve, but I was beginning to weaken again.

By late afternoon, my mind started to play tricks on me. Non-existent water shimmered on the horizon, and I'd seen Black at least four times. I couldn't complain about those visions, but when I reached out to touch him, he flittered further away, always out of reach. Bleeping hallucinations. And now there were camels. Camels and people. I shook my head, trying to clear it.

Then they came closer, and rather than disappearing like I expected, they solidified. Either I'd lost my marbles totally, or they were real. I'd never been happier to see a pair of gun-toting Arabs in my life.

"*Hal anti bikhair?*" one of them called, his accent harsh from years of living in this inhospitable environment.

Was I okay? No, of course I wasn't okay. I tried to roll my eyes, but they wouldn't cooperate. *"La. Ana 'atshaan."* No. I'm thirsty.

Their white robes identified them as Bedouin. They stared at this strange, dark-haired girl shuffling along in the middle of the desert, carrying half a bottle of blood and the remains of a parachute, like she'd dropped out of space. Which I suppose I almost had.

I'd pretty much collapsed by the time they reached me, but one of them crouched and held a canteen of water to my lips.

Thank you, karma.

I sipped slowly, resisting the temptation to gulp the water down. Black's voice in my head warned me of the danger of hyponatraemia, the low concentration of sodium in my blood, and I didn't want the sickness or seizures that could bring. A little strength flowed into my limbs, and I sat up on my knees.

"Man anti?" one of the men asked.

I wasn't about to tell them my name; not until I knew who they were. I shook my head and stayed quiet.

He tried a couple more times, but when I didn't answer, he gave up. Huffing under his breath, he motioned for me to get up on a camel. It knelt so I could climb onto its woven saddle. Then we set off, to where I didn't know, but the situation was a definite improvement on the state of things an hour ago.

Although they carried guns, that didn't worry me. Every kid worth his salt in these parts had an assault rifle of some sort, but they didn't tend to shoot random passers-by. In fact, the Bedouin were mostly peaceful and also bound by ancient customs to offer hospitality to anyone who requested it, even if they didn't like them all that much.

So wherever we were going, I'd get food, and with food would come strength.

As it happened, Lady Luck stayed with me, hitching a lift on the camel. Although I don't suppose her bottom was as raw as mine when I finally slid off the flipping thing. I liked riding horses. Camels, not so much.

We'd arrived in a tented village in the shade of a cliff, neat and tidy with a small oasis off to the side. The oasis I'd been looking for since I shot out of the plane over a week ago.

Thank goodness.

A few of the villagers came out to stare at me, children hiding behind their mothers and men staring me up and down. Then there was a commotion, and the small crowd parted as a man strode forward through their midst.

"Emerson?" the man asked, sounding a little surprised to see me. I couldn't think why.

"Hi, Salah. It's been a while, so I thought I'd drop in."

I'd first met Salah a decade ago when Black brought me to Jordan for my first bout of desert survival training. He'd been young, maybe twelve, when I found him slumped under a scrubby acacia tree, freshly bitten by a puff adder.

Being the good Girl Scout I was, I fished the vial of anti-venom out of my backpack and administered it before the symptoms got too bad. His father, and of course Salah himself, never forgot. We'd kept in touch over the years, and I stopped in to see him when I was in the area. Although usually my visits were slightly better organised.

"Emerson," he said again, reaching me and shaking my right hand with both of his. "How have you been? You look so thin." He turned to the waiting women and shouted in Arabic for them to prepare a feast.

"I've not had such a good time lately. Black died." Might as well get that out there.

He bowed his head. "I'm so sorry. He was a good man. So you're on your own?"

"Yes, just me. I need to ask you for a favour. Well, two actually. Firstly, can I borrow your phone? And secondly, I need to get back home."

"The second I can help with, but the satellite phone that you bought for me is not working. It will no longer turn on. Kaput, is that what you say?"

Great. Just great. Nate must be doing his nut, and I was desperate to know what happened to Logan and Jed. Did they get out okay? Escape would have been tough enough under normal circumstances, and with the state of Jed's leg, the situation had been even more messed up than usual.

And what if my team thought I was still in Syria? They'd try to come in after me, which would be not only dangerous but also completely pointless now I was hundreds of miles away.

But what could I do? Nothing right now but rest. I needed to save my strength for the journey home.

One of the women returned with a pot of sweet, spicy Bedouin tea, which she poured into tiny glass cups. Over that, and then a dinner of bread and well-salted goat stew, I worked out a plan to get home with Salah.

"I will send men to the town tomorrow to organise things."

"I need a boat to get across the Gulf."

"You want to go to Egypt?"

"Yes, to Dahab." The town lay west of Jordan and about sixty kilometres down the coast. It would be a long trip.

Salah nodded slowly. "For you, I will arrange it. Do you want to leave with the men?"

I shook my head. "No, I can't afford to spend time in town. I don't have any paperwork, and I'm not sure who might be looking for me. I'll need them to call a friend with a message, though."

"Very well. They will prepare the transport, and you can leave when it is ready."

As night fell, Salah provided me with blankets and a tent, and I got my first full night of sleep in almost a fortnight.

I woke feeling vaguely optimistic, but the morning brought bad news. Two of the Bedouin rode into the camp just after dawn to let us know there was a sandstorm approaching. Everyone scuttled around, tying things down and moving the animals to shelter as best we could. Within minutes, the winds arrived, kicking up sand everywhere and reducing visibility to zero. The storm was a nasty one, lasting through the day and part of the night. All we could do was shelter in the caves at the base of the cliff while the winds raged overhead and wait for it to blow itself out.

The next morning, the sky was calm again, blue

without a puff of cloud, but the storm left behind a layer of sand and dust that covered everything. As promised, Salah sent a couple of his tribe out on camels to the nearest town to organise my transport while the rest of us set about clearing up the mess. I'd given them Nate's phone number and a short message: *Valkyrie lives to ride again.* Nate would understand what that meant and call off the troops.

At sunset, the riders returned. "The boat is arranged for the night after next," the older one said. "It was the soonest the captain agreed to go."

"Did you get through to my friend?"

He shifted from foot to foot and looked at his feet. "We lost the paper."

For pity's sake, they had one job. Well, two, but neither of them was particularly difficult. Still, I couldn't do much about it now. I'd just have to hope Nate had his sensible head on.

The next day passed interminably slowly. As a guest and also a woman, I wasn't allowed to do much to help, although Salah did take me out into the desert to show me his new falcon. I wished there was some way to hurry things along, but unfortunately, life didn't work that way out here. The name of the game was *insha'Allah*, which meant "if Allah wills it," more commonly translated as "things will happen when they happen, if they happen at all."

So I had to wait.

The night in the desert dragged on forever. As the temperature dropped, I huddled under the extra blanket Salah found for me, grateful for the double layer of warmth. A group of kids woke me up at daybreak, and I spent the day sitting in the shade while they crowded around, asking questions about everything from England to elephants. Once they realised I didn't bite, they couldn't resist the novelty of a stranger. Then after another meal of delicious, if unidentifiable, food, the time came to leave. I had another camel trip to endure.

We set off as the sun dropped. Salah rode beside me until we reached the outskirts of the town, and then we said our goodbyes.

"Thanks for everything. I'll send you a new phone as soon as I get home. Same drill as last time, yeah?"

He nodded and grinned at me, displaying his lack of dental hygiene. "Next time, don't leave it so long before you come back."

Just before midnight, I crawled into the bed of a pickup truck and hid myself under a pile of blankets and some animal feed. At each checkpoint, the driver explained he was returning to his family after a trip to Petra and paid over the requisite bribes while I stayed silent in the back.

My muscles stiffened and my back ached as we bumped over the desert for a couple of hours. Finally, the truck stopped at a desolate section of coastline, and I smelled the sea air. I stood and stretched as the driver proudly pointed out the boat waiting for me down below.

I couldn't hold back my groan.

Because when I said down below, I meant down below. The boat was anchored at the bottom of a cliff that had to be almost a hundred feet of sheer drop.

I turned back to the driver. "Isn't there a way to drive round?"

He just shrugged. "Salah said you are good climber. This was best place to land boat."

"Can't it move a little?"

"No, you climb." He backed towards the truck, key at the ready.

Thanks, Salah. It wasn't like I loved my fingernails anyway.

I worked out the kinks in my back and tied the small bag containing my camera and other bits around my waist. I'd wrapped it in plastic and tape to keep it dry.

Then I started down.

It was a horrible descent, and I say that as someone who loves climbing. The cliff had plenty of handholds, but many of them gave way when I touched them, and I needed to be super careful not to cause a landslide that would take me with it to the bottom.

I somehow reached the beach safely, thanking Black, once again, for all those painful hours he made me spend scaling rocks with him, then clambered into the tiny boat. More of a dinghy, really, with a single outboard motor and a hard bench seat. Not particularly quick. Thankfully, the blue waters of the Gulf of Aqaba were calm that night, and with only a light breeze, we made the crossing in less than four hours, arriving just before sunrise.

Well, sort of.

We stopped a good distance offshore, and the boat driver wasn't keen to get any closer.

"No passport. You get out now," he told me.

Oh, for goodness' sake. I tried explaining to the guy

that the police would still be tucked up in bed at that time, but he kept shaking his head. Eventually I gave up, stripped down to my underwear, and dove off the side of the boat. I'd endured a week with no water. Now I had plenty of it.

My shredded hands stung as the salt hit them, but I gritted my teeth and set off. A mile of swimming brought me to the small spit of land that guarded the mouth of the lagoon in Dahab. I hauled myself onto the beach, skirted in disgust around a pile of discarded cigarette butts, and started off on the short trek back to civilisation.

A twenty-minute walk brought me to Dahab City, which wasn't a city by any stretch of the imagination. It didn't even have a Starbucks. Most of the buildings were high-end hotels and apartments set right next to the Red Sea. Keeping to the shoreline, I skipped the first two hotels before making my way up the private beach of the third: the Black Diamond. A red brick path wound its way through tropical gardens. Even in this arid climate, lush grass abounded, surrounded by fragrant trees and colourful bougainvillea. When I reached a white, two-storey villa with a traditional domed roof, I hopped over the low wall surrounding it and knocked on the door.

A minute later, the lock clicked and a sleepy-looking guy in his late fifties glowered at me. He rubbed his eyes, no doubt hoping that if he did it hard enough, I'd disappear and he could go back to bed.

"Morning, Bob."

"Emmy, it's not even five o'clock, and you're standing on my doorstep in...is that your underwear? Actually, you know what? I'm not surprised."

Bob was Captain Bob Stewart, a former Navy captain I'd trained with during my early years with Black. When Bob left the service, declaring he'd had enough of cold and wet, he managed to put up with two months-worth of DIY and decorating in the Virginia home he'd shared with his wife before declaring himself bored. While he may have had enough of cold, wet was too big a part of his life, so he and Sondra upped sticks and moved to hot. Hot being Dahab, where they ran the Black Diamond Hotel and dive centre.

How did I know this? Well, firstly because Black and I were friends with them, and secondly because when they announced their plans, we'd invested in the business. Hence it being badged as the seventh hotel in our Black Diamond chain.

"Nothing ever surprises you, Bob. Can I have the keys to my villa, please? Oh, and I need to borrow your phone."

Silently, Bob reached into his pocket and held out his mobile, then he disappeared back inside, rolling his eyes.

CHAPTER 43

WHEN LUKE WENT into the control room the next morning, he found Mack already at her station. Judging by the dark smudges under her eyes, she'd had as little sleep as him. Her gaze dropped to his hands, or more specifically what he held in them.

"Coffee? You're a lifesaver."

"Two sugars, right?"

"Mmm. I should cut down. One day..."

He took his seat beside her. "Anything?"

"Not yet. I still can't get into this server. Can we try again together?"

"Of course."

Side-by-side, they tried everything they could think of to get through the encryption, but to no avail. The clock ticked around to eleven, and Mack needed to head off to another meeting with some shadowy government department she wouldn't even tell him the name of.

"There's something we're not seeing," she said before she left.

Didn't Luke know it?

He had another go while she was gone, but got no further. They were sure the system held a backup of the email traffic between several army departments and the Syrian government, but their cyber security was proving to be far more sophisticated than that on the army base that Emmy had got into. Luke guessed they'd found out where a significant part of the military budget was being spent.

After almost two hours, he gave up, frustrated. Time to take a step back before he put his fist through the screen.

Lunch seemed a good idea, so he headed for the kitchen, only to bump into Ruth in the hallway.

"Oh, Luke, do you want something to eat?"

He took in her attire—coat, scarf, gloves. Welcome to springtime in England.

"Are you going out?"

"I can stay to make you lunch if you're hungry."

"No, no, it's fine. I'll do it."

A moment's hesitation, and she didn't quite stop her eyebrows from shooting up. "You?"

"It's no problem, honestly."

"Well, if you're sure."

In the kitchen, Luke opened the fridge, only to find a bewildering array of ingredients but no actual food. He'd mastered re-heating, but cooking from scratch? Way out of his depth here. Could he call his PA and have her arrange something? Actually, hang on, they were in London. There had to be an easy way to get food delivered. An app or something.

He was scrolling through search results when Mack walked in, and as soon as he saw her sombre expression, all thoughts of eating fled his mind.

"What's wrong? You look like someone just died. Is it Emmy?"

"None of the Brits know anything. It was another dead end. And when I spoke to Nate on the way back, he and Nick have switched everyone over from searching to mission planning."

"Which means what?" Luke had no idea, but from the look on Mack's face, it wasn't good news.

"They've given up hope she got out of there. They're preparing to send a team in to look for her, or more likely, her body. And it's worse—Jed's been analysing satellite feeds, and between those and intelligence on the ground, we think the security at the base has been increased significantly."

"So that means it's going to be even harder for the new team?"

"Yes. And Emmy described it as practically a suicide mission when she went in the first place."

"So who's going this time?"

Please, please don't let it be Mack.

"Logan's going back, Jack and Evan, who I don't think you've met, Dan, and either Nick or Nate. They're arguing about which right now." Mack put her head in her hands. "First Black, then Emmy, and now this. I can't believe it's actually happening."

Luke breathed a sigh of relief that Mack was staying put and gave her a hug. She looked as if she needed one.

"From what you've said, nobody can stop them going, so let's do everything we can to make sure they come home safely."

"You're right. Of course you're right. I need to pull myself together and get on with doing my job."

Lunch forgotten, Luke followed Mack into the control room. She linked up with the States, and the processes she worked her way through left him mystified. Not wanting to disturb her, he kept out of her way and carried on with his earlier search.

But he kept getting distracted. Every so often, Mack gave a little sniffle, and he knew she was trying to hold back tears. He'd never been one for emotional women, but he liked the way Mack wore her heart on her sleeve. Far better than trying to read a woman's mind all the time.

After she gave a particularly loud sigh, he reached over and tucked a few strands of hair behind her ear. "You okay?"

"No."

"We're doing everything we can."

"But it's not enough, is it? I've already lost two friends in the last year, without more dying."

"We don't know Emmy's dead."

"Even *she* isn't invincible, no matter what Black thought."

Luke gave Mack's shoulders one last squeeze and turned back to his laptop, holding back his own sigh. All he could do was carry on trying to crack this code.

Except when he looked at his screen, it had changed. The frustrating, blinking cursor from his previous attempts was gone, replaced with a string of Arabic words. What did it say? He ran the text through his newly improved translation software and found it was the beginning of a file directory.

Luke let out a yell. "Get in there!"

"What? Get in where?" Mack asked, distracted.

"Nowhere, it's just an expression. I finally got into that email system we've been trying to crack for the last couple of days."

She scooted her chair over and pressed against him, her body heat turning the words on the screen into a blur.

"How? What have you found?"

He forced his mind out of the gutter. "I think it's to do with timing. I didn't type anything while I was talking to you, and when I went back to where I left off, it had advanced through the process by itself."

"You mean if you constantly keep trying to get in, it throws more locks?"

"Something like that."

Together, they tried the same trick on Mack's laptop. "Holy guacamole, it worked!" she squealed, then threw her arms around him. "Now we're getting somewhere."

With Mack pressed against his chest, Luke most certainly agreed. But did the computer trail lead anywhere?

They set the search program they'd written together to work, leaning forward on their elbows as they watched it scroll through files, looking for keywords. Every time it flagged a message, one of them would scan through by eye to see if it looked important.

It was close to midnight when something piqued Luke's interest. "This is odd. It seems Emmy wasn't the only person irritating the Syrians that night."

"In what way?"

"One of their own pilots tried to defect. Stole a plane and tried to make it to Saudi Arabia. The Syrians chased him and shot him down over Jordan. By the looks of this memo, the Jordanians are furious. They say the Syrians should have asked permission before flying into their airspace."

"Where did the plane originate? Does it say?"

"No. The interceptor took off from just over the

border with Jordan. Oh, wait, now the Israelis have joined in. They seem disappointed they didn't manage to blow up both of the planes."

In an instant, Mack was on her feet, leaning over Luke's shoulder. "Find out where that plane came from and where it ended up."

"Why? Do you think it might be important?"

"Emmy's a seriously good pilot."

"The emails are talking about a fighter jet. Do you really reckon she could fly that?"

"If it's got wings and an engine, she'd have a good chance."

They couldn't find the plane's exact origin, but they did manage to find an approximate location for the crash site. Jed woke up one of his buddies at the CIA and wheedled, cajoled, and threatened until they promised to have a satellite take photos of the area at first light.

After this new development, the rescue mission, which had been due to depart that morning, was put on hold for a few hours until they were able to get a look at the plane's final resting place. The images started coming in just before lunchtime. Mack stared in dismay at the charred, twisted body of a plane surrounded by scattered pieces of wreckage.

From the state of it, the Syrians hadn't lied about shooting it down. The damage in the photo was clearly catastrophic. Mack zoomed in, trying to get a good look at what was left of the cockpit, but the plane had rolled as it hit, leaving the top buried in the sand.

"What if Emmy's in there?" she whispered. "Nobody could have survived that."

"We still don't know for sure Emmy was even flying

it."

Mack couldn't keep her hands steady as she swiped across the screen in front of her. Luke tried to comfort her with words, but they fell on deaf ears.

Nate took control, live from Richmond. He hadn't gone home since Emmy disappeared, according to Mack, and this morning, his customary scowl had been replaced with a frown.

"We need to send a team to Jordan right away. I want that cockpit checked before any of our people go back into that Syrian base."

Jed shook his head. "If we have any further delays going into Syria, that could cost Emmy her life. This is eight days now. If you'd seen what they did to Phil, you'd know how little time we've got in that respect."

"We're not sending a team when Emmy might not even be in the same country. And from the way you described Phil, we'll only be looking for a body to recover if they caught her."

Jed slumped in his seat and Dan snapped, "There's no need to be so blunt, Nate."

"Someone needs to tell it like it is. If Black was here, you know he'd say the exact same thing."

"If Black was here, we wouldn't be in this situation."

"She'd still have gone. You know that. Black wouldn't even have tried to talk her out of it."

"That's not what I meant. I'm talking about that weird connection they had. He'd have got inside her head and worked out where she was by now."

"And even if he hadn't, he'd be sitting in that seat..." Nate motioned to the desk where Jed was leaning back in a chair with his cast propped up on a stool. "Saying 'let her get on with it, the woman's indestructible.'"

"Then he'd rub his nose to remind himself," Dan finished.

In London, Mack sat stiffly, gripping Luke's hand out of sight under the table. She'd grabbed it when Nate so kindly reminded everyone of Emmy's possible fate. Luke squeezed it back, trying not to let on how worried he was himself. Until now, the only death he'd suffered through was his father's, and he'd passed away in the hospital. Mack's world scared him more than he cared to admit.

"Why would he rub his nose?" Luke asked her.

"Emmy broke it for him once. That fight they had when they first met, remember?"

"Wasn't Black a big guy?"

"Huge. About six and a half feet tall, muscles on muscles. But Emmy fights like a caged tiger."

How different was this new Emmy from the Ash he'd known? Luke was glad now that he'd never got into a serious argument with her.

Turning his attention back to the screen, he listened as Nate dispatched a group to Jordan to do the necessary. The second team would fly out to Syria at the same time to prepare on the ground, and if the answer came back negative at the crash site, they planned to hit the base the following day.

He saw in Mack's eyes that she didn't think this story was going to have a happy ending. All the money in the world couldn't buy the fairy tale she craved. As he wrapped his arms around her and hugged her tight, he wondered if what he felt for her, this strange kinship mixed with heat that sizzled in his veins every time they got close, would end any better.

CHAPTER 44

THE PHONE RANG once, twice, then a crisp voice came through.

"Control room."

I recognised Matt, one of the shift supervisors in our Richmond headquarters, although he sounded tired. Overtime or too much partying?

"Hi, it's me. Is Nate or Nick there?"

"Nick's not available, but Nate's here. Who is this?"

"Come on, Matt. You've been working at Blackwood for, what, six years, and you don't know what my sweet, dulcet tones sound like yet?"

"Emmy?"

Well, duh. "Who else?"

"B-b-but we all thought you were dead."

"Do I sound dead to you? No. Anyway, when have I ever died before? That's right. Never. Can you pass me over to Nate now?"

A few moments of silence passed before Nate came on the line. "Emmy, is that really you?"

"Oh, for Pete's sake, not you as well. No, it's a ghost. A ghost who's learned how to use the telephone. Did Jed and Logan get out?"

"Jed's here, but Logan's on his way back to Syria."

"Why's he going there? Does he not think we stirred up enough of a hornet's nest already?"

"He's on his way to rescue you. And don't worry, the hornets are well and truly furious. Congratulations."

"Well, for goodness' sake, call him back. And Nick, who I take it is with him? Why did you let Nick go? I already said no when he offered the first time."

"Nick's about as easy to stop as you when he decides he's doing something. Hang on, let me contact everyone."

Nate put my line on speaker, and I listened as he recalled two teams—one from Syria and one from Jordan. Smart cookies—at least they'd found the plane. I felt bad about trashing the MiG, really. I'd liked it. How much did a second-hand model cost? The running costs would be killer but the fun factor might make it worth it, plus I could seriously reduce my commuting time.

Nate interrupted my mental calculations. "Where on earth are you?"

"Welcome back, Emmy. Nice to hear from you, Emmy. How are you, Emmy?"

"It's been nine days. The time for pleasantries ran out a week ago. Just answer the question, will you?"

"Dahab. And I would have called sooner if I'd had access to a phone that worked. But I had more important things on my mind, like not dying."

He ignored the last part. Typical Nate. "How on earth did you get there?"

"A rough summary would be fly, walk, camel, more camel, truck, climb, boat, swim, walk. If you want more details, you'll have to wait until I'm on a secure line."

"Fine. When will that be?"

"Gimme twenty minutes. I need to collect my house

key and put some clothes on. I'm standing outside in my underwear, and the hotel guests are gonna start waking up soon."

"We'll be waiting with bated breath," Nate replied, before softening his tone a little. "Emmy, I'm glad you're okay."

"Me too."

Captain Bob came back with my key, and after promising to have breakfast with him at a slightly more sensible hour, I walked to the villa next to his. It wasn't a massive place, just three bedrooms each with an en-suite, a kitchen, and a combined living and dining area, but it did have a decent-sized terrace out the front with a magnificent sea view.

Although clean, the place smelled musty. Hardly surprising when it hadn't been used in almost a year. I'd always remember that scuba diving break as the last proper holiday Black and I took together. Five days, just the two of us and a bunch of fish. Oh, and he spent most of the time with his shirt off. Happy days.

But no more.

My closet was exactly as I left it, and I rummaged around for a pair of shorts with a drawstring. I'd lost so much weight in the last week anything else would have slipped down low enough to become indecent. I caught sight of my ribs in the mirror as I pulled a tank top on. Thin, far too thin. My donut diet started now.

I gazed longingly at the shower as I left the room. Gritty salt crystals covered me, leaving my skin dry and cracked in places. And my hair? Ugh. I tried to think positive. At least I'd washed the sweat and dirt off on my swim over.

Beyond exhausted, I hesitated on the threshold to Black's bedroom. Had he left it tidy? I couldn't stand to see his personal belongings. Not today, when I'd already faced my own mortality. What if he'd left clothes out? What if...? *Oh, just get on with it.* I stepped inside, letting out the breath I'd been holding when I saw it devoid of reminders. Now I needed to get what I came for.

I rolled back the rug next to the bed, revealing a small vault set into the floor. A ten-digit combination got me into it, and I pulled out a secure phone and a laptop. Months without use had left the batteries dead, so I plugged both in before powering them up.

The computer whirred to life, and I logged into the Blackwood intranet. Within a couple of minutes, the control room in Richmond appeared on the screen, bustling with quiet activity as always. Nate was there in his usual seat, looking more haggard than I'd ever seen him. Was that all because of me? We'd had our ups and downs over the years, so I guess I was a bit surprised to find he'd been so worried. I'd have to wind him up about that when I got home.

Beyond Nate, I got my first glimpse of Jed, sitting at Black's old desk with a heavy-duty cast propped up on a wheelie chair. As I watched, one of the interns brought him over a slice of cake and a cup of coffee, served with a smile. Now, that didn't surprise me at all.

"Hey, Jed." My voice came out as a croak, and I sounded like a frog. "What did the doc say about your leg?"

"Broken tibia and ligament damage in my knee."

"Hang on a sec." I found a leftover bottle of water in the kitchen and sipped from it before I sat back down. "The bone will heal quick enough. What's the verdict on the ligaments?"

"Six weeks of rest, then they'll reassess and see whether I need surgery."

"Six weeks stuck behind a desk. If you're lucky, I might give you a break from that. You owe me a very expensive dinner."

"Darlin', I'll buy you the whole restaurant."

I laughed. "Just dinner will be fine. And maybe a decent bottle of wine."

"Deal."

Nate huffed and broke in. "If you two are quite finished arranging your date, can we talk about work?"

"Shoot."

"No more shooting. You've already done enough of that. We've heard what happened up until you crawled away from Logan and Jed through that pipe, but can you fill us in on the rest?"

I briefly explained the events of the evening and the following days, starting with the missile and finishing with my swim into Dahab. Nobody bothered taking notes—Nate recorded everything.

"Jed, can you set me up a debrief meeting with the CIA?" I asked once I'd finished. They'd have a million questions, no matter how thorough my report might be.

"Sure."

"Sloane?"

She beamed at me from her spot beside Jed. "Yes?"

"I need you to send a new satellite phone out to Salah. He'll pick it up from the local post office again." Well, local-ish. A hundred and twenty kilometres counted as close by in that desolate wasteland.

A quick nod, and she made a note on her iPad.

"Mack, are you there?"

"Yes, I'm here."

A picture feed from the control room at Albany House popped up. Normally, Mack got the most stressed out of all of us, and after seeing how rough Nate looked, I'd been a bit worried about her. Thankfully, she didn't look as bad as I'd feared, although I did note the plateful of pastries beside her. She'd been using sugar as a crutch again.

"I'm going to send some photos over. The ones of the weapons need to go to the CIA, and they can clean those up themselves. Just make sure they know about the Stinger right away. I got photos of the serial number, and someone needs to find out where that missile was supposed to be because I'm fairly certain that place was not on a Syrian military base."

"I'll get right on it."

"The photos of Philip aren't for general consumption. Believe me when I say they're nasty. There's a tattoo you can blow up for identification, and if that's not enough, I'll bring back a DNA sample." On my knife blade, which I'd managed to keep dry on my trek.

"Thanks for the warning."

"Mack, are you okay?" She'd squirmed in her seat again, the second time I'd seen her do it.

"Yes, I'm fine."

"Are you sure? Look, if it's about the photos of Philip, I'm sure Nate could deal with them instead."

"No, really, it's okay. I just need a bathroom break."

Come to think of it, I could do with one myself.

"Right, I'll leave you alone then." I switched back to Richmond. "What does my schedule look like for the next few days?"

Sloane hesitated for several awkward seconds. "Uh, I cleared it, so it's empty."

"For Pete's sake, not another person who thought I was dead?"

Okay, so I'd come close enough to touch the reaper, but that wasn't the point. I'd been used to Black's unwavering belief that I could do anything, and it hurt when others doubted me. It had been Black's confidence that gave me confidence in myself, and if people started thinking I'd fail, I'd need to be very careful that negativity didn't transfer to me.

"We were just worried, Emmy. I'm sorry."

"Forget it. Anyway, if I don't need to rush back, I'll stay out here for a bit. It's been months since I did any diving."

"Shall I schedule a flight to Virginia for you in a few days? A week?

"Let's go for five days. Is Bradley back yet?"

Before I left, I'd told him he might as well take a break while I was away. He'd borrowed my plane and flown to Italy. Miles, his boyfriend, was on another archaeological dig out there, but Bradley had convinced him to take a week off and spend some time at my Italian villa.

"No, and we didn't tell him you were missing, either. We didn't want to worry him."

"Good. He'd probably end up on medication if your optimistic attitude rubbed off on him. Can you let him know when my flight is?"

"Will do. See you soon."

Now, what should I do with myself? A few days without meetings or missions or Alex hounding me promised bliss. Although I'd had plenty of downtime with Luke, that hadn't been a holiday. In England... Well, if I hadn't lost my marbles, there was certainly a hole in the bag. I hadn't been able to relax.

Today, I'd start with a long, hot shower, and by the time I'd got dressed, the hotel would be serving breakfast. The thought of waffles with maple syrup made my mouth water. After that, the sun lounger on my terrace seemed like a good place to rest my aching limbs. My muscles needed a couple of days to repair themselves after what I'd put them through, or I'd risk further injury. Maybe afterwards, I'd go diving. Or wakeboarding. Or windsurfing.

Or maybe I'd simply sleep.

CHAPTER 45

LUKE WATCHED MACK'S fingers fly across the keyboard as she came up with another permutation to add to the mission simulation program. With two teams on the way to the Middle East, they couldn't afford to miss even the smallest issue. Her shoulders were rigid with tension, and she muttered under her breath as she stared at the screen. Luke didn't understand enough about the logistics of the operation to be of much assistance, but he waited on hand, just in case.

"Anything I can do?" he asked.

She shook her head then changed her mind. "Maybe a cup of coffee?"

"Sure."

He'd put it next to the other two she hadn't touched from earlier.

When he came back with drinks for both of them, Mack was staring open-mouthed at the screen. With his attention on her, it took a few seconds to register the voice flowing from the speakers, dripping with sarcasm.

"Nice to hear from you, Emmy. How are you, Emmy?"

Luke barely recognised his ex's voice. Although the line was crystal clear, she sounded much harsher than he remembered. The girl he knew had been soft and sweet, not confident and slightly antagonistic. But when Mack's face relaxed, he knew it *must* be Emmy.

Luke listened as she condensed her nine-day journey into a single sentence of "fly, walk, camel, more camel, truck, climb, boat, swim, walk" and when she hung up, he squeezed Mack's hand.

"That's good news then, huh?"

Mack hesitated, motionless, then leapt up and danced around the room. Her happiness was infectious, and Luke couldn't help laughing. On her second circuit, she jumped into his arms, and he swung her in a circle, her feet narrowly missing the cups of cold coffee sitting next to her mouse.

"She's back! She's really back!"

"Certainly seems that way."

Mack touched her feet back to the floor and smiled. On tiptoes, she was level with Luke, and when her arms wrapped around his neck and her chest pressed against his, their lips were only an inch apart. All he needed to do was lean forward and...

No. He couldn't. Not with Mack. Not when Emmy was coming back. Luke needed to give things some serious consideration.

Mack seemed to have the same thought because she pulled back and put her heels on the floor.

"Thank goodness," she whispered, and Luke wasn't sure whether she meant Emmy's return or the fact that they'd narrowly avoided kissing.

He sat back down, feeling drained. "We were right about the plane too—she said she flew."

"You were the one who cracked the puzzle. If you hadn't, the new team would have gone in by now, and they'd probably have been killed. So thank you. Everyone is more grateful than you could ever know."

"It was you who put two and two together about her flying."

"But I couldn't have done it without you finding the plane in the first place."

"Let's call it teamwork, then."

Mack paused for a second. "I don't normally work well with other people, apart from Nate. Not on computers. But we make a good team, don't you think?"

She grinned at Luke and the effect was dizzying. His heart started to beat faster, and he nodded. "We do."

"And we need to celebrate. This calls for champagne."

"I saw a bottle in the fridge."

"No, Emmy keeps the good stuff in the cellar for special occasions. I'd say today qualifies."

Mack went off to hunt, and by the time she got back with a bottle of Cristal, Luke had found a couple of glasses and a box of chocolates.

He held them out to Mack. "For your sweet tooth."

That earned him another smile. He really needed to buy shares in a chocolate manufacturer, because he saw himself buying a significant amount of the stuff over the next few months.

Luke had a happy buzz from the alcohol when Emmy called back, and he listened with growing admiration as she described how she'd escaped Syria. The woman may be a few sandwiches short of a picnic, but she was undeniably resourceful.

He was just musing over how different she was to the Ash he'd known when Mack yanked him off his chair and shoved him under the desk.

There was no need to be quite so forceful—honestly if she wanted him down there, she only had to ask. He was about to say something when he heard Emmy address Mack directly and guessed, correctly, that Mack must be on camera.

Although it was uncomfortable being wedged in front of Mack's knees, Luke couldn't complain about the view. He stifled a groan. Really, he shouldn't be thinking like that, although it was hard not to with his face so close to the jackpot. Judging by the way Mack squirmed on the chair, she may well have been having the same thoughts.

Eventually, she told Emmy she needed a bathroom break, and the speakers fell silent.

"I'm sorry," she whispered. "I didn't know how to explain to Emmy that you were here."

Luke understood that. It wasn't as if their last words had been amicable.

"Maybe I could call her or something. You know, apologise for shouting at her about Tia."

He didn't relish the thought, especially as he was still sore over Nick, but if it would make Mack happy, he'd do it.

"That might help. I'd give her a day or so, though. She needs some rest, and she'll already get interrupted with the CIA's debrief call."

Hmm...A debrief. That sounded like a pretty good idea to Luke.

"Why are you looking at me like that?" she asked.

"Like what?"

"Like I'm lunch."

"Oh, uh, I didn't realise I was." He needed to be more careful. "Do you want another glass of champagne?"

"Better not. Emmy's sending through some files she wants me to look at."

She was? Luke hadn't heard that part of the conversation. Most likely because he'd had other things on his mind.

"I could do with checking in at HC Systems, I guess. My staff have probably all started partying with me out of the office for a couple of days, and I've got at least fifty emails I need to go through."

They went back to their desks and sat side-by-side, relaxed in each other's company. Luke could get used to that. He already dreaded the thought of going back to his big, empty office with only his PA to talk to. Sure, his picture window had a great view over the city, but the one here was prettier. Each time Mack moved, her waterfall of red hair did funny things to his insides.

He was trying, and failing, to focus on a particularly dull contract when Mack suddenly retched, then grabbed the waste paper bin and threw up. Okay, maybe that wasn't quite so lovely.

"Sweetheart, what's wrong?" he asked. "Are you ill?" Then he looked up at Mack's computer screen. "What the...?"

A scene that made *Silence of the Lambs* look like a fairy tale filled the screen. Surely that couldn't be real?

"Is that...?"

"Philip? Yes."

"I was going to say 'real.' But I guess you've answered that."

"Sorry, I didn't mean to be sick. I just couldn't help it."

"I almost lost my lunch myself. Did one human being honestly do that to another?"

"The world's full of monsters, but most people never realise how vile they really are. You can see why Jed and Logan were so worried about Emmy being captured now, can't you?"

"Yes, I can. I can also see why Emmy has nightmares."

"If history repeats itself, she won't get much sleep for a few days. It's a good thing she's got some time off."

Luke slowly began to understand why Emmy was the way she was. How many more of these unspeakable horrors had she witnessed? No wonder she'd hardened her soul.

And what about Mack? Seeing that...that... He closed his eyes, picturing Philip's insides spilling out into that rusty bucket. The vision would haunt him for a long time. He put an arm around Mack, needing to feel her warmth to counteract the darkness that threatened humanity.

"Is there anything I can do to help?" he asked.

"No, it's sunk in now. I'll be fine." She gave him a sheepish smile. "It's not the first time this has happened."

Luke closed his eyes, struggling to hold back his true thoughts, none of which were polite. "What more do you need to do with the pictures?"

"Just zoom in on certain parts and clean them up."

"Do you want me to do it?"

"No, I'll manage."

Luke kept a careful eye as Mack opened the files again. She did what she had to without further incident, but he suspected she was putting a brave face on things. He couldn't help glimpsing more of the gruesome images, and his appetite deserted him come dinnertime.

After spending so much time looking for Emmy, Luke and Mack both had work to catch up on. Two days passed in a blur of emails, programming, and meetings. Apart from a quick visit to Lower Foxford to check Tia hadn't destroyed his house again, Luke spent all his spare time with Mack.

On Thursday evening, they ate a delicious meal of beef stroganoff, courtesy of Ruth, and after coffee, they hacked into the servers of a well-known dating website. After spending an hour or two reading who'd messaged who, they fired off a polite email suggesting the company update their security, signed Loki and Diablo.

"I can't believe that guy sent a photo of himself dressed in that rubber outfit."

Luke shuddered, wishing he could un-see the overweight man stuffed into the gimp costume. "And I can't believe she agreed to meet him for a date."

"And that guy who tried to sue the website when he burnt himself... What was he thinking?"

"Exactly. He really should have worn an apron when he tried to cook his date a bacon sandwich."

Good food and a broken firewall—every hacker's

dream. Despite the money, the cars, and the made-to-measure suits, Luke was a geek at heart, and he'd finally met his soul mate.

Mack lingered outside his door as they headed for bed, and it took all his self-control not to invite her in. What would she say if he did? Apart from the near kiss in the control room after Emmy came back, she'd kept him firmly in the friend zone. He tried to see her the same way, but every time she bit that bottom lip or arched her back as she stretched, blood flowed straight to his little head. Life with Mack was hard, but without her? That didn't bear thinking about.

"What do you want for dinner?" Luke asked Mack the next afternoon. His last meeting had dragged on for hours, and all he'd eaten since lunch was a packet of digestive biscuits.

"I don't know. It's Ruth's day off, so we're on our own."

"In that case, why don't we go out to eat? Call it a late celebration of Emmy's return."

"Why not? As long as we don't have chocolate for dessert. I ate most of that box of candy you bought me while I upgraded the secondary database this afternoon."

"You didn't save me any?"

"I left the Turkish delight."

Fantastic. The only ones he didn't like. "Thanks."

"I'll make it up to you."

Oh, she'd better. "How about Japanese?"

"I love Japanese. There's a great place in

Kensington."

He smiled at her. "Give me the name, and I'll make a reservation.

"Perfect."

Yes, she was.

CHAPTER 46

"I THINK I drank too much sake," Mack giggled as Luke helped her back into the car after dinner.

He made sure he stood behind her as her skirt rode up. Not just for his viewing pleasure, but because he didn't want anyone getting an eyeful but him. His own throat burned—he'd been matching her shot for shot.

"It's only too much if you pass out."

She laughed again, and he felt the sweet sound all the way through as he slid into the seat beside her.

"You're right. Maybe we should go back and get another bottle."

"That's not a good idea, sweetheart."

Two Macks already floated fuzzily in front of him, although that was no hardship.

The driver lingered before closing the door behind them. Luke's regular chauffeur was on holiday, and the car service had sent a replacement. The way the man eyed up Mack's assets didn't escape Luke's notice.

"We're ready to go," he snapped.

"Of course, sir."

The car pulled away from the kerb, and Luke settled back in the seat. Mack didn't. She scooted closer and wrapped her arms around him. "Thank you for helping, and thank you for taking me out tonight. I had a great time."

She looked up at him with those big green eyes, and her lips parted just a little. Something passed between them as the resistance Luke had been clutching onto for the last few days crumbled. He glanced forward. Was the privacy screen up? Good, it was. He had a feeling they might need it tonight.

Mack's breath caressed his cheek, and an invisible thread pulled him towards her. He was unable to contain his elation when she kissed him back.

Everything about Mack was perfect—her stunning flame-red hair, the way she cared for her friends, the little gasp she gave when he tightened his arm around her waist. But most of all, her mind. Luke loved her inner geek even more than her outer beauty.

Yes, they'd definitely be needing that privacy screen...

Luke barely remembered the trip through London's streets, only the journey he went on with Mack as they let all those simmering feelings boil over into heated passion. By the end, he could barely remember his own name.

Then the speaker crackled, stirring him out of his lust-induced stupor, and Mack sat bolt upright.

"We're here, sir."

Luke hit the intercom button on the door console. "Just give us a few minutes."

Good grief. Had he lost his mind? It seemed so, but he didn't want to find it again.

"Are you okay?" he asked Mack.

"I think so. I mean, I've never..."

"Me neither."

Thank goodness for tinted windows.

"We should get dressed. What if someone notices

us? What if the driver—"

Luke pressed a finger to her lips. "He won't."

"My shirt's torn."

"I'll give you my jacket."

Mack tucked the remains of her blouse into her skirt while Luke fixed his shirt, stealing glances at Mack as he fumbled with the buttons. Her hair was all tousled, her mascara smeared, and most of her lipstick was on him. She'd never looked more gorgeous.

"Okay?" he asked, and this time she nodded.

Luke opened the door himself and half lifted her out. At least the chauffeur had enough sense to avert his eyes this time. Mack wobbled as Luke helped her up the path, and he wasn't too steady either. Not just from alcohol, but because he'd just had his mind blown.

Mack stayed quiet as Luke took three attempts to get past the retina scanner. Flipping security. At times like this, there was a lot to be said for simply having a key. Eventually, they got inside, and she collapsed back on the sofa in the hallway. In a strange way, it reminded him of the night they first met.

"Want me to carry you upstairs?" he asked.

"We shouldn't have done that," she whispered.

Uh oh.

"We were two consenting adults, and we both wanted it. Didn't we?"

No way had he misinterpreted that. Had he?

She sighed. "Yes, we did."

"Then what's the problem?"

"Emmy."

"Emmy's in my past."

"But she's not in mine. She's one of my best friends. How do you think she'd feel if she found out what we just did?"

Anger at the injustice of it all bubbled up inside Luke. He couldn't lose Mack, not because of a two-month mistake with a woman who'd done the dirty on him then done a runner.

"Oh, come on. If Emmy disapproved, she'd be a hypocrite."

"A hypocrite? What are you talking about?"

"Well, she didn't exactly hesitate before she cheated on me, did she?"

"Cheated on you? Are you kidding? Emmy doesn't cheat." Mack leaned back and groaned. "She's gonna kill me."

"Yes, she did cheat. With Nick."

"Nick? You think Emmy cheated on you with Nick? Who on earth put that crazy idea into your head?"

"I saw them together, dancing at her charity fundraiser. He's the fiancé she had problems with in the States, right? And then there's her ex-husband."

Mack half choked, half groaned. "Emmy and Nick were over a decade ago. They're just friends, and that's all they'll ever be now."

"You mean she's not engaged to him?"

"No!"

Could he have been wrong? Mack seemed pretty convinced, but Luke knew what he'd seen. That tango Emmy and Nick danced had been filthy.

"Are you sure?" he asked one more time.

"Nick doesn't even date seriously. Not since his fiancée got killed by some lunatic."

Oh.

It seemed that possibly he'd done the man a disservice. Luckily he'd still been reasonably civil, or that would be yet another black mark against him in Emmy's eyes.

"So, what now? What do we do about..." He pointed between them. "This?"

"We've got to forget it happened." Mack sure had sobered up in a hurry. "Go back to how things were."

"But..."

"No buts. We can't have any buts." She let out a shuddering breath. "Don't look at me like that, because if you do, I won't be able to keep my head. Please."

Luke stepped backwards, further, further, until he sagged against the opposite wall. How could the best evening of his life have turned into such a disaster? He may have only known Mack for a week or two, but he'd already lost his heart to her.

How could he get her to give him a chance?

The situation only got more awkward the next morning, and the atmosphere in the house turned cold enough to ice skate on. Luke was fifteen minutes into his battle with the coffee machine when Mack walked into the kitchen, and the flipping thing was still flashing an error message at him. In Italian. According to the translation app on his phone, *The filter is broken. Fix it.*

Luke couldn't even find the flipping thing.

"I'd offer you a coffee, but the machine isn't playing ball."

"It doesn't matter. I'll stop at Starbucks."

"You're going to the office?"

When they'd spoken about it yesterday, she'd

planned to work from home all day.

"I haven't been in for a while."

That wasn't a proper answer. "What time will you be back?"

"Don't know." She shrugged. "Late."

"Want me to get a takeaway for dinner?"

Ruth had another day off, and Luke's pitiful attempts at cooking wouldn't help in his quest to win Mack over.

She sat on a stool at the breakfast bar and sighed. "Look, I've been thinking. It's best if you go home. Emmy's coming back today, and after last night..." She trailed off and stared out the window.

"Emmy's coming here?"

"No, to the East Coast. Sloane's booked her a flight to Dulles. But it's probably a good time to draw a line under this...this...thing."

"By 'thing' you mean the best thing ever to happen to me?"

"I guess."

Luke took a seat beside her and cupped her cheek, turning her to face him. "Tell me you didn't feel it too."

"You know full well I did," she snapped. Then she closed her eyes and her voice softened. "Sorry."

"Don't throw it away. Please."

"Look, I like you. I really like you. But Emmy's been my friend for years, and I don't want to hurt her. Don't you realise how much she's been through already?"

"No, because nobody will tell me the whole story. But we can fix it. I promise, we—"

"I won't add to her problems."

"Mack, let's—"

"I'm going. I can't talk about this anymore."

Luke's heart seized as she strode out, leaving him short of breath. First Emmy, and now Mack.

Why did the good ones have to be so complicated?

Luke almost cancelled his morning meeting, but it was an important one so he dragged his sorry backside into the office. With Mack kicking him out, he packed up the few belongings he'd left in the guest room and took his suitcase with him in a taxi.

After months of thought, weighing up the costs and benefits, he'd chosen where to base the new American branch of HC systems, and the relocation specialist was sipping a cup of tea in reception when he arrived. Now Luke needed to convince his key staff to assist with the setup out there.

"So, what made you pick Richmond?" the man asked, making notes on a leather-bound pad.

"Virginia has a large pool of skilled employees, but the establishment costs tend to be lower than in California."

The city had been on Luke's shortlist since before he met Emmy, but he couldn't deny a certain redhead had swayed his final decision.

"And what's the timescale?"

"I want to get things moving straight away."

After a long discussion about logistics, the man agreed to get back to him with proposals within a fortnight. Luke should have been pleased—after all, overseas expansion had been on his wish list for years— but now he started to second-guess himself.

Had he made the right choice? Would Mack be

angry about him spending so much time near to where she lived? Or worse, would she think he was stalking her?

He picked at the sandwich his secretary brought him for lunch, half-inclined to call the whole thing off. Or perhaps he could expand in Europe first?

Stop being such a coward. This was a purely commercial decision, and Mack would just have to accept it.

Yeah, right. Who was he kidding?

His next discussion promised to be even more difficult.

Last time he'd spoken to Tia, she'd been even frostier than Mack, but now he needed to swallow his pride and apologise. He stopped off at home to pick up her phone and laptop then carried on to their mother's house, praying she'd gone to the country club as usual.

Tia answered the door and scowled at him.

"Can I come in?"

"I can't stop you, can I?"

He followed her through to the lounge, where she sat on the sofa and glared at him.

"I'm sorry I shouted at you. You should have told me where you were that night, though. What if something worse had happened?"

"Oh, please, with Emmy around?"

She had a fair point there, one he couldn't really argue with. "Just call me next time, okay?"

Tia brightened and even cracked a small smile. "Does that mean I can go and see her again?"

"If she agrees to it. I'll admit I misjudged her a little."

Tia scoffed at him. "More than a little."

"Okay, a lot. She wasn't entirely blameless, though."

"I know that. She knows that. She said your entire relationship was all kinds of screwed up."

Just when he thought his self-esteem couldn't get any lower.

"She really said that?"

"Pretty much."

Curiosity got the better of him. "Did she say anything else?"

"Just that one day she hopes you'll meet a sweet girl who'll give you what you need."

Well, he had, hadn't he? Trouble was, the one woman who he'd clicked with on a deeper level was also the one woman he couldn't have. What if this was his only chance at true love? He knew he'd never meet another Mack, so perfect for him in every way.

"I hope I'll get the right girl too," Luke said.

"Is that all you wanted? I'm going out with Arabella in a minute."

Luke handed over Tia's gadgets. "Do you want to move back in with me?"

"Maybe." Tia folded her arms. "I'll think about it."

Great. She was still angry. Should he push her or hope she got over it on her own? Being a big brother was hard, especially when their mother was so hands-off with parenting.

In the end, Luke decided to take the safe option and leave. At least he'd tried.

"Do you want me to drop you off at Arabella's?"

"Would you mind?"

"Driving my favourite sister around? Of course not."

"I'm your only sister."

"Exactly."

Well, at least she was smiling again.

He'd thought the talk with Tia would be his most difficult of the day, but as he pulled out of Arabella's driveway in his Porsche, he knew a tougher conversation awaited.

Mack may have told him to leave, but he couldn't stay away. Even if she only agreed to be friends, that would be better than nothing. The thought of going the rest of his life without seeing her secret smile again left him hollow inside.

Well, he wasn't going down without a fight.

All he had to do was convince Mack to give him a chance, and then deal with whatever Emmy decided to throw at him. He recalled her deadly aim during the snowball fight they'd had when she was in England and groaned.

Great.

He'd better practise ducking.

CHAPTER 47

EIGHT MEN STAGGERED past me, singing a painful homage to Ol' Blue Eyes at the tops of their voices. One of them dropped the blow-up donkey he was carrying and spilled half his pint as he stooped to pick it up.

"Stupid plane's late," he slurred at me.

"I got that."

I hated the airport in Sharm el Sheikh. I'd asked Sloane to book me on a scheduled flight because it seemed more sensible than sending a private jet to Egypt for just one person, but having spent three hours sitting in the departure lounge as it became ever more chaotic, that was a decision I very much regretted. The first hour had passed quickly—I'd spent it people watching, and there were some *very* odd people going through Sharm airport, let me tell you—but after that, the lack of edible food and clean toilets began to irritate me no end.

Then the check-in staff went on strike, followed by half of the ground staff. Nobody seemed to understand why. When I eavesdropped on their conversations, it appeared not even the staff on strike knew. My flight to the States was already an hour late when a garbled announcement over the Tannoy informed me a technical problem with the plane meant further delays. Judging by the row of maintenance staff I could see out the window, who had all downed tools and started praying to Mecca, it wouldn't be taking off any time soon.

But not to worry, staff would be stopping by with complimentary bottles of water.

Fantastic.

The mob around the ticket counter was getting angrier by the second, and the nervous-looking man behind it repeated over and over that there were no seats left on any flights, anywhere. I backed away, thinking up plan B. Call for my jet? Try to charter a plane?

My gaze alighted on a backpacker lazing on the floor beside the duty-free shop. He'd brought his own picnic, and a well-thumbed copy of *Treasure Island* lay in his lap. He appeared to be the only person in the airport not sick of the bedlam.

I wandered over, crouched down beside him, and smiled. "Hey, where are you off to?"

Half an hour and two thousand dollars later, I sat in economy class, trying not to murder the toddler screaming in the seat behind me. Swapping the name on the ticket online had proved easy enough, and the backpacker decided to spend an extra week at the beach with his windfall.

"We're flying into a slight headwind, so we should reach London in approximately five hours and twenty minutes," the pilot said. "Temperature on the ground is nine degrees Celsius, and there's currently a spot of rain."

The child bawled louder.

In the cab from the airport, I tuned out the driver's chatter and concentrated on the punchbag waiting for me when I got home. I'd already got Sloane to reschedule tomorrow's meetings, and next week I'd be lucky if I got time to breathe. But tonight I was blissfully free. I'd spend an hour in the gym, and if Mack didn't have plans, we could go out for dinner. According to Sloane, she was still in London.

The rusty taxi belched smoke as the driver sped off from Albany House, unhappy because I didn't give him a tip. But when the inside of the vehicle smelled like McDonald's and he'd talked non-stop about football all the way back from Luton, no way was I paying him extra.

I slammed the door and dumped my carry-on bag on the couch in the hallway. The oversized, decorative thermometer Bradley had installed next to the window told me the house was at nineteen degrees Celsius, so I turned the thermostat up a notch. I'd been freezing in a pair of denim cut-offs and a tank top ever since the plane took off.

Three steps up the stairs, I froze as a man's voice called out from the kitchen.

"Sweetheart, is that you?"

Now, I could have sworn I recognised that voice. Except there was no way the owner of it should have been in my house, and even less way he should have been calling me sweetheart.

But it turned out my ears weren't deceiving me. Because when I walked into the kitchen, I found a shocked-looking Luke Halston-Cain perched at the breakfast bar, drinking a cup of tea.

I spoke first as he seemed incapable. "Well, I can honestly say that if I'd had to make a list of people I expected to find in my kitchen today, your name would have been somewhere near the bottom of it."

And judging by the look on his face, he wasn't expecting to see me here either. So who was "sweetheart?"

"Uh...what are you doing here?"

"Shouldn't that be my line? I mean, last time I checked, this was my house."

"Yes, I know. It's just that Mack said you were on your way to the States."

Interesting. He clearly knew my schedule. And he knew Mack. I was going to make a wild assumption here and say that Mack and "sweetheart" were one and the same. What on earth was going on?

"If you must know, my flight to Virginia got intolerably delayed, so rather than sit around for hours watching the sandals, socks, and shell suits brigade, I flew to London instead. Why are *you* here?"

"Er, I lent a hand with the search when I found out you were missing."

"I called in five days ago, so that doesn't explain why you're still here. Or how you knew I was missing in the first place."

"I ran into Mack after a meeting at Sector 8. I mean literally ran into her, because I wasn't looking where I was going. The Tube drivers were on strike again, so I offered her a lift home, and we ended up here. That's when I realised you'd disappeared."

I supposed stranger things had happened. It wasn't

as far-fetched as the initial meeting between Black and me.

"Why did you offer to help?"

"I felt like I owed you one after you found Tia. Plus Mack told me you didn't just call her up and invite her clubbing. She said you helped her out with a problem in the middle of the night the weekend before."

Thanks, Mack. What else had she told Luke?

"Yes, there was a small issue, but it's been resolved. Tia won't make the same mistake again."

"What happened?"

"That's up to Tia to tell you, if she wants to."

I thought he might push it, but he backed off. "For what it's worth, thank you. For whatever it was you did. I can see how much you care about her."

"She's a great kid. So, the second part of my question. What are you still doing here?"

"Uh, Mack and I were helping each other with some computer programming."

The front door opened and closed, and I heard the click of heels on the tiled floor. Seconds later, Mack stopped in the doorway, the tiredness etched on her face turning to dread when she saw Luke and me.

Dread with a hint of omigosh-what-have-I-done.

I'd seen that look before. Once when she arrived at my place in a cab, minus her underwear, unable to remember the name of the man whose apartment she'd woken up in. A second time after she got drunk and slept with the ex she'd found in bed with another woman two weeks earlier.

"Oh, Mack. You didn't?"

"I-I-I thought you were going to Richmond," she stammered.

ELISE NOBLE

"So I've heard."

"Really, I can explain."

"Please, I'm dying to hear it."

She burst into tears and ran from the room. Oh, marvellous. Now I'd need to find tissues.

Luke swore under his breath and blocked me from going after her. "We didn't mean for you to find out."

"Were you going to try and keep it a secret? Because I'll let you into a little secret of my own. I'm a great liar. Mack isn't. Mack's an open book. Anything that went on between you and her would have remained a secret for about two and a half seconds."

"It only happened once, then Mack stopped it. Look, it was my fault, so don't take it out on her."

"Why did she stop it?"

"She was worried about how you'd react. She didn't want to upset you. Because of our history."

"It's just that, Luke. History. We were never right for each other. You need someone like Ash. Sweet and docile, and that isn't me. I'm anything but easy to live with when I haven't lost my mind like I had when I was with you. No offence. Mack's that, though. Sweet and docile."

"You're not angry?"

"Look, the time I spent with you, I was messed up in the head, and I ended up hurting you. I'll always be sorry for that. So if some good can come out of that episode, and by good I mean you finding Mack, her making you happy, and you making her happy, then it might cancel out some of the rubbish that happened. So no, I'm not angry. If I was angry, you'd be lying on the floor right now, twitching."

I watched a sliver of fear cross Luke's features

before I continued. "Mack's one of my best friends, but unfortunately she's also a magnet for the wrong kind of man. And I know from living with you that you're the right kind of man. So I don't care what the pair of you do together as long as you look after her. She deserves it."

"She's had trouble with men in the past?"

"Believe me when I say everyone will be relieved if we don't have to pick up the pieces after another idiot. I should probably mention, though, that if you pull this stunt with her—bring another woman round and expect it to be okay—I'll personally remove parts of you that you're rather fond of and roast them on a spit." I smiled sweetly. "Have you got that?"

My words had the desired effect. He gulped. "I-I-I won't hurt her; I promise. I think I've fallen for her."

Luke seemed surprised as the words left his mouth, but I could tell from his expression that they were true.

"Good." I patted him on the cheek. "Now, smile for Pete's sake." I looked around the kitchen. "I need coffee."

"I just made a fresh pot."

"Okay, you can stay."

I poured myself a mug of liquid caffeine then grabbed a box of Kleenex. Now, where had Mack gone?

Mack's already pale face went a shade lighter when I walked into the music room. Was I really that scary? I mean, I didn't even have a gun in my hand. All I had on me was the single knife I'd snuck through airport security in my bra. The dudes working the scanner missed that, although they did get spectacularly excited over a stray tampon in my pocket. That necessitated a conference before they decided it was harmless.

"I'm so sorry." Mack started with the apologies before I'd even closed the door.

I sighed as I leaned back against Black's piano. The smooth wood was cool against my back, its presence another reminder that I'd never hear Black play the ivories again.

"It was a twist of fate," she whispered. "I'm sorry."

"Enough with the apologising."

A-w-k-w-a-r-d.

"I didn't mean for it to happen. We'd had too much to drink and things got out of hand."

I sucked in a deep breath. "Did he treat you okay?"

"Yes! More than okay. He was..."

I held up a hand. "Spare me the details, yeah?"

"Sorry."

She hovered in front of the door, close to an escape route. Hmm, I needed to work on my interpersonal skills. Again. I walked over and hugged her, and after her initial surprise, she hugged me tightly back.

"It's okay," I whispered. "I just don't want you to get hurt."

She pulled back and stared at me. "You don't mind?"

Sure it stung, but I wasn't about to show her that. "When have you ever known me to get possessive over a man?"

"Well, never, but I haven't dated one of your exes before. I mean, I know you're okay with, say, Nick seeing other women, but none of them have been me or Dan."

"I wouldn't have a problem with you dating Nick, or Jed, or any of the others. Except Black."

"But I thought you and he didn't...you know? I thought he saw other women like you saw other men?"

"We didn't, and he did." I closed my eyes. "Somehow I could deal with the nameless, faceless women. The one-night stands and his little rescue projects. But if it had been you or Dan, that would have destroyed me."

My voice was all lumpy, and I knew I'd said too much. I tried to walk away, but Mack squeezed me tighter instead.

"Oh, Emmy, I'm so sorry. You deserve happiness as much as anyone."

"I exist to do a job. Being happy was never in my stars." That was my life now. My job. I pulled back again, harder this time, fighting tears that threatened to erupt. "I'm going to the office now, and I'll fly back to Richmond tomorrow morning."

I ran upstairs and changed, then caught the Tube to Blackwood. Mack and Luke needed space, and they weren't the only ones. It hurt to watch them have something I never would.

Work occupied me for the rest of the day, or at least I spent hours staring at my computer screen. When I couldn't keep my eyes open any longer, I pulled out the futon next to the desk and slept, my door firmly locked.

By the time the sun rose, I was in my jet, heading for the East Coast.

CHAPTER 48

OKAY, OKAY, I knew exactly what I'd done.

I'd run away again, but avoiding my feelings was easier than facing them. I was happy for Luke and Mack, really I was, but I still found it hard to see two people close to me find the kind of partnership I'd had one chance at and lost.

At least when I got home, I found plenty to keep me busy. Not least Bradley, who'd returned in my absence and wouldn't stop gushing about how wonderful his trip to Italy was, not to mention the fact that Miles had finished his dig and travelled back with him.

"The flight was fantastic. Your jet's lush."

"Glad you had a good time."

"And I even bought you candy at the airport."

See, this was why I loved Bradley.

Jed had also been waiting for me when I got back to Little Riverley. With his broken leg, he was officially on sick leave, although he was still going in for meetings and spent hours on his laptop at home. Or my home, it appeared.

"Bradley invited me to stay. I was bored, and you have a games room," he said. "And my apartment's on the sixth floor. Those stairs aren't easy with my leg."

His building also had an elevator. I was about to point that out, but then I thought, hey, having Jed around for a while could be entertaining.

"Just don't walk around naked. You nearly gave Mrs. Fairfax a heart attack last time." I'd heard her scream from the other end of the house.

"I thought it was her day off."

"Wear boxers, Jed."

The next day, I finally got in for my meeting with Jed's bosses.

"You certainly got a result, didn't you?" the director said.

"Yeah. Sorry about that. The bang was slightly larger than I anticipated."

Another grey-suited clone got out his laser pointer and highlighted an area on the video screen. "The satellite feeds show the whole weapons plant went up as well. Which puts the Syrians years behind schedule and saves us from having to send you back in again. Job well done, Emerson. We owe you one."

"Thanks. I'll remember that."

Only the CIA could be thrilled at the amount of mayhem I'd created. The director pushed a plate of biscuits towards me, and I took two. Even though I'd eaten four meals a day in Dahab and binged on falafel and ice cream sundaes, I still needed to gain half a stone.

"I didn't see you at Philip's memorial service," he said.

"That's because I didn't go. I didn't think it would be appropriate."

How could I face his family when I'd been the one

who killed him? No matter why I'd done it, his blood still stained my hands.

"We told his family he was lost in a light aircraft crash over the ocean. It was better that way."

"Good thinking."

At least they'd never know what he went through at the end. Sometimes a lie was better than the truth.

"Are you ready for more work?"

"Give me a few weeks, would you?"

I'd had a medical and thankfully my kidneys and liver were still functioning as they should, but my muscles had suffered wastage, my back still hurt in the mornings, and Toby and Alex needed to work their magic before I got back to full fitness.

"Fair enough, but don't leave it too long. I've got a number of interesting projects I think would be right up your street. I'll send the details over for you to take a look at."

Patience, for the director, was a hindrance rather than a virtue.

The job in Syria, for all its horrors, had at least reminded me of my purpose in life. I threw myself back into life at Blackwood, and as long as I kept busy, I found I could live with myself again.

And then there was Jed. He took me out for dinner as promised, and despite what I'd said, I didn't pick the most expensive wine on the menu. Jed ordered himself a bottle of white, but I was driving so I stuck with water.

"What are you having to eat?" he asked.

"Goat cheese salad to start, then grilled tilapia. You?"

"Lobster to start, then steak."

"That's two mains."

"When I was stuck in that hole, I never thought I'd see the inside of a restaurant again, so I think I deserve it."

"Fair enough. How are you healing up?"

"My leg's getting there."

"And your head?"

I knew firsthand what seeing Phillip in his final state could do to a person. I'd sleepwalked every night since I returned to Virginia and destroyed a sofa while I was at it. Jed had that to deal with, plus survivor's guilt and his own torture.

"Work sent me to see a shrink. Twice a week, Mondays and Thursdays."

"Any good?"

"I guess she helps a little. Are you having dessert?"

"I'm actually quite full now, and you know what they say: a full mongoose is a slow mongoose."

Rudyard Kipling was a very wise man. I never liked to eat until I couldn't move.

Jed raised an eyebrow and gave me his dirty smile, the one I hadn't seen in a long time. "How about a different kind of dessert?"

We didn't bother waiting for the bill, just flung some cash on the table and ran, well, hobbled in Jed's case, for the car. The engine screamed, and the Viper took off as I floored it over the bridge a couple of miles from Little Riverley.

Jed laughed and braced himself against the dashboard. "That the best you can do?"

"Nah, I'm saving the best for later."

The tyres smoked as I accelerated up the driveway and parked in a hail of gravel. I hopped out of the car, metaphorically, and so did Jed, literally, dragging his crutches behind him. We burst in through the front door and Jed eyed up the stairs and then his cast.

"Elevator," I gasped.

It turned out that with the right incentive, Jed could be remarkably agile even with his leg in plaster, and I sure was smiling by the end of the evening. Oh yeah. Having Jed as a houseguest definitely had its advantages.

And the best part? He didn't bat an eyelid when I rolled out of his bed and went to my own. He understood me. No questions, no awkwardness.

Exactly what I needed.

Over the next couple of weeks, things started getting back on track. Jed stayed at my place most of the time, ostensibly because of my gym and housekeeper, but we both knew the real reason. Let's just say more than one person commented on my smile.

Life was...well, not good, but better.

Except I'd forgotten just how sociable Jed could be.

"What on earth's going on?"

Eight in the evening, I'd been stuck behind a pile-up on I-95 for an hour, and now I'd got home, my lounge was filled with twenty men and a sea of beer and takeout boxes. I could hardly hear myself shout over the ball game on TV.

"I just invited the guys over, darlin'," Jed said.

"But you forgot to invite me? Or did you just assume I'd come along, seeing as this is my freaking house?"

Bradley threw a pretzel at me. "Take a chill pill, Emmy. It's only a bit of fun."

Those words struck fear into my heart. I'd seen the aftermath of Bradley's fun before.

Nick grinned at me from the couch. "Relax baby, it's just pizza and a few beers. We'll clear up after."

"You won't clear up. You never clear up." Nick was the untidiest man I'd ever met. A complete mess. It constantly amazed me that he ever managed to wear clean shirts and matching socks. I suspected he bought them in bulk and binned them once they were dirty. "And it's hardly 'just a few beers.' What did you do, buy a brewery?"

"No, but seriously, that's not a bad idea." Nate turned to the rest of the gang from his perch on the coffee table. "Guys, if we all put in a few dollars, we could probably do that."

Cue an animated but drunken discussion about starting their own beer label until someone scored and their attention turned back to the screen.

"Are you gonna sit down, baby?" Nick asked. "There's space between me and Jed."

No way. I refused to spend the evening wedged between their massive thighs, nice though they were. The British version of football was bad enough, but the American version sent me to sleep. How did they manage to turn a sixty-minute game into five hours? And when I started to nod off, Nick would poke me, constantly.

"You must be kidding."

"Or you could sit on my lap," Jed offered.

My eyes rolled so hard they got halfway to Alabama. "Nick, give me your keys. I'll sleep at your house." Next, I turned to Bradley. "And, party princess, if the house doesn't look pristine when I get back tomorrow, I'm holding you responsible."

"Don't worry. We'll all be good."

I returned the next morning to find a very hungover Bradley balanced precariously on a stepladder, trying to scrape a slice of pizza off the lounge ceiling. Boy, was I glad I'd escaped the night before.

"How on earth did that get up there?"

Bradley shrugged and wobbled, so I grabbed the ladder to steady it.

"I literally have no idea. I passed out around four."

I ventured further into the house, marvelling at the skill it must have taken to hook a shoe on a branch of the ridiculously expensive chandelier that hung in my two-storey high atrium, and almost tripped over Logan, who was asleep in the entrance to the dining room. As I wandered through the place, I counted another six men unconscious downstairs, before finding Nate in the kitchen concocting what had to be the most vile-smelling alleged hangover cure I'd ever come across.

"What's in that?"

"Lemon, raw egg, fresh oranges, vitamins, kale, pickle juice."

"Pickle juice?"

"It restores electrolytes."

"I'd rather just go teetotal."

I heard a gasp from the doorway and swivelled to see Mack, looking fresh as a daisy and followed by Luke and a very excited Tia.

Uh oh.

What on earth were they doing here?

CHAPTER 49

I HUGGED TIA then covered her eyes as Jed hobbled into the kitchen in his boxer shorts and cast, scratching his unmentionables.

"For Pete's sake, put some proper clothes on!" I snapped at him. "Tia doesn't want to see you half-naked."

"Actually, the bit I saw looked quite good," Tia mumbled, her face still squashed against my hand.

"Jed—clothes!"

He ambled out of the kitchen and Mack stared after him. "Ah, Jared Harker, the CIA's finest."

I turned to Luke with a groan. "My house isn't normally like this, I swear."

"What happened?" Mack asked. "Did your harem escape from the basement again?"

Not helping.

"Mack, be serious. This isn't setting a good example for Tia. Honestly, I wasn't even here last night. I left them to it and stayed at Nick's. Although to be fair, his place looks worse than this, and he didn't even have a party."

Luke didn't look as though he believed me, but when he laughed at Nate's attempts to work the blender, I breathed a sigh of relief he wasn't cross.

"Perhaps we should go to the office instead?" Mack

suggested.

"Good idea. Give me fifteen minutes to shower and change, and I'll come with you."

I took twelve, even after I stopped to tell Bradley he'd better have the house cleared by the evening or I'd confiscate his company Lamborghini. I also paused to check the body lying across the upstairs landing was still breathing.

"Tia, do you want to ride with me or Luke?" I asked.

"You. Do you have a sports car? I bet you've got a sports car."

We took the Viper, and on the way, she told me what happened after our interrupted night at Black's. I already knew most of it. It seemed no one had filled her in on my Syrian escapade, and I wasn't about to either.

I could tell she had mixed feelings over Luke being with Mack, and a lot of that stemmed from worrying how I felt about it. I tried to convince her I was happy about the situation, even though the pretence took an effort. My issues were my own, and I didn't want to make things uncomfortable for the two lovebirds. And honestly, I hoped it lasted. If it didn't, the fallout would be huge.

At Blackwood Headquarters, I parked in my reserved spot next to the front door. Nick's space beside it was empty. I hadn't seen him this morning, and I dreaded to think where he'd turn up.

Tia eyed up the *Director* sign in front of my car. "So you're the boss around here, huh?"

"One of them. Nick and Nate are also bossy."

"Nate?"

"The smelly guy in my kitchen who was struggling to turn the blender on."

"Really?"

I couldn't blame her for looking doubtful. If my first meeting with Nate had been this morning, I wouldn't have believed he was capable of running a multi-billion dollar company either.

"Yes, really. He comes across better after a shower."

Mack and I showed Luke and Tia around, from the shooting range to the forensics lab to the tech department. Tia seemed peculiarly fascinated with the surveillance room.

"It's awesome. You can watch people and they don't even know. It's like a real-life version of *Big Brother*."

"It's also interminably dull."

"No way! Oh, wow, that guy just reversed into a fire hydrant."

In the end, we left her there with Jorge, the shift supervisor, determined to help out. Give her a day or two, and she'd soon realise monitoring CCTV footage was the most boring thing ever.

Luke and Mack followed me upstairs, where I was still borrowing Nick's office. We paused in the kitchen to grab coffee on the way.

"I'd offer you a biscuit, but we only have these weird crackers with seeds in them."

"Toby again?" Mack asked.

"The one and only. So, what are you doing here?"

Luke settled back on the sofa. "I've decided to open an office in Richmond."

"You mentioned a while back that you might. I'm glad things are progressing. How long are you staying for?"

"A couple of weeks. Mack offered to introduce me to some people."

"And Tia?"

"Just a few days. She's got mock exams next Wednesday."

"It's nice to see her."

"She asked if she could stay with you, but I didn't want to say yes without asking first."

"Sure she can. I promise most of the guys will be gone by this evening."

"Most of them? How many are you planning to keep around?"

"Don't worry; my house isn't some debauched playground. Bradley might stay, plus Jed. He's on sick leave, and he's developed an addiction to my games room. I'll make sure he's got clothes on at all times."

"Just the two of them?"

"Just two."

"In that case, I'll tell her she can stay."

"What are your plans for today? Do I need to keep an eye on her?"

"If you wouldn't mind. I've got an appointment with a realtor at three, then Mack's going to show me around town."

"If you need an office, I've probably got a vacant one."

"You own real estate?"

"Don't look so surprised. Just because I was elbow-deep in horse poop when you met me doesn't mean I don't know how to invest."

"Oh." He glanced at Mack, who nodded. "In that case, what have you got?"

I'd met with my property agent not long ago, and my portfolio was doing nicely, thank you very much.

"How about a vacant floor in a building on Forest

Avenue? You can have it free for six months if you want."

Generous? Not really. I still felt like I owed him for providing me with room and board and other forms of, ahem, entertainment back in England, and besides, if he stayed, I'd make a profit on the rent in the future.

"In that case, I'll put it at the top of my list."

"I'll get someone to take you over there, and in the meantime, I'm borrowing Mack for lunch. I've barely seen her for weeks."

Mack and I went out to Claude's. The restaurant was French, but because I was a good customer, they allowed me a bit of leeway with my menu choices. I took a secret delight in seeing how far I could push it.

After a quick perusal of the specials' board, Mack ordered first. "I'll have the *Sole Meunière, s'il vous plait.*"

The waiter nodded.

I grinned at him. "I'll have a Kobe beef burger and fries, extra tomato, no pickle, and could you do me a side order of crispy seaweed?"

He gulped and gave me a sickly smile. "*Mais oui, madame.*"

Mack shook her head as he scurried off. "Why do you always do that?"

"Claude bet me a few months ago that he could serve up anything I ordered, and I like to challenge him."

"Have you beaten him yet?"

Much to my annoyance, no. "I had ostrich in satay

sauce last week. It was disgusting."

That was met with a peal of laughter. "Serves you right."

I was pleased to see Mack upbeat. After the idiot before last, she'd moped for weeks, so it seemed as if Luke was doing her some good. I said as much to her, and when she blushed, I knew I was right.

"I really like him," she confessed.

"You're good together. Two techie-freaks. I bet when you mention logic gates and 'if' statements he actually knows what you're talking about."

"Yeah, and he doesn't think Java's a type of coffee."

"It *is* a type of coffee."

"That's beside the point."

"Nothing's more important than a good, smooth espresso."

Nothing more than having the old Mack back, anyway. The last guy had come dangerously close to a body bag after what he put her through, and I was as confident as I could be that Luke wouldn't do the same. Just to be on the safe side, I'd done a full background check when I got back to the States. Apart from a couple of speeding tickets, a caution for urinating against the wall of the local cinema when he was seventeen, and a tendency to answer back to his geography teacher, his history came back clear.

We finished dinner with dessert—pineapple upside-down cake for me and orange sorbet for Mack.

"I thought you always had chocolate something-or-other?" I said.

"Luke's been buying me so many boxes of the stuff I'm going to have to ask him to slow down."

Yes, they worked well together. Mack's eyes lit up

every time she talked about him, and while she may not have admitted it, even to herself, I knew she'd fallen in love.

At least somebody was happy.

CHAPTER 50

WHEN WE GOT back after lunch, Mack disappeared with Luke for the afternoon, partly to look at the sights of Richmond and partly, I suspected, to look at each other.

Blackwood offered flexible hours for senior employees. People could work whenever they wanted as long as they got the job done. For some projects, like the Syria incident, we stayed in the office twenty-four seven, but everyone needed downtime. If Mack wanted to take a few days off and her schedule allowed it, that was up to her.

I went back to the surveillance room and found Tia watching video feeds from a shopping centre beside Jorge, who appeared to be her new best friend.

"Oh no, lady. You need to put those back!"

"Shoplifter?" I raised an eyebrow at Jorge.

"No." He rolled his eyes. "She just doesn't think a woman with a butt that size should be wearing leggings."

A couple of the other guys sniggered. Clearly Tia was their entertainment for the day. As she seemed to be enjoying herself, I left her to it, telling Jorge to call me if she got too annoying.

Nick rolled in just after lunch with bloodshot eyes and two days' worth of stubble. Although judging by the looks he got from the ladies as he strolled through the office, that hadn't diminished his sex appeal.

"How are you feeling?"

"Coffee."

Sloane heard his answer as we walked past her desk. "On it," she said, dashing off.

"You look terrible."

"Thanks. Believe it or not, this is an improvement on earlier this morning."

"Where were you?"

"In the boathouse. I don't suppose you know how I got there?"

"Not a clue, but I suspect beer was involved. Why did you bother coming in?"

"I have a video conference at four. I'm hoping Mack can do some fancy computer magic to make me look more human."

"Bad luck—Mack's out for the day. You'll have to try an hour of sleep instead."

I steered Nick over to the black leather couch in the corner and shoved my jacket aside so he could lie down. With Tia occupied too, that left me the afternoon to get on with some work. I'd received a request from the DEA the day before. Well, more of a re-request. We'd actually had the job on the books for a while, but it blew hot and cold, and we'd never managed to make much headway with it. For almost two years now, bad batches of cocaine had been turning up in New York and the surrounding areas, including Richmond.

The dodgy coke was cut with levamisole, a veterinary dewormer that could be fatal to humans. It killed off the white blood cells that made up the immune system, meaning small things like a cut or mouth ulcer escalated into deadly infections. The end result wasn't all that dissimilar to AIDS. And if the user didn't die from that, there were the added side effects of seizures and damage to the heart muscle.

Nice.

The flow of the drugs into the area hadn't been constant. Every couple of months, another batch turned up and more users died. Dan had interviewed a couple of them in the hospital a year or so back, an unpleasant task by all accounts, and one she'd told me about over a working lunch.

"They had these huge open sores covering their faces and bodies. One guy could have been an extra in a horror movie. And the dude in the morgue had pus leaking out all over the place."

I hadn't got past the appetiser.

The tipping point in the case had come a month back with the death of Steven A. Trent, a young, wealthy, and very stupid investment banker. In his case, the A stood for Addict, because according to his acquaintances, he couldn't get through a party without snorting a few lines. Not only was he rich, his levamisole-induced death got extra coverage because he happened to be the son of a prominent New York senator.

The day after the funeral, Herman Trent had announced his mission to win the war on drugs.

I spent the afternoon reading through our files before my video conference with the DEA at five. It wasn't the first time I'd seen the notes, but I wanted to refresh my memory. Black had been one of the previous investigators, and his connections with that scene were better than mine, so I wasn't sure I'd be able to add a lot to the party.

But I needed a project to get my teeth into, and as with everything in life, I'd give it a good go.

"So, do you have any new ideas?" I asked Damon Belcourt, my primary contact at the DEA.

He twiddled his pen around on his fingers, a nervous habit he'd had for as long as I'd known him.

"Nothing but whispers on the street, and most of those contradict each other. The lab's done chemical analysis that shows all the bad coke's come from the same source, but we're no nearer to finding where that is than we were two years ago."

"What do you want me to do?"

"What you usually do—rattle a few cages, shake a few trees. See what comes loose. You're not bound by the rules of paperwork like we are, and we're short of manpower. Everyone's too busy taking out low-level street bums so we can make it look as if we're fighting Herman's crusade."

I hated having to read through Black's notes. His spidery scrawl, not the easiest to decipher but something I'd learned to read with ease over the years, would never straggle across the page again. But I trusted his instincts, so I needed to know what he'd written. He believed the coke was being cut with the levamisole before it got to the States, which was strange in itself because smugglers usually liked the drug as pure as possible when they shipped it. It took up less volume that way, making it easier to hide.

Why the smugglers wanted to cut the drugs at that

stage was anyone's guess. Black hypothesised that the smugglers had a misguided belief the levamisole would act as a fungicide and prevent the coke from going mouldy when it was shipped in damp conditions, and nobody had come up with a better theory.

I'd got through most of the files when Tia bounced into my office, beaming.

"I spotted a shoplifter. He took a bottle of vodka, and I saw him getting arrested and everything."

"I'm proud of you. Are you done for the day?"

"I can hang around with the guys downstairs if you've still got stuff left to do."

"No, we can go home." She wouldn't be in town for long, and I wanted to enjoy the time we had together. "You want to get pizza? Watch a movie?"

"Awesome!"

At least when we got back to Little Riverley, the house was back to its rightful state. Bradley would be keeping his car after all.

"You want to go back to the surveillance centre?" I asked Tia the next morning.

"Can I? The guys said they'd buy me a donut for every thief I spot."

"Sure. You want to try and up their offer, though. I'd hold out for at least a Happy Meal."

While Tia headed off to work, I took a trip to New York. I spent the day tracking down acquaintances, something easier said than done when I'd been out of the game for so many months. Some had moved on, others had changed occupation, more had simply disappeared. The highlight of my afternoon was winning two hundred dollars in an underground poker game. By early evening, I'd got no further with the drugs case, but I was sick of hanging out in dive bars, so I got one of Blackwood's pilots to bring Tia into the city to catch a Broadway show.

After *Phantom of the Opera*, we went out for dinner.

"How was work?" I asked.

"I loved it! I caught two shoplifters today. One of them ran off and the security guard rugby tackled him. Can I come and work for you when I leave school?"

I choked on a prawn cracker. "I'm not sure Luke would be too happy about that. Besides, I thought you wanted to be an artist?"

She shrugged. "Art doesn't pay. Everybody says so."

"Some artists make money. Or what about something else creative?"

"I like textiles, but fashion design's really hard to get into."

"Get good exam grades, and you might be surprised. Somebody's got to be the next Vivienne Westwood."

"You think?"

I smiled at her. "I don't think; I know. You need to follow your heart. If you do something you love for a living, it won't seem like work."

"Do you love what you do?"

"I'm compelled to keep doing it."

"But you don't love it?"

"Maybe once, but not anymore." Not without Black beside me.

"Couldn't you leave? Do something else?"

I shook my head. "I can't."

The evening before Tia flew back to England, a group of us went out for dinner. Jed was still wearing his cast, which, strangely, seemed to behave like a magnet for women. At first, it was amusing, but by the time the eighth one came over to coo sympathy at him and leave her phone number, just in case he wanted any help, with *anything*, it wore a little thin. He waved me next to him, fastened his arm around my shoulders, and rolled his eyes dramatically.

"Save me!"

"They didn't teach you how to deal with horny women in the Army Rangers?"

"Not officially. And not in a fancy restaurant."

I was glad to see Tia among those laughing. She hadn't been happy to see me with Jed at first, but she was coming around to the idea now she realised I'd still give her the same amount of attention as when I was with Luke. At least she hadn't reverted to her brattish self when her brother and I split. It would have been all too easy for her to go back to her spoiled ways, but she'd turned a corner.

I lent her my big plane to fly back to London, which I think made her year. That wasn't as wasteful as it sounded because a team from the London office needed it the following day to take some equipment to Japan. When I left Tia at the airport, she was taking photos of everything from the cockpit to the bathroom fittings. Her Facebook page wouldn't know what hit it.

Tia's departure left me free to start working nights, which meant I could catch up with the drug dealers working the evening shift. Nothing like a good fix at six.

I tapped into my network in Richmond, slowly clawing my way up the food chain. After three days, I came across a guy who interested me. A key player, perhaps? He masqueraded as a bar owner, but no way had he earned the Porsche he drove through an honest living. I put him under surveillance, and it turned out I was right. Couriers brought him shipments two or three times a week, and after a few dead-ends, we tracked a batch of levamisole-laced coke back to one of the man's New York acquaintances. While the DEA followed up at that end, I went to have a little chat with our guy in town.

"All I want is a name," I said.

A perfectly reasonable request, especially when one considered the knife in my hand.

The prisoner didn't seem to think so. He spat at me, but the disgusting glob fell a foot short. I stepped forward and ran the edge of my boot down his shin. That earned me a whole array of curses.

"Would it help if I said please?"

"I'll kill you. I'll kill you!"

Really? I jammed my fingers into the spot between his earlobe and his jaw, wincing as he yelled loudly enough to wake an Ambien addict. Good thing I'd turned the music up.

"I'd like to see you try. Last chance. A name."

I pressed down on his carotid artery. He held on

almost to the point of passing out, then whispered, "Louis Santos."

"Thank you. And I meant what I said. Try and kill me. Just try."

I carried on pressing until he lost consciousness, then I untied him. I no longer cared for my own life. I was on borrowed time, anyway.

Although in the great scheme of things, today had been a good day.

I should have known the peace wouldn't last. Less than a week passed before my world turned dark again, in the control room at Blackwood this time.

The red blob of the tracking device on Louis Santos's car moved slowly across the screen. I'd planted it last night while he ate dinner with his wife, an easy enough job since he'd left the Mercedes in a dark parking spot behind the restaurant. Green blobs followed him as Blackwood vehicles played a game of follow-my-leader. The map Nate had designed reminded me of *Pacman*, and I wanted the greens to gobble up the bad guy.

My red phone rang, flashing "Unknown caller" across the screen. Unusual, but it wasn't unheard of for me to get a wrong number.

I didn't take my eyes of the car-blobs as I picked it up. "Yeah?"

An electronically distorted voice came back at me, one I hadn't heard in over six months.

"Good afternoon, Mrs. Black. Or is it Ms. Black now?"

Mentally I was in a lot better shape than the last time this son of a biscuit called, so rather than acting dumb again, I hit a button to record the call and start a trace.

"What do you want?"

"Come now, is that any way to greet the man who holds the lives of your friends in his hands?"

"Oh, I'm sorry. How may I help you?"

"There's no need for sarcasm. I heard you were back from your little sabbatical, so I thought I'd give you a friendly reminder to keep your nose out of my business."

"Which I've been doing, you murdering freak."

"Under different circumstances, I could enjoy you getting feisty."

"And under different circumstances, I could enjoy peeling your skin off your body, piece by tiny piece, but circumstances are what they are, aren't they?"

"I'm glad we're seeing eye to eye on this."

"We'll never see eye to eye. Just keep out of my life, and I'll keep out of yours."

I hung up on him, exercising the only bit of control I had over the situation, then stared at the screen for a second before hurling the phone across the room like I was pitching in the World Series. It hit the wall with a crunch and dropped to the floor.

Silence spread as people turned to stare at me. I'd never lost my rag like that in front of anyone except Black before, so I suppose I deserved the shocked looks.

As time stood still, I felt something creeping through me, flooding my veins and seeping out of my pores. Rage. Pure, unmitigated fury. All the anger I'd been missing after Black's death finally came.

How dare he?

Nate materialised beside me. "That was him, wasn't it?" he murmured, too quietly for anyone else to hear. He didn't have to elaborate on who "him" was.

"Yes. It was."

"What're you going to do?"

I looked at the faces around me. Nate. Nick, sitting at his desk, watching me closely. Dan, halfway across the room, carrying a cup of coffee. Behind her, Mack waited for instructions, mouse in hand.

Then I saw Black the last time he looked at me, his expression of confusion, soon to become death. I couldn't face that again. I couldn't watch the soul of another person I cared about leave this earth. I didn't want their blood on my hands.

No more.

Decision made, I turned back to Nate.

"Nothing," I replied through clenched teeth. "I'm going to do...nothing."

WHAT'S NEXT?

The Blackwood Security series continues with Forever Black...

> "Shouldn't you play it safe?"
> "I prefer to play it dangerous."

Diamond's back, and this time she's angry. All she ever wanted was the one man she could never have, and now the shadowy figure who took him away from her is going to pay.

Her special ops training has equipped her to handle the most dangerous situations, but controlling her own emotions isn't so easy. Is she broken beyond repair? As Diamond takes off for South America with her team in tow, she doesn't care. All she wants is justice.

Can love conquer all?

Or will it die trying?

Forever Black is available via this link:

www.elise-noble.com/forever-black

The tale of how Emmy got out of her court appearance in Chapter 29 is available in the FREE Pitch Black bonus chapters, available via the following link:

www.elise-noble.com/pb-bonus-clean

If you enjoyed Into the Black, please consider leaving a review.

For an author, every review is incredibly important. Not only do they make us feel warm and fuzzy inside, readers consider them when making their decision whether or not to buy a book. Even a line saying you enjoyed the book or what your favourite part was helps a lot.

WANT TO STALK ME?

For updates on my new releases, giveaways, and
other random stuff, you can sign up for my newsletter
on my website:
www.elise-noble.com

Facebook:
www.facebook.com/EliseNobleAuthor

Twitter: @EliseANoble

Instagram: @elise_noble

I also have a group on Facebook for my fans to hang
out. They love the characters from my Blackwood and
Trouble books almost as much as I do, and they're the
first to find out about my new stories as well as
throwing in their own ideas that sometimes make it
into print!

And if you'd like to read my books for FREE, you
can also find details of how to join my review team.

Would you like to join Team Blackwood?

www.elise-noble.com/team-blackwood

END OF BOOK STUFF

Well, I managed to break just about all the rules of writing in this book, and you know what? I enjoyed it. I hope you did too.

My favourite part was the research, though. I galloped wildly through fields on a Spanish horse, I learned how to shoot, I spent time in Dahab, Egypt, fell off a wakeboard too many times to count, and travelled to Jordan because I wanted to see what the desert there looked like for myself. And huge thanks to Aston Martin for letting me borrow a V12 Vantage for the day :)

I also need to say thank you to everyone who helped me to put this book together—Abigail and Amanda for making the cover and the words beautiful, and my proofreaders—Lisbeth, John, and Noel—for finding my typos. Plus big thanks to Cindy for the wonderful feedback and for fixing my Britishness.

I feel I should also acknowledge the following for their contribution: Lindt Truffles, Nescafe, Walkers crisps, and the vineyards of France and Australia.

Thanks for reading, and I hope to chat to you in future!

OTHER BOOKS BY ELISE NOBLE

The Blackwood Security Series
Pitch Black
Into the Black
Forever Black
Gold Rush
Gray is my Heart
Neon (novella)
Out of the Blue
Ultraviolet
Red Alert
White Hot
The Scarlet Affair (2018)

The Blackwood Elements Series
Oxygen
Lithium
Carbon
Rhodium (2018)

The Blackwood UK Series
Joker in the Pack
Cherry on Top (novella)
Roses are Dead
Shallow Graves (2018)

The Trouble Series
Trouble in Paradise
Nothing but Trouble
24 Hours of Trouble

Standalone
Life
A Very Happy Christmas
Twisted

www.ingramcontent.com/pod-product-compliance
Lightning Source LLC
Chambersburg PA
CBHW030753260626
47169CB00001B/35